THE GENESIS PROJECT

THE GENESIS PROJECT
KILLING THE SONS OF GOD

A NOVEL

MICROWAVE

iUniverse, Inc.
New York Lincoln Shanghai

THE GENESIS PROJECT
KILLING THE SONS OF GOD

Copyright © 2007 by Microwave

All rights reserved. No part of this book may be used or reproduced by any means, graphic, electronic, or mechanical, including photocopying, recording, taping or by any information storage retrieval system without the written permission of the publisher except in the case of brief quotations embodied in critical articles and reviews.

iUniverse books may be ordered through booksellers or by contacting:

iUniverse
2021 Pine Lake Road, Suite 100
Lincoln, NE 68512
www.iuniverse.com
1-800-Authors (1-800-288-4677)

This is a work of fiction. All of the characters, names, incidents, organizations, and dialogue in this novel are either the products of the author's imagination or are used fictitiously.

ISBN: 978-0-595-41687-5 (pbk)
ISBN: 978-0-595-67930-0 (cloth)
ISBN: 978-0-595-86031-9 (ebk)

Printed in the United States of America

CHAPTER 1

"OG WHO?"

There was a soft knock on the door as Michael Zarkuhn finished the last of his tea. He opened the door to witness the whitest teeth he'd ever seen; although this may not have been the case given the contrasting black complexion to that of the gaping enamel dancing before Michael.

"Good morning Mr. Zarkuhn. How are you sir?" The thin black man was holding a small note in his right hand which he handed immediately to Michael Zarkuhn.

"A gentleman asked me to give you this note hur sir."

"Thank you Chuck. How's the family doing these days?"

"They fine sir, just fine and thank you again for helping us get little Charles into that famous, fancy school up Nothe. We ain't goin to let you down, no sir."
"I know little Charles will do just fine. Is my car ready yet?" Michael's question came quickly as he attempted to avoid idle chatter.

"Yes sir. Got hur right out front; can I load yo bags sir?"
"Sure, if you could just grab that small one there Chuck. Thank you."
Michael grabbed his jacket and gently closed the door behind him. He remembered the first time he met Chuck, Charles Grandier, the porter, for the small quaint hotel on the Mississippi Gulf. Mr. Grandier was extremely helpful; he knew everyone within a 500-mile radius of Biloxi, Mississippi making him a genuine asset. A year earlier Michael Zarkuhn had made phone calls to some contacts in Boston, Massachusetts arranging for young Mr. Grandier, Jr. to enter Harvard University. Michael figured why not; the young man was brilliant and he knew Junior would prove to be a tremendous asset in the future, a key for the "Quickening". Michael enjoyed the Gulf Coast area as he thought to himself while crossing over the state line, but now it was time to perform some serious work.
"Hello!"
"Michael I can barely hear you."
"Can you hear me now? Michael asked."
"Yes. Hey, I appreciate your interrupting your vacation we desperately need your participation."

Margarite's voice always seemed to be hiding something, but Michael could never pin point what.

"It's okay. I had a wonderful time. By the way I'll be there say around eight o'clock."

"Do you have a place to stay Michael? You know you're welcome."

"Thank you, however, I'm fine. I'll see you at eight then."

Margarite Plantard was the epitome of the librarian's librarian. Her pale, narrow, features concealed her enormous maternal strength and noble character. She was graceful like a gazelle, possessing extraordinary elegance. She wore her raven colored hair up in a tight small bun with long locks cast to each side; they provided symmetry for the pointed, horned rimmed glasses attached to a strand of pearls dangling from her flamingo neck. The glasses besmirched her natural beauty as did her taste in clothing. Despite Ms. Plantard's eccentric style of dress and matronly hair style, she was indeed a very attractive and ebullient woman. Michael always enjoyed her company at the dinners hosted at her family estate. She'd inherited a tremendous cache of wealth estimated to be $700 millions; however, her closest confidants knew this figure was greatly underestimated.

Michael Zarkuhn soon arrived at the bed and breakfast he was to stay. He reached behind the passenger seat and grabbed his tote and headed for the lobby to register. Approaching the lobby he noticed a few people in the area which prompted him to exercise additional caution. Circumspection and vigilance were an intense part of Michael Zarkuhn's character.

A man in the hotel lobby speaking to the desk clerk was a big man. Correction, he was a huge man with a round face and a nose that indicated he liked to drink and fight. His nose was red and bulbous, his hair white as snow which reminded Michael of Santa Claus on an extremely bad, bad hair day. Michael had no idea who the character was but he unnerved him. The stranger continued talking and greeted Michael at the desk.

"I'm not sure we've met. Who are you?" Encounters such as these always pushed Michael's primal alert button. The man limped on his right leg indicating a possible sports or military injury. A boxer a brawler, who knew but the scar tissue over his eyes spoke to a violent past. Michael's bet was brawler. The desk clerk and an elderly bystander drinking coffee almost seemed to disappear as Michael observed their actions.

"Szmesh Ognorski is the name. I have a tiny financial interest in this bed and breakfast."

Ognorski turned to the desk clerk as he leaned against the counter and began tapping it with his massive fingers. A sudden feeling of uneasiness surged through Michael's body. A big voice said don't stay here, which was offset by the little one asking, why not? This gargantuan seemed docile enough, but he was talking far too much. Michael detested too much talk. He could visualize every morning, where you going? Do you need anything? You need a ride, yakka tee, yak? Zarkuhn was trying to place the blushed faced, blonde monster but couldn't.

"Mr. Zarkuhn, please sign here. Thank you sir", the young freckled faced clerk handed him the key.

"Here's your key and your room is."

Michael abruptly cut her off feeling uncomfortable about the whole encounter he read the room number off the lodging folio. "I'll find the room thanks."

"See you around Mr. Zarkuhn."

Not if Michael saw him first. Damn, he wanted to shout that out. As Michael entered his room he scanned its surroundings and then remembered he'd forgotten to read the note given to him in Mississippi by Chuck, the porter at the Millard Inns Hotel in Biloxi. The note read Iraqi conflict imminent due to manipulated intelligence. Sons of God behind the diversionary agreement with terrorist leadership in Middle East; he burned the note and recapped his last four years. The group he worked with was aware of three main Secret Societies determined to carry out schemes to dominate and control Earth. Michael Zarkuhn's group had dedicated themselves to the task of discovering which of these organizations was ahead in the effort and what could be done to thwart their plans. More importantly were the issues of who the "Sons of God" were and how to identify them. In the last four years Michael had spent most of his time in the Middle East and Eastern Europe gathering data towards the effort.

A genome laboratory owned and funded by the Collective had narrowed down some specific DNA and RNA markers believed to link certain humans as "Sons of God" as referred to in Chapter Six of the Christian Holy Bible.

There were twelve members at the core of the Collective who controlled the group. Michael Zarkuhn's lodging room door knob rattled.

"Yes who is it? Who is it?"

Repeating himself he retrieved his weapon from his tote. Pressing his face against the opposite side of the wall from the door handle he knelt on one knee. The first bullet entered where Michael calculated it would, right through the center of the door followed by a barrage of 9mm rounds. The intensity of the assault increased on the room to an unbelievable magnitude.

"Ognorski"! He suddenly remembered the face. The hell storm of ammo now forcing their way into his room helped to improve his memory but what a bad time to recall a bad guy's face. Zarkuhn had seen the giant ugly Santa in Florida on the pier in Clearwater, Florida. Ognorski was buying a hotdog as Michael was being escorted to a yacht. That day it had to have been 100 degrees outside and Ognorski was sporting a long sleeve shirt under a tattered flight jacket. His attire should've prompted suspicion from the group escorting Zarkuhn but it hadn't and that oversight cost them their lives as it now would cost Michael his.

"Ahh!

The shearing pain was indescribable. One of the bullets shattered Michael's tibia while he was still airborne attempting to dodge the showering storm of bullets. Michael landed in an unflattering position unto a bed quickly falling to the from the onslaught on bullets. Tears rolled from his eyes as he grimaced from the intense pain from his wound. He tried to pull the mattress and bed on its' side but had no success and he realized he would soon expire. The tiny missiles were entering from every direction as he sarcastically thought to himself that getting a room here was definitely a mistake that would cost him his life. Soon other bullets found their mark as his face slammed against the floor his gun and his consciousness slipped away.

CHAPTER 2

"REMEMBER GENESIS"

"Yah, I have dah body. He's dead ah!"

Michael could barely hear Ognorski's voice with an Eastern European accent. The accent was probably Estonian or Lithuanian and Michael had dealt with persons from that part of the world. It was so dark but the void was familiar. There it was a bright light glowing and his body now felt weightless. Michael had this experience before and it unnerved him simply because he wasn't in control. Always he questioned if he were dead or in a state of suspended animation? Michael panicked the first time this happened. It occurred during a battle at Edrei against the King of Bashan, King Og. He, Michael was wounded by the giant king as he stepped between him and Moses in order to shield the patriarch from a deadly blow. However, later while he lay in a tent awaiting a hero's funeral service Michael woke up fleeing the tent which housed him only to be found by Moses later jubilantly announcing Michael's miracle resurrection to the tribes of Israel. His anxiety always subsided having experienced the same phenomenon over the many centuries. He referred to the experience as "dead light periods" where he would reminisce his past while in the unconscious state. Obviously he was deceased, but Michael could clearly hear.

"Wait! Maybe if I, no hands, no movement and no sense of smell. I'm dead". Suddenly there was an orb in the void. Now instead of darkness Michael could only see a tremendously luminous light engulfing him.

Suddenly there was sensation in Michael's limbs and he could hear voices harmoniously chiming a mantra.

"You have always fought the good fight against the enemies of ALL.

"But you still haven't told me." He recognized that voice it. Hearing it eased his tension. Suddenly and without warning the trunk opened, Michael felt alert.

"Miles I'm worried. Michael is late. He was due to arrive hours ago." Margarite realized she always recited the same script whenever Michael Zarkuhn was late. It did not matter if he was a minute late she still worried.

Miles slowly sat down by the large bay window lowering his pipe in his lap while exhaling a cherry tobacco cumulus from between his bearded lips.

"You know Michael can handle himself and very well if I might add. The man is pure hell should anyone dare to cross him my dear you know this."

Margarite felt little comfort in Mile's comments though she knew Miles was perfectly correct in his assessment of their most lethal black ops security chief.

"Do you remember when Michael first came to us Miles?" Margarite asked in a low motherly tone while pinching her teacup between her delicate elongated fingers. "He was so innocent, so naïve and yet he possessed so much knowledge of all things."

That day was four years ago on the morning of September 11th, 2001. Michael had knocked on Margarite's door and asked for an audience with her. Miles was at the mansion that morning to watch a polo game later that afternoon on the grounds. The man servant, Peter was not amused at the stranger's request. Peter was very terse in stating to Michael "madam was not available without an appointment so please go away".

"Yes. He is quite an enigma isn't he?" Miles inhaled a slow puff from his pipe. "Margarite, I must admit I had thought both of you crazy when you first shared Michael's mission with me and yet I somehow felt that Michael could be trusted to work with us, the Collective."

Miles cleared his throat, "I never knew he had met your father, much more that they were so close; Michael's stories are truly fascinating, and intriguing. Michael's friendship with Joseph did aid in the Collective Inner Circle developing a comfort level with him. My dear I can assure you of that."

Michael had shared information of the September 11th terrorist attack early that morning. What a conundrum this had caused for the Collective Inner Circle.

"Yes, he did create quite a stink the first time we met. Remember we considered calling a special meeting of the circle without so much as verifying the information he'd shared with us, but the aftermath, frankly shocked the hell out of me. How could this stranger have known what he knew? That's what I couldn't figure out!" Margarite reflected on that horrific morning remembering she soon had all her answers.

"Well my lady he's not quite human if you ask me? According to our esteemed comrade Doctor Sabat his physiological and neurological makeup is quite unusual. Not to mention his extraordinary intellect; yes Mr. Michael's rather a superman." Miles folded his arms and took another puff from his pipe. Margarite once more thought back on what Michael had first said to her, "madam I need your help. I humbly proffer my services to you and your associates. We must not let what I'm about to share with you occur!"

Margarite stared at Michael as though he was insane, and felt inclined to call the authorities. Peter and Miles were both present which increased her feeling of security and kept her from the rash action.

"Speak! What is it sir? What is so pressing a matter that drives you to barge into my home, my life with this nonsense?" Margarite ordered, removing her matronly glasses from her thin face.

"Today a terrible thing will happen and we must stop it. You know the leadership of this country, the President, well you must contact them."

Michael could not believe the startled looks his request conjured up. In fact, everyone possessed that dumfounded expression which baffled him. Michael Zarkuhn brandished his own look, that what's everybody so surprised about look. The deer meets headlight look."

"Sir please sit." Miles requested. "Now, please expound on the matter because frankly you've lost me sir." Smirking as he looked at the other two persons in the room as Michael sat.

Margarite was taken by the man's statuesque appearance. The stranger was tall, about six feet five inches, with a clear bronze complexion. His hair was jet black tinted gray balanced the frame of his face; indeed he was comely. His full lips and dark almond shaped eyes were accentuated by his clean shaven face. He presented a powerful aura which lit up the whole room. As he moved Margarite Plantard could see the muscles bulging through his French tailored suit, obviously he was a man of means with impeccable taste.

"Mr., Mr., Mr. Ahhh!." Margarite remembered having second thoughts because it was so difficult to get the stranger to acknowledge her when she desired to know his name at one point.

"I'm sorry Madam, please forgive my bad manners. I'm Mr. Zarkuhn, Michael Zarkuhn, and I possess knowledge of a plot against the people of this country, a crime of omission by those whom you trust. A plane, in fact, several aircraft will be flown into buildings killing thousands of innocent beings." Zarkuhn was sincere and adamant in his delivery about the terrorist plot.

Everyone was stunned and un-choreographed silence befell the room. Peter, the man servant was the first to speak.

"Mr. Zarkuhn, if what you say is true, how is it that you are privy to this matter? Are you one of the benefactors or participants of these alleged acts of terror?"

Peter never slept, rarely spoke, was never seen eating and breathing was believed to be optional with him. Mr. Peter Stuart was a bit of a mystery. He had been with Margarite's family since before she was born, a whopping sixty two years of loyal service. Margarite knew very little about him or his family. What she did know was that she loved him and considered him a grandfather not merely a plebeian or servant. Peter Stuart was rumored to be originally from Great Britain and she had overheard while at her father's lavish parties that he was of royal blood. She knew he spoke French, German, Hebrew, Greek and Latin fluently. Peter would assist her with homework and she remembered asking him one afternoon how he came to be so adept in so many different tongues, knowing so much.

Peter just simply smiled and said "I truly love you little one, but you must concentrate of the quest at hand so you'll be ready for the Quickening". She did not wish to be a bother and never probed the term nor soliciting an explanation.

"Yes that is a good question Peter. How is it you know this information?" Mile's inquiry turned mildly hostile in tone. I demand you explain yourself and I suggest you do it quick, fast and in a hurry. Peter, please call the authorities!" Miles ordered.

Michael quickly interrupted "that will not be necessary, but which would you prefer I answer first? Quick, fast in a hurry or, right I see? There are terrorists on four aircraft and they are going to crash two aircraft into the World Trade Center Tower buildings, the Pentagon and one into the White House. The aircraft for the White House has a sky marshal and undercover Secret Service agents on board and an air interdiction aircraft, a modified T-38 will take it down somewhere over Pennsylvania unfortunately killing all on board."

"Wait!" Miles shouted. You're talking as though these events have played out for you, as though you watched it on a video or something." Margarite could tell Miles was losing patience.

Miles was Margarite's childhood friend. Miles had grown up in a lower middle class household but through his special gift he was able to achieve great status as a professor of law and prominent attorney. His gift, perfect recollection, a photographic memory had pulled him out of the ranks of mere pedestrian, a commoner to one of super intellectual elite. Graduating from Cornell and receiving an advanced degree as a Rhodes Scholar at Oxford he amassed wealth and numerous influential positions in both academia and the world of commerce.

"Madam, I think perhaps you should address the telly." Peter had been missing for minutes before reentering the room again. He slowly proceeded towards the big screen encased in a very innate hand carved mahogany wood and turned it on. Margarite winced at the carnage, the billowing charcoal smoke, the burning towers being blitzed on every channel. They all watched for over twenty minutes with what seemed like hours in utter disbelief at what no one would've believe could or would've ever happened on American soil. Yet there was a stranger in their midst who had predicted the event one hour ago.

Yes, they remembered their first meeting with Michael Zarkuhn. Nothing was ever to be the same for the Collective Inner Circle from that meeting on. An emergency meeting was called that night to further probe the mysterious stranger and what he could offer the group.

The silence was broken with the sweet smell of Mile's pipe which intoxicated Margarite as she glared out the large windows. She pulled back the rich purple velvet drapes which appeared to sprout from out of the twenty nine foot sculpted ceiling. Margarite closed the curtain and sprinted for the front door, "It's Michael, he's arrived!"

CHAPTER 3

"WHAT'S SO SECRET?"

"Michael we were worried. Oh my God! You've been injured! Peter, Miles come quickly, hurry, Michael's injured!"

Margarite had never seen Michael or anyone in such a battle weary state. She'd only seen Michael in suits and once naked, however, she'd no recollection of that piece of information. She could see tattered holes with discoloration like burn markings on his clothing which were covered with dried blood and dirt.

Michael was shocked at her reaction, he felt her concern was genuine enough, but he tried to assure her he was fine. Taking the shoulders of both Peter and Miles he settled into what was known by all to be his favorite chair located by one of the two large draped bay widows. The warmth from the fire dancing in the large stone fireplace caressed his cold limbs. Michael graciously accepted a glass of sherry from Peter who seemed quite calm in contrast to Miles and Margarite. Peter was smiling at Michael and there was something very knowing in his smile which made Michael feel even warmer. Michael took a sip of his sherry and laid his head back on the chair exhausted from his ordeal.

"I must tell you that tonight I was put through the grinder. It is so good to be here with you even in my present condition." Michael Zarkuhn reached into his left pocket while arching his stomach up managing to pull out a bundled white cloth.

"Margarite would you see that Doctor Teranez receive this at tonight's meeting? I cannot wait for Cheryl to tell us the stuff these guys were made of, and Margarite in the future would you please insist on my staying at Plantard Mansion the hospitality industry is not so hospitable these days."

Michael's joking was an attempt to deflect concern about his coughing. He'd hoped not to cough as much, but there was still congestion in his lungs. Although his body was healing the damage and trauma was intense, it would take a little more time then he was accustomed to getting in back to par, but the aged sherry accompanied by the warm hypnotic blue flames waltzing in the fireplace were proving to be therapeutic in his healing process. Margarite took the handkerchief which Michael had handed her and with both hands cupped as though she was palming water to cleanse her face and carried it towards the door.

"Michael what is this anyway?" Margarite inquired as she walked away curiously unfolding the cloth. By the time Michael had sipped the sherry and rolled it in his mouth it was too late to warn her.

"Oh my God! Margarite screamed as a finger softly bounce up off the thick carpet along with the other two nestled in the handkerchief.

"Sorry Margarite, you were not to open it, just give those to the doc for DNA analysis," Michael explained.

Within seconds Peter appeared wearing gloves, sporting a dust pan and plastic bag.

"I shall make sure Doctor Teranez receives this immediately upon her arrival sir, madam", remarked the most elderly servant.

"Michael do you feel up to telling us what happened?" Miles and Margarite asked at the same time. Peter left the room glancing over his right shoulder at Zarkuhn and he was still smiling. Margarite had to have noticed, but tried to play it off, but she knew how unusual a smile from Peter was.

"I'll bring you up to date soon," he swallowed another sip of his sherry. Through all of the excitement he had forgotten the mud, blood and bullet holes scattered all over his tattered clothing, he just wanted to clean up and rest. He quickly jumped up and attempted to clean his favorite chair to which swift admonishment came from Margarite. "No, Michael. Stop that we shall care for the chair. Please go rest."

The meetings for the Collective were always held at eleven o'clock in the evening and it was already a little after ten o'clock. There would be ten other members arriving. All were influential and prominent figures representing a multiple array of talent on a national and international level. However, their membership in the Collective was clandestine.

"Michael, go ahead get cleaned up and rest. We shall get you before the meeting. In fact, you may exempt yourself if you wish. Peter please prepare", Margarite was cut off before she could finish her request.

"Madam, Master Zarkuhn's room and bath are ready," Peter announced.

Zarkuhn loved the old cogger. He was high octane in the efficiency department. Alfred, the butler for the comic super hero Batman had nothing on Peter. He was simply the most attentive professional anyone could ever meet.

"Peter, thank you", Michael beckoned the aged man servant over to him and embraced the British gent. He helped Michael up the long winding staircase to Michael's room he'd prepared for him.

"From the look of things sir I'd say you were shot at least thirteen times, at least that's how many bullet holes are in your garments so this would be a logical conclusion."

"That's what I figured too Peter, but really whose counting." Both men found this amusing and chuckled like little school girls trying to keep our voices down.

"Peter it happened again the lights and then the resurrection. I was shot and now I'm here same as always. I regained consciousness in the back of a trunk where my body was stashed. A hit man by the name of Ognorski had terminated me at the Pilgrims' Bed and Breakfast where I normally stay outside the city.
He had two accomplices with him. I believe he was the same person who attempted to hit me in Florida last year."
Peter continued to fold fresh towels which he laid at the foot of the bed. He pulled down the bedding and stood in the middle of the room as though he was standing guard in the front of Buckingham Palace.

"Sir, it is wonderful that you managed to get out of that rather precarious predicament?"

"Well Pete my good man when the trunk opened my assailants pulled out some shovels leaving me in the trunk under a tarp. Later two of my attackers pulled me from the trunk tossing my lifeless body on the ground as they continued to dig my new home. I guess you could say they were preparing my new "digs."
Peter's raised his right brow, "I got the joke sir, ha."
Clearing his throat Michael continued, "I used one of their weapons against them, now they have new digs." The attempt to make joke solicited another raised brow from the butler.

"You are lucky sir, to possess such ingenuity but what of Mr. Ognorski?"
Michael thought about the question and it never dawned on him at the time to just wound his attackers, hind sight being what it is he realized he should have salvaged at least one of the men for interrogation.

"I did notice tattoos on the inside forearm of all three men."
Peter's blue eyes lit up before he asked his next question.

"Describe the tattoo Sir." Peter appeared intense as he awaited an answer. Zarkuhn described the tattoos he had seen.

"It was two serpents each devouring the tail of the other with the Goat of Mendes in the center."

"Sir, you've seen this before correct?" Peter asked.

"Yes, I have." Michael responded slowly. "It's the mark of the Clan of Nimrod. They were descendants from those punished at the Tower of Babel mentioned in chapter 11 of Genesis, in the Christian Bible."

"My wounds are healing quicker this time considering the large amount of trauma inflicted." He sat on the edge of the bed removing the tattered clothing and dropping them in a large pull tie trash bag left at the side of the bed by Peter.
"I shall dispose of these items sir."

"I appreciate it, thank you Peter."

The attackers' were descendants from the bloodline of Cush, the grandson of Noah whose father Ham was cursed by the patriarch Noah for an unclear reason. Michael remembered the day as though it were yesterday when he arrested King Nimrod, "the Mighty Hunter" and the son of Cush. Michael's Armies camped on the out skirts of Babel where men were attempting to build a tower to reach the heavens in the valley between the two rivers in the land of Shinar. This place was to be later called Babylon which is located outside Baghdad, Iraq. This was the first "World Order" led by Noah's great grandson Nimrod, "the great hunter". Michael always thought it peculiar that the Great Grandson of a cursed son, Ham, would become the Earth's first great king. He thought it ironic that the second so called "New World Order", through its surrogate the United Nations would represent the descendants scattered throughout the Earth thousands of years ago would later go back to the historical site; there they rebelled under the auspices of waging war against Saddam Hussein. They gathered to serve notice that the children of the once scattered by God for uniting had come back to claim what was theirs, thus, thumbing their noses at God.

Michael could still see the chaos caused by Jehovah that day. Wars immediately began because of the chaos caused from different languages. God had divided in order to make it easier to conquer his pets.

"Kneel before your God!" The archangel commanded the soldiers while massive spaceships landed one by one carrying the armies of God. Michael's armor glistened beneath the brutal sun on the Fertile Crescent Valley as God came down to observe the progress that the beings he called Adamu had made. Adamu was the primitive worker God's brother Enki and his wife had genetically engineered to mine for gold, or as it is written in Chapter two of the book of Genesis "to care for the garden". The precious gold was being sent back to the home world of Jehovah, courtesy of the labor from human slaves.

Michael slid into the hot tub and sighed as the warm water embraced his battered limbs. He wiped away the beads of sweat running down his face and tried to retrace how he ended up on Earth. He remembered, Admonishment, punishment, and retraining were all the words used by his Master, Jehovah.

"But how could I have sinned so? Master, Holy of Holies I do not understand." He asked as he kneeled before the thrown on his master's ship, the very ship the prophet Ezekiel would later describe after his visit before God's thrown in the book Ezekiel. Oh, how he beckoned an explanation from his lord. Completely innocent, Michael's only desire was to understand the hidden wisdom of his great God's actions.

"Speak Michael. What is it you do not understand?" Thunderous was the voice of the lord Jehovah, Yahweh, Enlil, Lord of the Mountain.

"Master I tremble before your awesome power, wisdom and your glorious beauty. I beg of you to help me gain your understanding with matters of governing your vast realms. Why did we use the neuro-chambers on the creatures below? They posed no military threat that I could see Master. They merely gathered as one people and remarkably spoke the same tongue in the spirit of great brotherhood; gathering in the valley below with no wars amongst them. Is this not what you desire amongst all your subjects, throughout your realm?"

"TWICE YOU HAVE ASKED ME QUESTIONS. TWICE I HAVE BEEN TOLERANT OF YOU MICHAEL. BECAUSE YOU HAVE LED THE ARMIES OF THE ELOHIM WITH DISTINCTION YOU SHALL RECEIVE YOUR ANSWERS IN THE FORM OF RETRAINING, AS ADMONISHMENT AND AS PUNISHMENT, SO THAT YOU MIGHT GAIN THE UNDERSTANDING YOU SEEK. UPON YOUR RETURN TO US YOU WILL POSSESS YOUR ANSWERS. UNTIL THEN YOU WILL FIGHT THE ENEMIES OF THESE INFERIOR BEINGS WITH THEM UNTIL I AND THE COUNCIL OF THE ELOHIM THINK YOU ONCE AGAIN WORTHY OF RETURNING TO JOIN US."

CHAPTER 4

SECOND WORLD ORDER

Doctor Amin Sabat was the first guest to arrive. Sabat was a short thin man whose gangly appearance despite his small size made him appear rather tall. He reminded one of a short Abraham Lincoln with a Persian accent. He was however, quite noted for his work in the dual specialties of neurology and psychiatry.

"Where is he? I wish to checkout Michael's health." Amin hurriedly handed his gloves and scarf to Peter trying to remove his coat all at the same time without much success.

"Of course sir, Master Michael shall be with us in a moment." As Peter attempted to grasp all of the doctor's items under his chin he turned and walked briskly away mumbling as he glided across the shiny hard wood floor. As Doctor Sabat entered the study he was graciously greeted by Margarite.

"Amin welcome how are Tamika and the boys?"

"They are fine Margarite, just fine and how are you Miles?" Miles finally lowered his pipe, but for a moment.

"Never better my good man, never better."

The long heavy drapes were pulled together now and the grandfather clock in the hall chimed. It was now eleven p.m., a light haze filled the room. A loud knock on the door was literally a wakeup call for the room's occupants. Three more guests had just arrived. As Michael slowly walked down the winding stairs tugging on the smoking jacket provided courtesy of Peter, he tried to clear his head of the thoughts, memories of his expansive secret past.

"Greetings, cheers!" Markovitz handed Peter a bottle of red wine as he greeted everyone.

"Mmm a Shiraz from your own vintage no doubt; this is truly a treat sir," remarked Peter with an unenthusiastic murmur as he shuffled to and froe. His arms full of coats and winter wear left a trail in the hallway as he walked. The room seemed to come to life with the six members of the Collective greeting each other and the busy chatter back and forth between each of them.

"Michael, please come join us. Are you alright? Anish Markovitz motioned to Zarkuhn. Seated beside him was Miles and to his left brandishing a bottle of whiskey in one hand, an empty glass in the other and a cigar at the right edge of his mouth was J.P. Rockdale the oil magnate. "Let me pooor ya ah drank ma boy! Ya luk lak ya cood uze ah stiff one."

"No thanks sir. I think perhaps a glass of wine will do me just fine."
Like clock work Peter appeared with a silver platter in hand and one beautiful wine glass embracing the richest body of wine.
"Shiraz Master Zarkuhn? Courtesy from Mr. Markovitz' very own vineyard; yes his very own wine yard."
Michael winked at Peter as he gracefully removed the glass and quietly whispered to Peter, "do tell, his very own vineyard you say."
From the beginning of Michael's relationship with the butler he and Peter seemed to be on the same wave length always humoring themselves at the expense of most of the Collective members. They justified their cheeky actions by citing the need for some type of amusement to break the monotony.

Knock, Knock, Knock. All eyes turned towards the atrium as Peter motioned one of the other man servants back into the kitchen gesturing that he would get the door.

"Blouuh it's very chilly out there!" Ted and Alice Martin were making their arrival. Ted was a well respected attorney in criminal law and his lovely wife a noted Doctor of Classics & Ancient History with a specialty in Mesopotamian Archeology.
It was now getting late and the meeting would soon start without the remaining four members.

"Wait! Hold up my good fellow." It was Bishop James Terrell and Makesh Patel bringing up the rear. Bishop James Terrell was the Regional Archbishop for the Northeast United States. Bishop Terrell possessed the calmness of a Buddhist monk which is desired by most Catholic clergy. His insights into sensitive missions reflected the cunning and craftiness of a seasoned intelligence operative. Michael often wondered if the Bishop was an intelligence operative, perhaps undercover because his of brilliant acumen in black ops.

Mr. Makesh Patel was an electrical engineer and programmer by trade. He had made his original fortune in the hospitality industry boasting a portfolio of over twenty five hotels under various flags. More recently he started several ITT firms in his native country of India and was making a bundle with all of the outsourcing being done by major American corporations. The ITT firms as well as the Hotels allowed the Collective human assets a means with which to base overseas operations and intelligence gathering.

"I note we are missing Karen, Cheryl and Mr. Tashido" remarked Miles.

"Let us wait five minutes and then begin?"

"I think that would be perfect if everyone agrees," suggested Margarite politely.

Ring, ring. "Plantard residence may I help you? Yes, of course I shall relay the message at once Doctor Teranez." Peter lowered the telephone and approached the study. Doctor Cheryl Teranez and Senator Karen Stinger are two minutes out. Their limo will be arriving shortly madam."
The chatter and conversation started up after Peter's announcement.
Michael made his way to one of the large windows. He needed a little space to continue clearing his head. He pushed the curtain back and marveled at the night sky outside. Hundreds of tiny white lights glistened in the tree line along the lengthy, winding driveway. The lights brought memories deep within the recesses of Michael's past; memories of being there above in the heavens.

"We will miss you Michael." His friend and battle companion Gabriel stated to him as their vessel hovered high above the planet.

"Gabriel, I do not know why I am being punished so harshly!"

"Lower your voice my brother, shhhh." Gabriel looked around the laboratory to ensure no one was present.

"I do not even remember asking questions of my lord and if I have asked what was the harm?"

"Michael we all have questions, however, you questioned our Lord frankly that is why we were stood behind you. We all wondered, yet you were the bravest proven by going forth."

Just then a technician entered and bowed before both of them as it gathered a piece of equipment that would be used in Michael's surgical transformation.

"Michael was bewildered as to why Adam, the first human slave and his mate Eve did not die upon violating his Lord's commandment not to partake of the "Tree of Knowledge. His curiosity bated him into asking the question of God.

"But Gabriel, neither the man nor the woman died as our lord had decreed they would."

"Michael we were there, we all bore witness, but ours is not to question why or why not? I do not understand your need to know these things. Clearly these are matters for the Lords, the elders to deal with. Their kind have always made the decisions governing such matters, we are merely the emissaries Michael. We are Malachim and this is the way it has always been, since the void and after. Please my friend do not persist in these foolish inquiries anymore, look what it has gotten you. Uriel, Raphiel and the millions of others you command are as the beings of that planet below there, we're inferior to our masters, let us act as such in dealing with our masters. Do not forget the fate that befell our brother, Satanail."

The window pane was cold to the touch and Michael watched his breath condensate on it as a limousine approached from the distance. It would be good to see the Senator and Doctor Teranez when they arrived.

"Ted do you have Louis' cell number on you," Miles shouted out.

"Yes, I'll give him a jingle."
Margarite placed her hand on Michael's shoulder startling him just as a knock rang out from the front door.

"Are you okay? You must forgive me if I seem a little too solicitous, but I had never seen you so battered and the blood, well I." Michael cut her off, "It's okay Margarite. I really appreciate your concern and your hospitality." He gently held her arm entwining it with his and turned to her as they strolled towards the dining room. He could feel her clinch his arm tightly and see from the periphery of his eyes she was content, maybe a little too content.

The group wasted no time being seated and bringing each other up to date on the latest two hours inner circle gossip and hot stock tips.

Michael caught Peter's eyes as he answered the phone in the foyer outside the dining room. As two male servants who lived on property served a wonderful dinner and filled glasses. Peter seemed uncharacteristically shaken.
Michael leaned over and whispered to Margarite "please excuse Margarite I'll be right back."
Peter looked at Michael as he followed behind him, and as they reached the edge of the side kitchen door Peter spoke quietly, "Mr. Tashido, he's, I am sorry to inform you sir, Mr. Tashido has been compromised."

CHAPTER 5

"FRIEND OR FOE"

As the aging man servant opened the door to receive Doctor Louis Tashido the room became deathly still as though a death sentence had been handed down to a loved one.

"Louis welcome. Please come join us," Miles bellowed as though all was well. "We will now address the minutes of the last meeting. Alice if you would be so kind."

Alice adjusted her glasses and began reading.

"Open item number one, the cell in our Philippine operation needed increased funding due to Al Quedas' surge in activity in its surrounding geographical region. The Collective agreed that the monies should be forthcoming via our two hotels and the chicken processing plant outside Manila."

Alice looked up and waited for a response from Bishop Terrell who had oversight for the region's operations for the area.

"I am very pleased to announce that this operation has moved $1,322,161.80 and has recruited six new local assets according to our Asian Chief Mr. Murray. It gets better, five of our new recruits are Muslim and outstanding prospects. Last week's report from the station chief indicated that the use of the Mosques and Catholic churches in volunteering to help find jobs for its attendees through laundering donations using religious institutions has produced a multitude of new possibilities which I myself am planning to present to you all tonight."

The Bishop was grinning from ear to ear and once more Michael Zarkuhn couldn't help but ask himself again was he really a priest? No way was this guy's a priest he loved this cloak and dagger play too much. Michael was just glad he was on their team.

"That's all I have thank you" the priest remarked snuggly as he sat down.
"Number two is the drug smuggling operation in the gulf coast area which was moving the contraband in order to fund future American government sponsored black ops fake terrorist strikes in the Southeast Region of the United States. This operation was also an open item and is overseen by Mr. Zarkuhn.

"Michael, Michael we are waiting for your report!"

"Oh sorry Miles I was daydreaming." It was Michael's turn to report as he tried to clear his thoughts of his distant memories which were increasing in frequency.

"I too was successful in establishing a counter intelligence network using two students and one mole in the operation."
An objection came from the left side of the table.

"If I'm not mistaken didn't we tantively agray to fry those responsible", rattled J.P. Rockdale with a southern slur of speech which if you did not know him you'd mistaken for symptoms of intoxication mixed with Ebonics. However despite his continuous torture of the English language he was quite bright drunk or sober. In fact he was the Collective's first lesson in "looks can be deceiving".

"Yes that was the case as I remembered it but after evaluating the situation and conferring with Bishop Terrell and Miles it was decided that by leaving the operation alive and providing a "tick" to suck valuable information out of it, sources as well as substantive data could be gain. This would strengthen the whole counter operation as well as give us persons to exploit via extortion and termination for their unforgivable role in supporting the secret terrorist actions against the American people."

"Not bad … I lak tha ideah. Dun't know tha parteculars but it sounds good," the pseudo drunk remarked.

Miles rubbed his chin and looked around the room, "all in favor of this action" he softly asked? There was a unanimous show of support. Once more that big grin reappeared on the face of the bishop and once again Michael couldn't help it he was still wondering about the bishop there's something scary about this man of God. Then it hit him; that was it. The Bishop was a man of God capable of anything in the name of his belief. Yes, this guy was dangerous alright. He was no different than some of the Muslim fanatics only the Christians justified their killing innocent Muslims, Jews and anyone else they chose in the name of "War on Terror".

Michael sat back in a more secure state of mind feeling he knew the Bishop's secret to coolness.

Now the Collective Inner Circle peered at Louis Tashido, Ph.D. of Oriental and Islamic Religions at the University of Munich. He had also been a superior member of the Great White Brotherhood, Bavarian chapter. Louis was tasked with assisting the Collective's genome laboratory in Atlanta, Georgia and with finding religious relics thought to possess great powers.

His oldest and most important project was the Genesis Sons of God project, which he Doctors Teranez and Alice Martin were tasked to pursue. The official genome laboratory name was "Gynysyx". Tashido was to report his findings during a recent trip to the Middle East, but it would appear that with the new order of business he would report failure because of his deceit. The anticipation was on their faces. What would Louis say? The inner circle liked and admired him but member who had been compromised could not be tolerated amongst their ranks. It was understood without exception each member's area of operations was compartmented only known by one other member in the group who provided advice, guidance and backup for the other member during each operation. This was verified by the Chairperson who was the senior member of the collective.

The Controller was a member not present for security reasons and by all the bylaws of the Collective was the most powerful individual only known by the two most senior members of the Collective inner circle. The Controller would communicate special requirements to the group in various discrete and often times unorthodox ways. Unfortunately the last Controller was elected during Joseph Plantard's tenure meaning even the oldest members of the existing inner circle had never met him or her. However, security measures to verify the person's identity were used. Nevertheless, Michael had never trusted the Controller system citing it made the Collective vulnerable to an intruder. Unfortunately, old traditions are hard to get rid of, but he was patient and would wait until the day the others would rid themselves of the Controller.

Tears rolled from Louis' eyes as he gazed down towards his lap he quickly looked up wiping the tears with the back of his left hand. "I've been compromised. My ... my family has been taken hostage in Hong Kong while we vacationed."

He began to sob uncontrollably as Senator Karen Stinger and Doctor Cheryl Teranez released each others' loving grip hidden under the table. They stood over him and embraced him to offer comfort. Michael suddenly noticed Karen looking towards him as to beckon his presence. He wasn't the only one who noticed the Senator's flag as each member automatically took defensive postures as subtly as they could.

Mr. Tashido pulled out a pistol. J.P. moved in as well as Anish Markovitz the chubby Jewish CPA.

"Let me go, let me go. I must, please!" Louis kept yelling as every man in the room subdued him on the beautifully woven Persian rug gracing the dining room floor.

"Give me that," Miles pulled the gun a snub nose 38. caliber which was in poor condition from the hysterical man and gave it to Michael Zarkuhn. Everyone was noticeably shaken by the event.

"Tea anyone", chimed Peter holding a tea tray and brandishing a most devilish smile in the doorway.

CHAPTER 6

INFILTRATION

"Louis, have you lost your mind? My god man! What were you going to do with this damn antique, ah? Excuse me ladies."

They'd all seen Miles mad but never this incensed.

"Wait one moment Miles, let him up gentlemen. Please." Zarkuhn requested. As all hands released Louis from the floor he slowly adjusted his shirt and tie. He seemed surprisingly composed; acting as though the event which occurred never transpired.

Louis calmly sat in his seat and looked around the room.

"I'm sorry, I apologize. Sincerely, please accept my humblest apology. I kind of lost it there huh?" The word understatement resonated throughout every single member's mind as they met eyes satisfying each one of their needs not to repeat an overused cliché.

Margarite finally took a deep breath sat panting deeply as though she were about to faint.

"Louis, yes I'd say so." Margarite continued hyperventilating while Doctor Teranez attended to her.

Michael sat next to Louis and stared into his eyes. "Louis, tell me what happened."

"Sure, of course Mr. Zarkuhn. I had just landed in California when I received a call on my cell phone from Merie. She is still in Hong Kong with my son on vacation. I came back for the meeting. Merie was informed me she was not alone at our residence and that some men wanted to speak with me."

Louis once again began to weep.

"Louis, please try and maintain your composure!" Miles exasperatedly begged.

Michael stared in Miles' direction. Miles was now testing Zarkuhn's patience and Zarkuhn let him know it.

"Miles please refrain from anymore harassment of this man." Michael's eyes seemed to glow brightly ... it was not normal, but Miles and the others anchored their seats as though the school principal had walked into an unruly classroom.

"Go on Louis please continue," Michael requested.

"Thank you Mr. Zarkuhn trust me this is not easy for me. My family ... I'm afraid. You see I had just joined my family in Hong Kong for vacation after spending time in Iraq and Syria. I touched basis with some of the world's best and brightest authors Charia Stitch, James Mars, Andy Collinsworth and Larry Gardnier the list goes on. Their books and their research provided desperately needed information. I sought to gather data that would prove relevant to validating our own genome project "Gynyxys". The meetings went very well and most unanimously agreed with our findings. But, Sir Gardnier cautiously warned me that pursuit of this research might create problems for me and he gave no explanation. Of course I never doubted the group would not concur, after all they had all written books regarding the subject long before our recent more proactive needling."

Michael couldn't take it. The yaka tee, yak prompted him wave his hand in the blabbering man's face, "Stop, just stop! Louis, please stick to the issue at hand, your family's peril."

Louis' face went sullen again and he shocked the room with his next statement.

"Of course the issue right excuse my rambling. The men who are holding my family I believe may belong to a secret society aligned with "Papa Nero's" division some you may be familiar with them. They can be terribly ruthless." Bishop Terrell's, voice rang out with noticeable concern "The Black Pope? No offense Ms. Stinger."

"None taken Bishop Terrell." The black senator from Florida responded with a nod of her head.

Michael had dealt with this group on more than one occasion. The more serious dealings with them were in the 1300s while he was a Knight Templar trying to help his brethren flee Portugal for Scotland. The Vatican's Roman family branches were no cream puffs. They were a part of the Catholic secret infra structure created by some of the most brilliant farsighted men ever to walk this planet. Michael knew all so well of the Catholic Church's wolf in sheep's clothing style and had his bets on its secret group to be the forerunner for one world government.

The Pope was known as Pontifex Maximus, but his secret military counterpart was known as the "Black Pope", or Papa Nero and for centuries just another puppet of the God Mercury and all unbeknownst to the world.

Michael had known him well the God Mercury, but by other names. In fact many different names have been used. The name Marduk in the city of Babylon, Merodach in the Christian bible, in the Torah he was called Enoch and Thoth by the Egyptians. There were other names as well, but what was important to know was that his representation through the Church and Secret Societies was formidable and steadfast.

"Are you sure of this?" Michael asked with concern in his voice sitting down very slowly his wheels were turning with all kinds of possibilities for exacerbated trouble. It was serious business for this group to be so openly aggressive against any group. Those in the room familiar with the topic wondered how the Collective had managed to threaten this secret faction. They couldn't know about the groups' efforts unless someone informed them.

Bishop Terrell sheepishly raised his hand, reminiscing, the glare focused in Miles' direction from Michael Zarkuhn earlier.

"If I may ... Mr. Tashido, did you in fact speak with a member of the "Nero Clan", yes or no?"

Mr. Tashido snatched someone's wine glass from the table and guzzled its contents down nervously.

"Yes! Yes for the love of creation yes! He said his name was Paul and that he merely wanted to talk with me. He said I should return immediately, but I knew ... or I think. Well, anyway I asked to speak with Merie and he told me that was not possible until I complied. He warned me to speak to no one of this matter. I've sentenced me family to death by showing up here tonight I should've returned.

Doctor Alice Martin was Louis' co-researcher on the project he was assigned to. She possessed knowledge of his findings and was aware of how close they were to breaking ground for the next level in their research. However, she'd some reservations as to whether or not her fellow associate had shared all data and information he knew with her and the group. Alice generally quiet abruptly stood up and slammed both hands firmly on the solid shiny table, slowly raised her redhead and angrily bellowed, "we simply must help Louis in anyway we can. Compromise aside I motion we retaliate against this action with the utmost prejudice."

Not that anyone at the conference table disagreed with her, but flags, whistles, fireworks, bells, and hell freezing over was picked up by all present. Something was wrong with Louis' story and Alice was either demonically possessed or trying to alert key members of the inner circle that Louis was full of excrement by her uncharacteristic display.

"Yes I agree," shouted Doctor Amin Sabat, exuding the enthusiasm of a collegiate athlete in a locker room.

Michael now noticed his palms were sweating which was rare for him. He stood up and with the command presence of a battlefield general turned his back to the group. Quickly he turned back around and looked at each member as they sat in anticipation of his next move. "As head of special operations I need to meet with the two senior members and you Ms. Martin after we've adjourned."

"Will there be anything more madam?" Peter asked loudly from the large double doorway with an exaggerated smile on his face. Suddenly everyone in the room burst into hysterical laughter even Louis could not refrain. The butler always took the edge off.

CHAPTER 7

THE ARCHANGEL GOES TO HONG KONG

As the meeting concluded with the last members filing their reports and giving parting goodbyes until the next inner circle conference Peter scurried towards the kitchen. Louis still remained to assist the strike team which was put together at the conclusion of Michael's security meeting.

"How's the tea Sir?" Peter asked Michael who entered the kitchen behind him. Peter put away the last pieces of china used earlier at the meeting.

"Peter somehow I've sensed you know more about what it is we are trying to fight then you let on. Don't answer just listen I'm not from here I'm immortal in fact I've been here for thousands of years." Michael didn't know why he was telling the old man this but he felt compelled to have at least one ally who knew his secret and well why not the butler.

Peter looked down at the floor, looked up at Michael and looked back down.

"Bloody hell if I've told the staff once I've told them a thousand times clean the floor. Always make sure the floor is cleaned before you retire for the evening. I'm sorry sir you were saying?"

"Never mind Peter thanks for the tea it was perfect."
Peter knelt down wiped the floor and apologized for being inattentive, "no problemmm sir."

Margarite, Miles and Louis were still sitting in the conference room when Michael returned from the kitchen. He knew Peter had heard him what he still didn't know was why he'd told the aging butler his secret.

"Well do you understand the tentative plan?" Mr. Zarkuhn asked the crew.
"Michael, try this on for size." Miles was smiling as he pulled out the seat next to him so Michael could sit next to him. Ms. Plantard then handed Michael a couple of papers and asked him to review them. Michael reviewed the protocol and plan and responded.

"We can do this. There will need to be a few changes, but this is viable, quite good. Who came up with this extraction plan? It's really quite innovative. However, you know that if we terminate any of "Nero's" agents we will incur serious repercussions should they find out it was us. They will seek retribution in a very serious way."

As Michael made eye contact with each occupant of the room they looked at each other trying to determine if what they'd decided was indeed prudent in light of what he'd just shared. Each member could almost hear the other's thoughts and those thoughts were singular and unmistakable, "If we do not retaliate with a strong resolute answer to this egregious act we and countless other innocent will suffer later."

Michael smiled at Louis "very well we will save the family of Mr. Tashido. Louis are you completely comfortable with what you must do and how? Remember the microchip and nano-surveillance unit will record all that occurs once you leave this room. The chip will be placed under the skin behind your left ear. Both are undetectable we used organic Salmon DNA from our techno lab outside Washington. Do you have any questions?"

Mr. Tashido shook his head from side to side as he stared into the massive stone fire place in the conference room. "Yes I understand. When do we leave?"

His mind appeared to be elsewhere and although he may have seemed okay with the direction the Collective was going Michael could see he was concealing something, something important and that made his colleagues cautious.

"Our flight departs tomorrow gentlemen. I've reserved our tickets with Delta. We leave at 06:22 for Hong Kong with stops in Atlanta, Georgia and Hawaii." Miles seemed proud of his small everyday accomplishment making reservations. Probably because this was something alien to him.

"Michael you have a call." Peter announced from the door of the conference room. Michael took the call and peered in the room at Miles and Louis. Margarite paced the hall next to Michael as he spoke on the phone.

"I understand", he stated and hung up the phone.

Michael walked over to Margarite who stopped directly in front him with her arms folded, she was obviously anxious.

She spoke to Michael in a low almost sultry tone, "do you really understand Michael, because I don't understand. Why must we do this?"

Margarite turned and walked briskly upstairs to her room. Michael could feel Peter's eye upon him as he looked down the hall at him to only see him turn and disappear into the kitchen.

The next morning after arriving at Atlanta's Hartsfield-Jackson airport the three men spoke maybe three words between them in two hours. Later in Hawaii Michael directed Louis to make an attempt to call his wife and the abductor. Louis removed his cell phone and made the call in a secluded corner.

He was surprised by who answered.

"Baby it's me. Are you and Tashi alright? Yes, I will speak with him put him on. Paul I apologize for the delay." The Michael and Miles heard him explain.

Michael and Miles sat on the edge of their seats with great intensity trying to gage this gist of the conversation and that of the man on the other end of the call. Mr. Tashido hung up and looked at the phone as though it had offended him.
Michael noticed he was once again in a daze so he tried to get his attention with a low whistle. "Louis what did they say? Is your family okay?"

Louis sat back in his chair sighed, "my family's okay but I must meet with their captors by Friday or they won't be for long."

"Well we have two days so we'll make it", offered Miles.

Michael put his chair back and as the pilot made his flight announcement about an altitude 30,000 feet Michael settled in he felt relieved that his two associates were not seated with him. As he drifted off into semi-consciousness he was not so sure Louis Tashido was as innocuous as his situation and character suggested.

Suddenly, Michael was dreaming about his past once more. He'd met Mr. Joseph A. Plantard in 1917 in Germany before the war. It was at a clandestine party in a castle outside Stuttgart, Germany. This meeting was a precursor to the later secret society meetings of the Bilderberger conferences which now meet once a year in extreme secrecy at plush and luxurious hotels around the world. Its' guest were the elite and as well as the scourge of this beautiful planet, because of the ways and means by which those who met designed their projected domination of Earth and her indigenous peoples. Most of the planet's human population were without the blood of the Gods and therefore considered Goyim or cattle.

Michael felt honored at the time at this 1917 meeting with the elite of Europe, America and Asia. Of course he had not known that the main theme of the meeting was to help design the theatrics of World War I.

Mr. Plantard was a short gentleman with an athletic physique and was known for his sublime strategic and critical thinking. He'd made his money through mining and shipping. Michael also remembered he was drawn to him and they spent many hours at the meetings and after discussing literally everything. Plantard reminded Zarkuhn of another close friend he had hundreds of years prior by the name Count de Saint-Germaine born 1710. A mysterious gentleman who some say was immortal. Saint-Germaine's death was never really confirmed although most agree it may have been 1784. How Michael wished his new friend Joseph was immortal.

Mr. Plantard told Michael of a secret group he belonged to and asked him to consider joining them. Michael explained that he was not able to at that time, but would keep the matter confident and ask if the offer to join at a later date would be extended. That is how he was able to meet Margarite the day of the 911 tragedy Michael replayed the day in his mind. He had spoken to Plantard while visiting his mansion right after Margarite had graduated from college in 1983. A smile across his face as he could see her face the morning she walked in on him while he was stark naked in one of the guest bathrooms. It was funny to him that she had not remembered him some 18 years later when he returned to warn her of the impending doom.

Mr. Joseph A. Plantard was indeed a good friend. He always had dinner with Zarkuhn whenever he visited Europe or Asia. Plantard preferred the anonymity when he leisured with his more trusted friends. Michael thought back on a meeting that took place in Italy at a quaint Italian bistro near the Vatican. He could see the faces of the tourists who came strolling in raving the praises of having just seen the Vatican and the Pope. The expression on Plantard's face said it all. Later, Michael asked him about the matter. He was very garrulous in his position of the church, Christianity and religions in general.

Suddenly Zarkuhn woke up. The flight attendant was asking him something.

"Sir", she asked, "would you like some refreshments?"
Michael replied in kind, "no thank you."

Zarkuhn strolled back into his memories recalling the shock he received when his long time friend explained why he did not trust religion and the churches, synagogues, temples or mosques. He shared his secret with Zarkuhn the same year he was mysteriously killed.

CHAPTER 8
SANCTIONED KILL

The three men avoided all contact with one another in the airport once their flight had landed in Hong Kong.

Zarkuhn called out for a taxi as the terminal traffic and passengers shuffled pass him. Miles was met by the Asian station chief, Maurice Murray who had flown in the day before from the Philippines.

"It's a pleasure to see you Maruice," Miles greeted the station chief.

"Hop in Miles we have our rooms already", Maurice yelled across the roof of the rental car before jumping in.

Louis Tashido paid his parking fee and headed straight for the small vacation home owned by his wife's family. He placed a call to Merie.

"Merie, baby I will be there shortly let me speak with Paul."

Paul took the phone, "hello Louis you are here already that is good. Please hurry we have business to attend to. However we will not be here when you arrive, but you know what we want when we do. As a show of good faith we're letting Merie go okay. Don't let us down."

"Paul let me speak to Merie," Louis requested.

"Baby, take Tashi and leave for home immediately; I have it from here. Don't worry all will be okay; now just go, hurry."

Merie was afraid and Louis could hear it in her soft voice, "Louis what is going on? Who are these people? Are you in trouble Louis?"

Louis shouted, "please do as I say woman, enough is enough. Take Tashi and go home now!"

He cut off the call wondering why simple instructions were so hard to follow for most people even his loving wife. Why did he have to always manipulate situations in order to achieve his desired results? Perhaps it would all change in the next couple of hours.

Meanwhile Zarkuhn was tailing Mr. Tashido. He had picked up a rental from Moma & Sons Rental which was located a distance away from the airport.

Thanks to the latest technology Zarkuhn had no difficulty tracking the corrupted Collective member. Michael knew the importance of Mr. Louis Tashido's research with regards to project "Gynysyx". Michael knew that the Collective's findings were as accurate to what had actually occurred in the history of humanity without his direct input.

Zarkuhn once again retraced Joseph's argument, "Michael, I've always execrated religion as you know. My abhorrence with the institution of religion is the mind control it has uses to mislead the ignorant and innocent. Religion is simply riddled with hypocrisy especially Christianity. Not to mention religions who have Gods' that will promise you your fill of under aged virgins in gardens for eternity if you blindly follow the bloody mis-teachings of some Islamic extremist. Most of the takers are usually illiterate, underage or so high on drugs they are already dead and with their God before they execute their deplorable acts of attacking and killing the innocent children of Allah. I mean does Allah require you marry these virgins first? These fanatics make God sound like a bloody pimp mind you."

"Where was I? Yeah the Christians worst of the bunch! Anyway I'll never forget sitting in a Baptist church while visiting one of my Negro friends during the height of the civil rights marches in support of equal rights for Blacks back in the Unites States. Have you ever been to a Southern Baptist Church Mr. Zarkuhn? It's an experience saturated with entertainment, dance and much lively song even some rather interesting theatrics. It makes for great superb entertainment. Well, half way through the sermon the preacher as they refer to him states that women were more prone to sin by nature. This was justified with referencing the fall of Eve via her transgression in the Garden of Eden." Michael noticed the zeal with which his friend Joseph was gearing up for the attack and prepared himself for his friend's sermon.

Plantard took a drink of his espresso and began his assault. "Michael I nearly fell off the end of my chair. There I was, down South, way down South in Dixie doing my part to support the rights of Blacks in America. Yes, sitting in a Black Southern Baptist church listening to a sermon about how Eve was tricked by some snake thus, making women were more likely to commit sins. Bullshit! Total, unadulterated bull the most appalling part of the charade was that the cattle, sheep, that whole congregation just sat there and let the shepherd get away with stereotyping women. The congregation couldn't see that their rights were being violated by a Black man right there in God's on home."

"So Joe what happened? Surely there's more." Michael asked anxiously.

Joseph tried to catch his breath. "What happened was almost my lynching by the entire Black community for my volunteering to point out a few transgressions of Mr. Man, Adam, after the sermon that day. Some of the congregation gathered in the lobby after services and I asked them to go to Genesis which their minister did cheerfully. I'll tell you by this time we had gathered half the congregation in the lobby of the church. Everyone wanted to see the white boy preach or teach whatever.

Once we verified everyone was at Genesis I referred all present to chapter 3 of the "King James Version of the Holy Bible". Well that's when all HELL broke loose. Wow! I made a joke. Get it? All hell, the Bible, church."

"Yes, once there I asked everyone to read verses 3:1 through 3:5 and asked them to repeat after me. The serpent asked Eve "what did God say" and the woman, Eve, replied "that we may eat of all the trees in the Garden, but of the tree in the midst of the Garden we shall not eat of it, nor shall we touch it, for the day we do we will die".

"Then I asked them to go to chapter 2 of Genesis verses 2:16 to 2:17 and read out loud. By this time I'd caught the "Baptist Bug" myself, hot flashes and all shouting loudly, "and what did God say to Adam?" I repeated what I read aloud with them, "and God commanded the man saying of the tree in the Garden thou may eat freely. But of the tree of "knowledge of good and evil", thou may not eat of it for in the day thou shall eat you will surely die!"

Zarkuhn felt a chill at the last statement his friend had made. He was venerated by what he had heard that day in Italy with from friend. Michael Zarkuhn realized where Joseph Plantard was going with the passages. Michael was sentenced to live on Earth for asking his lord why Adam and his mate had not died that very day. He had also wondered why the act they had done was such a sin, because since their transgression they reflected the attitude, judgment and intellect of his very Masters, the Elohim of God himself.

Plantard continued to grow more excited, "it was that preacher and my friend who noticed the discrepancy in what Jehovah had said to Adam and what Eve told the "Nachash" or serpent. I asked all who were present to read the two passages again and to compare what God had said and explain it. Then I admit I went over board sounding a bit like a home grown Southern Baptist Minister myself ... yes ... yes ..., "Eve said touch, yet God clearly said to Adam eat and eat only. Does God say what he means and means what he says I shouted?" The house yelled "yes, oh heavenly spirit yes", "then I shouted well why did Adam lie to Eve telling her that God said not to touch the blasted fruit either. Ladies sounds to me like a husband who says don't write any checks honey, no don't even touch the check book or something in the account will bounce. Just like men to lie. Michael I tell you, you could have heard a pin drop. All of a sudden there was the rustling of paper back and forth and then conversation, lots of it."

"The last thing I remember was that big black preacher snarling and trying his best to turn purple in the face. That black preacher nearly passed out right there on the spot do to that effort. My friend hurried me out of Georgia not just the church. We've spoken over the years but he's never invited me back. So that's just one of my reasons for mistrusting religion and clergy."

Michael thought back on that day in the Garden of Eden and recalled that it was Adam's over zealous attempt to protect the new naive Eve from committing a violation of his lord's command that set Eve up for failure. For when Eve had come to him he acquainted her with the animals, the lay of the land and the food that was provided for them warning her not to eat from the tree and the middle of the garden. But Eve was so innocent and more naïve than Adam so he told her God said not to touch the fruit either a lie that would change humanity's destiny.

Well the serpent now had a way of discrediting the whole law now if he could only show her that the touch would not kill her. So he showed her the fruit and quickly touched her hand with it. She was already confused when the magician did not die because he was handling the fruit. That touch convinced Eve the fruit must good to eat. The fact there were no deaths that day did not help Michael's God's case either. Gabriel, Uriel and Michael were duly perplexed.

Zarkuhn could now see Louis' car turning into a driveway up ahead. The neighborhood was quiet, upscale and had plenty of trees and vegetation which Michael knew might come in handy. There were no other cars in the driveway or on the street which struck Zarkuhn as a bit strange. He wondered where Paul and his entourage might be hidden. Mr. Tashido removed an attaché from his car and made his way to the back then to the side door and entered the small house. Michael patched into central in order to exploit the devices located on Louis Tashido so he could listen in.

Michael could hear him answer the phone, "yes you're correct this is he I have it. I'll wait for you ... oh did my family get out okay?"

Louis headed for the kitchen. He approached the refrigerator and opened it reaching for the freezer compartment he suddenly saw a flash. He fell to his knees at time same time his head violently struck the frame of the refrigerator. "Oh God no," he yelled but nothing came out. As he lay on the floor gurgling blood from his mouth his vision was gone he could not see. Tashido was fading fast loosing consciousness, loosing his life. In his final moments of silence he panicked and struggled. He was a competent enough scientist to know he had taken a gunshot blast to the back of his head.

Louis' last thoughts were who did this and what would happen to the relic? Darkness won over him as he slipped away the last temporal experience he had was hearing a door shut.

CHAPTER 9

LOUIE, LOUIE, LOUIE

Zarkuhn saw the headlights in his rear view mirror and slid down in his seat as best as he could. The approaching car was a Jaguar with three men inside. It passed him at a slow rate of speed. Whoever it was were casing the place. The door behind the driver opened and a body ran out towards the back of the house. Michael Zarkuhn reached under the seat for his alternate weapon. He pressed a button on his cell phone which alerted Miles that the bait was being taken.

Zarkuhn had fought soldiers loyal to the Superior General of the Church before and if these were some of them they would be very proficient students of "contemplativus in actione", or active contemplation. This practice of strict obedience made them reliable and formidable and was practiced by the Swiss Guard, Jesuits, the Knights of Malta, American government officials, etcetera, etc. each group was very motivated and extremely loyal. Loyalty was such a rare and precious human character trait worth the weight in gold of those practiced it. Zarkuhn had decided that taking prisoners for questioning would not be an option on this gig. He knew with the Vatican's vast resources hidden deep in the coffers of their archives that even his immortality could be threatened by some ancient concoction or bad backdoor non-secular contract signed by some bureaucratic heavenly saint cast out from his home world eons ago.

The Jaguar returned heading in the opposite direction with the lights turned off. It parked parallel just in front of the house near the curb and the other two men in the entered through the side door.

Michael could hear them talking through the hidden device concealed on the dead Louis Tashido.

The first voice he heard was that of Paul, "oh no!
What the hell happened here?"

Zarkuhn had been around for centuries and as such he could sense certain telling emotions in the actions and voices of humans. The response he had just heard in Paul's voice was telling him that Paul was all too familiar with the deceased. Paul questioned his man who had apparently entered the kitchen first and found Louis' body.

"This is the way I found him." The man answered. "Just like this and I can tell you the kill is fresh, within the hour."

Paul noticed something on the body that peaked interest. "I see two bullets to the back of the head, but what is this incision behind his left ear? Kev hand me that knife there off the sink. Was there anything else, a package, were his hands just like that, was that refrigerator opened or did you open it? Move Kevin what is this here? Look here a tracking probe. State of the art these little babies are."

Paul wondered who else his associate Louis Tashido may have been working with. Paul would miss this valuable source. He'd done much for the Brotherhood and the Church over the years. They were not close, but recently their common goals had pushed them closer. Their partnership was producing results towards the unification of the two more influential secret societies and the Vatican who Paul had sworn his allegiance.

Zarhuhn now felt some palliation about his hit on this compromised member. He was elated to have executed the order by the Controller and Collective to terminate this loose end. However, Michael still felt a loss for Doctor Tashido's family. He knew Louis' young wife Merie and his little boy and was fond of them both. Although he could not fully understand nor comprehend the concept of family his many years on the planet aided in him respecting the importance of the need for the family unit amongst the humans. He had come to the conclusion that in the societies where this family unit concept was strongest the species tended to survive and prosper more efficiently.

Paul was now on his cell phone with someone, "your Eminence why would the Collective kill their own member? Their more like a boys and girls club from what I've heard it doesn't add up. I agree with you your Eminence there most certainly has to be another player in the game, but who? Yes of course that would be my job, yes at once."

There was a pause and then Paul began to speak again, "We will sanitize the site. No all is well with our latest shipments." He hung up and could be heard directing his team.

Michael was concerned as to why the men continued there chatter when it was now known that an active bug was in their midst. The answer was clear they wanted him to feed off what was said. No problem he thought he'd play along.

Miles was trying to call in when the three men under surveillance loaded up their car. Zarkuhn maintained his stealthy position in his rental. He wanted the kill he show them the bad guys the ends and outs of "the boys and girls club" as Paul put it. Something was driving him to clean this matter up with Paul right then. This desire unsettled him it seemed his aspiration was driven more by instinct then reason. To want to engage and terminate Paul and his two soldiers as much as he desired only meant that he could make no mistakes during this mission. Michael had learned as a Supreme Commander of the Armies of the Almighty to attack using surprise, force and no mercy. It had become second nature to him to conquer ... not wait to be conquered.

The men were now in the jaguar and pulling off with the headlights off. Michael laid his head down towards the passenger side of the seat and waited. There was a bright light followed by an explosion that shook his car as he glanced up. The Tashido's vacation home was literally obliterated. Smoke and fire was bellowing up in cycles as the sky was illuminated by the bon fire. This action was expected in order to sanitize the scene. Michael was now turning his vehicle around and heading in the direction of the character called Paul. He could see fire trucks and emergency vehicles headed up the hill towards him as he drove down. Fear that the authorities might stop him or the bad guys raced through his mind as he trekked away from the inferno.

He called Miles, "Miles I'm tailing the bad guys. Did you get all of that activity recorded?"

"Yes, I did. I don't understand why this guy did not destroy the devices, since he obviously found them, Miles asked? He's a pro; surely he knows we could exploit this against them."

Zarkuhn did not respond to Miles' inquiry. He was acutely aware that he was being led by the man referred to as Paul to a trap. He could see the Jaguar was approaching what appeared to be a fishing district. It was an industrial area with warehouses and dilapidated buildings and ships along the wharf. The bouquet from the salt and algae from the ocean was extra heavy as Michael drove closer. Its' swells could be seen dancing against the docks to a beat orchestrated by the encroaching moon. It made a great deal of sense to Michael that at least a portion of "The Black Popes', operation would be located in such a strategically sound place, the docks.

Paul's car pulled next to a badly painted warehouse on the end of one of the wharfs. Zarkuhn parked his rental some 300 yards away and concealed it behind another warehouse and some crates. His adrenalin was running high as he holstered his Glock 18C and double checked to ensure the other two weapons on him were locked and fully loaded. Zarkuhn carried two Glocks, both fully automatic packing fifteen rounds a piece. His other favorite was the Llama 87, a

Spanish sporting handgun which he carried in a back braced holster. A most unlikely weapon for combat kills, but it was a special gift from his friend Pablo Picasso, the famous Spanish artist. He was now feeling ready for the turkey shoot.

Voices could be heard accompanied by laughter echoing from the warehouse a short distance away and before he realized it he could see the doors were wide open. There was a night operation going on inside but he couldn't make out what kind from where he stood. He sat down behind some large boxes just east of the building's front opening. He could see boats making there way from the back side of the warehouse to two large ships in the bay. Michael slowly removed his camera to take zoom shots of all the vessels supporting the operation. The tracking devices that had been hidden behind Louis Tashido's ear went off line. This was his cue to stay alert and prepare for anything from that point on. As Zarkuhn took a glimpse around the large box concealing him he noticed Paul with four other men walking out front. In the distant on the same side as the warehouse he saw another person discretely dart along the side of one of the shacks in the shadows. Zarkuhn sensed Paul's might be an ace, but he had seen it coming so he'd be prepared. Paul left the men outside and walked back in slowly. As Zarkuhn watched Paul suddenly stopped and walked hastily back to the men outside. One of the other men called inside … he was screaming for the others to come out. A mental hemorrhoid for Michael was the physiological reaction of perspiration, he hated sweat. The former Archangel detested this biological feature of his new existence. He had become accustomed to the physiological phenomenon even though it had taken some 9000 odd years or so to do. Subconsciously it was what his sweating represented psychologically … fear and anxiety. He loathed being physically reminded that he felt threatened that he could experience fear. This emotion was entirely too human for his emotional palate.

What was going on inside he pondered? Paul and ten men were now outside in front of the warehouse all armed. Michael slowly eased away from the large crates towards the side of the warehouse further east of Paul's location. The men began to separate into small groups. They were now searching the docks in all directions. As Michael retreated slowly into the crevasses of the murkiness of the dock he maintained vigilance on the spot where he had seen the mysterious figure earlier. He was in no mood to be killed again. Twice in one week would be a new record for him, one he was going to try and avoid at all cost. It did not matter he was immortal … dying hurt like hell. There's no good or easy way to accomplish the task of dying. He reminisced all the ways he'd become acquainted with the

Grim Reaper and none were welcomed. No, death was not an option, no pain damn it not tonight. There would only be pain for the others, those who got in his way. Zarkuhn locked and loaded. Suddenly the shadow a darker presented itself at his feet.

CHAPTER 10

PAUL'S NO SAINT

"Don't shoot!" Maurice begged with both hands in the air.

"Miles was worried you might need help and asked me to join you. I had a little trouble locating you. The tracking device stopped working about fifteen minutes ago."

Michael was now agitated at the man's arrival. Maurice was an outstanding station chief, but Michael knew little of him. He had not hired Maurice as he had most of the other station chiefs. Maurice had been with the Collective prior to Michael joining leaving a void in Michael's mind as to Maurice's marksmanship and martial arts abilities.

"Suush"! Zarkuhn patted the grounded beside him getting Maurice to kneel beside him. "No talking do you understand?" Michael whispered and before the station chief could answer Michael's hand was on his mouth and a big index finger in Maurice's face was going from one side to the other. "No talking". Maurice nodded realizing he had almost messed up the request. He held his pistol, a SIG P228 with both hands between his legs as he kneeled. At least his side arm selection was acceptable a weapon made by the Swiss and holding a thirteen round clip. This reflected sound judgment and strong prior training with side arms for this was not the weapon of a novice.

Zarkuhn had always worked alone in the field for the three years after he'd joined the Collective only using his agents as occasional messengers.

He moved closer to Maurice, "let's move further east I want you to place yourself on my left flanking the center of the warehouse, okay? When you see me move cover me. If I do not move cover me anyway. Whatever, happens you must not be compromised do you understand", Michael asked? Maurice caught on but cringed at the thought of taking his own life, but he gave thumbs up and nodded. Maurice assumed a prone position and began to crawl slowly thirty meters away from Zarkuhn's position. Once Maurice was in position he noticed two men approaching him. He began to move as far back from the boxes and crates concealing him as he could towards the edge of the peer. Maurice desperately tried to get Michael's attention but without success. As he peered around the corner from his location he could see why. The men approaching clearly had an agenda and it appeared to be to flush out Zarkuhn not him as he had thought. Four more men were approaching Zarkuhn's spot from his west and two from his front position. Paul was now lighting a cigarette and walking towards Zarkuhn behind the two men preparing for the frontal assault. Paul swaggered as though he were taking a leisurely stroll with a companion in a park.

Paul could now be heard by Zarkuhn and Maurice as he spoke through the headset he sported. "We think he's directly in front of us. No we have not made contact yet. What is your wish your eminence, should we terminate the subject? Paul was standing about 150 meters directly in front of Zarkuhn and his stature clearly revealed to Zarkuhn a physically superior specimen. Zarkuhn could see that he did not have to wonder about Paul's martial abilities or his confidence in matters relating to what was about to occur.

The other men had stopped as Paul began to speak to whomever he was conferencing with. Zarkuhn looked to his left to check on Maurice. He had vanished and Zarkuhn was pleased, but puzzled at the same time. He cautiously moved back to take a look further towards the water behind the wharf and caught the shadow of what may have been Maurice entering the choppy surf. Michael felt a weight off of him, now he felt like being proactive about the given situation he no longer had to worry about a team member's safety.

Paul looked to his right and then to the left. He adjusted the frequency on his headset at the waist and directed one of the groups to move in. It was the group furthest from Michael, the group east of him.

Michael Zarkuhn took a deep breath and picked his mark. With literally supernatural speed his first shots hit the men closest to him before they could react. The first man dropped in a limp pile of flesh breaking his right leg from the weight of his body as he crumbled. His partner fired off several rounds in desperation as Zarkuhns rounds had penetrated his right retina and left cheek. The second man's scream was so unnerving that the other attackers scurried for cover stumbling and temporarily loosing their professional mercenary composure.

Michael was now running and moving to his east where the two bodies of the first victims lie in what looked like an oil slick under the dark skirt of night. The moon was at a quarter and the clutter on the dock assisted in camouflaging Michael's large mass as he jetted to another set of crates. A hail of bullets began to pop off around his position bursting splinters of wood like confetti, but he knew the attackers had not beaded in on him yet. His night vision was superior a benefit of his supernatural DNA. He could see as though it was daylight and he saw an advantage as he hit the ground hard behind his next hiding spot. The next four rounds blast right through the hand and chest cavity of one of his attackers and two of the other rounds shattered the shoulder of the fallen man's wing man.

Paul was now moving parallel to Michael and delivering heavy rounds in Michael's direction in an effort to pin him down. Michael could see that unlike his men, Paul's rounds were hitting within inches of him. He now focused on Paul's attack. The six remaining men were now joined by others from the warehouse and they were sporting night vision goggles. Zarkuhn had that feeling it was time to get lost and quick. An opportunity presented itself in the form of an old wooden shack behind him. It was just what he needed to make his escape. Michael now pulled his other weapon and stood up both firearms were now catapulting hot projectiles in Paul's direction. The first bullet hit the blonde man in the right arm knocking him off balance and abruptly on his back. Paul although struck with a 9mm round lodge in his arm continued to scoot on his back as though he was performing a drill in Army basic training. Zarkuhn made a mental note that Paul did not cry out or even wince at the time the bullet made impact. He was now beginning to suspect something really nasty about his battle worthy adversary. But this moment was not the time to go over possibilities about the blonde superman. Michael turned and darted in the direction of the shack behind him as quickly as he could. Sweat raced down his face and his heart pounded so hard it hurt. All of a sudden a searing pain burned in his right side above his groin. One of the assailants had flanked him and Zarkuhn had run right into the bullet from the man's gun, but Michael's momentum propelled him and the shooter through the door of the shack knocking the shooter on his back; as the shooter fell backwards he released his weapon in an attempt to break his inevitable fall. Zarkuhn tossed the weapon in his right hand as he was falling on top of the unfortunate soul and using his right hand now free quickly grabbed the attacker's throat as he fell on his chest and squeezed his larynx hard with his massive hand crushing it. The man gave little or no resistance as though he had been sedated. Michael kept moving as his right knee rested on the man's chest his left foot continued pushing off the dead man's right arm he headed to the back of the shack still at full speed impervious to the wound he'd sustained. With the force of a professional football player he hit the back of the wooden shack while spinning so that the impact was absorbed by his back letting it do the damage to the aged wooden structure. Turning he saw two gunmen enter the shack with guns blazing. He answered their assault by emptying the remainder of his clip from the second gun in his left hand at them as he fell into a salad of wood and glass in the cold dark water beneath the pier.

CHAPTER 11

THOUGHT GOD HAD ONLY ONE SON

The telephone rang in the study at the Plantard mansion.

"Plantard residence may I help you", Peter answered. "Hello Doctor Teranez how are you. Yes, I'll get her at once."

Peter approached the intercom and paged Margarite. "Madam, madam."

"Peter what is it sir?" Margarite responded.

"Doctor Teranez is on the phone for you madam."

Margarite picked up the line, "hello Cheryl I take it you have DNA results for us."

"How did you know that?" Cheryl replied jokingly.

"The results are ... wait, is the scrambler on Margarite?"

Margarite glanced down to ensure the settings on her line indicated the conversation was secure.

"We're clear go on. What did you learn?" Margarite was really curious about the results on the three fingers collected by Michael on the men who had attacked him the day of their meeting.

"Two of the DNA markers indicate the men were in the family of Nimrod. Ted ran the fingerprints through our national and local identification data banks and they came back with negatives on two of them. We did get a lucky hit on one of the fingerprints though. The guy was a man by the name of Anatoili Ognorski, a former Russian Special Forces officer with the defunct KGB. But the funny thing is Mr. Orgnoski was reported as deceased as of 8 August 1987. How many times has the Collective seen this kind of resurrection?" The doctor asked sarcastically.

"Was Orgnoski one of the Sons? Did his DNA provide a link to one of the families?" Margarite knew the answer before the doctor told her.

"Yes and no; his genetic signature was strong with the line of the Rephaim family line. Essentially he's a descendant of the large reptilian guys with a drop of mammal. This definitely explains the large size of the finger and Mr. Zarkuhn's description of him being unusually corpulent. His relatives were probably those from the Caucasus Mountain region located near the Russian and Turkish border before they migrated southwest to a more hospitable climate. Well this Og gentleman definitely got his size honest as documented throughout the scriptures in Genesis, Exodus and Deuteronomy. The giants have been around since before Noah at least the documented accounts. It's a bit ironic that this character's family line may go back to King Og of Canaan who hid on the Ark and later married one of Naoh's daughters. Just think our Michael may have slain Goliath's great, great, great, great, great grandson," Doctor Teranez concluded.

Well this was interesting thought Margarite the Collective now had a faction of the Nephelim Order also showing aggression against them. Margarite thanked the doctor and hung up the phone. She tried to reason out the new data she had just been given. She was bewildered by the Collective's present volatile situation. There was the attack against Michael at his hotel, then a kidnapping of Louis Tashido's family by another secret faction. It seemed everyone was moving against their order. She remembered her father explaining that a day would come when "imbalanced forces" would move to destroy her family and the Collective. She had asked him why he didn't just say evil forces why "imbalanced forces". His reply and explanation was, "my dear one person's evil is another person's good this relationship can still provide balance; however, imbalance within any living thing is not the natural state of the thing proven by the mere existence of its imbalanced state, thus making it unsuitable to live with and negatively affecting all things it comes in contact with that are balanced dark or light. The imbalanced state must first be detected or recognized and then ultimately purged. So if a person kills my dear it does not mean they are necessarily evil murder may be consistent with their predatory nature which in truth does not constitute imbalance, yet the act itself of killing amongst most humans is an act which creates an imbalanced environment. The question that the Collective seeks is what constitutes a real human? As Solomon said, "know the nature of a thing". It may not be natural for humans to kill or murder one another without just cause, but what does a human look like? If a creature looked like a man but its genetic makeup was not truly what constituted a man then perhaps this creature's predisposition to violent acts which so offend us and create imbalances within our society could be explained. How would you be able to figure it out? Do the nonhumans have blue eyes are they Black, Asian maybe, or do you have to look under the microscope to get a closer look?"

Her father then put his arms around her as she recalled and said "just be aware that people are not what they may appear to be ... figuring out what they are will let you know their inherent nature and what they might be, no what they are capable of."

That was right before old man Plantard's death when he'd gotten back from Europe. Now she and the Collective continued the research which her father had so fervently dedicated the secret organization to. In the hope of someday being able to identify the others who looked like men and women, but in fact were different beneath the skin. He'd bought in on the belief that only through genetic technological advancement could the Collective really know who or what they were dealing with on the planet.

"Ooh my! Peter you scared me." Margarite was startled by Peter's entrance into the room with the afternoon mail.

"This came by courier Madam." Peter handed the express letter pack to Ms. Plantard and retreated somewhere into the abyss of the massive mansion as he always did.
The package was addressed to Senator Karen Stinger, O.W.O.W. Foundation which was a nonprofit cover for the Collectives philanthropic operations and language based educational programs. The package was from Senator Karen Stinger's office sent out from SOG, seat of government location, Washington D.C.

Margarite dared not open it without another Collective member present. She had become adept to C.H.A. "covering her ass", since becoming a member of the Collective. In fact, she found herself gingerly laying the express package down on her study desk and wiping the area where she had held the package.

"I'm becoming paranoid for heaven's sake. Margie get a grip", she mumbled."

Senator Stinger listened to the cell phone dial tones and then left a message, "Yo luva, how are you? I'm headed to Hotlanta this afternoon. Call me okay love you."

She slid her phone into her purse and continued to her car. Karen was feeling uuphoric. The last session before the holidays had just finished and the house and senate were able to pass the intelligence bill recommended by the 9/11 commission. She could finally get some R&R with her lover.

As Senator Stinger turned her ignition on a tap on the window jolted her. It was Carl, her page.

She rolled the window down, "Carl what is it? Is everything okay?"

The young freckled face man from Dade County Florida pushed his glasses up on his face from the center using his right index finger at least three times in one second. "Senator I hate to disturb you, but I hadn't seen you and heard that you'd already gone on vacation so I fast tracked some documents to your foundation office in Boston. I hope that was okay? When you come back I would like to show you something pertaining to the new Intelligence Reform Bill the house just passed."

Karen thought this to be a strange request but she had personally selected this young Opie looking teen to be on her staff because he was brilliant. He had scored a total of 2325 on his SAT and graduated valedictorian from his high school. He was a senior at Emory University, located in Atlanta, Georgia and maintaining a 4.0 with a major in pre-law with a minor in mathematics and if Carl was concerned than she was compelled to look into the matter.

"Carl it's alright and yes I'll get with you when I get back."

"Just when you get a chance ma'am please review section 14 of the bill very closely, okay", the young man begged.

"I'll do that Carl; most certainly I will and have a wonderful holiday. I like saying that sounds politically correct to me. Don't you think so Carl?"

"Yes ma'am and Merry Christmas to you ma'am."
The Senator rolled up her window and headed for the airport.

Carl quickly headed back in. The weather was bitterly cold and the city as bracing itself for a snow storm. He was glad the senator was taking some time off. Carl said good night to two of the other office staffers and headed out the door. The young page realized he could do no more with the draft of the bill that was delivered to the Senator's office apparently by mistake. The draft of the new Intelligence bill which had rested on his desk was routed to the office after the signing of the original but this copy had markers and notes in someone's handwriting with which he did not recognize. The notes and what appeared to be corrections were all done in red ink. The initials LEX were next to each change and on some pages HER was initialed. He believed the LEX and HER represented the Lexington Institution and Heritage Foundation. What baffled the young page the most was the notes and content on each marked page. The changes seemed to suggest or if he was correct in how he interpreted it a significant negative impact in civil liberties for American citizens; specifically during times of emergency disasters or increased threat indicators as forecasted by the hierarchy of the new governmental apparatus. The bill also appeared to have left openings as though it would work with some future bill or legislation. The young red head Opie looking page had compared this draft to the final bill and was confused by his findings. He knew the bill was too thick for his boss and most of the other senate offices to read in its entirety, but the flags and sticky notes had aided him in his findings. Carl took the draft home and made notes for the senator in order to make it easier for her to follow his concerns. Surely the document wasn't classified. How could it be? It was the law governing American people so he felt all was well and locked up his office and headed home.

Miles looked up from his paper work where he was seated in the lobby of his hotel and spotted Maurice.

"You're wet! What happened? Where's Michael Zarkuhn?"

"Maurice just kept walking until he got to the hotel elevators. Pushing every button frantically as though that would speed the transaction up he looked at Miles and stated, "Zarkuhn is mad the man is crazy. I left him on the pier back at the harbor."

Miles' expression was that of disbelief, "what do you mean you left him? You mean you disserted him?"

"That's exactly what I did and you know what Mr. Turner I think your Mr. Zarkuhn wanted it that way. Frankly I'm relieved. I hope the man's alright, but there must have been twenty or more hostiles after him. When I slipped into the bay to haul tail it out of there I could hear mega gun fire. It went on and on and on. You know that guy's not well. Where did you all get that lunatic? He loves that bang, bang stuff and if he gets himself killed betcha he'll die happy … bang, bang!"

The elevator door opened on that remark and Maurice soggy with shoes squishing rudely excused himself.

Miles packed his paperwork in his briefcase and sucked down his scotch as his cell phone rang.

"Miles is Maurice with you? Did he make it back okay?" Zarkuhn quizzed.

CHAPTER 12

SON OF A GUN (PAUL)

"Find out everything we have on that character. Something's wrong, there's something nasty about this guy and I want to know what it is. I've seen pros before but this guy's way above the bar. You see that there, right there." Paul pointed to the dock area outside the shack where Zarkuhn had made his escape. "That's the son of a bitch's blood. Our man clearly got him and got him good. I'd say probably around the waist area from the blood splatter; while I'm thinking about it make sure the technician collects his blood it may come in handy." Paul frowned as he held his injured shoulder.

"So then what does this gibronni do after being popped one? He crushes our guy's trachea while still running over him and crashes through a damn wall while no less shooting in an acrobatic position at our incoming troops. Damn I'd like a soldier like that one for Christmas."

Paul was now real motivated. He had not had this kind of mortal challenge for years. Holding his shoulder in the splint the company medic had made for him he planned in his head how he would proceed. Right now he needed to notify his superiors of his failure to get the relic and to neutralize the intrusive operative on his own turf. He had not kept his promise to his boss sighting how easy it would be triangulating Zarkuhn's position using the implants behind Tashido's ear to track the homing device back to Zarkuhn.

"Damn he's good," Paul mumbled tossing his cigarette to the wet soaked pier and walking away.

"Michael where are you? Yes, Maurice got in a few minutes ago."
Miles was tense as he spoke with Michael. He was no field agent prayed he would not have to assist Zarkuhn with the use of a firearm. Miles realized he should not have volunteered for this operation. However, the Collective charter stated with regards to violations of Security Protocol and Integral Sanitation was clear, "termination of a Collective inner circle member required at least two inner circle members verify that the order was ratified by two thirds of the inner circle members to include their vote and that the verification and execution of the directive be carried out by two inner circle officers or one inner circle member and by proxy the head of special operations." Head of special operations being Michael Zarkuhn and he represented J.P. Rockdale for this unfortunate arrangement. The vote was eleven to one against at the last meeting. Margarite insisted another solution could be found.

However, the intelligence provided to the Collective supported the fact that Louis Tashido's committed security violations, collaborated with known threats to the Collective and withheld an artifact which the Collective had tasked him to find an artifact that had cost too many lives, time and money. The initial search for this particular artifact was initiated with the support of Clement of Alexandria in 210 A.D. while he secretly served as one of the first Collective inner circle members. Another member and former student of Clement of Alexandria was Origen. Origen's teachings and works were banned by the Roman Catholic Church fathers. It was he who insisted that the Collective address the problem of the Fallen Angels and their bloodline here on Earth, thus the Genome research lab was founded thousands of years later to do just that.

Alice Martin and Louis Tashido headed this endeavor for the Collective and had briefed all the members on past initiatives which had been a quest of the organization for over 1800 years.

Miles briefly remembered being totally fascinated by Doctor Martin's presentation and learning about the "Book of Enoch" and a Christian work called the "Clementine Homilies."

Tashido had reported to the group that he and Alice Martin had come across a source in the Middle East that could lead to some positive results in locating the most powerful treasure the Earth had ever known. Of course the Collective approved any and all resources in acquiring this find. Unfortunately, Mr. Tashido's acute change in behavior coupled with unexplained expenditures and travel generated suspicion by his cohort.

"Miles did you hear me? Are you there Miles? Michael was beginning to wonder if bringing Miles along was a prudent move. But all of the other members were preoccupied with previous engagements leaving only Miles to accompany him.

Miles snapped out of his trance and answered, "yes Michael I heard you I kinda dozed off for a minute there. You say you're fine right?"

"Yes, Yes I'm okay look I can't talk right now Miles."

Zarkuhn's wound had already begun to heal by the time he had gotten to his vehicle. It was a miracle that he was not seen during the night under the pier wading in the water. Every few minutes he would swim along the perimeter checking on his enemies' movements. They had searched for him all night and into the early morning. They appeared to have called off the search when several police and ambulance vehicles showed up at the warehouse. The mass exodus of boats which made a bee line to the two ships located in the bay was reminiscent of fleeing refugees that he had witnessed in Vietnam. Paul had definitely cleaned up the warehouse location and probably concocted some story of attempted theft. Michael was lucky to be on his way out of the area in one piece. His main objective now would be to connect with Miles and determine the next course of action.

Senator Stinger walked to baggage claim located in the North terminal when she saw her lover and sprinted over to her.

"I missed you baby. You look so good", the Senator from Florida purred. She picked up her bag placed it on the floor in record time. They were soon headed for her lover's car. "Let's get out of here honey."

"May I help with one of the bags, maybe your tote? The gorgeous Latino doctor asked her girlfriend. She was so elated at her companion's arrival. Cheryl had worked very hard the last week with her research at the genetics laboratory on the project called "Gynyxys" and with her other daily projects that came with being CEO of one of the most influential research facilities of its type in the world.

She began to assess her tasks and the institution's challenges. Running the facility was made complicated by the fact that the facility was completely privately funded and owned. No government funding or assistance aided in any of its research. The board of directors, the distinguished staff and anyone who made contributions were always under the United States Government scrutiny. Any research involving DNA was a very sensitive issue. Doctor Cheryl Teranez found herself motivated by the last report given to the Collective's inner circle. A revolutionary leap could be made if the briefing given by Alice Martin and Louis Tashido proved to be fruitful.

"Have I thanked you lately Karen for doing all you've done for me?" Cheryl asked her Senator lover gazing into her eyes as they pulled onto highway 75 South.

The Senator smiled, "If you're referring to our special work there is really no need baby you have been a God send. Your talent has spoken for itself. Girl do you know where we'd be without you honey? However, tonight after dinner you can show me that appreciation anyway."

Ms. Stinger leaned over and gently licked the left ear of Cheryl and whispered softly with a husky overtone, "we don't have to wait for dinner if you feel like it."

Cheryl could barely keep her hands on the steering wheel as Senator Stinger nestled her sweetly scented ear lobe. She felt the fire run from the top of her head taking the lusty highway through every Chakra till it rested in the steamy oven of her woman hood. She made sure to do at least 5 miles over the listed speed limit as best she could of course Cheryl desired to speed but her lover's notoriety dictated no unnecessary attention such as a speeding ticket be forthcoming.

Anish Markovitz was chafed when he picked his phone to call Margarite.

"Come on pick up the phone," he said aloud.
"That's funny. Pamela is your line working?" He called out to his secretary.

She responded, "Mr. Anish my line is fine."

Anish picked up his cell phone and punched in a page. He then entered the pin number 1*61# and hung up once these characters were entered. The cell phone sang and Mr. Markovitz answered, "Yes, who is this?"

"Anish what's up?" Ted Martin asked the question again, "Anish are you there?

"Yes Ted I'm here. I did not recognize your voice. There is something wrong at the mansion."
Ted tensed up. "Why do you think something is wrong?" Before a response was rendered, Ted called out to his wife Alice. "Alice please attempt to call Margarite. Anish hold on one moment okay."
Anish was starting to chatter …, "Ted, Ted…."

Ted was watching Alice dial the Plantard residence for confirmation and Anish was again asked to hold, "Anish please I beseech you calm down."

"There's no answer", the verdict from Alice as she hung up the phone line and scrambled for her coat and purse. Ted verified the fact with Anish and hung up his line. Simultaneously the three members' grabbed their coats, punched in telephone numbers and put the mandated emergency contingency plan into action.

Senator Stinger's pager went off then Doctor Teranez's, Miles nearly fell out of his bed when his pager sounded. Miles looked at his clock. "What the dickens, it's 05:47 in the morning." Miles managed to locate his cell phone and noticed the 1*61#. Miles had not heard the page but he understood the new code. The numbers were 332666777 which was the code for trouble. All the members thought the premise behind having the code was sound but the numbers themselves were rather childish. Contrary to what the members may have thought, on at least two other occasions the silly little numbers alert had worked.

Miles contacted the front desk in order to make arrangements to check out. Meanwhile Cheryl had just finished her shower and was getting dressed. Karen had to make a quick call to notify her Washington office that she would not be available until further notice. Ted and Alice were on the New Jersey Turn Pike headed south. Anish had just got off the phone with Makesh Patel who was in Boston's Logan Airport headed for India. He turned around and headed back out of the terminal yelling for a taxi using impeccably perfect English shocking himself. Makesh never used perfect English unless he was cussing with his hands flailing in combination.

Dr. Amin Sabat apologetically excused himself from the chief of staff's weekly meeting at Boston General Hospital and pulling off his smock headed for the parking lot to his car. He would contact his partners at his practice to cover for him in his absence.

The Hong Kong Police detective seemed satisfied with Paul's statement and the sketch the police artist had ended up with describing the assailant would make his capture easier.

Paul looked at the sketch and commented, "yep, that's the guy". You know I can't figure out for the life of me why the guy would attack us like that? Detective Wu please let me know if I can assist your department in any other way."

Detective Wu closed his pad and reached out his right hand, "sure thing Mr. Constantine. I will keep you posted. Sorry I forgot about your arm." He smiled as he withdrew his hand.

Paul reached over with his left arm to pat the officer on his shoulder, "no problem. I'm told the bullet went right through," Paul volunteered.

The detective turned to walk away and abruptly stopped then turned back in Paul's direction, "Mr. Constantine who provided you the medical attention for your arm?"

"You know I'm not sure what the fella's name was. Why?"

"Well thanks". Detective Wu turned and walked away looking around the whole warehouse as he walked out. Detective Wu knew better than to tip his hand. He had worked this city for fifteen years on the wharf and docks these were his areas and it could be deadly work. The department had lost many good officers who failed to assimilate quickly enough to the quiet mean underworld of the Hong Kong streets. Detective Tei Wu had fought the Triad, the Italian Mafia and the British and American Intelligence networks on this turf; not mention the drug lords. Detective Wu knew Paul was not telling the whole story. The bullet holes in structures across from the warehouse, the back missing in the shack across the street and water in certain areas on the pavement even though it hadn't rained all pointed to a gun battle outside the warehouse not an assault inside as Mr. Paul Constantine had put in his affidavit.

The detective didn't give a rat's rectum about a few whites killing each other. What he did care about was his cut of whatever action there was involved in the warehouse operation. He'd find out what was at stake and then squeeze the white boy as he always had done the others in the past.

"Captain Kao I'm on my way to station "C". I will see you for lunch I have another investment opportunity."

Detective Wu knew this information would please his unit Captain. He had to make that call he thought to himself because everyone will be on board by tonight like clock work to help harass and squeeze his new investment. A horn was blowing and Detective Wu looked at his rear view mirror spotting a car headed for him but it was not slowing down. Instinct caused him to pull forward a little at the stop light to avoid the collision. The car hit his before he could react and the airbag in his vehicle knocked the air out of him. Two men jumped out of the vehicle that struck his and two others from an adjacent automobile leaped from theirs grabbing him by the arms. Detective Wu somewhat disoriented was explaining he was alright when the stun gun was used on him.

He felt drunk and droggy when he came to.

"Where am I?" Wu yelled. The room was dark and he was tied to a chair in the middle of what appeared to be large warehouse similar to the one he'd just departed. He shouted again' "do you know I am a police officer? Answer me this is a very bad mistake."

Tie Wu had been raised a Jain by religion, but he had moved to the dark side over the years. He became consumed with all that was temporal, the physical world of money, booze and women. A fear, a feeling of loneliness and despair entered his heart he had so much bad credit in the karma bank. He hadn't prayed, he hadn't meditated and he'd stopped believing in anything except greed and corruption. No one had to tell him this was the day of his death he felt it, no he knew it.

"Well, well detective Wu you've come back. This is a surprise." Paul was dancing from side to side and grinning as he approached the tied up detective. Detective Wu stared at Paul not knowing how to approach him.

Paul pulled a chair over and sat in it backwards with his arm resting on the back right in front of the police officer. Paul adjusted his splint and the sling and pulled out a cigarette and lighter. He lit it and offered one to Wu, "cigarette?"

Wu yelled indignantly, "I do not smoke you bastard!"

"Whoa, Wu, Wu! Settle down little doggy, just settle down. Why all the hostility? I just wanna talk with yuh mate."

Paul blew out a ring of cigarette smoke and scratched his nose with his left thumb cigarette still in hand. He leaned his head to the left then to right as though he was sizing up the detective. What am I to do with you Wu? I so confused. Wu is me, Wu is me. Now I know what to do. I got it!"

Wu panicked at the wild look in his captor's eyes. Wu cried out, "I know I shouldn't have pried into the injury and bandages on your arm I know that Mr. Constantine."

The young detective was now sobbing profusely. Tears were streaming down his tan face mixed with sweat from his brow.

"I beg you, please forgive me don't kill me, please. See I was never here, never."

Paul lowered his head appearing to be touched by the captive's plea. He stood up, bowed, and said, "That's an idea. Great, you were never here!" With his cigarette still in hand the captor looked back at his captive, "are you a Christian Mr. Wu?"

A puzzled expression fought its way through the face of the frightened detective.

"What?"

Paul put the cigarette out on the concrete floor stared directly at Wu and said, "It's not a trick question. There will not be a test later trust me on that. Are you a Christian? Because if you say you are you'd be lying wouldn't you Wu and that's a sin I'd have to kill you. However, if you're not a Christian, well then Wu I'll have to kill you. Well Wu which is it? See the way I see it detective you were going to make my life here difficult. Probably try to shake me down or something, maybe even arrest me. Well I already pay taxes to Caesar, in fact, I've been known to even collect taxes for him from time to time and you're not him. I'm gonna show you personally what our operation does out there."

"Boss, his car's in the bay." Jimmy, one of Paul's lieutenant peeped around the corner to inform him Wu's car had been pushed off the pier some three miles from their location. The car was doctored with Michael Zarkuhn's blood and his weapon that was dropped while crushing the neck of one of Paul's cronies was placed in the vehicle.

Wu began to scream as Paul Constantine slithered towards him. The screaming only excited Paul. The terror in the man's face was almost worth keeping him alive for a couple more hours. Paul thought of getting a babe to join him, but he didn't have time he wanted the superman Zarkuhn. He literally ached for another show down with Mr. Bad Ass.

The local authorities would find Michael Zarkuhn's weapon and blood in the car; he be a hunted man if he hadn't already bled out. When the authorities found one of Hong Kong's finest body mutilated and washed up on the beach they'd react like rabid dogs. Paul began to think that his plan was so full proof he might not ever meet Zarkuhn again. The more he thought about it the less he cared.

Paul violently grabbed detective Wu by the neck from behind in a sleeper hold. He squeezed with all his might trying to get the best leverage possible despite his wounded arm. The man struggled and gasped for air as the chair rocked back and forth scuffing the cement floor. When the body no longer revealed signs of life Paul ensured the officer's face was mutilated. This senseless act would intensify the heat on Zarkuhn by the whole island.

Paul and Jimmy tossed the body over the side of the boat. They knew it would not be long before the body would wash up on the near by beach. Jimmy looked on shaking his head. Paul turned patted Jimmy on the back and gloated at his handy work, "Jimmy my man I need a cold beer. It's been helluva day."

"Jimmy laughed and started the motor and headed for shore, "boss you're a son of a gun."

CHAPTER 13

SO WHO DOESN'T WANT US DEAD

The Police could see no one when they first entered the residence. The alarm was still going off but there was no sign of forced entry found at the back or front of the mansion. The first officer in was followed by ten others and S.W.A.T with eight of their tactical hitters.

"Gentlemen we're both okay", the voice announced. It was Peter on the mansion's intercom system.

"This is Mr. Peter Stuart, the butler for the mansion I shall join you in one moment."

By then the whole house was covered with law enforcement. The police sergeant and S.W.A.T lieutenant nearly fainted when Peter miraculously appeared wearing the hell out of his penguin attire from what was thin air.

"Where in Sam hell did you come from? Let me see some I.D. sir. Who are? All this was in one blurb from Sergeant O'Connell of the Boston Police Department.

Peter possessed a noticeable scowl in his voice, "may I remove my wallet officer? Here that should do."

He handed his wallet to the sergeant who was still dumbfounded at where the elderly butler had appeared from. Peter observed the S.W.A.T lieutenant in his own world obviously trying to locate something to kill and he worried about the taxidermies garnishing the wall of one of the small mansion bars. He would play this one close to the vest realizing law enforcement were known to break into killing frenzies at the drop of ... well anything.

Peter took a seat and filled the police sergeant in while the other officers insured the property was secure.

Peter told what had occurred, "our residence possesses state of the art detection you see and it alerted us that there was a breach in sector 4g and 6h. So madam and I ..."

Sergeant O'Connell interrupted Peter, "madam, whose madam?"

Peter explained' "Ms. Margarite Plantard of the Plantard Mansion here where you are now. She's the owner where was I?"

Again, Sergeant O'Connell interceded, "where's this madam person now? Why isn't she here?"

Peter sighed with exasperation and started to explain, "I should imagine she's calling off the dogs so to speak, but shall join us momentarily."

Just then Margarite appeared, "officer thank you so much for responding. It seems we were invaded by three men in two sectors of our back lawn areas. Peter may show you if you'd like. One of the dead is still out back behind the fence near the carp pond. I'm sure your men will want to secure the area and collect evidence. Oh! Here's the weapon that killed him."

Sergeant O'Connell and the lieutenant were tempted to call central to make sure they were not at a funny farm. The sergeant took the Desert Eagle hand gun Margarite handed him from the side of her long skirt and took statements from Peter and Ms. Plantard.

"So you see Peter warned them and when they refused to comply with his request he simply had no choice but to shoot the second attacker as well. Then the third man went running towards the grove taking one of his wounded accomplices with him." Margarite was glad her story was over. Now maybe the visitors would go home.

Sergeant O'Connell stood up put away his note pad shook his head and looked at the both of them in disbelief.

"Well Officer Mackie head out back with two others and search those groves and radio in air to assist. We're going to need a chopper, look for tire tracks, et cetera, et cetera." The officers quickly dispersed and carried out his requests.

O'Connell asked if he could do anything else for them and if they felt safe remaining at the residence. At this point he dare not mention to them to avoid the crime scenes, somehow he knew they already knew to do this.

But he was insistent that they not leave the city and informed both that he would be back with more questions. Before departing he shook Margarite's slender hand and asked her as discretely as the circumstances would allow, "Ms. Plantard how old is Mr. Stuart? I mean, he's got to be at least what seventy or so?"

Margarite smiled at the officer and leaned over and whispered in the officer's ear, "I think Peter will be 92 this August, in fact, please don't tell anyone. But officer shouldn't you have known how old he was, his birth date is on his license."

O'Connell grinned, "I thought it was a typo." He sheepishly remarked and quickly closed the large door as he left.

It was now 11:03 p.m. and both Peter and Margarite desperately needed to contact the inner circle of the Collective. They realized that each member had probably started the emergency contingency mobilization plan as required. Each Collective member would now be at their emergency location when they received the "all clear" email and page from Margarite. The "all clear" message was a simple statement which referred to ancient Hebrew lore regarding the book of Enoch referencing an angel by the name of Metatron. The message read, "Enoch was then 365 years old when he walked with God and then he was no more. God made him the liaison between himself and man." This was the message that indicated all was once again well at Plantard Mansion, the Headquarters for the Collective.

Peter picked up the phone in the study ensuring the scrambler was on and that proper COMSEC protocols were in place before speaking. It was J.P Rockdale, "hell man I bin tryin to geet yall fur tha last eight hours. Pleez tell may everythangs awhright thare."

Peter could only smile at the sincere concern J.P expressed for him and madam.

"Mr. Rockdale thank you very much sir perhaps you would like to engage in conversation with Ms. Plantard?"

J.P. replied, "Yeah! Pleez let may engage hurh, woodya."

One by one the emails came in from each member with confirmation of receipt of the "all clear". Peter verified all the calls and then reported to Ms. Plantard who placed a call to Miles one of the senior members on the Collective board.

"Miles I'm so happy to hear your voice." Margarite sounded exhausted as she spoke on the phone line.

"Are you and the staff okay? What of Peter?"

"Yes we are all fine," Margarite responded as she commandeered a chair and sat.

"I am delighted you are well. I can only assume you think it prudent to call a meeting as soon as it's feasible," Miles suggested to his childhood friend. Margarite's yes, rang out clear over the line.

Miles changed the conversation, "Anish informed me he was trying to contact you today in order to advise you that O.W.O.W.'s financial documents were audited by the IRS."

Margarite took a deep breath. It was acutely evident that the Collective was under attack from all angles, even the government was on the attack. She directed Miles to notify the others that the meeting would be held at the Atlanta locale. She continued, "Miles what about Michael? Have you heard from him?"

Miles' response was slow, "well Marge his face is on the front page of the Hong Kong newspaper this morning and it's not there because he's won the lottery. As best I can tell they're saying he shot up and killed some warehouse workers and a police detective. Looks like all Hong Kong is really mifted about the condition the cop's body was found in, the newspapers are reporting something about mutilation of it."

"Miles you and I know Michael did not mutilate anyone. Both of you need to get home." Margarite felt helpless as she laid the phone down. She was nauseated at the thought of all the week's whimsical events. The sordid business was taking its toll on her and she was sure the others were wearing down as well.

Miles assured Margarite he would come up with something, although he didn't have a clue of how he would get Zarkuhn out of this pickle. Miles was pre-occupied with the IRS audits. He wondered how long it would be before other assets and the genome laboratory would come under fire.

Miles was indeed an excellent attorney and represented the Collective and its legal matters impeccably, but he was acutely aware that they were going to have to battle for the life, the very existence of the Collective entity. At stake was all that the secret society had accomplished over its many years since its inception.

"Ahh! I can do this, yeah that's more like it, no taxes, no continuances, and no strings attached aaawwh," Miles then let out a menacing laugh in the hotel restroom as he shook the urine off the tip of his penis. He was startled as Michael Zarkuhn greeted him with a puzzled expression undoubtedly solicited as a result of the strange conversation and noises he'd heard resonating from the rest room before his entrance.

"What in the blazes! Michael what are trying to do? Damn it man, I almost cut my ... never mind. Here put the blasted razor over there would you? Let me call Maurice."

"No!" Zarkuhn shouted. "No wait a minute, okay go ahead on second thought that's a good idea. I think I've figured away to get out of the mess I'm in. You know The Black Pope's man Paul set me up?" Michael sat on the edge of the bed rubbing the hole in his pants where he'd been shot. "Miles go ahead call Maurice, get him over here, but don't tell him I'm here."

Maurice appeared at Miles' hotel door within seconds after the call.

"Miles, it's me Maurice."

"Come in Maurice. Good morning."

"Miles so what's up?" Maurice asked before seeing Zarkuhn seated on the edge of the bed. "Whoa! How did you, never mind. I don't want to know," he stated looking at Zarkuhn with an obtuse expression on his face. "Mr. Zarkuhn you realize the entire island is looking for you?"

Zarkuhn scrutinized the pedantic station chief. He didn't trust Maurice because he hadn't hired him and well he had run in the face of danger earlier on the dock. Michael was not entirely convinced that the station chief was dirty though, and he had to truthfully acknowledge to himself that Maurice's running had been a prudent tactical step. However, Michael wanted to share the scheme he had in mind with both men.

Zarkuhn broke his gaze and addressed both men. "Miles, Maurice listen to me very carefully as I know you're going to think this is crazy. I'm going to hand myself over to the authorities. It's the only way to ensure protection for the Collective. Plus no one here can disagree that I must consider myself compromised after I'm turned over to the authorities."

Miles couldn't believe what he was hearing, "Michael you've lost it. Do you have any idea of what those ingrates will do to you before they even question you?"

Maurice volunteered, "yeah much less try you before a court. You'd never make trial."

"Of course I know all of this Mr. Murray," smirked Zarkuhn. "That is precisely the reason Mr. Turner esquire will accompany me as my legal counsel. Maurice your role will be paramount in successfully completing this scheme for what I will ask of you will take nerves of steel. Are you up to it?"

"Well I need to know what it is first." Maurice could only imagine as he developed a lump in his throat the size of a jaw breaker. Zarkuhn frightened the hell out of him. He had never feared any man the way he did Zarkuhn, in fact Maurice's position was that every creature with breath probably felt the same way he did which justified his feeling of inadequacy and inferiority in the presence of the mysterious Collective's special ops chief.

"You Maurice will have to terminate me. I know I'm asking a lot of you but it's the only way to maintain the integrity of our operation. Miles I don't want to hear anything out of you, no arguments, nor a peep about this decision. The Collective's mission must be protected at any cost."

"I can do it," volunteered Maurice and rather hastily fashion while trying as hard as possible to subdue his excitement over getting such a desirable assignment. Maurice held his head down in an attempt to conceal the glee in his dilated pupils. He placed both his hands over his face with his elbows resting hard on his knees as though an implausible tragedy had taken place. Zarkuhn knew Maurice was trying to keep his eyes from being noticed by him and Miles, but all the better for he would surely hit the mark with that enthusiasm bubbling in him at the prospect of shooting the man who made him feel all so inadequate.

Doctor Teranez drove as fast as she could North on highway 75 from her home in South, Georgia. She couldn't get to the laboratory fast enough. The inner circle knew a raid would be coming, they just didn't expect the government to launch an investigation this fast on some anonymous tip. She wished Miles were there. His legal expertise would certainly be needed today.

Margarite was checking her email when she noticed a hot one right below the urgent one from Doctor Teranez about the government raid on the lab. The second email was from Makesh Patel notifying the Collective that his two ITT centers located in India had received prying telephone calls from an unidentified source. He believed something negative was on the horizon for the two firms.

Senator Stinger could not believe her ears. She started crying as she laid her cell phone down on the table after being informed that Carl, her young promising page was found dead in his Alexandria apartment. Carl didn't know many people in Washington D.C. He was such a good young man and she blamed herself for his death. The Senator's mind began racing back and forth between emotions. Sadness, helplessness and rage were tagged teaming her. She wondered if this may have had anything to do with what Carl wanted to share with her before she went on vacation.

Senator Karen Stinger broke down slamming her hands on the table she yelled, "Carl I'm so sorry. I, I pro, prm, prom, promised your, moth, mother that you would be safe." She cried out hysterically shouting out loud, "now you're gone, you, you, you're gone. Damn it. Why? Why, oh God why?"

Peter kneeled before the candles in his large room which was located in the alienated North wing of the Plantard Mansion. Smoke from the smoldering incenses dallied through the hazy orange glow of the room flirting with all it came into contact with. These incenses were his all time favorites the frankincense and myrrh. He began to chant his favorite mantra as he stared into the fireplace while his fingers pulled at the beads in his hands. Peter prayed for tranquility and peace, he meditated for knowledge and understanding and asked for tolerance and wisdom. He loved the warmth of the flames from the candles on his face as he knelt before his ornately mandala alter. Meditation and prayer purified and resuscitated his spirit ailing spirit providing him bliss. Without failure Peter had performed this ritual for three hours every night for as long as he could remember.

The old man spoke softly the words, "there is no greater gift than to breathe so that one may serve the Almighty. I give thanks and pay homage in knowing an unworthy wretch such as I may bow before thee. Contemptuous in my attempts to be humble, offensive in my very being of flesh and bone, arrogant to think myself worthy to be heard at ALL. Forgive me my failure to attain mastery of thyself and of this realm as you so graciously cast me down to do."

He continued for the next two hours to give thanks for the very breath in his aged body. Peter counted the beads as he pulled each one through his withered fingers. His knees ached and bore scar tissue, testimony to his dedication in performing the long arduous ritual which had become more than a ritual the act was his friend. The meditative prayer sessions were more than act of contrition. It was a social event that allowed Peter to imbibe all the elixir of truth the Universe offered. Peter had been blessed over the years in being able to realize the following:

Each meditation and session of prayer birthed an orgasmic twinkling in which the face of the creator was revealed through introspection. An honest glimpse into oneself revealed the true plan and intent the creator has made available for each one of us to carry out should we choose. The problem of proper selection of your path could be answered by merely establishing a relationship with God Almighty.

Peter would sleep peacefully again another night.

CHAPTER 14

PAYBACK'S A GLITCH

The crowd went into what looked to be soccer rage, the police could barley hold them back. They were rapidly morphing into a deadly mob as Zarkuhn and Miles were hastily escorted up the stairs into the Police Headquarters in downtown Hong Kong. Zarkuhn grabbed the back of his head as a sharp pain seared down his spine, the warm blood streamed from the gash he now brandished on the back of his head. It was just one of the many unsolicited assaults delivered to him in a short period of time, courtesy of Hong Kong's finest.

"You'd think we had the plague or at worst were related to the Queen of England the way we're being mistreated," Miles jokingly remarked. He looked around to view his client being tossed from one side to the other by two large Chinese police officers who appeared to be on enough steroids to manufacture at least fifty home runs each in the Major Leagues.

Inside the station Miles and Michael were greeted with cigarette smoke which resembled a musty fog hovering over the English Channel as they entered the station captain's office. Two men sat in the smoked filled room wearing expressions of discontent. Zarkuhn and Miles stood waiting to be invited to sit before doing so. They stood for two minutes, five minutes it had been eleven minutes and Miles cough a noticeably fake cough, but a cough nonetheless. They stood for another five minutes then another two minutes. They stood for almost twenty minutes before finally being addressed by an angry Buddha looking Chinese guy behind the desk.

"You are Mr. Mick all Zarchuhn?" The question was spat out by Captain Le Kao. Do you know the bad situation you have done my city? You make problem for me, make problem for your Embassy, you …," Miles attempted to speak.

"Captain I….," he was violently interrupted by Captain Kao.

"You, his lawyer? You shut up this not America. This is China jewel and you, your type try and do what you want in my country. You come and kill my detective." The captain turned his back and stared out the window. The other man a lieutenant stood and asked Zarkuhn and Miles to follow him. They went down a corridor and to a room on the right at the end of the corridor.

"I am Lieutenant Lehchin. Detective Wu was my subordinate and on a personal note a friend. Before you speak know this, that I have taken the liberty of pulling background information on you there was nothing derogatory found.

This was done after you contacted us this morning. Know that this room is secure so anything said will stay here. I think both of you can appreciate this act of discretion. Now what happened to Detective Wu?"

Zarkuhn glanced at Miles before speaking. Miles nodded and gestured with his hands accompanied by, "go ahead tell him everything that is why we are here."

Zarkuhn cleared his throat, "I was here in Hong Kong on assignment representing my employer the Manila Midas Shipping Company. We were trying to establish a working relationship with Barbarosa Shipping here in Hong Kong. A meeting had been setup for Monday with one of their executives Paul. No last name was given."

"Your story does check out about your firm. I spoke with your office in the Philippines this afternoon, with a Mr. Steeley, this was the person whom we spoke with he was on the floor so they patched us through. He's a very nice man Mr. Steeley. But you said you were going to have a meeting with a person on Monday and you didn't have a name that's strange don't you think?"

The lieutenant was obviously uneasy with Zarkuhn's statement.

Zarkuhn continued, "I had ask the gentleman on the other end for a complete name but he said the boss never gave out his last name."

The lieutenant stopped Zarkuhn by raising his palm in his face, "his name is Paul Constantine. He's the assistant vice president for Barbarosa Shipping. They have been in business in this city for over sixty years and we've never had an issue with them. Hold one moment let me get you a towel and some bandages for that wound. Sergeant, Sergeant!" The door opened and one of the steroid Siamese twins peeped in the room.

"Please get me a first aid kit and a towel ASAP", the articulate Chinese lieutenant ordered. The door closed and with in seconds his requests were met.

Miles leaned forward towards the table in the interrogation room and asked, "Lieutenant Lehchin I must ask you where you received your education? Your English is excellent."

"Thank you Mr. Turner I was schooled in the United States. My mother married an American Air Force officer when I was four years old living in Taiwan.

I'm a graduate of Stanford University, California. Now let's get on with it. Mr. Zarkuhn please continue."

Michael laid the towel down and picked up from where he left off, "Thank you, I went by the office on Friday so that I would be able to save time on Monday's visit, because I wanted to watch the dock operation without a show being arranged for my benefit. When I arrived I noticed the operation in full swing and several boats going back and forth to two ships in the bay. I wanted to get a closer look so I approached the front of the warehouse and I realized I could smell coffee. Not some coffee pot in the corner of some smelly back office, but the potent smell of coffee. The dock crew was putting coffee in the packages they were sealing and loading. Then I was approached by a man who identified himself as the foreman who insisted that I leave. I did attempt to explain that I had a meeting with Paul and he asked two of the workers to watch me while he trotted off and got Paul. Well this Paul pointed at me and the next thing I know the foreman pulls a knife and grabs some tape. I will share with you that part of my duties at the company is head of security and I carry a weapon plus I know a little self defense. Suddenly I started running and the whole dock is in pursuit and that's when the shooting started. I managed to get away after shooting some of their guys, but I never shot your friend the detective. I never saw him."

The lieutenant sat back and began to tap the table in a finger roll rhythm.

"That's how it happened and of course you're going to testify to that?"

Zarkuhn responded, "Lieutenant why do you think I'm here? Those people tried to kill me for something they think I saw that night on the pier. You and this police force are the only protection I have. Detective Wu may have lost his life in the warehouse for the same reason. Those men may have killed him. I'm telling you I never met Detective Wu. Your Captain and this city have pegged me for a cop killer and their wrong. This Constantine may try and kill me again.

"We will arrange to investigate the site further and I will personally handle the inquiry of Mr. Paul Constantine. If there has been any impropriety I will get to the bottom of it. However, in the meantime I will need you to hand me your passport and we have all your weapons correct? I will book you, but turn you over to Mr. Turner. Do not attempt to leave the Country. The only reason you are not going to jail is that I believe the evidence against you is suspect and you are here cooperating. Plus there really aren't many places you can hide on this Island. Do not forget the whole police force wants to kill you as well. Please come with me so we can process you out on your own recognizance. As we use to say back in the states in college, "see wouldn't want to be you Mr. Zarkuhn." The lieutenant laughed for the first time as he escorted both men to processing.

It was about seven o'clock p.m. and the lieutenant stood on the steps with Zarkuhn and Miles as Captain Kao watched from the police station door. It was no secret how he felt about Americans or Zarkuhn. It was not clear why he was so angry or why he was so agreeable with the lieutenant's move to allow Zarkuhn to leave, but his cooperation would allow for the next stage of Zarkuhn's plan to be executed. Suddenly two gunshots rang out from one of the buildings across the street. Zarkuhn's body was viciously propelled forward into lieutenant Lehchin's arms as everyone scattered for cover. Zarkuhn was pulled by the officer into the front door of the station. Blood was everywhere. Miles lay on the steps in a fetal position afraid to make any move. Several officers took defensive positions and ran across the street where the shots were thought to have been fired. The sound of sirens blasted the air and an occasional scream from some of the women prompted guns to point in every direction but the correct one. Michael's wound proved fatal. The first bullet struck him directly on the vertebra between his shoulder blades and the second exited from his left cheek bone beneath the eye. Whoever the marksman was found his mark. Lieutenant Lehchin and Captain Kao carried the lifeless body to one of the rooms just off the main desk in the lobby and covered the face with a police jacket. They were both communicating with their officers who had now encircled the buildings across from them that were suspected of harboring the shooter.

Lieutenant Lehchin darted outside and retrieved Miles from off the steps. Miles was so scared he would've been content to wait the full nine months in that fetal position he assumed before moving.

"What is it? Yes, go on," the Lieutenant shouted in his communication's equipment. "Excellent, my men have already located the shooter." Miles was not responding. Still numbed from the shooting and wondering if he were going into shock it suddenly registered what the Lieutenant had just informed him. If they believed they had the shooter that was not a good thing, because the shooter was the Collective's own Station Chief Maurice. Panic and doom, doom and panic amplified throughout over body and through mind. He needed to do something besides age another ten years as he had done ten minutes earlier. Miles wanted to see Zarkuhn's body, "excuse me where is the American's body," he asked the desk sergeant. The sergeant pointed to the room next to him and Miles proceeded to enter slowly. He could not bring himself to pull the jacket off Zarkuhn's face. Miles sat on a wooden bench in the room bewildered. Miles had not felt like this for years he didn't have an inkling of what he should do or where he should be. Logic and strong will had always provided his way, given him answers, but now he found himself a babbling idiot. He'd never felt as insecure as when he was on the steps of the police station. Right now he was needed by the Collective family and the moment appeared to be overwhelming him. He realized that his intellect was not going to be enough Miles would have to reach deep down into his soul for true grit and guile to pull this one off. It was paramount that the plan outlined for him and Maurice be successfully executed.

Miles wanted to know where Maurice was. He had fulfilled his part all too well having just killed the Collective's head of Special Operations basically Maurice had shot his superior.

Lehchin's communicator alerted and he answered, "What do you mean you lost the shooter? Comb the area and bring in the crime scene examiners behind you please keep me informed."

Lehchin was not happy with what he had just heard. He was informed that the room where the shooting had occurred from was empty, except there was blood in the room on the floor and scuff marks as though someone was dragged through the blood. As the Lieutenant entered the room of Michael's body Miles stood up and approached him. Miles wasted no time in informing the Chinese police officer that Michael Zarkuhn was of the Islamic faith and that it was imperative that his body be returned to his family immediately for properly burial preparation all a lie of course, but in adherence to Zarkuhn's plan.

When the police officers arrived to the room where the shooter had been they found the blood beneath the air conditioning unit in front of the window. A chair was on its side and the site commander ordered everyone out of the room except his evidence collection team as was directed by Lieutenant Lehchin. The site commander pulled his cell phone and made another call to Captain Kao once he was alone.

Lehchin couldn't help wondering if what the dead American had told him was true about Paul Constantine.

Miles walked up to the lieutenant, "Lieutenant Lehchin I must take my friend's body back to the states immediately for proper burial preparation, for my friend is Muslim remember."

Lehchin stopped and place his pistol in his holster and placed his hands on his hips and then pointed his finger at Miles, "I heard you the first time. You take his body and get the hell out of my country. I agree with my Captain. You are a plague and I'm sorry about your colleague, but you have caused nothing but problems. Please go.

"You insensitive bastard," screamed Mr. Miles Turner, "you've lost nothing young man. My friends and I have just lost a friend you merely picked up an investigation. This man came to you for help because he saw no way out. He didn't ask to be shot, but now he's dead and you say we're a problem well screw you and your damn country sir."

The lieutenant grabbed Miles arm, "that will be quite enough. Look I apologize for my statement, but you're incorrect I lost a friend too. Please come with me and I'll assist you Mr. Turner."

The lieutenant closed the door behind Miles as they both entered the interrogation room. "I'll need to be able to get into contact with you when you leave. An escort will be provided to the airport for you and Mr. Zarkuhn. Your friend's body will be in the ambulance behind you okay. I'll share this with you, I know this man Paul better than I let on. If he is responsible for killing my friend and Mr. Zarkuhn I will avenge their deaths. Any information you can provide me in the future will help us for this is a very powerful man in our city.

Captain Kao placidly watched from the other side of the one way mirror. He hated the new way business was done in the Hong Kong police force. Computers, e-mail, wire transfers and the like. He remembered in the old days when nothing happened or was approved without his police unit and his British Intelligence contact getting a piece of the action saying so. Now these young college educated types were complicating matters with their "holier than thou attitudes". They were entirely too smart for their own good. Thank Buddha for providing young loyal sergeants like the one who had just notified him of what was going on behind Lehchin's back. He would watch Lieutenant Lehchin closer in the future he might mess up his retirement plans.

CHAPTER 15

CAIN, OH BROTHER WHERE ART THOU

Michael began to have the dreams again, those memories of times long gone by. This time something was different though he was also thinking endearingly about his friends and associates from times past. He'd made more friends over the last four Millennia than he could count and he could reminisce something about each one of them in exquisite detail. He realized while in his slumbered state he loved all of them. It was an emotional trap that he hadn't realized snared him. A truth regressed deep within the recesses of his once naive mind was freeing him. Michael was free, truly free for he'd learned to love the Human race and himself, they were not beast, nor were they Goyim, as he'd been taught, mere cattle for the slaughter. They were worthy of him fighting for and his long prison sentence, his punishment was punishment no more. Now Michael Zarkuhn, the Archangel, understood the beauty of what his God and the counsel of elders had missed some hundreds of thousands of years ago not chronicled in the book of Genesis. These beings were as intelligent as he and as his master. He could see they posed a threat because of their unpredictability and their potential to soar to levels of spirituality that rivaled even God's. A level achieved by Jesus and few others, an ability that would some day allow the human race completion of the circle of truth about their existence and that of the true creator, the Mother, Father, the ALL of the Christ. For this they certainly didn't deserve to be used as food or slaves in the gold mines of Southeastern Africa, the so called garden by his Lord.

Why was he all of a sudden visualizing the face of Cain? Yes, he could see Cain's burnt face as Jehovah his master called out for him. "Cain where is Able your brother? I asked you where is Able, your brother?"

Adam and his mate, the one they called Eve were running into the thicket to try and hide from the chastising God as he called out to Cain. They had already ticked him off in numerous ways especially by mating after learning the secret of procreation and having the audacity to enjoy it. This they learned with the help of Enki, the creator of man and younger brother of Jehovah.

Jehovah, Lord of the Mountain was furious upon learning that his slaves, his pets now kept him up at nights mating as the other wild beast. Their primal sexual grunting noises, screams and panting infuriated Enki, the Christian God.

Jehovah eventually found Able's body covered with shrubs and dirt, he was uncharacteristically saddened by the sight as he cursed Cain for killing one of his favorite, most promising pets. He shouted out loud "You brought me fruit, grass an insult and your dead brother gave me a life through sacrifice, a gift indeed worthy of me, a God. Able copied his Master's way and slew the beast, then prepared the beast, a feast for me, to please me. He took the life of a beast to pay tribute to his God. You, you my own nephew, yes the one who was spawn from the loins of my wayward brother that serpent. You dared to bring me fruit and weeds and now you've slain him, my favorite."

Michael still heard the voice of his lord as though it were yesterday. Lord of the Mountains, the one referred to as Yaweh, Jehovah and by other religious names. He banished Cain to the East to the lands they called Nud in those days, Ethiopia today.

Michael now admired Cain, but he didn't quite understand why he killed Able at the time. However, thinking back on Cain's stated reasoning it made sense later. Michael listened intently from behind some trees while Cain addressed God.

Cain stated, "Uncle you looked down on me for bringing you the fruits of my labor. My gift was something that took me many months to grow and harvest. I was proud of my accomplishment as were the others, to include Able. But, you a God responsible for the lives of countless beings under the rule of your father, Anu, and the counsel criticized my offering. However, acceptance of a dead carcass, that of an innocent animal satisfied your natural blood lust and you'd rather I kill an innocent creature too, not for food or protection, but to merely satisfy your ego thus, proving your power over it and me.

So he challenged God under the law that his true father, the serpent, had shared with him. Since he'd possessed royal Annunaki blood, by way of God's brother's heated liaison with Eve, Cain brazenly informed God, "legally I had the right to take the life of that being Able and any beast on this planet by your own law. Furthermore, the beast Able, brother or not was inferior to me, bearing no royal blood; thus, relegating him to no more status than that of the very beasts he herded and sacrificed to you. Uncle I'm disappointed at your response. I sacrificed Able as an offering, the supreme offering, the life of your most treasured beast with my own hands for you."

Michael's mind raced back and forth in his trance state. Cain was in fact spared because of the law and allowed to travel east after receiving a judgment in his favor and confirmed by a mark for all to see.

A mark, the royal symbol was placed upon Cain's body so that all who laid eyes on him would see the "mark of Cain" also known as the "seal of Anu." Cain, however, due to his successful argument which supported his explanation for killing Able ensured a legacy for the "rule of law", for all with his bloodline in the future, for they would be tasked to achieve ultimate rule by law against all on Earth. All who laid eyes on him were aware of the origin of the mark, and also aware of its power. Only the royal family possessed the seal. No creature dared injure or harm anyone wearing the mark. To this day and throughout time the mark can be located on Masonic lodges, court room doors, the British Flag, the Vatican Square and various official government buildings.

Cain later used his new found status to build a city and to take a wife. The wife had to be worthy of him someone with royal blood, so he took Lilith, granddaughter to his uncle Jehovah as his wife. Interestingly enough, she was the first wife promised to Adam. However, she proved to be a good judge of character considering Adam to be a wimp and although the first man of his type, he was only half Annunaki and not of royal lineage. Her view of the Adamu proved to be accurate as Michael remembered Adam's excuses to God in the garden explaining that, "it was the woman who you gave to me that made me do it," when he was asked why he had transgressed by eating the fruit of the tree in the midst of the garden.

"What a pussy", the angels whispered amongst themselves as they watch the coward try and place the blame on his innocent naïve wife.

Michael and the other Malachim avoided Cain's wife Lilith, however. She was later known in the Hebrew Kabalah as a demon as well as the wayward granddaughter of Jehovah. She like Cain was of reptilian lineage and a pure blood royal, who'd start the secret reptilian bloodlines that would later be known as the Merovingian bloodline rooted throughout the majority of future European Royals. She was shunned by the Annunaki Royal hierarchy as well and later migrated south seeking her own lustful agenda via India accompanied of course by her new husband Cain.

Cain's punishment and life was later ended by the "blind one", called Lamech ironically one of his own bloodline.

Michael's had served with some of Lilith's children throughout the centuries, but today he waged war against her great, great, great, great, great-grands and the other "Sons of God". They were literally hell bent on the domination of the Earth, secretly claiming to be the rightful heirs via their bloodline, using any and all methods to achieve their goal. Cain's descendants were but one faction of the "Sons of God" that Michael and the Collective sought to thwart.

The children of Seth, "Sons of Jared" were another group that Michael had fought side by side with over the centuries. Unfortunately, their blood had been tainted with the reptilian blood of Cain's children after defying the patriarch Jared and descending down from the holy mountain.

The Collective had in the last two centuries combined forces with the "Sons of Jared" to fight the offspring of the Gods.

Michael felt the emotion of love for Earth and her inhabitants so strongly while in his dream state and consumed by the "dark light". He now knew he did not ever wish to go back to the Mother Ship or the planet Nibiru that had been the only home he'd known from the time of his inception.

He would miss Uriel, Ariel, Raphiel and Gabriel the closest persons to brothers he'd known. The questions he had in his head stopped, for there was only way, the way of truth and his path was growing clearer.

Miles wondered why he had not heard from Maurice as Michael Zarkuhn's body was being loaded onto the aircraft headed for Hawaii and ultimately Boston, Massachusetts. Miles put in a call to Margarite, he tried everything in his power to avoid making the call, knowing the news of Michael's death would crush Margarite, and stun the Collective but they would know sooner or later.

"Plantard residence may I help you", answered Peter with his posh British accent.

"Peter, hello it's Miles, how is everyone?"

"They are all fine Sir. And you, is everything there okay?" Peter could tell something was amidst. He could sense it. "Sir perhaps I should get madam. Please hold for a moment."

Peter found Margarite in the main study sitting in Michael's favorite chair drinking a hot cup of tea and staring out the large windows at the snow covered grounds. She slowly placed the fine china cup down and acknowledged Peter without looking in his direction.

"Is the call for me Peter?"

"Yes madam it is Mr. Turner."

"Miles tell me some good news." Margarite immediately felt something was wrong. The silence on the other end of the line seemed to linger forever. Miles' voice was somber, "Margarite, Michael is no longer with us. Michael was shot, the wounds were fatal. I am bringing him home. We'll arrive tomorrow morning and I can't say anymore than that I must go. I'm sorry love."

Miles hurried to get off the phone. He could not bare the pain and heartache which resonated even through silence from his long time friend. His heart hurt for her because he loved Margarite and at one time wanted to wed her. But, he knew that his asking her to wed might have changed their friendship forever. He was no fool and felt that Margarite's heart belonged to Michael Zarkuhn though Miles believed Michael never had a clue and Margarite would have denied her feelings for him if queried. His heart still wept for her. Nothing mattered to him but Margarite's happiness. Miles boarded the aircraft and sat trying to focus on the tasks ahead of him.

Peter stood at the door as Margarite started crying. He slowly approached with his arms crossed behind him and she realized that her emotional reaction would reveal her heart. Peter would know the truth as if he hadn't already.

"Madam it will be alright. Trust me for have I ever told you anything that was not true? I know you love Master Zarkuhn."

"Peter I never told him how I felt about him and now I can not." Margarite held Peter's hand as he placed it on her shoulder. She sobbed as Peter handed her his handkerchief. Peter had not done that for years. Only little Margarite could get a handkerchief out of him.

Peter wished he could cry, but he was all cried out. His tears dried up years ago. Still Peter wished she knew what he knew that time was Michael Zarkuhn's closest ally. He would be back, however the problem would be how to explain his miraculous return from death.

CHAPTER 16

COLLECTIVE INNER CIRCLE REGROUPS

Gynysyx, the genome laboratory head of security held the HomeLand Security and CDC inspectors in the lobby until Doctor Teranez arrived. He'd claimed to have no entry code sighting the sensitivity of the work done there. As the doctor entered the lobby she recognized the Department of HomeLand Security agent. It was agent Frank Todd, he as one of the first DHS agents to be brought into the American Gestapo Organization when it came into being. It was well known information that the government was uncomfortable with the Collective's involvement in DNA genetic research and Todd was going to rise through the ranks by bringing the lab down adding to his already numerous notches.

Todd didn't care for blacks, he didn't care for liberals and the only thing he disdained more than the before mentioned was a smart black, especially a woman. He had been put in his place by Senator Stinger during one of his visits four years ago to this very Gynysyx laboratory located in Atlanta, Georgia. While visiting Doctor Teranez's office the agent threatened to shut the facility down unless full disclosure of the labs' ongoing research was made available to the Department of HomeLand Security to ensure no violations of civil rights, biohazards or relationships with undesirables existed that threatened the United States National Security were mentioned.

When her guest returned from the restroom to hear the conversation starting to heat up she'd asked Dr. Teranez, "Doctor, am I interrupting anything?" Senator Stinger questioned her friend.

Agent Todd turned to address the intruder who he vaguely recognized, but started to take great pleasure in insisting she mind her own business. He asked her to leave and informed the black woman standing so confident in his face to depart at once. Senator Stinger had grown up in the South and she knew his type. Todd was the kind that hated her in daylight, but in the dark lit back rooms of a night club would do everything in his power to bed a black woman. The senator saw him for what he really was, a White weak minded insignificant small penis conservative. He was just like most of the colleagues she served with in the Congress. The Christian heterosexuals who unlike most of the gays she knew would rape the same sex if they thought they wouldn't be caught.

"What is your name sir?" The Senator from Florida asked the DHS agent. She walked around the front of him as close as she could without touching him and took a seat in the front of the doctor's desk.

"Lady I thought I told you to excuse yourself," the agent said trying to compose his temper as best he could.

The senator knew just how to push the buttons of a bigot and decided she was going to have her some fun. The fact that it was a man made it all the more enticing to her. Before long this White boy would make a mistake he'd err in his judgment. He wasn't very smart the Senator thought. He hasn't asked me who I am or why I'm not complying. Karen Stinger knew his nature was to instigate an unfortunate episode leading to her unfortunate arrest claiming she'd interfered with an official investigation and resisted arrest. She would play this patsy and have a laugh over a martini later about it.

"That's it I warned you lady," the agent shouted. The shouting prompted a security guard to enter Doctor Teranez's office followed by her secretary. To which they were told to please leave, "this is government business" as he grabbed the Senator's arm in order to try and handcuff her. Doctor Teranez started to inform the agent he was making a mistake, but was stopped by the Senator who pulled her other arm away and looked at the agent and asked, "you refused to identify yourself to me when I asked who you were agent and not once have you attempted to ascertain my identity why? Could it be that no matter who I was it could never have an affect on you or your job? The black woman went on as the agent asked her to please make it easy on herself by giving him her other arm.

"No I don't think so Bubba and as a United States Senator I find your actions deplorable, extremely egregious and criminal."

The agent froze. He suddenly saw his whole future flash by him in dust. Todd couldn't quite comprehend what had just happened. The only sound he could distinguish was senator. The handcuffs were removed in record time. It was if they were never out or even on the agent's personage. Special agent Todd felt short bus special. He had just accosted a United States Senator and what made matters worse were the witnesses present to seal his doom. The situation couldn't get worse. But the agent sensed the Senator had baited him. In fact, he knew he was and by a black woman to boot. Then the gravity of his err hit him it can get worse, his life was in the hands of a black woman with a authority, a big authority, damn!

Here we go the Senator thought, how long will it take him before. Suddenly agent Todd started talking, "ma'am I didn't know who you were" and ten seconds was the answer.

"It really shouldn't have mattered though right?" The senator responded.

"No ma'am not really. I, I was conducting an investigation," popped the agent.

"No sir, you weren't conducting an investigation you were harassing this doctor and this organization weren't you?" Chimed the Senator.

"Yes ma'am I suppose it would look that way if you." He was once again interrupted.

"I beg your pardon Agent Todd, are you now calling me a liar? Are you agent Todd?" The senator questioned with a big grin on her happy coffee colored face.

"Of course not Senator, I merely meant to say that." The agent swallowed real hard and looked the Senator in the eyes for the first time since their altercation. He knew was cannon fodder and wondered what his superiors were going to say when they got wind of this cluster fu*%$# of a situation.

"Special Agent Todd sit down!" Senator Stinger directed. "What in the hell were you thinking? This is not the way to climb the ladder of success. Do you realize you're two shakes from the unemployment line? Are you aware I sit as co-chair on the Senate Intelligence Committee; that I was instrumental in getting your head honcho his job? What do you think I should do about your actions here today? You above all others as a federal agent in this wonderful country of ours should be acutely sensitive to the rights of our citizens. You have been entrusted by the government of this great country, the greatest country this world has ever seen to protect the democratic process and the way of life carved out by our founding forefathers; yet your actions today witnessed by several of us casts serious doubt on your fitness to accept the baton of freedom. Again, what would you have me do?"

Special Agent Todd was embarrassed. He'd never been so moved with a sense of duty towards patriotism in his life as at that moment from the Senator's speech. Todd couldn't believe the feeling instilled in him by this black female. She'd summoned a sense of pride deep from within the spiritual coals smoldering in him. Yet, she verbally admonished him without attacking or denigrating his spirit something he'd already done himself. Todd saw that his actions had been offensive as well as being legally questionable.

He would take what the Senator threw at him, he deserved it. He spoke quietly. "I'm so sorry for my actions doctor, Senator. There is nothing I could ever say to exonerate my malfeasance of duty here today. Senator you should ensure that the full letter of the law and administrative remedies are met with regards to my actions here today ma'am."

The Senator smiled at him as she took a seat beside him and looked him straight in the eyes. "I'm going to forget this ever happened today. I'll ask the doctor if she'll trust me to handle this."

Doctor Teranez cut in, "but of course Senator."

"Agent Todd, I don't ever want to here of an incident remotely similar to this again concerning you. You're only human and we all make mistakes. We fall prey to our human frailties and succumb to poor decisions. I hope you have learned something here from this incident. I'm willing to bet you will go along way in the Department of Homeland Security and anywhere else if you just remember to always act justly and be noble."

"I'm so sorry. Thank you for this opportunity to improve, thank you." The agent was contrite and sincere as he excused himself.
That was over three years ago and now agent Todd was in the lobby holding a cup of coffee and joking with the security guards.
Doctor Teranez cautiously approached him not knowing what to expect from the man who had tried shut her down and arrest her lover years earlier.

The agent spoke first, "Doctor Teranez it's been awhile ma'am. I hope all finds you well."

This was not the greeting she expected, but her guard was still up as she asked the agent, "Mr. Todd what can we do for you?"

Todd's smile was different somehow he was polite, "southern gentleman polite". At their first meeting he'd been arrogant and offensive.

Todd smiled and stated softly, "I think there may be something I can do for you. By the way how's Senator Stinger?"

Doctor Teranez signaled security to clear the way for her and the husky agent who sported a "jarhead" haircut. Todd asked his companion from the CDC to wait promising they'd do lunch when he returned.

They entered the doctor's office where they had first met. Doctor Teranez hung up her coat and placed her purse in one of the drawers behind her large cherry wood desk. She sat in her oversized chair and asked her guest if he wanted more coffee.

"No thank you doctor, no more coffee for me this is my third cup. The reason for my visit Doctor Teranez is that I feel compelled to warn you that you have enemies on the hill. Now I know you are probably aware of this fact, but the million dollar questions are who and why? I want to work with you in order to protect you from what I feel is a witch hunt which is not in alignment with the good order of democratic principles."

Cheryl Teranez did not expect this, the agent's statements through her off guard. Her cell phone rang and she apologized to the agent as she looked at the incoming number. It was her house telephone number Senator Stinger was calling.

"Would you excuse me one moment," the doctor asked as he volunteered to step out of the office and into the hallway where a guard was posted on both ends of the hallway.

"Karen you will never guess whose here in my office. It's Special Agent Todd from DHS you remember him right, Teranez asked the Senator."

"Yes, I remember him what does he want?" The Senator asked defensively.

"He says we have enemies on the hill and that he wants to help us, but personally I think he's trying to win points with you for his screw up." Cheryl replied.

"I want you to ask him just one question for me and please don't ask me for an explanation okay. I'll explain when you get home. Ask him who killed my page, ask him that", the Senator hung up the cell phone leaving Doctor Teranez absolutely speechless as she went to the door and beckoned agent Todd back into her office.

The agent sat in one of the two chairs in front of the doctor's desk. He was concerned about the mortified look on the doc's face.

"Doctor is anything wrong?" the agent asked.

She responded by asking, "who killed Senator Stinger's page, Carl?"

Special Agent Todd pulled his chair underneath his buttocks and scooted closer to the desk whispering to the doctor, "that's why I'm here ma'am, we killed him."

CHAPTER 17

SETTLING DOWN

Doctor Teranez was not sure if the agent had developed a morbid sense of humor, insane or telling the truth. She was frankly afraid to pursue the issue any further. She despised the cloak and dagger world always insisting her girl friend change the subject whenever she would discuss it with her in bed. Of course, this would only incite the Senator to want to share more intrigue with her and she would be forced to listen.

"I'm not sure I understand what you mean by, you killed him", Doctor Teranez asked the agent.

He sighed and attempted to explain, "I personally didn't kill the young man I believe the job was carried out by my department because it was felt the page was a National Security Threat or NST. I personally object to such operations but my objections, well they're in vain. Believe me doctor this action changed my life. I could get into trouble if DHS and their sponsors find out I had this conversation with you. Look I've got to go, but I'll be in touch. By the way I'm the Field Agent Incharge for the Southern Region now thanks to Senator Stinger. Please let her know I appreciate what she's done for me and let her know she may be in danger."

"What do you mean danger?" Cheryl's eyes dilated as she stared hard at the agent. "You're saying someone may try and harm her too?"

"Yes, if they think she poses a threat," the agent replied.

"But why would they kill that poor young man?" The doctor asked with desperation ringing in her voice.

Special Agent Todd stood up and started to walk to the door. He turn back towards the doctor and said, "you really don't want to know that ma'am. One person is dead already for knowing and all he did was perform diligently with his work assignment."

The agent left two business cards on the doctor's desk before exiting the room. Doctor Teranez promptly scooped them up and placed them in her purse. There was no other business for her so she gathered her things and headed back home. She was glad that an investigation was not initiated on the lab. However, a new worry now ate at her the safety of her friend. Senator Karen Stinger may be the target for assassination by an agency she had oversight of is what the agent implied.

Anish was proud of the results of the audit by IRS. He called Ted and Alice Martin to share the great news. They were all happy with the results. Since they were in Atlanta courtesy of the last emergency emails they'd received they thought it would be great to get together. Ted remembered that Makesh Patel was staying at the Atlanta Ritz Hotel in downtown Buckhead near them and they called to invite him as well. Amin Sabat was due to arrive later that evening and J.P. Rockdale and Bishop Terrell would be arriving in the early morning.

Atlanta was bristling with consumer activity. It was the third week of December and holiday cheer was at full blast. The Collective members would only meet for a day and be back with their families in time to celebrate festivities with them. The atmosphere at the cigar bar in the Atlanta Ritz Hotel was laid back as the pianist played slow sultry jazz. Anish rarely drank but was enjoying a small glass of sherry while the Martins tickled their pallet with the bars scarcest Red wine. Makesh was drinking a Samuel Adams Lager mixed with Guiness Stout. Nothing was said, they were all happy to be together without an agenda or reports in front of them. Anish's cell phone went off it was Doctor Teranez and Senator Stinger. "That would be wonderful, please do. We will be in the cigar bar when you get here", Anish informed the Senator.

"Well gang I guess you heard two more of our comrades will be joining us shortly."

Anish's firm had successfully satisfied the IRS inspector's assault earlier in the week. The financials and all associated transactions regarding the non-profit entity were near perfect. Anish had fulfilled his fiduciary responsibilities to perfection for the Collective. Now it was time to party.

Margarite picked up the phone in her bed room it was Sergeant O'Connell. He was asking her if she knew the dead man from the shooting at the mansion. She explained that she never saw the body, but knew he was there by the pond because her man servant Peter had informed her after he had shot him.

Why? Who is he?" Ms. Plantard asked the sergeant.

O'Connell took a deep breath and sighed, "it's rather complicated ma'am this guy doesn't exist in the NCIC, our state data base or any place on Earth for that matter. The only identifying clue on him was a tattoo that I'm trying to zero in on. You know to see if it's a military unit or fraternity he may have belonged to."

"Sergeant would you mind describing the tattoo you saw me? That is if it wouldn't divulge too much of the investigation or anything?" Margarite pleasantly asked.

"No ma'am I don't mind at all, hell oh excuse me ma'am. I mean you might be familiar with the tattoo. It looks like two snakes and they are eating each other's tail and in the center of them is a goats head. Does that sound like something you've seen before?"

"No, I'm afraid not sergeant. It rather much sounds like some esoteric biker markings to me", Margarite shared.

"Mmm I was thinking that very same thing Ms. Plantard. Thank you for your time ma'am. I'm sorry to have troubled you, merry Christmas." O'Connell hung up.

CHAPTER 18

MORNING RUN

As the morning appeared Lieutenant Lehchin finished his tea at the little market shop he visited everyday without fail. He was determined to question Paul Constantine about his friend's death. He left a tip and grabbed his cigarettes. The young children were playing kick ball in the street near his car as they did every morning. The Lieutenant suddenly felt uncomfortable and began to scan his surroundings more intently. His mother had taught him to trust his intuition and over the years martial arts training and a strict spiritual regimen combined with her advice prove to be very helpful. Lehchin survived the mean streets of California and Hong Kong better than most.

A cyclist rode past him, an old man sold fresh fish on the opposite corner, a woman was shaking dusty rugs while the children chased each other and behind him the young boys kicked the ball in front of the tea market. He began to think about the shooting the day before and was unnerved when he noticed a man on the far corner east of him. The unusual thing about the man was his clean fade hair cut and a very expensive watch he sported. The guy was either brave, stupid, not from around these parts or a seasoned criminal. Either of these didn't work in his favor for attempting to be inconspicuous.

The Lieutenant pulled out his car keys and unlocked his door. He sat down behind the steering column as he watched the man on the corner being joined by another man. The man joining him was black and definitely American by his dress style and posture. Seeing blacks in this part of town was strange there were no hotels for tourist or sites for vacationers and it could be very dangerous for strangers. Okay so the possibilities were narrowing and what was left was that the men were either stupid or dangerous criminals, the short list.

The two men glanced in Lieutenant Lehchin's direction so he checked his rear view mirror as a precaution to see if he was clear on his rear. Lieutenant Lehchin hated being stalked if in fact that's what was being done. Sitting in his Aston Martin he noticed the residual of morning dew on the hood, but something was awry. On the passenger side very little dew existed despite the fact it was under the shadow of a building. That side should have had more dew on it because of its lack of exposure to the rising sun. So why was there no dew or moisture on that side of the hood? The Lieutenant opened his door and got out to walk around and investigate. He noted hand impressions on the chrome of the car. The two men on the corner gave up being discrete as they began gawking as though Lehchin wore a bikini or bore two heads. The officer was now maneuvering his coat so as to be able to pull his gun easier and both men clearly observed this move. Hand prints on the front side of the hood, a bomb he thought to himself. I bet someone has put a bomb under my car. He had to see if the suspicion was correct so he knelt down but could not see under the car. He got down on his side and scooted a little closer as he tried to keep the two men in his view as best he could while trying to verify his hunch. The lieutenant realized he was making a tactical mistake. Backup was needed a basic procedure taught to any rookie. He called in on his cell phone and requested two squad cars to his location. The Lieutenant also indicated to the dispatcher that he might be in danger. The dispatcher confirmed his location and gave him an ETA of three minutes notifying Lehchin that two cars were near him. He relaxed a little after the info and lit a cigarette while he waited for back up. The two men on the corner were now joined by a car. The car was a jaguar a new model with three occupants. Lieutenant Lehchin knew this car it hit him out of no where. The car was Constantine's vehicle and he knew now was the time to panic. No ego or heroics would flourish under these conditions. It was time to run. He looked for the best possible escape route. Then as luck would have it one of the squad cars pulled around the jaguar and headed for the Lieutenant. Lieutenant Lehchin threw his cigarette down and mashed it out; pulled his weapon and was now going to question the suspicious onlookers. As the police cruiser got closer he could tell the officer had two other persons with him. Great, the more the merrier the young Lieutenant thought. He was really perturbed about almost being forced to flee the scene for fear of his life and for that he would take great liberty playing the bully as soon as his boys arrived.

The cruiser pulled up next to curb in front of the Lieutenant's car and Lehchin approached it. In the back sat Captain Kao and one of his sergeants. The lieutenant thought to himself that this was just the type of support he needed. The window rolled down slowly as the lieutenant bent down, Captain Kao was smiling and at that very moment the soccer ball the young boys across the street were kicking hit the roof of the Captain's cruiser scaring the daylights out of Lieutenant Lehchin. He instinctively dodged to the ground as the gunshot from the Captain's widow rang out over his head. It didn't take a rocket scientist to put together what just went down. Lieutenant Lehchin rolled to his feet as the car doors opened. He could see the jaguar and men on the corner still standing there as though they were taking notes. He heard another gunshot as he scurried across the street to the area he had determined earlier would make his best escape run. The adrenaline was pumping through him as he finally mustard up enough guts to return fire on his own team. When he shot he shot at his team for keeps this was the only way he would survive.

*"Aaahhhh, why?" Officer Lehchin yelled as he capped one the oncoming police officers who was shooting at him. The round hit the running officer in the abdomen dead center. The officer fell to his knees and balled up on the pavement as the other officer jumped over him. Captain Kao was behind him in hot pursuit waving his gun in his left hand and his other fat hand widely in the air as though he were drowning in a pool of water.

Lieutenant Lehchin ran hard he knew his attackers wouldn't be able to keep his pace. He weaved and turned around the corners of the Hong Kong neighborhood slum he'd entered and nearly knocked over an elderly lady as he hit one of the corners. He thought perhaps he should attempt to enter one of the houses, but leaned against the idea of putting any innocent persons in danger. He grew weary and his lungs burned and ached. He could see nobody was behind him and entered an ally to his right walking quickly behind a dumpster he bent over with his hands on his knees and his head lowered gasping for air. Glancing up every couple of seconds he thought about how he was going to get out of this mess. He knew the Captain would cover his tracks and the best way to do that would for Lehchin to be found dead. No one at the site where the chase began could say Lehchin was a police officer because he had civilian clothing on and what was worse he had a gun. The Lieutenant remembered he could call the chief with his cell phone and then if things couldn't get worse realized he must have lost the cell phone during his roll to avoid the ball which he thought was an attack. That ball had saved him from having his head shot off by the Captain he'd served with for two years.

Lieutenant Lehchin decided it was time for him to put more distant between him and his present position. A car pulled up blocking the ally way it was the jaguar. Lehchin stopped cold in his tracks and looked around for an exit. To his left was a restaurant door all blocked up with garbage and directly across from him on the right was a brick wall with graffiti. He laughed inside after taking time to quickly read the graffiti. Painted on the wall in multiple colors next to him was some gangster art which read, "Angels of Death Territory Dare to Trespass" ironic he thought this was his hell.

The car window quickly rolled down and Lehchin recognized Paul Constantine right off. Paul's right arm was in a sling he sat smoking a cigarette just staring straight ahead. Lehchin had slid a fresh clip in his gun but his back was literally up against the wall. He could try and shoot it out and if it came down to it that's what he'd rather do go out fighting.

Paul flicked the fag from the window of his car and turned his attention to the cornered police officer.

"Lieutenant may I give you a ride somewhere? You look a bit lost. Doesn't the Lieutenant look lost to you Jimmy?"

The driver leaned back and looked over his right shoulder and smirked at Lehchin, "Yeah boss he sure looks lost to me." The driver said as the occupants in the car rang out in laughter.

Time slowed down like the movie Matrix as the Lieutenant Shot directly at the figure sitting in the back of the car. The Jaguar door seemed to fly open automatically and Paul fell to the ground on top of the smoldering cigarette he'd tossed out earlier, he was now in the prone position. Jimmy the driver took position on the driver side shooting rounds over the front driver side hood. The other passenger in the back seat took position from the trunk's driver side. Lieutenant Lehchin dove behind the dumpster his gun blazing.

Blood poured from his right shoe as one of the attacker's round tore away the top of his shoe as he dove. He would miss his big toe and the balance it once provided him.

Paul maneuvered his way to his feet and ran to the wall opposite of Lieutenant Lehchin. Paul was now shooting from the corner of the graffiti wall. He knew that Lehchin was in a strategically strong position by being in the ally. He had a one way in and the metal dumpster to provide protection. It did not take Lehchin long to figure this fact out either. He realized the attackers could not come in without him taking them out.

The lieutenant was in serious pain. He wondered why he hurt so badly. His wounded foot ached beyond imagination. If he wasn't killed by the assailants' bullets the pain was going to kill him. Under the present circumstances of possibly being shot and the possibility of being dead within the next few minutes he couldn't understand why the pain was so excruciating.

The shooting started to subside a little and Lehchin suddenly had an idea. He peeped around the trash bin to recon the positions of his attackers. His glance solicited multiple hot rounds which smashed and drummed a tuned against the metal bin and the stone walls of the alley. It was a plan that just might work. The Jaguar's gas tank was the key to the success of Lehchin's plan. The Lieutenant would attempt to ignite the fuel. If he could saturate that back part of the car with bullets he might get lucky. He also noticed that the trash bin was on wheels. This was going to help as well in the event he could blow the car up. He'd push the bin forward while gaining ground on the enemy and fighting his way out of his cement trap.

Paul shifted his location to the wall opposite of Lehchin's spot. He now had a tactically better shooting angle on his target. The Lieutenant shot at Paul and then placed four bullets into the area near the trunk of the Jaguar. The shooter at the trunk ducked and covered wondering why he was incurring the policeman's wrath. A smile grew on Paul's face as he appreciated the Lieutenant's adroitness.

"Hey Jimmy, oh Jimmy your boy's trying to hit the gas tank. Kudos lieutenant great thinking you should be working for me." Paul howled.

The Lieutenant once again shot in Paul's direction and then a couple more rounds at his planned target. He lucked out with this round of shots. Liquid was running from under the car and he could hear the gunman from the trunk area screaming like a banshee.

The gunman couldn't be seen, but he could be heard by all of Hong Kong. "I'm hit oh god I'm hit Jimmy. Damn I'm bleeding to death here. I need a doctor. Oh god I'm hit." The gunman squealed.

Paul was embarrassed he shook his head and remembered why he disliked this guy. He glanced at Jimmy and yelled, "Jim help the poor bastard. Shoot him, kill him. I can't take the whining its annoying do me a favor and help him, help me."

Jimmy had been with Paul five years and he'd learn to trust him without question. Although the gunman was someone he sponsored Jimmy did not hesitate to place two bullets in the man's head as he was directed by his boss to do. "Boss is that better? That should be better, okay. Sorry about the annoying noise", Jimmy stated and burst into a giggle.

Lehchin felt chills crawl up through his limbs. These people were the coldest criminals he'd ever encountered. Even the Triad who were known for their ruthlessness didn't rival the lack luster butchery of these killers.

In the background the yelling of the natives could be heard and in the distance now the roar of police sirens growing ever closer. Paul was now edgy as he looked at the pinned lieutenant and called out, "whoops sirens that's our cue. We must be leaving now let's just say it's a "Pavlovian" response. You know dog here's a whistle he comes, criminal here's a siren he runs. Okay?"

Lieutenant Lehchin fired a couple bullets in Paul's direction a futile effort to shut the man up. He grew tired of his foot hurting but listening to Paul's lunacy was worse pain.

Paul motioned to Jimmy and directed his number one to start the car. Jimmy hopped in and started the Jaguar up. He pulled up next to Paul who hustled into the car next to Jimmy. The car pulled off with tires screeching as the smell of fresh burnt rubber assaulted the air.

Lehchin couldn't move, but he knew he couldn't wait for his boys from the precinct to arrive. Chances were the Captain had already cooked up a dirty story placing him in the quagmire of this whole panorama.

Lieutenant Lehchin attempted to stand, but he was not fairing well in the effort. Without notice a car pulled up with the same screeching noise that was made by Paul's fleeing vehicle. Please not again he thought. Could it be his assailants had returned to finish the job? This car had one occupant a studious looking white man who was waiving at the lieutenant to get in the car.

The man jumped out of the car and yelled from over the roof of the car, "get in damn man hurry. I'm a friendly come on we can't stay here, come on," the stranger begged.

"I'm wounded I can't make it go on," Lehchin responded. Right about now the young lieutenant did not trust the stranger he couldn't trust anyone. "Go on!" He yelled again.

The stranger left the car running and looked in both directions. The sirens were now getting closer as the man ran towards the wounded officer. Lehchin placed his gun directly in the man's face.

"Sir I don't know you and you need to go." Lehchin informed the stranger. Grimacing in pain the officer was now about to pass out. He felt himself getting faint and he felt cold.

The stranger said, "I have no gun you see? You're going into shock please let me help you to the car. We must escape now."

Lieutenant Lehchin woke up reaching for his weapon. He was in a car and the trees racing outside his window made him noxious as he watched as they raced by outside the window.

"We'll have you in front a doctor in a minute, I'm certainly glad you're still with the living. Oh, and don't worry about your safety son, this doctor is a friend, a bit of a quack but he'll help us."

The stranger was hoping that what he had just told the wounded man would come to fruition.

"Where are we going? Who are you?" Lehchin was still worried as he asked the questions.

"Well we're going to a friend's house and which answers the where. My name is Maurice, Maurice Steeley and that answers, "the who."

CHAPTER 19

RESURRECTION

Miles was greeted in the airport lobby by Peter. Miles looked terrible. His weight loss was noticeable and he definitely had become closely acquainted with his clothing they were gamey and well worn.

Peter moved in Mile's direction with his cane over his arm. "Miles I'm so sorry you had to bare this heavy burden alone. A hearse is out front. Where is Master Zarkuhn's body being held?"

Peter was there to collect the body of Michael Zarkuhn. Margarite could not bring herself to come. She had barely come out of the study since being told of Michael's death. She explained to Peter that when she saw Michael again it would be to say her final farewell.

Peter was there to pick the body up, but there was another reason that he was there a reason he could not share with anyone on the Collective's board. He realized that Zarkuhn would be revived at some point in the future. It was a secret that Michael Zarkuhn had only imparted to the butler, Peter. Michael's casket was picked up by Peter after completing what seemed like hundreds of forms at the heavy freight pickup area. Miles sat quietly up front while Peter and some of the dock workers loaded the metallic coffin into the rented hearse. As they pulled through the security check point Peter presented the necessary documents to the TSA and civilian security gate guard. They had desired to verify the contents of the coffin and were obviously in a hurry to re-enter the heat of their little hut.

Miles fell asleep quickly his snoring drove the poor butler crazy. Peter was tolerant of the raspy noise realizing this man had gone through a lot and Peter was sensitive to it. Peter would drop Miles off at the mansion and take the coffin to the cottage located on the west side of the mansion grounds and there he would wait for Master Zarkuhn's resurrection keeping anyone curious from discovering the ultimate secret.

Michael basked in the light wondering how long he'd been deceased and if all the work he'd plan went according to his design, questions and curiosity flooded his mind. This was the most vicious attack he had ever experienced rivaling the fatal injury he'd received in the same battle Alexander the Great received an arrow under the armpit in Persia. Michael in an effort to join the Macedonian king at the top of the wall received sword across the bridge of his nose.

As always it appeared as though he would survive his latest trauma indicative of the symptoms and dreams he was experiencing now.

Back, back into his past he would once again spiral. The memories were forever replaying themselves in the annals of his mind. Michael began to dwell on the treachery and ill will his God had wreaked on mankind.

He clearly remembered God repenting for the evil he contemplated against the children of Israel while Moses communed with him on Mount Sinai. God wanted more than anything to destroy man. The Deluge was his attempt to do so before he had made a covenant with Noah and later with Abraham. He would have succeeded were it not for his brother warning Gilgamesh better known as the patriarch Noah. The covenant was made with Noah to never flood or destroy man again because he, God was so over taken by the savory smell of barbecued meat on Noah's alter. Michael began to detest and feel contempt for the God he'd served for some many ions. God was jealous, unforgiving, merciless and forever making covenants with what seemed to Michael to be the worst of mankind.

Michael laughed to himself while still in his dead light state when he recalled how Jehovah had made Abram rich and powerful at the expense of others who were not in league with him and his plan for controlling this wealthy planet. He remembered how he and Peter one night the year before discussed God and the bible over a bottle of brandy. He was so inebriated he proved to be totally out of control.

"So Abraham, Abram tells his wife by the way honey do not tell the pharaoh we're man and wife because they'll kill me. Poor Sarai, later referred to as Sarah is confused and says to Abraham what shall I say husband? Aah, say I'm your brother okay. Then sure as the old guy predicted the pharaoh and his whole court were talking about the beauty of the desert prince's sister."

Peter attempted to ask an intelligible question even though Michael was almost ten sheets to the wind, "You were there then too? I mean you actually saw this happen?"

Michael recalled laughing while trying to finish the story as best he could in the drunken state he was in. "Yes Peter I was one of the herdsman for the patriarch Abram at the time and I also served duty with Akhenaten, I mean Moses. It was very interesting to say the least. So this pharaoh takes Sarah into his palace and makes her his sweet thing. Well my Lord gets wind of it and boy did he get pissed. I mean really P. O.d. You know you would have thought Sarah was his sweet thing the way he put it on the pharaoh and his posse."

Michael thought back on how hard Peter had laughed, so hard he had to stop telling the story for about ten minutes before the old butler caught his breath.

Michael continued recounting his story in his mind.

"Here was my God mad as hell, excuse the expression, totally outraged about his boy Abraham's wife being porked by some Egyptian definitely not wearing a Ramses and doing so all because of Abraham's lie about her being his sister.

Well then God plagues the whole city and the pharaoh is freaking out trying to figure out what he did wrong, you know wondering why corporate is pissed. Then wah lah! The poor bastard finds out he's been porking another guy's wife and not just some guy, a guy who's connected very, well connected. So to stop the madness he pays off Abraham with sheep, cattle just about anything he could think of east and west of the Nile and begged him to leave Dodge. So now it's about three days later and we're headed towards Sodom and Gomorrah, I'm thinking to myself why hadn't Abraham simply told the Egyptian Pharaoh the truth upfront? With the backing of Jehovah he would still have been protected, right? Well I'll be a suck head mule if Abraham doesn't pull the same pimp trick on another guy in the new land we entered. This time it was King Abimelech, you know son of Gideon, the King of Gerar, oh that's right you wouldn't or couldn't know him I did. Well anyhow, anyway he tells this poor slob, "Yeah she's fine huh … yeap and she's my sister." So Abimelech takes her into his fold, but unlike the first sucker this King has some kind of vision or dream or something as told to me later by Brother Daniel. Well the dream warns him he's screwing up and Abraham's God is going to kill the lot of them. This Abimelech dude had the right idea even though his God was Baal, a son of Jehovah, he in no way desires a falling out with any God especially Daniel's God. He summons Abraham to his court to explain his treachery and asked him what he and his kingdom had done to deserve placing the King's family and country in such grave danger. He was genuine, I mean his delivery to Abraham was filled with what I thought to be integrity and he seemed to have desired good relations between his people and Abram's tribes. Peter on that note more wine is in order. Peter I was there in the court with old Abe for that one. There's continual questioning from the King and Abraham really doesn't have a good answers and all of a sudden he pops out with "well she is my sister on my father's side, but not my mother's side", as though that would make a difference.

"Well what did you do sir?"

"I just stood there shaking my head thinking of what bad habits the Hebrews had picked up from the Egyptians you know the marrying sister thing and all. Next thing I know this kings giving us more sheep, more cattle, you name it and asking us to please leave Kansas.

Abraham ends up rich, rich, rich just like God had promised him he would be. Then it dawned on me that God had set the pharaoh and the king up by using some sacred law or something that was on both the poor soul's law books. Well take King Abimelech for example his God was Baal. Do you know who Baal was Peter? Or did I already tell you? I'm drunk I can't remember. I'll tell you its God's, Jehovah's son or El Elyon's which is another name for Jehovah. Of course Jehovah insisted the Israelites stop worshipping Baal around 1059 B.C."

"Let me get this straight, you mean the whole time Abraham was telling the truth? Sarah was in fact his sister?"

Michael would never forget the puzzled look on Peter's aged face as he took another drink of his brandy.

"That's nothing Peter let me tell you the whole damn family was dysfunctional, Abraham, Lot, David, maybe not Solomon. I mean most of them were stark lunatics like Republicans and as sex crazed as Democrats. But the thing that got me was the invitro-fertilization program my former boss, God Almighty initiated once he found those patsies. He promised the world to Noah, Abraham, Moses and list goes on. He'd hand them Nations if they would just follow him so to seal the deal he literally placed his seed in certain select women connected to these guys in order to justify and ensure his future interference in this world's affairs, specifically via Israel. One thing I can say is God keeps his promises and especially to his kin. He may have to be reminded from time to time but he'll keep'em."

Zarkuhn suddenly heard a car door slam. He snapped out of his dead light dream state. However, he sensed he was somehow different. The change was more acute than ever it was the beginning of his extreme dislike for the one he had called Lord, God Almighty. Some love still remained, but the erosion process was continual. Michael felt he never wanted to see the great manipulator again; nothing God had ever done was for the betterment of human kind and Michael Zarkuhn now realized it even if the human race didn't. Why couldn't God have been more like Jesus he thought?

"Michael, Michael can you hear me it's Peter this is your wake up call."

CHAPTER 20

FRIENDSHIP A PREREQUISITE TO LOVE

Senator Stinger was on the patio drinking coffee when Doctor Teranez arrived home. "Karen, honey I'm really sorry about your page. Do you know anymore than the fact that he's dead?" Teranez joined her friend on the patio as she tried to console her.

"I know that kid did not deserve to die Cheryl." Karen started to cry as she continued to talk with Cheryl. The D.C. authorities told me he was strangled in his apartment. They said it looked like a robbery, but I'm skeptical."

Cheryl sat next to Karen and hugged her, rubbing her shoulder in a circular motion ever so lightly. She asked her friend, "Why are you skeptical?"

"It was something Carl said to me before I came here for vacation, oh, Carl was his name. He stopped me in the parking lot and asked me if I'd review the Intelligence Reform Bill with him when I got back from vacation. He seemed concerned about something in it."

"Well, what could it be Karen? My God! Something as important as an intelligence bill I would think is pretty serious. I mean I don't know much about those types of things, but I cringe at the thought of something being wrong with the thing. I mean wasn't the purpose of the bill to bring about remedies for incidents like 9/11?"

"Thanks to Carl I may have a copy at the mansion waiting for me to review. Margarite left a message that I received a package from my office. Carl forwarded a copy to me the day I left. The same day he lost his life." The Senator wiped her face as she mentioned the loss of the young man.

"I want you to rest okay. Don't forget Special Agent Todd's appearance either. I have a sneaky suspicion he's going to prove valuable in getting to the bottom of this matter. Oh! You asked me to ask him who killed your page and his answer was that his agency had him killed." As Cheryl informed her lover of this new information she could feel Karen's back tense up. Cheryl squeezed her even harder to keep her from going ballistic.

Karen held Cheryl's hand and looked her in the eyes. "Todd gave you a number where I can call him right?" Cheryl nodded.

"I think I should get up to Plantard Mansion. I feel compelled to read that bill and try and figure out if it may have had something to do with this murder." Karen knew this would not fare well with Cheryl as she stood up and headed towards the bedroom. Cheryl also stood up quickly and ran to her grabbing her around the waist at the same time swinging her around. Cheryl embraced her and passionately kissed the left side of her face as she held her waist tightly.

"You're wrong baby I know you're thinking I'm disappointed, but I'm not and baby I'll be with you." Cheryl kissed her lover with a kiss wet enough to put out a major fire. Karen looked into her lover's eyes, "thank you, I love you so much." Senator Stinger returned the kiss in kind holding her lovers head with both hands as she sucked the nectar from the Latin beauty's lips.

The two ladies held each other tightly as they rolled their hips and pressed their loins against one another. Soon they were engulfed by lustful flames rising from the sweet wells of their womanhood. Before the two realized it they found themselves on Cheryl's king size bed with their legs wrap around each other like two serpents entwined, a feminine helix of hot sweaty love.

Michael thought he had lost his mind. He could have sworn he heard a voice say, "wake up call, this is your wake up call sir." The sounds were starting to come and he could see blurs. Great he thought I can feel my toes wiggle. His vision was clearing up quickly. There was a light directly over head, but something kept flashing or blocking the light intermittently.

"Hello sir, how are we?" Peter asked Michael as he leaned over the open casket. Peter noted some scaring and dry blood on Zarkuhn's face that seemed to heal before his very eyes. Zarkuhn was surprised, but then again not surprised that Peter was present during his return to the living. He erred in his plan neglecting to go any further than the hit on himself and return to Boston. He completely forgot that he would need to be at the right place at the right time before he could all of a sudden rise from the dead.
It could've been worse he could've have been buried alive.

"Welcome sir," Peter greeted the sore martyr as Michael attempted to sit up from his metallic sarcophagus. "I've taken the liberty of stocking the cottage with the necessary provisions for you. I've also been entrusted with arranging your funeral. Madam Margarite has also allowed me to take vacation and should she require my services I can be reached here at the cottage."

"Wait a minute!" Michael stopped Peter by placing his right hand in Peter's face with the traditional "speak to the hand" gesture. "You're telling me you take your vacations in this cottage? Peter for Christ sakes it's on the same property as the mansion it's less than half a mile. Peter the idea behind vacations is to get away far away as possible."

Peter raised his right brow which reminded Michael of the Spock character on the series Star Trek as he answered, "and?"

"Peter never mind, do you have any Asprin, Tylenol, anything? My head's killing me."

Paul was pissed as he stormed up and down the long dock cussing and ranting at his rag tag group of mercenaries. He simply couldn't believe the week he was having. He started yelling, "It was all going so well we killed a copper, we moved record shipments of product, we framed ourselves a troublemaker and then someone kills the poor bloke for us. Of course there's the downside of loosing six of my men. Loosing the bloody copper in the alley, and, and what else Jimmy? What else happened that was a negative? Help me out here."

Jimmy looked up at the ceiling of the warehouse and then down at his feet, then up, then back down, "Oh the Jag got shot full of holes by that chink cop. That's a bad thing right boss?" Jimmy sheepishly answered shrugging his shoulders.

"Well yeah Jimmy you could say that. Yeah we'll use that one until I figure something else to bitch about boys." Paul responded.

"I want the cop. I want that damn cop. I want that Lieutenant Lehchin, do you all hear me? I don't care what it cost or what it takes you to get him by tomorrow night he'd better be toast. If that cop is not toast soon, I'm going to set some examples starting with you Jimmy and you may ask yourself why. Because, I didn't like the damn answer you gave me a few minutes ago. Now there are twenty of you including numb nuts there and I'm going to have this picture of the target circulated. The object is to terminate the bastard with extreme prejudice and bring me proof he's dead. Are there any questions ..."

"Ah, boss," Jimmy slowly raised his hand"

"Jimmy if you ask me anything I'll shoot you even though I luv yah," barked Paul.

"Never mind boss", Jimmy murmured.

Margarite was not sure allowing Peter the responsibility of handling Michael Zarkuhn's funeral service was the correct or fair thing to do, but Peter was Michael's closest friend that she was aware and cared for him as much as any one and he was so very insistent. She felt such a comfort whenever Peter tended to a matter. Margarite could not have held it together if she were to have to arrange the service for Michael. The door bell grounded her and she raced to the front door beating both servants who promptly stopped and returned to their duties. Both servants had agreed to fill in for Peter in his absence although realized half a Peter was better than no Peter would be the general consensus.

"Miles, oh Miles," Margarite hugged Miles and pulled him in from the biting cold. Margarite was truly happy to see Miles. Her heart beat was rapid and her breathing uncontrollable. Miles' presence provided relief the same relief and calm she found when Michael Zarkuhn was often in her midst. She was confused by her emotions, not knowing or really understanding her response to Miles' arrival.

Miles felt at home in Magarite's slender embrace. He couldn't remember ever feeling the way he felt right then in his childhood friend's embrace. Hugging the woman he had loved for years only reaffirmed that he still loved her. That moment Miles felt uncomfortable in the long, pale slender arms of Margarite, he was not worthy to receive such affection. She deserved better than him, Margarite was a queen who deserved a king, not a frumpy, balding, pompous intellectual pipe toker. He only wished Margarite could feel for him the way he did for her.

"Miles I missed you so much. I'm so elated you're here, safe," Margarite shared with him as she continued to clutch him tightly. Miles turned his bearded face to her gently released his grip from around her. Looking into her luminous brown eyes as Margarite still held him with her long elegant arms gazing at her lovingly a tear made its way down the right cheek of his face. She never thought of Miles as anything but a friend, even closer a brother. However, here she was now embraced in his arms feeling a love which could only be the fruit of lovers.

Margarite was tired, she felt worn down and longed for stability in her life something she could count on, someone that would be there, that had always been there. She needed the affection and the touch of a man. Margarite asked herself how she could have been so blind to miss that what she needed was right there in front of her. Miles and Margarite now found themselves chest to chest, cheek to cheek and eye to eye. Not even Aphrodite, the goddess of love could have created a better elixir for this moment of love. The intimacy through the closeness of a man and woman is the oldest concoction for love known to man and woman. Miles and Margarite could feel the passion oozing from the spontaneity of the moment. The lusty union was inescapable brought on by all of the years of suppressed pheromones the two nerds had packed away and now they were simply over powered. Unexplored pools of desire boiled in the beads of sweat simmering out of their pores. Margarite's pink perky lips met Miles' bearded mouth in a light and gentle liaison in the foyer of Plantard Mansion.

"Miles I'm sorry, I don't know what in the world came over me, heavens!" Margarite explained as she continued to hold on to her childhood playmate. She politely apologized for what they both knew was no indiscretion but mutually assured affection. It was an affirmation that they loved each other. They had without realizing it successfully completed a long course which would ensure both of them a long life of mutual respect, love and admiration, trust and happiness. They had been friends first openly accepting one another wholeheartedly, human frailties and all. The long years of friendship they'd purged all pretentiousness, expectations and suspended all petty judgments of each other while depositing positive emotions in their repositories of trust before this their morphing into lovers.

"I must say no apology is really necessary my dear. To put this as blunt as possible, I love you, I love, I love you Margarite. I have always cared for you and I, oh how I cherish you. Please do not apologize for giving me hope that this could be the beginning of us. Fair Lady I beg of you not to toy with my emotions for woman I do so love you." Miles whispered this to her as he fought fainting. Margarite decided she would exercise a bit of selfishness and indulge herself. She'd allow her instincts to lead in this moment of passion not her head. Margarite now knew she loved Miles and today she'd consummate the fact.

"My dear sir would you please accompany upstairs." the beautiful, slender lady requested of Miles as she stared into the eyes of a long overdue opportunity for companionship. Miles smiled as the woman he had always loved held his right hand and slowly led him up the long winding staircase while leisurely pulling the blue ribbon from her long raven hair as they trekked towards bliss.

CHAPTER 21

TWO TABLETS PLEASE

"You're going to be okay son. I've stopped the bleeding and although you can't grow the toe back, in a year or two you'll have forgotten you had a big toe on that foot."

As far as Lieutenant Lehchin could discern he was receiving medical advice from a very smelly old white man standing directly over him. Lieutenant Lehchin was conscious enough to start cussing, "where the hell am I? Old man who are you? Where's the guy who drove me here?"

Doctor Lester Kry was an eighty year old physician transplant from Midway Island, having served in the Army Air Force during World War II, he'd migrated to Hong Kong to make it his home. The doctor had a strong distaste for American imperialism and British delusions of Grandeur, so he moved to Hong Kong with his young Japanese wife and raised four children, realizing the British would eventually go away. Dr. Kry was also a contract agent for the Collective secret society and had been since the war.

Maurice entered the room with a cup of coffee and sat across from the lieutenant. "Well you look better don't you," he remarked sarcastically.

"Doctor Kry when might we get moving?" asked Maurice the Collective's Pacific Station chief. Lieutenant this is Doctor Kry."

"Well Maurie you can hit the road now provided this young guy adheres to his regimen of medicines he'll be just fine," the old white crusty doctor responded. Don't forget to send me my money for the patch work you sorry toad!"

"Yes of course you'll get it, hell how much is the bill," asked the station chief.

Doctor Kry gazed up in the air to the right and then to the left, back to the right and pulled a number out of the air, "$600.00 he blurted."

Maurice reached into his back pocket removing his wallet and finding the exact amount requested by the doctor, "here you are sir, a worthwhile business expense", Maurice stated as he handed the money over.

"Lieutenant Lehchin I'm sorry, but we have an appointment to make. Please get up and be careful not damage the good doctor's work, we've gotta move or we're going to be fish food."

"Okay," the Lieutenant stated as he gingerly managed his way off the table that supported him. "I don't feel anything. Hey Doctor Fry this is great you did alright. I don't feel a thing, in fact I feel too good!"

"Thank you son, that would be the drugs you're feeling and its Kry, with a K, and don't worry in a couple of hours you will feel all the pain you and your injury are due. So take this when you feel pain coming on just one tablet okay, not two, not three just one." With that Doctor Kry laughed and disappeared from the room.

"Where are we going?" The Lieutenant's medicine was making him hyper and he felt uneasy not knowing the stranger's game plan.

Maurice was preoccupied with how to execute his escape from the Island. He finally heard his passenger talking to him. "I'm sorry Mr. Lehchin what did you say?"

Lehchin answered, "Where are you taking me?"

"It's us, where am I taking us and I'm getting us the hell off this Island. Is that a problem Lieutenant because if it is I'll be happy to drop you off at some other destination of your choosing?"

Lieutenant Lehchin had not thought clearly about his situation. There really hadn't been much time too, but now that he weighed his options he realized he was screwed. He couldn't go back to the city because Captain Kao would surely have him done in. The Lieutenant couldn't be sure of how high up the corruption went in his police department.

"I'm screwed. I think I stand a better chance of surviving if I hang with you, but it would really help if I at least knew your name. If you've already told me thanks, but I'm not good with remembering names when my toes are being shot off and I'm high, so what's your name?"

"Maurice."

Both Lehchin and Maurice laughed as their car vanished into the Hong Kong countryside.

"Not a problem your eminence, I will take the next aircraft for America. No your eminence, I know the area fairly well and if I'm not mistaken we have a possible contact on the east coast who might prove resourceful. Yes, I shall keep you informed." Paul hated taking orders from the church. He had outgrown religion years ago and thought of his superiors as being weak, over fed depressed men who did not truly follow the dictates of Catholic doctrine. Paul Constantine knew he was what the church needed, new blood, the right blood, his royal blood. Paul had used the church's archives and his inside contacts to aid him in his research for over fifteen years and he made startling discoveries, one so amazing and wonderful that it changed his life and his goals.

One night while conducting an experiment to see how many bottles of wine were required to get himself drunk, Paul traced his family tree back to none other than Emperor Constantine. With this little known knowledge the then ambitious and inquisitive young Paul continued his research as well as performing his other duties tasked to him by the Catholic Church, but his dream was to someday exercise his power, to enforce his birthright as a "ruler of men".

"You realize this is not a good idea particularly now Captain, so make it quick I have a plane to catch. You've acted in our best interest and represented us to our mutual benefit and prosperity in the past, but of all times you asked to meet, now was not prudent. What could be so important as to risk your connection to me," Paul asked Captain Kao with a strong resonance of disgust in his voice.

"I wanted to inform you of all the measures I've taken in order to neutralize our recent problem," the Captain informed Paul like a groveling weasel, his type sickened Paul Constantine. He couldn't wait to kill the Captain. That would be a great day and worthy of opening up some of his finest Irish ale.

"I have no need to know what you are doing Captain, only that it be done when it need to be done. You need to do something for me though."

The Captain's posture stiffened as though he were a Doberman Pincher reacting to his master's command. "Yes, of course, no problem, what can I do?"

Paul pushed his chair back and stood up, put on his most fashionable shades, leaned over to whisper in the Captain's fat ear. "Remember this, if you don't get me that lieutenant by tomorrow night, I'm going to pick the most inopportune time imaginable and gut you. Yes Captain, you resolve the problem or die. It would be quite a pity, for all that dirty money and pension to go to waste simply for not finding one man, don't you think?" Paul stressed as he slammed the table and exited the quiet little restaurant.

Paul arrived in Boston Saturday morning, full of anticipation about his assignment, he loved America. To him America was truly the land of opportunity and extreme decadence. He loved partying in the U.S. of A, all the drugs, booze, women and the homicides ensured his cup ran over. This was the land of plenty, the land founded on an experiment to allow anyone, and everything under the flag of freedom and justice for all to prosper in sin. Paul called his contact and arranged for a get together at one of his favorite spots. His hotel of choice was a hole in the wall. He enjoyed the type of hotels which had a distinct smell of despair that hovered in the hallways and clinged to the walls, unknowingly draining all the hope from the occupants entering its domain. Constantine felt he could literally swim in the atmosphere of despair and depravity fostered by the unforgiving environment. It was a cesspool he always indulged himself with a swim in, like a swine in mud he was happy. A bit of poverty, hopelessness and immorality acted much like Popeye eating a can of spinach, Paul was energized from by chaos and sadness of others. As Constantine strolled down the sidewalk admiring all the endless possibilities of potential criminal acts, day dreaming that someday he might move his operation to America where he could buy the protection of politicians, law enforcement and then it came to him as though a light switch popped on. He didn't need protection from the Americans, for they would need protection from him. Paul Constantine burst into laughter at what was he thinking ... protection, hell he would be in a position to rule several nations if this operation were to go as he'd plan. He entered the little neighborhood pub and went straight to the back booth near the restrooms. The bar tender walked from behind the bar and took his order. Just then the men's restroom door open and there stood Paul's contact, "Father Terrell, Bishop how the hell are ya?"

It was Bishop Terrell, inner circle member of the Collective. Bishop Terrell had known Paul Constantine for years and knew he must have been the Paul mentioned by Louis Tashido at the last inner council meeting when Tashido said that the perpetrators were from the church. Terrell was once a part of the Papal Army and there was none better except for Paul Constantine. The bishop was nervous about what Constantine could possibly want from him or why he was even in the States. He was not aware of what had taken place in Hong Kong or that the Plantard Mansion was attacked by factions related to the church.

"Paul I can't really say it's good to see you. What is it that I can do for you, what do you want? Your message sound urgent." The bishop asked with serious anticipation.

Paul sat back as the bar tender placed a bottle of Jack Daniels and two beers in front of him and hastily disappeared. Paul took the bottle of whiskey and chugged a big swallow then picked up a beer to chase it. "Well Padre' what do you know about the "Tables of Testimony"? The tablets, come on two tablets or something like that and father I'm not talking about asprin okay.

CHAPTER 22

THE CLEANSINGS

Cheryl and Karen were on their way to Plantard Mansion when Cheryl's cell went off, "hello this is Cheryl."

"Yes, my dear, this is Miles how are you?" Miles asked.

"Miles I couldn't be better. I am so glad you're safe and here with us, isn't it so sad about Michael? How's Margarite taking it? I know how fond of Michael she was."

"Well, yes it is sad he and Margarite were quite close, but somehow she's proving to be quite the lady. She's handling his loss just fine thank you, when might we expect your arrival?"

"Karen is with me and we'll be there around three O'clock."

Miles was relieved at this information.

"That's perfect I will inform Margarite. Please be careful. See you at 3 p.m."

"Well my beloved that was Cheryl. She and Karen will be arriving at approximately three O'clock. I'd say we can lie here in each other's arm for at least another hour."

"I'd thoroughly enjoy that my love, Miles would you do that thing again?"

"What thing would that be my love?"

Miles was stomped. He had no idea of what his new love was talking about. Margarite gave Miles the look. "Oh that thing, you mean with the beard. I'd be most obliged my love, but of course." He climbed back into bed wasting no time in performing the magical beard trick.

Makesh Patel had enjoyed Atlanta with his associates from the Collective, but he could not wait to see his family and check on his businesses. He was very uncomfortable with the events that had transpired over the last two weeks with the Collective. Makesh felt it his patriotic duty to be a member and to provide as much support via the assets he owned as he could, but not at the expense of his death. When he came into the Collective four years earlier things were different.

He remembered experiencing discrimination for being Arab and Muslim even though he was neither. He was East Indian and Hindu, but he had an accent and brown skin and for that he was nearly killed by some over zealous Boston police officers. If it were not for Ted Martin who provided legal representation for him after witnessing the abuse he suffered first hand by the thugs in blue he wouldn't be headed home right then.

Makesh realized then that when he was approached two months later by Ted and Miles and ask to join the secret group that he owed them and more than that he wanted to contribute some good himself. Now Michael Zarkuhn was dead and he was the best they had at smiting the bad guys. Not to mention the government was now singling out the members and what about the other secret factions who were now seeming to wage war against the Collective none of it was good. Even Anish and J.P. were having reservations. They had all discussed it amongst themselves. They felt they had too much to lose and that there was not enough protection should they be targeted as Margarite was last week. He sat in his car at the airport and knew he had to make a decision. Well right then it wasn't going to happen. What he needed was the loving attention of his wife and children.

Makesh noticed two men watching him as he adjusted his mirror and strapped on his seat belt. It was time to get moving. With the turn of his key none of what he wanted or needed mattered any longer. Patel's car went up in smoke and flames as the deafening noise shattered the windows of nearby vehicles and the debris killed one and injured four innocent bystanders. The two men walked silently away acting as nothing happened got into their car and drove off. Security waived them through as they attempted to leave the area. These men were not only immune to the loud noise from bombs, fire, and cries for help they were government agents void of the ability to think on their own or to realize they had taken innocent lives as is usually the case.

Another good person was now gone. The Collective would not know of their loss until roll call the next day at eleven p.m. when each member was to leave a status report on voicemail to indicate all was well.

"Peter that was perhaps the best Beef Wellington I've ever eaten." Michael was tempted to lick the plate.

"Thank you sir, I certainly appreciate the compliment. You know the British are not known for their culinary skills, however, other than fish and chips we seem to do well with Beef Wellington."

Michael was antsy, he could feel something terrible was pending, the Collective members were in danger he knew it. Michael desperately wanted to get back on the job, but the problem of his miraculous resurrection had to be convincingly addressed. How could ... and then he birthed an idea.

"Mr. Stuart, I think we should give Miles a call. My reason for this is that he is the only person in our group who can verify my death. My other reason is that my body cannot be kept on ice forever a funeral will soon be expected," Michael was pacing the cottage floor as he made his argument.

"Sir, I'm not sure Mr. Turner's heart would survive the news. However, it would be an asset to have another member in our group aware of your little secret. I will not be here forever you know. Well, perhaps I'll get him over here and, and then, well bloody hell the rest is on you Sir."

Anish was still on cloud nine with his pass on the audit given by the IRS. As he sat at his desk with his arms crossed behind his head as he leaned back he thought of who hadn't told yet of his success. He began to talk to himself, "who's the man? I'm the man. Who's the man?"

Anish heard a thumping sound and called out to his secretary. He had given her the day off or at least he thought he had. He went to check on the noise in the next room.

"Who are you? The office is closed gentlemen." Anish inform the two men standing in front of the secretary's desk. They were wearing suits and just stared at Anish. The black man looked at Anish and smiled as he sat on the edge of the accountant's desk.

The White man with him sat on the couch and removed his hat. The black man spoke, "so you da man! That's what I heard, that you da man. I tell you what."

Anish interrupted, I'd like you gentlemen to leave at once, please leave or ..."

"Or you'll call the police. Hey this guys going to call us", the black intruder said looking at his partner.

The white man sitting on the couch smiled at his partner and politely recanted with, "would you kindly inform da man we're already here." Both men laughed as the black man walk over to the front door to lock it. Anish ran to his office and grabbed the phone the white assailant casually got off the couch and followed. The phone was dead. Anish's next action was not one he thought he would ever conceive himself doing. Anish removed the gun from his desk and pointed it at the white intruder as the black accomplice entered behind him.

"Now what the hell do we have here? Da man has a gun. You see that he has a gun. I didn't think he had the balls. You know you really do not look the gun toting type Mr. Markovitz." The black man remarked.

"Who are you? How is it you know my name?" Anish rambled.

"Well it's on your sign outside isn't it?" The black shared with him.

"But putting that aside Mr. Markovitz all we want is your help, that's all. You see I like you to give the financials on these two companies." The black man handed Anish a piece of paper with Gynyxys and O.W.O.W on it. "By the way I'm Mr. Andrews and that's Mr. Bellows we're with the government, DHS to be specific."

"Gentlemen please let me see some identification please," requested Anish while he still brandished the weapon. "I don't care who you are. You're not going to see anything here today particularly information on these clients without a warrant."

"Sir we don't need no stinken warrant", the white burly agent stated as he walked closer to Anish.

"I'm warning you if you come any closer I'll shoot and what's more if you don't leave I'm going to start shooting."

Both men were trying to move further apart from each other in order to flank Anish, but he realized it and decided to show his visitors he meant business. The blast from the bullet startled Anish all though he knew it was going to shoot. The bullet lodged above the entrance door next to the exit sign. Anish fired the shot to warn the men but he was praying that someone was in one of the other offices and would report the gunshot. The men shocked from the totally unexpected behavior of what they had perceived to be a wimp were noticeably more apprehensive now. This person was obviously unpredictable and killers did not enjoy the unpredictable. Predictable meant fun, the opposite meant room for mistakes which might cost them.

"Calm down sir, just stay calm okay we're not going to do anything okay, just stay calm," begged the black agent as he backed up slowly having miscalculated the little fat man's resolve.

The two men realized noise from gunshots was not going to work in their favor they had to work quickly. Time to get what they came for was slipping away. What both men did not realize was that Anish had turned on his recorder and placed it next to the phone in the bottom of his file basket.

There was an eerie silence in the room. It seemed to last an hour as each man evaluated the "Mexican standoff".

Anish knew they could not let him live to possibly identify them. They were Homeland Security Agents as indicated by their badges. These two could not risk the slightest suspicion Anish's whistle blowing might cause. They obviously knew his connection to the Collective and were attempting to collect financial and tax information for their quasi Nazi masters. Anish Markovitz remembered his family, his grandparents how the majority of his family perished at Auschwitz one of the Nazi death camps. His tough grandfather became a hero while at the death camp by fighting off then attacking his captors as he refused to enter the showers of death. As the old man fought he yelled, "I don't need a shower I had a bath last night you putts, so get your filthy hands off me I'm clean."

Consequently because of his actions the Markovitz' family was spared death by the guards who admired his spirit after they shot him on the spot. Anish would fight as his grandfather did. America now had what the Collective knew to be silent Nazis. Those of the elite' race didn't matter only the cause at the expense of the innocent. The thought pissed him off he turned and pointed the gun at the white agent and with eyes burning fired his weapon screaming, "Nazi, Nazi, die Nazi, die."

The black agent was already firing his sidearm at Anish hitting him in the chest multiple times as the white agent was propelled against the corner wall he cried out with his hands flailing in front of him as though he were trying to stop the onslaught of bullets from hurting him. In seconds both men lie crumpled in pools of blood on the CPA's office floor.

Mr. Andrews, the black agent approached Anish's body in text book fashion to ensure he was dead before trying to attend to his partner who he knew was dead. Andrews had popped Anish with four rounds and he'd loss count of how many times his partner was hit. He needed to get his accomplice out of the office and fast.

Agent Andrews hoist his buddy's lifeless body up on his shoulder and proceeded to flee. Anish hated Nazi's and all who oppressed the innocent in the name of legal authority. Today he'd balance the "book of justice", he would make sure justice reflected to proper credit due it in order to ensure just reconciliation on the book. Anish raised his sidearm and squeezed the gun with what little strength he could muster. As the sound from the barrel rang out in the office Andrews the black agent felt a chill. He knew he had not been thorough enough as the hot thrust of the blast whistle through his spine like a hot knife through butter. The cracking and buckling of his spine from the bullet and weight of the body he was carrying left him on the floor in a paralyzed state of remorseful motionless flesh.

Anish could die in peace as he reconciled his book of justice by ridding the Earth of two American Nazis.

CHAPTER 23

PAYBACK

"Karen, Cheryl how are you doing? Please come in. Miles and I are in the study come join us." Margarite sounded so damn preppy both women couldn't help but think to themselves, "sounds as though she's been laid."

Miles met the women with wide arms and a strong hug wearing a velvet smoking jacket and his signature pipe in hand. Cheryl looked over at Karen as she received her hug. No way could this be happening, the women thought. The signs were there though. Damn, Marge and Miles had got their groove on. Both women were in disbelief. At one time they had thought Margarite gay because of her life style, but here she was radiant and Miles, well he was prancing around like Hugh Hefner in that damn velvet jacket.

"Ladies what can we get you? I can not tell you what a joy it is to see you." Miles stated as he waived the kitchen servants into the study.

"Miles, Margarite we are so sadden by the news of Michael's death."

"Karen shared as she took a cup of tea and saucer as she leaned forwarded.

"Frankly my concern is who might be capable of replacing him. His foreign connections, his control and ability to get things done alleviated such stress off of us in the inner circle. I'm a little concern. Perhaps we should call an emergency meeting, I mean Karen and I are already here and Miles appears to be well recuperated doesn't he?" Cheryl said with a sly look on her face as she glanced at Margarite. Miles thought that Cheryl's suggestion made a great deal of sense. The inner circle needed to regroup and evaluate its present state given all of the new occurrences and changes that had happen to it in the last week. He would also have the specifics from Peter on funerary arrangements for Michael. Margarite was thinking along the same lines. This would give her time to inform everyone on funeral services for Michael Zarkuhn. And to try to put together the assassination attempt at the manor, unwarranted investigations by the government and a station chief, Maurice, who'd met Miles in Hong Kong was nowhere to be found.

"You're right Cheryl we need an emergency meeting." Margarite stated glancing at Miles and Karen. Karen nodded.

Miles answered the telephone on the second tone. It was Peter. Peter asked him not to mention his name as he was on vacation. He explained that he was happy Miles got the telephone because he needed to speak with him at his earliest convenience. Miles thought Peter's request peculiar to say the least, but agreed to meet with him at the cottage.

"Not a problem. I'll meet you at say 7 p.m. will that be alright," Miles asked.

"As you wish sir seven O'clock will be just fine, and sir tell no one of the meeting, execute the utmost discretion."

Miles explain that he would have to leave shortly in order to take care of a pressing personal matter.

"Surely Miles it can wait until tomorrow, beseeched Margarite."

Miles grimaced at the very thought of trying to explain.

"No I afraid I must take care of this matter tonight. Trust me my dear. Ladies I shall be back momentarily. Please feel free to contact the inner circle and arrange the emergency session."

Miles removed the keys to the Audi from the key box and quickly disappeared out the side door from the kitchen. Margarite was connected to Miles now more than ever. She would not pry and snoop, but she could tell something strange was going on. But considering all the strange and bizarre things that the group had happen to it in the past two weeks she could not get as much of a rise out of his unusual behavior.

Maurice and Lieutenant Lehchin had been gone 20 minutes before Doctor Kry heard the knocking on his front door. He hobbled to the door and opened it slowly. Standing in front of him was a man in his early thirties but the ware and tear on his body, cuts, scars and a very conspicuous healed bullet hole on his chest push his looks twenty years up. Jimmy was scrawled across his chest as he sported the biker attire. Jean pants, jean vest and enough chains to anchor a yacht.

"Hey old man my name is."

"Let me guess its Jimmy, Dr. Kry coughed up to Jimmy's amazement.

"How did you know my name," Jimmy asked.

The doctor walked over to Jimmy and using his stethoscope placed it on his chest in then pointed to his chest, "I heard it through the grapevine."

Jimmy looked at his chest, but Jimmy was too stupid to be insulted. Right now he felt a strong desire to beat the hell out of the old man though in order to get information, but the polite thing to do would be to ask for the information first and at no time in the past had anyone ever given information he wanted to hear, so inevitably he'd always have to beat the right stuff out of them.

"Old man have you seen this chink?" Jimmy forcefully asked as he held the picture of lieutenant Lehchin in the doctor's face.

Jimmy was now putting on his gloves. His favorite black leather gloves were the weapon of choice for Jimmy. He enjoyed the way the soft leather felt on his knuckles as he pummeled some poor slob.

"Yeah I've seen this Asian man. He stopped by here almost eight hours ago for medical treatment. Had a bullet in him which I removed and he went on his way. He left about say three hours ago. He was driving a ... a ... let me see, he was driving a horse and damn carriage you socially challenge misfit", the doctor shouted.

Jimmy was in absolute shock. This man was either crazy or had a death wish. The two thugs accompanying Jimmy couldn't believe the old doctors gall either and laughed at Jimmy's reaction. That is until Jimmy turn to give them the eye.
Jimmy looked on the table and saw the bloody rags and syringe.

"Hey most of what you told me was true wasn't it old man?" Jimmy could see the doctor had operated on someone and he knew only nine cars had passed them on the main road none of which had the cop. He knew because it was important enough for him to check each one out. Paul had told the men he was going to kill someone and Jimmy knew Paul always kept his word. He'd be first to be killed to set an example and that wasn't going to happen. Jimmy was going to catch the cop.

"Let's go guys."

"But what do we do about this old geezer?" Jimmy's two twisted associates were not sure they should leave the old man alive.

Jimmy sounded adamant, "I said let's go. Leave the old man alone. I think he's cool, anyway I might change my mind and come back and kill him later. I need to think on it. Let's go."

CHAPTER 24

TABLE FOR TWO

Dr. Alice Martin sat in her favorite chair with her favorite tattered robe on enjoying the fire in front of her. She couldn't stop thinking of her findings and results of her research regarding the search for data pertaining to her and Louis' project directed by the Collective's inner circle.

All of the indicators pointed to the probability that her colleague had either found and ascertain a very special artifact or that he was very close to getting it, she shivered at the very thought. It would be the greatest discovery, the most fantastic archeological find in history and yet no one could be told. The Ark of the Covenant would be a phenomenal discovery, but the Collective desired something more valuable. The Tables of Testimony, also known as the Table of Destiny would be the real find. There would be no power in communicating with an alien megalomaniac who assumed the title of God. No the Ark was a communicator, what the inner circle wanted were the secrets to the past, the future and more importantly the bloodlines of all those who possessed the blood of the "Sons of God".

"Alice, Alice honey!"

"Ted I was daydreaming." Alice was still excited at the prospect.

The phone rang. "Martin residence how may we help you?"

"Yes, Ted its Margarite. We are having a get together tomorrow and would love for you and Alice to attend."

"Well I don't think that will be no problemo. Same time as usual?"
Margarite answered, "but of course we'll see you bye."

"Margarite huh?" Alice asked still curled up in her favorite chair.

"Yes. There's a meeting tomorrow. I wonder what's up. That's two meetings in two weeks, mmm."

"Well I've notified Alice and Ted any luck with Anish?"

Cheryl looked up at Margarite, "no I'm having no luck getting Anish on his cell or at the office. Oh and I tried to contact J.P. and Makesh no luck with them either."

"I tell you hold off for right now. I forgot tonight is security report night."

Cheryl admitted she forgot herself. Each inner circle member was required to make contact after eleven p.m. tonight to ensure all was well.

"Margarite do you have that package that came for me last week I would like to review it", asked the Senator.

Margarite exited the room and returned with the package requested by Karen Stinger.

"Thank you. I'll be in the study if you should need me. May I get something from the kitchen, I'm famished."

"Ladies please forgive my aberration. I shall have the staff provide us sustenance immediately." Margarite quickly hit the intercom button.

"Marge please Cheryl and me, we can get our own food if that's okay." The down to earth Senator begged.

"You are both too kind, but we have our own work to do. I'm just sorry I have not provided anything but tea up till now. Sisters we will have a feast shortly," Margarite spouted.

"Did she say sista?" Karen looked at Cheryl and asked with a huge look of surprise on her face.

"I do believe she did say sista," repeated Cheryl as she sipped her tea and then turned to Margarite and smiled.

"Did I offend you", asked Maragrite.

"No o' contraire we are thoroughly enjoying what we believe is the new you. We love it sista," shared Karen as she got up to go and review the package sent to her by Carl her former page.

As Miles entered the cottage he immediately keyed in on the metal coffin in the middle of the floor of the large living room. The cottage was warm and presented was a rustic, trailer park decorum. The smell of incense tickled Miles' nose as he entered further into the abode.

Peter closed the door as Miles attempted to hand him his coat.

"Sorry sir I'm on vacation you'll need to dispatch the attire yourself," barked Peter with a stiff poker face.

Miles was somewhat taken and thrown for a loop with Peters' curt remark.

"Well where should I?"

"Just kidding sir, please allow me. Peter took the coat and chuckled all the way to the closet."

However, laughter could also be heard from one of the back rooms. It was low and brief but someone else was definitely finding the whole charade by Peter funny. Before Miles could solicit an explanation for what had just transpired, Peter began to speak.

"Sir the reason I asked you to visit with me. Sir I've asked you here in order to. Perhaps I should say. Well I say now that you're here I wanted to inform you that. Would you care for some tea Sir?" Peter just couldn't get it out. Michael was realizing that this was a difficult matter. It would be for anyone. Maybe he should help Peter out. Michael coughed.

"Who in the world is that Peter? No I do not desire any tea. What I would like is an explanation for your bizarre behavior," demanded Miles.

Peter glared towards the back room and placed his palms together and sat on the edge of the sofa.

"Sir, Miles I think it best that you be seated. For what I'm about to tell you is astonishing. It is indeed unbelievable, quite remarkable actually and ..." Miles grew impatient.

"Blasted Peter what the hell is it!"

"Well sir see for yourself," as Miles turned and looked behind him towards the bedroom there stood Michael leaning on the door waving at Miles as Miles found his way to the floor surprising even gravity at the speed of his descent. With the help of a bit of smelling salt Miles was brought to consciousness. He could not understand, contemplate, comprehend, relate to, or deal with, or even fathom the vision in front of him. Miles reached forward with outstretched hands very slowly to touch the figure before him. He started sweating and shaking. The image looked so real, but it couldn't be Zarkuhn for he was dead. Miles had witnessed the whole grotesque incident. The blood, the flesh, damn, the brain matter not to say the least, there was no way anyone could survive what he witnessed.

He pulled his hand back quickly. Miles looked up at Peter as he still caressed the rug on the floor where he fainted.

"Peter how did you, who is he? I mean it's great, this is an imposter right?" Miles queried.

Michael spoke, "no my friend it's me. I know this is difficult for you to understand. I will explain this event to you as best I can. Come on get off the floor and let's get this over with."

"Hurry Mr. Lehchin we're in time. Come on grab that bag from the back come on." Maurice, the Asian Station Chief, hurriedly headed towards a little fishing boat. Three Asian men were preparing the vessel as they spotted Maurice approaching. Lieutenant Lehchin grabbed the large bag from the back seat and quickened his pace catching up with his rescuer.

"Who are these people? Are they apart of your group? Where are they ..." Maurice stopped dead in his tracks stopping the lieutenant's barrage of questioning.

"You know I'm beginning to think saving you may have been a mistake. Please refrain from asking any more questions."

The two men were met by Lin Ho the ship's owner.

"Mr. Maurice good to see please you come aboard, quickly we must meet the big ship." Mr. Ho moved with purpose as did his small crew. Within three minutes the small vessel was departing and headed for its destination. Maurice had arranged for one of the Collective's cover shipping corporations, the Manila Midas Shipping Company to provide a ship to take them back to the Philippines to his head base where he would sort out his situation and contact the Collective hierarchy with an in depth report. Maurice Steely would not forget to mention the unsanctioned kill committed when entering a room of the building across from the police headquarters where he took the fatal shots killing Mr. Zarkuhn. Maurice knew there would be no negative impact for the incident. It all happened so fast. He remembered entering the building and as he made his way up the fire escape and then down the hallway of the seventh floor. He knew that the building was pretty vacant because it was undergoing renovation. Most of the lower level offices were still being evacuated by some slow business owners but there were not many people around which would work out fine.

Luckily for Maurice the man who was already in the room Maurice had chosen to make his hit had not assembled his weapon. Startled the dark skinned man turn and attempted to attack Maurice using Savate, a French style of martial arts which Maurice was vaguely familiar with. The station chief countered with a stiletto to the man's lower abdomen and then repeated the recipe as was needed until a bloody mess remained. The shots to Zarkuhn were easy. One to the back of the head and one to the upper torso, but disposing of the body before he took the shots was another matter. He figured the corpse would eventually be discovered on top of the elevator once the smell became too intolerable.

"Once we get to our destination Lieutenant you will have some tough decisions to make." Maurice turned and walked below leaving the young lieutenant to his dilemma.

Karen Stinger slowly laid the papers down on the desk. She placed her palms together rubbing them in an anxious dance as she tried to reason out what she was reading and had read. It was apparent that Carl was trying to warn her about some of the contents of the document. He was too inexperienced and too young to completely comprehend the full relevance and impact of the legislation she and her colleagues on both sides of the floor had passed.

Senator Stinger now having read most of the Intelligence Reform Bill more thoroughly came to the conclusion that the legislative body of the government had stolen some more of the Constitutional Rights of the American people, because she had not read the damn thing and scrutinized it as was her responsibility to do. The bill was written in such a way that under certain conditions, conditions which could be manufactured by departments within the government itself, but not verifiable to disinterested or objective parties, rights of American Citizens could be violated without legal representation. The bill was designed using vital input of some of the country's strongest Republican funded think tanks. The senator knew this much because of the notes left on the document throughout it, obviously left there as markers for those insiders who wanted to evaluate its' more toxic content.

She immediately retrieved her clutch and scrambled through it finally locating the business card of Special Agent Todd she dialed his telephone number. There was a cell phone number and she ensured her scrambler was operable on her end and called.

"Hello, Special Agent Todd may I help you?" The voice on the other end was definitely his.

"Yes Mr. Todd this is Senator Stinger I wish to have you see me as soon as possible."

"Ma'am I'd love to see you but its 11 p.m. can this wait until tomorrow? I was headed up that way tomorrow anyway"

"Sure it can. I meant tomorrow. I will call you in the morning okay and agent Todd please come alone."

"I understand senator. I'll be there and I think you may want to alert your associates to be extra careful. I cannot go into detail right this moment. Just watch your back."

Karen looked up and caught Cheryl standing in the doorway. She was going to tell her something bad Karen could read her. Margarite joined her at the doorway moving fast past Cheryl.

"Have you told her yet," Margarite asked.

"No I can't bring myself to say ..." Cheryl started to cry as Karen shot around the desk to console her.

"What is it?"

Margarite shared with the senator that Makesh Patel's body had been identified as a victim in a bomb blast at the Hartsfield-Jackson Airport in Atlanta, Georgia. They found out from J.P. Rockdale who was at the airport on his way out when his flight was canceled due to a bomb blast.

"J.P. explained that's why he hadn't answered his phone when contacted earlier. The only way he knew anything about Makesh being a fatality was because he was pulled aside by a government agent man who refused to give him his name, but told him who the victim was and asked if he knew him." Margarite took a deep breath and continued.

"When J.P. asked why, the man said I know you belong to a secret society and that J.P was in fact in danger and that he should cooperate with him. This agent got J.P. a flight out on a private jet cleared by the agent with the security authorities."

"How's J.P. now?" Karen asked.

"He's shook up and get this he's sitting at the Boston's Logan Airport. He decided to come here after the incident feeling that we would all wish to gather after this event."

Margarite took another deep breath.

"Wait a minute it maybe a trap!" snapped Senator Stinger.
Karen Stinger suddenly recalled her conversation with Special Agent Todd earlier that evening. Todd said he was headed up this way. Up this way. How was he aware of location? Todd was in Atlanta, she was now in Boston up from Atlanta.

"Ladies J.P. has a tail and probably the plane he was on was bug and hell it may get worse. Margarite can you contact him?

Tell him to remain where he is. Do not come to the manor whatever he does." The senator sat down to try and figure what else should be done.

"Margarite I'll be there in say about ten minutes." J.P. sound a bit relieved when he shared this with Margarite.

"No J.P. Listen very carefully. We think you've been set up and we think you're being tailed."

J.P. began to look out the limo window from side to side and back to back. All he could think of was how he needed a drink. It wasn't fair to have this much pressure without a drink.

"Hon I'll handle this on my end. Dont ya wurry ya sweet lil head about a thang. Daddy J.P. goin tu handle bizness."

"J.P. don't!" Margarite looked at Cheryl.

"J.P. hung up. I'm afraid he may do something rash. I'm going to call Miles and Peter. Right now sistas we need a miracle.

The cottage phone rang as Miles sat in total disbelief from what he had just been told by Michael and Peter over the last few hours. Peter answered the phone and listened intently before slamming down the phone and quickly moving across the room towards the closet to retrieve his coat was the signal that the call was not a good one.

"Gentlemen it seems that Plantard Mansion may receive some undesirable guests shortly. I'm grieved to inform you Mr. Patel is no longer with us and Mr. J.P. Rockdale may be in danger."

Miles was moving in high gear already at the door with Peter. Zarkuhn made a decision to reveal and kill despite possibly exposing his secret to the other members. Miles looked at Michael and smiled, "I'm sure glad you and staged I that death in Hong Kong."

Peter smirked and added, "Yes it's nothing short of a miracle, lets hop to it lads. There are reservations for a table of two at the mansion."

CHAPTER 25

WHOSE WHO IN THE GAME

Bishop Terrell was calling in his report to the mansion when his cell phone went off. It was a call from Plantard Mansion, the Collective, was contacting him but why?

"Bishop Terrell speaking may I help you?"

"Father this is Senator Stinger we have an emergency here at the mansion. You need to be extremely careful. We are apparently being targeted by hostiles and some of our inner circle may have already been terminated."

"Senator Stinger, are you and the others alright? Look I am willing to come in to assist. I may have some information which might be useful. I think I need to come in."

"You sound serious Father. If you have something that may help by all means come, but stay in constant communication with us. Miles, Cheryl, Margarite and some of the others will be present." Karen was now very concerned as she briefed the others that the bishop was coming in.

Ted and Alice secured their weapons and put on the house alarm before loading up in their Lexus to head for the Plantard Mansion. They were both silent as they traversed the back streets and trekked towards the countryside to be with their comrades. Ted couldn't take it any longer the silence was a little too uncomfortable.

"Honey what does all this mean? I mean this has really gotten serious. I never thought I'd say this but it feels like Vietnam. I can't believe this Michael dead, Makesh now dead and may be others."

"Ted you know the project Louis and I are, I mean that he was working with me on? Well I haven't done a complete report to the Inner circle yet...."
Ted stopped her. "Should you be telling me any of this?"

"Damn straight I should", responded Alice his wife. "Ted listen I think Louis may have found one of the relics. To be specific I think he found the "Tables of Testimony", or at least the first copy given to Moses by God before Moses broke it. God made a second copy for him, but ... look out."

Ted could not avoid the tree in the road and the tree's accomplice ice took over to do the rest.

After Doctor Amin's call Margarite briefed the group. The group did not blame Doctor Amin for wanting to dispatch his family and himself out of the country to a safe haven. He explained that Makesh and Louis were good men and how he had served eight honorable years without question or failure but the stakes were too high. The Collective felt uncomfortable with him not being where they good provide him some protection. If he was out of the country or not accessible he could end up like their other comrades. Margarite understood and asked him to be cautious. He would stay in contact as required and he stated he would be ready to serve once he could secure his family.

Margarite and the others hadn't heard from Anish either, but no one wanted to bring the matter up or speculate on whether or not he was also a casualty.

J.P. instructed the limo driver to continue driving. They had long passed the Plantard Mansion. He had not formulated a plan yet but he was able to find some whiskey so it wouldn't be long before he could think straight.

"Driver keep on I'll tell ya whan, thanks, podna." J.P. took a nice long shot of the whiskey the driver was able to get for him from the bar he hadn't noticed.

Bishop Terrell knew his meeting with Paul Constantine did not go well. He left it with giving Paul information on the "Table of Testimonies". The Bishop pretty much ran down the whole story from Exodus and added a few theories as to what may have happened to the Ark and its contents. He did not know how Constantine knew to ask him about the tablets or whether it was simply a coincidence. He did know that his former colleague was a killer, a supreme hunter and survivor. If Constantine was looking for the tablet given to Moses by God then he would eventually find it.

The priest had been tempted to do him at the bar when he had what he felt was a chance, but Paul amused the Bishop and plus the father knew Paul would have eaten his lunch gone were the days when he could have ended it. Terrell had been out of the operations game for years since being assigned to America by the Vatican. He was retired and out of the fight game and he had no compulsion to be treated as a defenseless choir boy, at least not by Constantine.

Special agent Todd was still groggy when he attempted to answer his telephone. "Hello, Special Agent Todd may I ..." he heard the voice on the other end cut him off.

"Todd listen to me you should check on the whereabouts of two of your agents. Specifically Andrews and his side kick. I suggest you look into this matter yourself try 352 Phoenix Blvd., Suite 13. Oh you should probably take some cleaning supplies.

"Who in the hell are you," asked the Homeland Security Special Agent as he tried to see if the telephone number was being reflected." It was a pay phone, but that in no way impede Todd's movement. Strange things were happening and he didn't want any surprises especially since he was possibly meeting a United States Senator in the morning. He had worked hard to get his position as the Regional Director and he was not going to throw that hard work away.

When he arrived at the address given by the anonymous caller he could see the lights of two police cruisers parked in the parking lot of the business complex. He approached slowly so as to evaluate the situation. This was not the kind of night for coming out in particular at one o'clock in the morning. It was wet, very wet and cold to beat. Special agent Todd parked his vehicle and pulled out his badge. He hated rain in the face and he hated city cops.

"Officers I'm Special Agent Todd. What's going on?"

"Sir we got a call of gunshots being fired so for the last 20 minutes we've been checking every building. Sir, were you monitoring our radio scanners? How did you know to show up?" One of the young City of College Park, Georgia Police officers inquired.

"No. I was coming from the airport off an operation when I show your lights. So any progress yet?"

Todd knew he had to get to the office mentioned by the unknown caller soon.

"What areas have you checked already?"

"We're almost threw sir. We found nothing out of the ordinary so far just a few lights on in some of the offices. Is there something else you need Sir?" The same young officer was becoming suspicious as was expected of a good law enforcement type. Despite dealing with a fellow law enforcement puke or not cops were suspicious of anyone.

Todd noticed something that the young city cops hadn't. He saw the unmarked government vehicle parked under some trees. The tag was one of his. He pondered the situation had his people left the car here only to return later or were the two men still inside somewhere on surveillance. He quickly excused himself.

"Guys I'm tired good luck on your hunt. Oh! Please be safe."

Todd sat for another twenty six minutes before the two city officers gave up their search. He got back out of his car and finally located the office the caller gave him. The door was locked but there were lights on which could been seen fighting its way from underneath the front door.

The rain was relentless in pelting him. Todd carefully removed his all purpose tools from his utility jacket. He was inside the office in less than a minute. The sight was not registering. He immediately visualized what had transpired in the front office by the placement of the two bodies piled on the floor. Todd locked the door behind him and put on his gloves. He stood in the same spot long enough to drip most of the rain water off before proceeding inside. In front of him lay two of his employees. Special Agent Andrews was on the floor with the body of Special Agent Bellows in a prone position on top of him with Bellows head pointed away from the front door. Andrews' body was in a sort of sitting position, but his torso and legs were contorted in such a way as to defy physics.

Special Todd entered Anish's office with his side arm pulled. He found the owner of the business on the floor in a pool of coagulated blood with a weapon in hand.

"I'll be damned." Todd thought to himself. The little fat guy had somehow manage to drop two of Todd's most seasoned agents; also two of his most dubious as well. The special agent had been monitoring the two men for over a year for suspicious signs and activities. His mind raced with questions like who his agents worked for, why they had popped this guy and who all the players were in the game?

Todd noticed a piece of paper on the floor next to the dead owner. He picked it up and read it, Gynyxys and O.W.O.W was scrolled on the paper. Todd would have lost his lunch if had eaten lunch. He knew both of these organizations were tied to the secret society "The Collective". He had investigated the two organizations years earlier and now was attempting to align himself with their parent group, the Collective. Todd was not aware of the secret group's name but he sought to establish a rapport with some persons he felt were influential with the groups.

"This is not good, this is real bad." Todd stated before completely realizing the political damage was before him, but what he did know was some serious sanitation was in order. Think about sanitation, the thespian was fighting to come out, that recondite actor in every good agent. Now was the time to write a script, to design a play around the terrible career destroying circumstances staring him in the face. This ability was just one of the keys to a successful existence in the intelligence community, "spy world International". He had very little time to develop the scene for the dead agents' bodies and that of the little dead accountant. Unfortunately, the truth about what happened to the dead accountant on the floor who probably died for being associated with the secret society that the government cronies wanted information on would be obscured, lost forever with the rewritten play Agent Todd would create before the night was over. He would clean this up before dawn using every once of energy and will possessed in him.

As Peter entered the side door to the kitchen of Plantard Mansion with Miles he grabbed Miles by the arms. Three large guns were pointed at the men and Peter knowing Mile's weak constitution for that sort of drama attempted to keep Master Miles from hurting himself as he waxed faint and headed for the floor.

CHAPTER 26

CONSTANTINE GOES TO KANSAS

Lieutenant Lehchin hadn't left much back on the Island and although he would miss Hong Kong there was no family, no property, no girl friend, not even a dog to go back to. He was lucky to be alive and wondered what Constantine and that damn crooked Captain Kao were doing at that moment.

Captain Kao was finishing his second pack of smokes when he got the call from the local authorities that a man fitting the description of Lieutenant Lehchin left from their harbor four hours ago. The Captain erupted in a fit of rage, slamming chairs across the room, cussing and finally taking a seat as his heart raced and breath shortened. He tried to loosen his shirt collar, but his arm hurt, it was numbed. The Captain felt noxious and faint. The fat chain smoking man attempted to get up but found he had no strength. Suddenly he tried to laugh for he realized all his bad habits and bad life caught up with him. He thought to himself, "I'm having a heart attack," as he tried to call for help he clinch his chest. Finally his assistant heard the noise and promptly entered the Captain's office only to find him on the floor dead.

"Ladies please I beseech you lower the weapons," Peter asked while trying to keep Miles in the upright position.

"We're so sorry Peter, Miles. We didn't know who you were." Margarite helped Peter with Miles as she put the Desert Eagle special down on the kitchen counter.

"What took you so long? I thought you were at the cottage." Karen asked as she too lowered her M16.

"We took the liberty of checking the grounds before coming in Madam. Sir, are you alright now? I'm letting you go now, please release my arm Mr. Miles." Peter sometimes couldn't understand how he put up with such a group as this one.

Michael had also performed reconnaissance of the mansion grounds before stealthily entering one of the upstairs rooms. He would wait for the right moment to make his presence known as all three men had planned on their way to the mansion. Michael had regrets now. He regretted not taking out Constantine and he regretted killing Ognorski before questioning him. To his estimation the Collective was under attack from possibly three different factions. He also came to the conclusion that he would have to inform the Collective inner circle about a most interesting discovery he'd made. But for now he'd wait and protect.

Constantine had known Bishop Terrell a long time. He and the bishop had worked a lot of special projects in Eastern Europe and Northern Africa. Terrell was his handler and had taught Paul much in his early days. As Paul paid the two prostitutes leaving his room he remembered the most important tool learned from Bishop James Terrell back in the day, and that was how to tell when you're being lied to or when someone is holding back. Constantine knew his old friend was hiding something and it must be something juicy. If it had not been for the fact that Terrell used himself as a training tool to help his young student practice this art form Paul might have been fooled, but he practiced on Terrell for almost a year at the Bishop's beckoning. Terrell was a stickler for perfection and now that obsession might cost him.

The agent tailing the Bishop was due to check in that morning and Paul was willing to bet it would reveal some valuable information about his old mentor. But for right now he was hungry. He had had his daily orgy now he needed to try that American breakfast food he'd heard about called "grits".

"Hey dude." Paul greeted the smoking front desk attendant as the man lowered the sports section of the newspaper.

"Where can I find some grits?"

The man cough and laughed at the same time exhaling smoke from the cigarette as he tried to stop laughing before he answered with, "Mississippi."

Two black youth sitting in the lobby breaking from a hard night of serious drug sales joined in on the laughter. Paul decided hell it must have been funny and his participation in the roar made four laughing men.

"Hey man what do you know bout grits?" One of the youth asked Constantine.

"Yeah man who told you about grits you not from this hood are ya?" The other youth stated. This one was high and Paul unconsciously postured like a shark. The man addressing him was not only high but he was not white people friendly. Paul was oversensitive to threat and could instinctively sense an asshole when it was in his area. Yes Paul fancied himself an "asshole magnet". He smiled as he thought up the new term, "asshole magnet".

"You know honky I think you were trying to be funny. Where's da grits and all that shit. Bitch I don't think that shits funny." The big black youth stood now also posturing and smoking a joint.

His companion turned to him, "bruh chill the dude didn't mean nothin bout it."

"Take yo monkey ass over there and sit down man."

No way was his associate going to take his advice and chill. He was looking for conflict. This black boy hated whitey.

"Now, now, Rodney look here I don't want any trouble man." The desk clerk was trembling as he tried to calm the belligerent black man down.

"Cracker shut up was I talk'n to you? Hell no I was talk'n to you bitch," as the young black man addressed Paul in a most belligerent manner. He was approaching Constantine slow as he spouted more obscenities. Paul was getting a buzz a mental high. To him the situation he now found himself in was exciting. He thought to himself, "this is cool just totally cool I'm going to get to kill an American Negro, a bad ass, a keffer, a nigger. Wow!

Paul adjusted his right arm that had been wounded days earlier and started to shout back. He figured he have some fun while in America getting in to a brawl with a native.

"You dumb son of a bitch, you ingrate. Do you even have a mother? Where is she? I want sex so call her mate. Yeah, yo momma boy I bet she's a good cow aye." Paul figured what the hell I'll get him real pissed so as to heighten the intensity of hostility.

Now the other young black man stood up. The expression on his face said it all.

"I don't believe this white guy just said what I think I heard him say."

The desk clerk was an old hand at street life. He knew his white tenant must have an ace or he trying to get himself killed for some damn insurance money for his white family in some upper middle class suburb. Right then it really didn't matter he was going to make his move out the lobby quick. He ran stumbling towards the back office and locked the door. The large black aggressor moved with surprising agility and swiftness despite his intoxication from the marijuana and liquor. He swung at Paul and landed a beautiful blow to his left cheek. His accomplice wanted to join in after hearing the insults hurled at his buddy from the strange grit seeking white man but the lobby's small size prohibited it. Paul fell back against a column directly behind him. The attack was followed by another blow to his chest and then the top of his forehead. Hitting the floor on his right side Paul glanced up and licked the blood off his lower lip.

"Whoo! Damn boy you hit hard." Paul critiqued his beating with his attacker and smiled.

Both black men were stunned. Both began to sense something was not in order. The stimuli they were being exposed to at that moment was not computing. This was not the norm. This white guy should be crying, begging, running, or least fighting back, but not complimenting a brother on his butt whipping.

The onslaught of the attack stalled for a moment and that was all Constantine needed. He'd taken his belt off without being seen during the assault by the large black youth. Paul Constantine stood up and looked at both men as he adjusted his jaw. "Yeah you hit hard son, all good things must come to an end, right?"

The young black man never saw it coming. The belt buckle crashed into the side of his left eye. The buckle was special. It was made of stainless steel and perforated around the edges. To make matters worse for the receiver of this meg shift tool, it weighed three pounds. The speed and precision ensured a most efficient fracture of the bone enclosing the eye of the young man. He screamed out as the metal crashed against his skull. Blood made its entrance and was not shy. The target tried to retreat as the pain and the blindness in the eye started to impose themselves on the black bully.

The sight of his buddy retreating and the blood only made the accomplice madder. He pushed his friend aside only to hear the cracking in his mouth followed by what felt like a foot to the left knee. The second black youth too tried to retreat. Clutching his mouth and dragging his left leg backwards he fell onto the couch which he had been sitting on earlier. He knew dental work was going to be in order that is if he got out of this situation. Paul knew he had both men in a bad way. He decided he would be surgical in his destruction of the two men. Whether he would kill them or not was a matter he would take into great consideration.

Paul felt a rhythm flowing through him as he always felt right before he dished out a thrashing to some poor unsuspecting victim. His attention immediately focused on the larger and stronger of the two men. As the big youth saw his friend fall on the couch behind him he yelled and ran at Constantine again.

"I'll kill you." Is as far as he got before realizing he didn't have the use of his left knee. Constantine dislocated the man's knee cap with a powerful front kick angle upward and added a palm to the attacker's left cheek. He had debated a nose job which would have put the poor guy's cartilage up in his frontal lobe tilting the game. Instead he opted for door number one which meant pain for the winner.

Constantine's mind was racing back and forth with the possibilities of damage he could dish out. He had read about the American justice system. He knew he was in a great position being a white man attacked by two, not one but two of what the American white use to call, "niggers". He could kill them both and not go to jail. No hiding or disposing of bodies necessary. Damn this truly was the land of honey. "I love this f$#**)(# country," Constantine shared with his two prey. Then it happened his phone was going off. This could only be.... no it was his eminence. "Yes your Excellency. No I'm in the middle of something right now. Of course your eminence it is very important that I complete your will. I was, or I think I was successful in finding a lead to your little notebook." Paul paced back and forth across the lobby floor as the two wounded black men moaned on the furniture and floor. He occasionally looked down at them as he passed by ensuring a good hard kick to choice body parts. Both men wondered who he could be talking too. This bastard was too mean to take orders from anyone they both thought to themselves. The larger of the two became increasingly upset at the caller because whoever it was; was pissing off the white guy kicking his butt. With each "yes your eminence," the kicks got harder.

"He yelled out to the caller get off the damn phone you dumb son of a bitch."

Unfortunately the insult was heard by the Cardinal. There was silence and Paul stopped his pacing. He glared down at the large black man who had yelled the insult as he held the cell phone. With a heavy Italian accent the Cardinal finally spoke again.

"Paul do you understand me?

"Yes your Excellency I understand fully."

"Good son, that's very good my son." The accented man repeated.

"Oh and Paul before I let you go please kill the man who I heard insult the church."

The Cardinal hung up his line never doubting his request would be carried out.

Paul was heart broken. Here was an opportunity to have some real fun and now because of one lousy insult overheard by his boss he had to end the carnage.

"Rodney right? The desk clerk called you Rodney earlier. That is your name right?" Paul asked the large black man as he moaned on the floor in front of the couch in a pool of blood.

"Yeah, hell yeah that's my name. Look man we need a doctor. I'm bleeding to death here and my damn leg."

"Look Rodney you've placed me in a bad situation by calling by boss that rude name and to boot I know he was not born out of wedlock so you told a lie too … tiss, tiss."

"What the f$#@. Man look at us I'm a mess and you say I've put you in a ahh … it hurts. I don't want to here that shit man. I need medical attention bad."

"No you need a hearse my friend." Paul walked over to the man and knelt down in front of him as the man tried to fight him off. Constantine managed to fight passed his large arms and grabbed his trachea squeezing and twisting with precision the struggle was over in short order. Paul wiped the blood on the dead man's jacket and gazed at the other man. The large black youth's friend was crying and scooting away in the corner across the room trembling and shaking so violently that the counter next to him sounded as though it was going to break.

Paul stood up approached him and knelt in front of him.

"You were looking out for a friend and see what it's got you, but I admire that and because I like that bit about, "sitting your monkey ass down," that you stated to your dead friend there earlier I going to grant you life. However, if I am mentioned or even implicated in any way with this unfortunate incident my phone friend will send ten more just like me. Get my drift monkey?"

"Yes sir. No problem, I got it." The young black stated right before he passed out.

Paul got the second call from the tail he placed on Bishop Terrell.

"A mansion really! What's the address? No kidding.

No don't do anything. Just observe until I get back with you. You say there are others watching the place too? Have they seen you? Good make sure they don't see you."

Paul wondered why the padre was out so early visiting rich big homes. He needed to set up shop. He dialed and listened to the answer on the other end.

"Boss don't be mad we're close I know he's on some ship out here...." Jimmy blurted out in a pleading tone.

"Jimmy please shut up. I need you to get the blue team and come to Boston A.S.A.P."

"Boston, Boston, Massachusetts?"

"No you dumb ass! Kansas."

CHAPTER 27

HOMELAND INSECURITY AND BLACK CARDINALS

Lieutenant Lehchin poured a cup of coffee and walked over and sat down at the table next to the Collective's station chief, Maurice. Maurice had a dilemma on his hands. What to do with Lieutenant Lehchin was his problem. In thirty minutes they would be ashore and headed to his headquarters. He wondered why he had intervened with the men trying to kill the young lieutenant.

"How are you feeling Maurice?" The young lieutenant asked Maurice.

Maurice sat back and lowered both his arms by his sides took a big sigh of relief and looked at Lehchin.

"I'm at a quandary you see. I don't know what to do with you young man. I mean I saved your ass back there, but I'll be damned if I don't know what to do with you."

"Look sir I need to let you know you owe me nothing okay. You saved me and for that I'm grateful, truly grateful."

Maurice had tracked the lieutenant on the microphone and appreciated the way he handled himself. He continued to track him because he was not sure if the lieutenant was a part of the problem or the solution. What he found out was that he was an innocent, good law enforcement officer in the wrong place at the wrong time.

"Do you need a job son?"

The lieutenant was speechless as he sat back in his chair.

"Welcome Bishop, we were just about to eat breakfast. Are you hungry, would you like some coffee?" The Senator from Florida asked Bishop Terrell.

"I would enjoy some coffee thank you." The bishop walked over towards the fire place and warmed his hands as he loosened his scarf from around his neck.

He was worried, he felt concern, worry escalated to fear. He contemplated the danger that Paul the predator posed to him and the Collective. Suddenly he felt ill. What carnage, what damage had he done already? Who had fallen prey to this masterful killer? Whose son, daughter, or innocent had gotten in Paul's way?

"Here you go bishop. Do you require coffee sir?" Peter asked as he handed Terrell a cup of coffee in fine china. So fine was the china that the bishop thought his nerves and the stress would over power it and crush it to dust.

"Thanks Peter."

"Sir I may be out of line with saying this, but perhaps you should take the floor and enlighten your colleagues. You know tell them what ails you. Anyone can plainly see that you are uneasy about something sir, so please get it off your chest. Oh would you like cream and sugar?"

The bishop always sensed something unusual about Peter, but he could never read him as he could every other person he'd ever met, except Michael Zarkuhn.

Michael sat quietly in the room as he smelled the beautiful scent. It seemed to pull him towards it. He always loved rituals mainly because of the scents a by product from the incense ceremoniously used at the gatherings. Michael became curious about its origination. Maybe it was from one of the other servants' rooms who knew. He opened the bedroom door and looked out into the hallway as he continued to sniff the air for the origin of alluring fragrance. He realized the wing he headed for was rarely used by guest or anyone, anyone except Peter. Peter lived in this wing. Michael was already in the room before he realized he was going to have to apologize to his friend. He couldn't explain his magnetism to the room.

As Michael stepped into the room his body relaxed. He succumbed so completely to the venue he nearly passed out. The ambience was so serene and tranquil it was hard to believe such a place could exist in such a barbaric corporeal plane. It was just like home, home in heaven on the planet he knew as home. Michael noticed the most beauteous alter and precious artifacts around the room. He was drawn to the center of the room where he found a mandala with a symbol, a symbol he knew very well but had not seen for thousands of years. Then he saw it, an artifact that puzzled him beyond belief. Peter was definitely a serious collector and he possessed some very rare pieces. The door opened before Michael could react and suddenly Peter stood in front of him. Both men stared at each other and then Peter approached Michael.

"Come, it's time sir. Some day perhaps I shall consent to a proper showing of my possessions. Did you find what you were looking for?"

"Peter, please forgive me. I, I was not spying or going, I mean looking for anything. But regardless I am sorry for invading your privacy. This room drew me to it. It has such solace and peacefulness. My apology Peter I have never felt such peace on this planet as in this room."

"Well having said that we have coffee down stairs so come on and let me serve you breakfast okay sir." Peter guided Michael out and slowly closed the door behind him glimpsing in as he shut the door.

Cardinal Giordano Ricci was not content. He knew Paul was not to be trusted and that he was the most efficient soldier in the, "Society of Jesus'" army. Paul was the only man for the job. Eventually he would have to deal with Paul, but only after he accomplished this last most important task. Cardinal Ricci needed the artifact that Louis Tashido informed him he had in his possession, but the holy soldiers found nothing on or at Tashido's property. The Cardinal was a practical man and he knew true power must manifest itself in the temporal world not through blind faith or money, but through the tools left here by God himself. What he sought if possessed would make him supreme power on the planet. The secrets of life of virtually everything pertinent to the creation and existence of man would be his.

Meri Tashido, Louis' wife missed her husband terribly. They had been together from childhood and Louis was not just a husband, he was her closest friend. Merie wondered if the piece Louis had acquired in the Middle East had been destroyed in the explosion of their Hong Kong home.

"No, no Tashi. Don't touch that sweetie." Merie spoke softly to her little son as he made his way around the periphery of the coffee table.

Merie accompanied Louis on all of his trips and she herself was quite an accomplished self taught intellectual with regards to archeology and ancient history. The petite Indonesian repeatedly warned her reckless husband about playing sides in the clandestine esoteric community. She was quiet and subdued in her duties as a wife to Louis. Merie was a master at the art of acquiescence. She read what her husband read, research what he and his colleagues researched and what Louis and his astute colleagues missed she somehow always discovered.

The telephone startled the little boy prompting him to cry. Merie picked the toddler up as she answered the phone.

"Hello. Oh thank you, thank you your eminence. I appreciate it really I do. I just hope they find who did this to my Louis."

Merie bounced the toddler up and down in her right arm as she held the phone to her ear sobbing now with a smorgasbord of emotions swelling in her heart.

"My daughter I am confident that the persons responsible for this heinous crime will be brought before justice and ultimately God. If there is anything I or the church can do for you please contact Merie. I am here for you, you do know this."

As Merie began to cry she was able to respond," yes Cardinal Ricci, yes your eminence I know, thank you so much for calling."

"Believe me it's my pleasure dear. Remember if you should feel you need to call me please do. Bye my dear."

Merie felt the weight on chest get heavier. She knew the call from this high profile man who was her husband's boss was a reminder to keep him in the loop and worst that he may feel she had the package he desired; this despite the fact that his henchmen found nothing while she was held at her home in Hong Kong. She hugged her baby close to her bosom as she tried to think of who could help them and what she should do next. All she could see was doom. "Damn you Louie, damn you" she sobbed holding he baby child close to her chest.

"We have forgotten a member of our family and we must make amends." Miles stated as he sat at the kitchen table.

"Who?" Asked the black senator from Florida.

"Oh no! Merie, we've neglected Merie and her baby. I'll try and call her at once," blurted Margarite.

Sergeant O'Connell was not buying what he was hearing. The first officer on scene explained to him that according to the hotel desk clerk a white man from one of his rooms had killed one man and almost killed the other. Yet an interview with the survivor presented a different story. As he walked over to the ambulance containing the surviving witness he recognized him as a regular check in for his station downtown.

"Buster what the hell happened to you? Man someone messed you up. You want to tell me who?"

"Sarge it was a gang of 'em. It was so quick.... aah. I mean they killed my boy. I'm hurt'n man I got to go man. Let's go," the young man yelled.

"Keep it down Buster they'll get to you. Now your story doesn't jive with the skeleton inside. He says some white tenant did you and your girlfriend. Now to be honest with you I don't think anyone from this hood's going to miss your boy or you if you get my drift. So why don't you come clean. What really happened?"

"Sarge I toll ya what happened. We were jumped by some gang that's all. That's my story hell I'm the one with broken shit over here." The young man turned away from the Sergeant as he moaned in pain. The Sergeant needed the white tenant. He would interview the desk clerk to try and make some sense of the homicide that took place in the lobby, but O'Connell knew he needed the mystery Caucasian to get to the bottom of the killing.

The Atlanta Journal Constitution Newspaper read "Prominent CPA Found Dead in Office," and Special Agent Todd of the Homeland Security Department had loss ten pounds in sweat just reading that blurp. He and his men had managed to clean and reconstitute the dead CPA's office making Anish look as though he were involved in some questionable activities with shady foreign nationals. This was made possible using some choice pieces of data and materials from other on going cases.

Todd knew this would give his department purview over the investigation allowing him time to get his story together and to try and solve what really happened that night he lost two bad agents.

The loved ones of the agents had already started calling on the missing men. Agent Todd was confident that the discovery of the two agents in the bottom of the gorge outside North Atlanta would also prompt his attention so that he and the HLS team could investigate and ultimately cover their back sides. The worst part of the whole ordeal was how damn insecure it made Todd feel. He was also loosing pounds over the thought of meeting with the tough black senator from Florida, Senator Stinger. He would have to put a call into her as a courtesy and to inform her of Mr. Markovitz's unfortunate death. Otherwise the suspicion would burgeon out of any hope of cooperation with her and her group.

"Oh my God! Michael." Margarite fainted and approached the floor first followed by one or two others. Surprisingly Miles remained steady thanks to prior knowledge of the event. Michael walked very slowly towards the kitchen door. Peter was in front of him and helped to gather Dr. Cheryl Teranez off the floor. Senator Stinger's knees were weak, but she held on to the back of one of the kitchen chairs as Bishop Terrell held her shoulders steady. Miles was jealous of the ladies falling faint around him. Fainting had become a national past time of his and he was bloody damn good at it.

"Ladies I give you Mr. Zarkuhn." Peter announced.

Miles began to explain. "Forgive us the deception, but it was the only way we could get out of Hong Kong in one piece." Miles stated he would explain in detail later.

"I too apologize for the pain I caused you all, but what Miles has stated is true. I had no way out, but to create a mendacious scenario and feed it to the local authorities and our assailants." With that everyone hovered around him for a cliché "group hug."

CHAPTER 28

SMASHING THE ROUND TABLE

"Let's see so the white man gets struck by one of the youth and that's when you took off right? Well then how do you know the tenant, the white guy did the damage to the brothers? According to you he should have called us for the beating he was getting."

The emaciated chain smoker escapee was behind the desk was still shaking as he started to answer the police Sergeant's question. But not before Paul strolled into the lobby.

"I said I don't know any more than that officer," the gaunt unshaven man spouted as he hastily headed for the back office before the sergeant could stop him.

"Hey mister!" Sergeant O'Connell called out to Constantine.
Constantine looked at him with an element of surprise and at the two uniformed officers at the doorway talking.

"Yes officer what may I do for you? Paul asked as he approached the sergeant.

"I'm sorry to bother you sir, you live here?"

"Yes, yes I do," Paul answered politely.

"There was an altercation here this morning and a man was killed. Here's my badge, I'm sorry I'm Sergeant O'Connell with homicide here in Boston. Do you have any I.D. on you sir?"

Paul reached into his back pocket and noticed he had everyone's attention now as he pulled his wallet free.

"Here you go officer." Paul handed the wallet over to the sergeant.

"I'm sorry sir I need you to remove the drivers license from the wallet for me, company policy."

Paul laughed "of course no problem officer O'Connell."

"That's Sergeant O'Connell, well I guess I am an officer too once you get down to it right lads?" The sergeant stated loudly.

"So you're from Italy. Wow! So what brings you to Boston?" The sergeant inquired with an anticipated look on his face.

"I'm a sociologist with the Vatican. You know Italy and I'm doing research on the ghettos of your country and those who inhabit them." Paul was rather pleased with his answer as the explanation rolled off his tongue like butter. It was the same cover he always used in America or at least for his last three visits.

"I know Italy, I know Vatican too. Growing up we had Catholics in my ghetto. Now, did you see any thing earlier this morning? There are reports of a white man's involvement and frankly the hotel clerk says you're the only person void of color in this ghetto. So how about it ... you see anything?" The sergeant asked with a grin on his face.

Paul was beginning to take an extreme dislike for the Irish cop. He didn't particularly like law or order and he detested those who sought to maintain it, especially smart ass cops.

"Officer If I had witnessed something I would have tried to get it on camera especially if I were the victim, you know reverse Rodney King and all. No I saw nothing."

The sergeant could see the man was becoming irritated, but he could see more than that. The sergeant asked Paul, "where did you get that abrasion on you face and are you some kind of Karate student? I notice your knuckles have like a ring around your hand not just your knuckles."

"Sergeant, officer, copper or whatever, am I under arrest or may I go?" Paul was starting to salivate. He was reaching his piss factor. Constantine had too much to do today and the cop was starting to annoy him. He knew he was being jerked around and even if it was warranted Paul didn't like it.

"I tell you what lad I neglected to get your passport earlier, so I'll be taking that passport now if you would hand it over sir. You do have it on you right or is it in your room?" The sergeant could not see the man in front of him taking down the two thugs, but there was something not right about him. The sudden disappearance of the desk clerk sparked by fear aided the sergeant's suspicion.

"Here's my passport," Constantine handed it to the sergeant and walked over to the couch in the lobby and sat.

Sergeant O'Connell walked over to the other two officers and handed the identification to one of them and told him to run them.

"Oh you can go in a few minutes Mr. Constantine just sit over there."

Constantine considered an assault on the law enforcement officers but only for a millisecond. The task would take far too long and he was under the gun, literally. He could tell the sergeant suspected him and wanted anything on him to hold him so he could buy enough time to make something stick.

Sergeant O'Connell turned and glared at the man he suspected of something, anything. The background check on the visitor reflected no criminal history, but did initiate an inquiry from Interpol. Interpol stated in a message back to the sergeant's headquarters that further communication was forthcoming, but that no derogatory information was mentioned. What the sergeant and his superiors found unusual and somewhat alarming was that a liaison law enforcement representative would be there in Boston the following day to assist them.

Sergeant O'Connell now knew his hunch was correct. The man sitting on the couch was into something nasty church affiliated employee his ass he thought as he approached Constantine.

"Mr. Constantine you're free to go, however, we will need to keep your passport until we close this matter."

"Well how long will that take? I need my passport." Constantine protested.

"I'm sorry Mr. Constantine but that's...."

Paul finished the sentence before the sergeant, "company policy right."

Paul proceeded upstairs to his room. He needed to ensure he would be able to continue his task unimpeded by any police snooping.

Sergeant O'Connell was called by his station chief and asked to report in A.S.A.P.

"Hello." Merie barely recognized the voice as Margarite spoke.

"Merie this is Margarite Plantard, I called to check on you.

We have not heard anything from Louis and we were worried. He disappeared while in Hong Kong."

"Ms. Plantard my Louis is dead. He was murdered in Hong Kong. You did not know?"

"Merie I'm so sorry. I did not know. Is there something we can do for you and Tashi?" Margarite's heart was heavy, heavy with sorry, shame and remorse. "No madam we are fine. I, I am afraid me and Tashi may be in danger Ms. Plantard. I have no family with which to seek refuge for little Tashi."

"Merie I can offer you sanctuary...."

There was silence throughout the entire room. Everyone listened to what Margarite was proposing. A key few of them knew as inner circle members of the Collective that they had authorized the killing of Merie's husband. What Margarite was suggesting made them all feel awkward and uncomfortable. It was one thing to sanction a kill it was quite another to look the family members of those killed in the eyes and try and convey veracious sympathy.

"I will contact you later today Merie, are you familiar with Louis' communication protocols? He had told us that because you assisted him in some of his explorations and research and that you knew how to call us. Do you understand what I'm asking?"

"Yes madam I am familiar. I shall call you back in say three hours." Merie then hung up the phone.

"Now that was interesting," remarked Miles.

"Yes it was." Stated Bishop Terrell having mixed feelings and still wondering when would be the opportune time to share his time bomb with the group.

"I did what I did for two reasons. One Ms. Tashido may have the item we seek and two she feels as though she and her baby are in danger and we caused it, okay."

Margarite having offered her position scanned the room for a response.

"I'm waiting. Does anyone have anything to add?" She asked.

"More croissants anyone," Peter added.
Once again there was the roar of laughter in the Plantard Mansion.

CHAPTER 29

WHY CAN'T WE ALL BE FRIENDS?

J. P. Rockdale couldn't believe his eyes. He quickly opened the door and nearly slipped on the ice not so much because it was slippery but due to his sloshed physical state.

"Wha tha hell happened dear? Yall had sum kine of axadent, huh? J.P. slurred. The chauffeur joined both J.P. and Alice as she showed them her car. Ted was knocked out from a head wound and took the three of them to get his limp body out of the wrecked vehicle and into the limo.

"To the bat mobillll Robban." Yelled J.P. as they all got into the limo. "Hospetall Robban."

"No!" shouted Alice Martin. "J.P. get us to the mansion, I believe Ted may have a concussion and he's cold. We can care for him at the mansion, trust me we must get there."

"Vary well, Manchen it is, to tha Manchen James." J.P. shouted to the driver.

"I will give you directions driver. You passed it about five miles back so turn around somewhere up here." Alice directed.

The driver complied and they were headed back towards the mansion.

The senator was growing impatient. She had asked that Agent Todd contact her first thing and it was already going on eight thirty in the morning. Agent Todd once again remembered the tongue lashing he he'd received from the tough black female senator some years earlier and was damn scared to call her for fear of being verbally thrashed again.

"F" it he thought, what's the worst that could happen and then put the phone back down to really think out what he was going to say.

Michael and the other men monitored the security system located in the basement opposite the massive wine collection. They had identified three positions on or near the mansion that were probable threats. The infrared and ultraviolet detection system picked up the heat signatures of the persons. With this information a sense of calm was once more present in the group. Now Zarkuhn would activate directional microphone technology listening devices and possibly neutralize and capture one of the sources later.

Peter picked up the telephone and promptly alerted Senator Stinger of her call.

"Karen Stinger speaking may I help you?"

"Senator Stinger I apologize for the late call, but we've been a little busy here in Hotlanta". I have some unfortunate news, Mr. Anish Markovitz, do you know him?"

"No I don't think so", the senator answered.

There was silence and Agent Todd continued.

"Anyway this Mr. Anish Markovitz was found dead here in Atlanta in his College Park office. College Park is a suburb of greater Atlanta near the airport here."

"Agent Todd why are you informing me of this? I stated I was not familiar with this person."

"Well Ma'am he had a piece of paper in his possession and other tax documents with the names of corporations you are either familiar with or associated with if you get my drift."

"No I'm afraid I don't get your drift agent Todd." The senator needed Todd in front of her. She still did not trust him or know his motives in the whole scheme of things. He had touched the lives of too many in the circle and that was unsettling to her.

"Agent Todd I had stated the last time I spoke with you that I desired a face to face meeting with you, didn't I say that?"

"Ah yes ma'am, but …" The agent was abruptly cut off.

"But nothing I suggest I see you before days end or I'm calling for an inquiry one that's sure to get some dirt out."

"I see you today Senator."

Karen put the phone down slowly and sat down. Now Anish was dead. She could here his wonderful accented voice ringing with enthusiasm about everything no matter the subject or area. "Mr. Markovitz is dead."

"I'm sorry my dear, what?" Miles asked the Senator as she murmured in a low tone.

"Anish Markovitz is dead," she repeated in an elevated voice.

Miles still could barely here her, but Dr. Teranez heard it loud and clear only to repeat it. "What! Anish is dead?"

Miles stood and called Margarite while at the same time buzzing the security area for Michael. Once in the large study the announcement was repeated by Miles again, "Anish Markovitz is dead."

All eyes turned to Senator Stinger as she explained the conversation she had with Special Agent Todd.

"Todd is due to speak with me in person today and there will be several questions I task him to answer if any of you can think of anything I should ask him inform me prior to our meeting please. I can tell you the first question will be who killed my page? Second did he or a representative of his help J.P. at the Atlanta airport when Makesh was killed and now that Anish is dead why is it that wherever he is one of us gets killed?"

Senator Stinger was noticeably furious.

"Mr. Zarkuhn would you do me the honor of assisting me in the questioning of this agent and escorting me to wherever we set up the meeting?" The senator asked Michael as his massive structure graced the study's double door entrance.

"But of course I will senator," Michael responded graciously.

The alarm went off in the Mansion's many rooms. It was a low three tone intermittent ring which was known to all as indicating an incoming vehicle near the Mansion's front gate. A vehicle had broken the unseen barrier through the front gates one mile from the Mansion's front doors.

Miles, Zarkuhn and Peter watched the approaching limousine as it raced towards the mansion on one of several monitors. They also noticed the heat signatures scurry for what would be better positions to spy and observe.

"This is a prime opportunity for me to pay our visitors a special visit. Right now they'll be paying attention to the activity with the car." Zarkuhn smiled at the thought of dropping in on the unsuspecting observers.

"You're quite right sir," remarked Peter.

"We'll continue to monitor the limo and keep you informed as to the bodies" movements," Miles added.

Michael Zarkuhn completed a sound test and weapons check and then vanished into a tunnel leading from the basement cellar into the woods behind the mansion.

Bishop Terrell armed with an M16 stood guard with the women of the inner circle upstairs awaiting the arrival of the unknown limo.
The telephone rang out scaring everyone present. Margarite was too afraid to answer. All of the others standing around her could understand. They could not take any more surprises, no more death. Bishop Terrell answered her prayer and grabbed the phone.

"Plantard residence," bishop greeted the caller on the telephone line.
"Peter, Peter is that you? The voice on the other line asked. "No this is Bishop Terrell, who is this?" The Bishop queried.

"Bishop, thank god. It's Alice, Alice Martin. We're in the limousine headed towards you. I have J.P. and Ted. Ted is hurt he'll need a doctor I have minor injuries."

"Alice we can see you dear you are clear. Who's driving?" The catholic priest's background for thoroughness was gleaming with that question.

"I'm afraid he's an unknown, sanitation may be required," Alice whispered.

"We shall pray not," the bishop hung up.

The others were told the good news and all precautions were taken within seconds to ensure only the bishop and Margarite would be in immediate sight upon the arrival of the limo.

As Michael Zarkuhn exited from behind the thick brush and boulders concealing the tunnels' hatch which he locked back and reset the alarm to he got a call from Miles. His ear mike rang with my Miles' voice. "Michael one of the bodies has just been joined by another body there are now four bodies to be dealt with so be extra careful."

Michael could feel the cold dampness through his gloves as he lay on the partially snow bitten ground. He realized his camouflaged clothing with its base white would offer little cover. The snow was not as heavy on the grounds and with it being daylight Michael knew he would need to exercise great patience in his movements towards the targets.

In 1968 working as a sniper in Laos and Cambodia he'd mastered the art of being stealthy and patience. Once waiting twenty one hours on a mountain in high snake infested grass in order to pop an American CIA agent turned drug dealer in order to make the self professed good guys antsy about their new money making endeavors. The kill was accomplished at just a little under a mile, but with great weather conditions and contracted by Margarite's father Joseph Plantard who despised the CIA.

One group was located on the eastside of the front gate in the woods with a clear view of the front of the mansion while the other sat directly in front on a hill 100 yards up under cover. The latter was the position just joined by a second person. Michael had exited North West from the back of the mansion. This placed him in the woods North East of the closest position and only two and a half clicks from them as he decided to make his way towards the west position first.

The limo stopped and Alice woke J.P. up shaking him strongly on the shoulder. Ted was directly in front of her and she had continually shoved, poked and prodded him in order to keep in from falling asleep. She opened the door and attempted to pull Ted up and out with her as she exited the limo door, but he was too heavy. J.P. was trying to bring up the rear but decided it was a brighter idea to get out on his own side and walked around to help Alice remove Ted.

"Driver, driver I could use your assistance please. Alice couldn't figure out why he hadn't jumped out as he had before on the road to help.

The driver's door opened and he and J.P. Rockdale walked quickly around to help Alice get Ted inside.

It was extremely cold, but the sun was threateningly bright that morning and the water from the thaw rebelled with the offspring of puddles virtually everywhere. The entourage carried Ted towards the front door accosting the melted snow puddles as they sluggishly trounced forward.

J.P. could barely remember where the front door bell was when the door opened with Margarite standing before them beckoning them inside into the warmth of the large beautiful stone structure.

"Come in, oh come in please it's cold out there," Margarite shared.

"Thank you, Thank you Margarite." Alice looked a mess as she thanked her hostess. J.P. was slighted intoxicated but thinking clearer because of it.

"Please lay Ted on the couch their," Margarite pointed towards the couched in the formal living room. The chauffer was helpful and quiet as he almost single handedly carried Ted to the couch. Bishop Terrell and Doctor Teranez showed up hugging Alice and greeting J.P. as Teranez quickly approached Ted. She spoke, "Ted I want ask how you're doing as I can see you need help. I'm going to attend to you now okay. Do you recognize me? Ted wake up. I need you to stay awake as I'm sure your lovely wife has told you okay."

"I know you Doctor, I understand," Ted said in a slow graspy voice.

The chauffer was quiet and paused as though he was waiting for a tip or instructions as to what he should do. The moment was made even more awkward because of the Collective's quandary over how to handle him was now upon them. Each member was thinking is he a spy? Is he an assassin or is he just waiting for his damn money? Timing is every thing and Peter of course was blessed with this amicable trait.

"Madam I shall pay the chauffer now?" Peter appeared as usual from Michael Jackson's ranch "Never, Never Land" or somewhere. Peter's sudden suggestion of paying the dumb founded, Lurch look alike was the catalyst to getting the chauffer out of the picture so the group could proactively start its healing process. Once generously paid by Peter the chauffer quickly sped off down the long trail lined by tall barren trees leading out to the mouth of the Plantard Mansion.

"Dispatch I'm headed back from my morning run. You will not believe the morning I've had. Dude I've been keeping company with a bunch of idiots. But they sure give good tips."

The chauffer shook his head at the experience he'd had.

"Did you get that?"

"What!" the blonde stout man responded.

"Did you see the old geezer get into the limo with that object before the limo driver got in and left?" He was asked by his comrade who was for all intent and purpose a serious poster boy for "Killers R Us".

The observer was irritated at being assigned such a novice in the field and it was reflected in his tone.

"You didn't see. No you tell me what you saw Tony? We've been here on surveillance for two days now and we finally get some activity other than a brief arrival, now you tell me what you make of what you just saw. Come on … what you waiting on Tony?"

"Well Max I don't know why you're so wound up. I saw the old butler looking guy come around the corner and look around then he got into the limo and he got out, okay, so what?"

"You're kidding me, you're kidding me right. Look the old guy just scanned the car. Yeah he went through the car like a football player through a Prom Queen's dress on prom night man. To me he may have even planted a listening or a tracking device in the limo. You notice when he got in he slid the back glass divider open and leaned over in the back. I bet you he bugged the passenger area when he did that after he bugged the driver's spot."

"Well if you are right that means we should have that vehicle tailed too, but to be honest with Max I think you're paranoid."

Max could hardly believe his young apprentice's attempt at deductive reasoning or his psychological diagnosis his partner shared with him.

"What! I don't damn believe it. You know there may be some hope for you yet kid. I am a little paranoid."

With that comment both men felt a thump. Max grabbed his chest right above where the bullet proof vest he was wearing stopped below his neck. His apprentice, Tony was hit in the leg by the dart that struck him.

"What the … Max I've been shot! Max I…."

"Tonnneeey shhhuuuuut uuuppp," was the response from a very irritable and tranquilized supervisor.

Zarkuhn wasted no time in going through his prey's equipment and other items after sedating the men. What he found shocked him. They were not from the Catholic soldiers from church nor were they from the "Clan of Nimrod", these were possibly new players from a secret society all of which would lead a person to believe they were members of the "Sons of Jared", but Zarkuhn smelled a setup. While defiling the sanctity of his prey in spray painting them and giving them special haircuts he notice a necklace around the neck of the younger man and a tattoo, but what was so strange about both items particularly because they were worn by a white was that the items were Islamic.

"I smell Al Queda. Nice try guys you must be "Mercs R US" well you get what you pay for."

Zarkuhn took what he needed from both men making his recon mission a most fruitful one. As the men awoke later dealing with excruciating headaches they immediately noticed their painted faces and other superficially vandalized anatomical parts such as the black stains on their fingertips. Not having their pants and missing patches of hair did nothing for their comfort levels. Clearly they'd been made and all Max could think of was "thank god not I didn't get laid," having spent eight months once in a Turkish prison he still suffered human frailties in the masculine department of his psyche.

Both men retreated from the perimeter of Plantard Mansion in haste, but not before Max briefed his young study on what to tell their superiors had happened once they reported in.

"You know we can never tell what really happened here? We were attacked by four no five attackers and humiliated, right?" Max stated not looking at his young study as he provided the script.

"No you're wrong," the apprentice murmured, "I counted at least eight of them." The study grabbed what was salvageable and scurried out of the woods with Max as quickly as he could.

Michael had already started making his way towards the second position known to have set up shop across from the entrance to the mansion. However, that target location had witnessed the whole assault by Zarkuhn on the unsuspecting "Sons of Jared" operatives.

The church operative glanced at his newly arrived partner and commented, "so what you think chief?"

"What do I think? I think the guy's a bloody genius that's what I think I'd love to have that son a bitch working for me that's what I think. Did you see how smooth he was? You know he reminds me of. Well I'll be damn," commented Paul Constantine.

Constantine had joined the agent he assigned to watch the bishop and now he'd just found his long lost friend from Hong Kong Michael Zarkuhn.

"How did he survive? Captain Kao said he was killed by an assassin." Paul was not really concerned Kao was a screw up and Paul couldn't wait to get rid of him.

CHAPTER 30

LET'S GET READY TO RUMBLE

Merie picked up the phone to call Margarite. The Regional Director for the Department of Homeland Security Special Agent Todd arrives in Boston, Massachusetts. Maurice formerly hires and briefs Lieutenant Wu on the do's and don't of Collective House. Cardinal Ricci hears about Paul's indiscretion in Boston and contemplates a meeting with Merie. Bishop Terrell spills the beans. Michael spills the beans. Alice spills the beans. Margarite and Miles spill the beans. Paul would love to have a meeting with Michael Zarkuhn over a plate of beans. Sergeant O'Connell gets the okay to arrest Paul Constantine. Sons of Jared get on a Subway. And head home. Senator Stinger meets with Special Agent Todd about the death of the bean counter. Doctor Teranez's secret laboratory makes a break through. J.P. Rockdale sobers up momentarily and Peter refuses to serve beans.

CHAPTER 31

POWER PLAY

"Merie I've been trying to call you." The voice was that of the Cardinal, Cardinal Ricci.

"Yes, I'm sorry. I was on the line with a friend." Merie answered nervously.

"Ah, I see, but I was under the impression you had no friends; anyone I know?" The Cardinal inquired.

"It was just a colleague of Louis' and mine, no one important.

"But of course they're of no importance, just a friend right. We must meet Merie. I've so missed your company Merie. How's little Tashi? I really would like to see you both."

"That may not be possible your Eminence I have a full schedule and Tashi isn't feeling well … I, I." Merie was cut off.

"You, you owe me. I protected you and your family. I was particularly generous with you my dear. Especially in light of your husband's past transgressions against the church. The church protected you and you must give me what it is I paid you for." The cardinal's voice was getting loud and intense.

"What was that?"

"What?" Merie asked nervously.

"I heard the click Ms. Tashido. Tell me you are not recording our conversation, tell me please."

There was silence and it seemed to last for hours. Merie hung up, she had been instructed by Margarite to come to Plantard Mansion on the next available flight and when Cardinal Ricci had called she was completing her reservations and had called for a taxi.

"Tashi come on honey. That's a good boy mommy's going to take you on a trip okay."

There was a knock on the door.

"Who is it?"

"Bandor Taxi lady you call a cab?"

Merie grabbed Tashi and her bags.

"One moment please, one moment okay."

"Okay lady sure."

"I'm sorry it took so long I was...."

"Come with me lady we're going to confession."

"No please!" Merie cried out as she struggled to release the man's grip from her arm, Tashi began to cry.

"Ma'am I will hurt the child. You, you I was paid good, no great money for, him no one mentioned him okay. I'm a professional you get my drift I'll kill the kid so shut him up and please cooperate. Get in the car" The Arabic looking man was truly a professional and Merie could tell.

"Well every one Merie will be a guest in our wonderful home by day's end, "announced Margarite.

"That's good news. Has anyone heard from Michael?" Senator Stinger asked. She wanted to make sure he was available for her meeting with special agent Todd.

"You know, I guess the limo driver was okay huh?"
Doctor Teranez said anxiously.

"Yeah I guess" responded Senator Stinger.

"Hello, yes Senator Stinger please."

"Senator tellee for you madam," announced Peter.

"Senator Stinger speaking."

"Ma'am Todd here, where to now?"

"You tell me."

"We could meet at the Homeland Security office here downtown."

"I don't think so Todd are you crazy or on drugs or something? You guys are crooked as hell. You've got issues you need tissues damn it. I can't trust you or your organization. I tell you what. Where are you right now?"

"I'm at the airport."

"Wait there, I'll send a car for you." The senator stated.

"Sure no problem senator, as you wish I'll be here ma'am."

"Let's get out of here before the superstar finds us," stated Paul.

"Why? We've got the drop on him. He's surely on his way up here and we can eat his lunch boss, the element of surprise."

"Do I have to repeat myself," stated Paul.

"No sir, you do not have to repeat yourself."

"Then I suggest we disappear quickly. This guy's good and he'll try and pop us in a minute if we don't puff smoke bloke."

"Ted are you hungry honey? Peter made your favorite beans just for you. Lima beans soup Ted can you believe it. Come on sit up." Alice sat near her husband and started spooning him the soupy beans.

"That's funny my pager just went off. It's the genome lab," stated Doctor Teranez.

"Miles I neutralized the targets …"

"I saw them leaving rather hastily Michael, but not until they had a little nap ay?" Miles was laughing sheepishly.

"Your next targets are also vacating their location Michael."

"That would indicate that they possibly saw my attack on the first group, but it doesn't explain why they didn't take advantage of having a tactical jump on me."

"You know Michael maybe it has something to do with the person who arrived later at the sight. Remember that was the location which initially had one body and later another came."

"Miles you could be right especially if it were someone who never expected to see me again because I was suppose to be …"

Both men said the word at the same time.

"DEAD!"

"You don't think it's one of the Hong Kong connections do you?"

"What I think is that they could have waited and ambushed me, but they didn't."

"But I would have warned you of their movements before they could ambush you."

"Miles they didn't know that you had me covered."

Miles rubbed his chin, "Right, you're right."

"I'm headed back to base, but first I'm stopping by the cottage okay. Oh and let the senator know I've got her back"

"Master Miles are you hungry?"

"Yes, Peter as a matter of fact I'm famished. I'll be right up." Miles spoke into the intercom and headed upstairs.

Bishop Terrell put his tea cup down and walked into the hall of the big mansion.

"Whoa! I'm sorry bishop."

"No, I'm sorry it's my fault, where did you come from?"

"I was in the basement looking for a palatable wine for dinner tonight."

"Miles may we talk I need to make a confession."

"Ha … ha, you a killer. What a hoot! That's funny as hell bishop. Oops. I'm sorry bishop didn't mean to say hell."

"That's perfectly okay Miles I deal with the hell issue daily."

"Father stop please you're, you're killing me here with your wit."
"Yes of course I am."

"Is the study okay Bishop?"

"Yes, of course."

"Well bish what is it? What do you need to get off your chest? You did get any one pregnant did you? Ha!"

"Miles really this is serious. Where in the blazes are you getting this energy from? You're normally subdued and …"

"Yes father, oh padre' lighten up. I'm just happy that's all I know I'm a little more lively than normal but it could have something to do with the fact that I've found love. Can you believe it in my late forties and I'm in love."

"Yes I can as a matter of fact. I am indeed happy for you and Margarite."

"How did you know? Is it that, or was it that obvious?"

"Well Miles really I need to discuss another issue and it is serious. I …"

"Father I think we should perhaps have another member present if this is as serious as your face suggest."

"Perhaps you're right, but who, which member?"

"I'd like to invite Michael in on this. What you think?"

"Yes it's perfect because he's not a member although he carries the weight. He is our security guy as well and somehow I think he's going to want to hear what it is I've to say."

"Fine let's wait until he returns. He should be here soon. He's stopping by the cottage first."

Michael had been notified by Peter that his belongings were placed in the guest room at the cottage. He wasn't really concern about belongings he was interested in one piece of luggage.

"Where is that special package?" Michael always disliked the cottage because of its' rustic appearance. It was so dead and sad looking even inside. Looking for anything in this wooden tomb could depress even the most acute hypo-maniac. He noticed a duffle bag in the far right corner with a lock on the top running through four of the holes. This was what it was all about. Michael approached the large bag and quickly opened it pulling out several pieces of distasteful clothes and rags. He continued to clean out the bag until he felt what it was he sought.

Holding the bag with the prize still inside he entered the living room and sat down on the couch gently he pulled out the jewel and placed both pieces of the most beautiful stones on the coffee table. They seemed to glow as he observed them. They were more beautiful then Michael had remembered; brighter than that day Moses had slammed them down on the jagged rocks at the foot of the mountain in his rage at the weakness of his Hebrew followers.

"Senator Michael is on his way here."

"Great! Thank you Miles, Margarite would it be too much of an inconvenience if we used one of the cars?

"Senator of course not you may take which ever vehicle you'd feel most comfortable with."

"Margarite thanks I'm going to get my things. We'll leave as soon as Michael gets here."

"Well I need to speak with him first before he leaves Senator if that would be okay?"

"No problem bishop my appointment will wait."

Paul was not in any mood for Sergeant O'Connell when he and his associate arrived at the dive Paul was staying at.

"Ah, Mr. Constantine how are you mate? I need you to come down to the station with me. It seems that we have a visitor who has been following your travels and wants badly to ask you some questions."

The sergeant opened the lobby door for Paul.

"Sir after you, no not you only Mr. Constantine, thanks."

Paul looked at his associate and glared at the burly cop.

"Jimmy, do not forget to make our plane reservations."

"What!" The associate who's name was Edward responded.

"I said don't forget our flight." Paul walked away with having said that in a "you'll die," if you don't tone.

"Gotcha! Yeah gotcha boss, sure I'll take care of it."

Edward realized Jimmy and four of his crew were due to arrive at the airport later that day and he would ensure they were greeted and briefed.

"Please get in Mr. Constantine this will not take long."

"I most certainly hope not. I'm on a strict diet and I can not take too much pig, makes my blood pressure go up."

Sergeant O'Connell found the comment amusing and laughed.

"I have her with me don't worry she is fine where do you wish to have her deposited Padre?"

"Take her to the location on Baker Street Father Mitchell will accept the package. Oh! This should be our last communication you will find your blessing at the usual place. God be with you."
The Cardinal mistrusted this operator but he'd always proved to be most effective at every task assigned.

"Yeah thanks appreciate it."

"Damn I hate dealing with these religious guys. Weird man their totally weird, I don't trust them."

"I think they're strange too." Merie was still scared but tried to distill some of her fear by talking to her captor."

"Yeah I mean I've been working for these people for awhile and they are heartless bastards. I've never seen so many fags and degenerates working for one organization as I have these Catholic vampires. Hey I shouldn't even be talking to you about a client. I'm a professional."

"Of course you are, but you have a view right?"

"Well lady I don't know what you did to these guys and frankly I don't care but for your sake I hope they let the kid go. You know it could be worse you could have been a guest of Opus Dei their really jacked up and not as forgiving."

"Well that's not gud atall."

"What's not good Master Rockdale" asked Peter.

"I'm getting Sober."

"Well not to worry we have plenty of spirits in the old castle Master Rockdale."

"Well damn man fetch me somthan queck I starting to lose my mind."

"Doctor Teranez and the senator could not stop laughing and Miles had to join in the laughter.

"J.P. old chap, really that liquor will be the death of you."

"Well hell, better the likker than the S.O.B.s who ben killen us I say."
The room was cast in silence. There was a twisted kind of agreeable logic to J.P.s' statement.

Cardinal Ricci instructed his secretary to arrange his visit to America. He had never been to America and even though his trip would raise many eyebrows and be extremely newsworthy he felt it a necessity to make the trip. The Pope was not well and with the recent scandals the church was fighting a trip might be what was needed for morale and good public relations for the Vatican.

"Ah I am the Secretary of State for the Vatican that is why I'm taking the trip to the Americas … that's what you shall print," he stated to his press secretary as he smiled to himself and swayed out of the room.

Max was not happy with his new haircut and the paint on his face. Everyone at the subway had some sort of reaction to him and his apprentice and even the blind guy playing guitar at the entrance of the subway station starting laughing profusely at Max's arrival. This action by the blind guitarist brought immediate retribution from the few gatherers who then departed at seeing his reaction to Max's appearance.

"This is really humiliating. We're members of an elite mercenary unit and where are we in a damn subway being laughed at by a bunch of capitalist imperialist waiting on a damn train.

CHAPTER 32

I BELIEVE IN JESUS NOT GOD

"Hello everybody."

"Michael good you're back. How was it? Margatirte was too perky with the question.

"Well it was alright. I mean I neutralized the threat so it was great right?"

"Michael what's in the bag?"

"Good question Doctor Teranez It's my lunch. No it's some of my surveillance equipment. Excuse me right now I have a meeting with Bishop Terrell."

"Miles you're with Michael and I so come along if you would be so kind."
The bishop politely cleared the way for Michael to enter the study with him and Miles.

Michael slowly removed his gear and placed it on the floor next to the large chair by the window he loved so much.

"Drink anyone."

"You know, I think I will indulge."

"Sure Bishop what's your poison?"

"Miles make it Vodka on the rocks please."

"Michael anything for you my friend?"

"I'll have one of those sparkling waters. The Senator and I will be going back out later so I want to stay frosty."

"Of course" stated the Bishop Terrell with an assured professional knowing in his tone before addressing the two men.

"Gentlemen an old associate paid me a visit a couple of days ago a person from my past and his presence may have something to do with the killings and other problems we've had over the last few weeks."

"Who is this person father?"

"Miles I'm getting to that." Bishop Terrell was obviously nervous as he took a drink from the glass he was religiously rolling between his palms back and forth.

"Before I joined this wonderful family I worked for a similar group attached to the church. Michael you've mentioned them on occasion and I'm confident you may have even dealt with them in the past."

"The church! What do you mean a similar group? You mean like Opus Dei or some splinter like that?"

Miles was not following any of this he too was beginning to perform the roll your drink in your palm routine as he leaned forward on the edge of his seat. Michael wanted badly to ask Miles if he thought by leaning more into the direction of the speaker he would comprehend the material better; but his accomplice Peter was not there to embellish the essence and full scope of the joke so he abstained.

"I was a black ops type one each, yada, yada with the Vatican." Michael couldn't help but think of how much the bishop sound like some of his old Special Forces associates from the old days.

"One each, yada, yada yep Michael always knew that puke, the Bishop was a spook and now it was coming out, it was truly confession time.

"Okay so what are you saying father? Either my drink is too strong or I'm an idiot or ... don't touch that last statement."

"Miles perhaps you're not leaning into the Bishops direction enough. Try a more acute angle." Michael couldn't help it he had to make a remark about Miles' posture.

"Bishop I always felt your instincts, skill and acumen for our wet jobs and clandestine work was top of the line particularly for a man of the cloth and this explains why."

Michael couldn't help but notice Miles falling further into the abyss of "I'M CONFUSED".

"The man that kidnapped Louis' family you said he called himself Paul. Well that man I believe was been Paul Constantine."

"Well let's see the man who I met and that's putting it lightly, was about six feet, 190 pounds with very blonde hair a muscular lean built and oh yes a real bad attitude. How's that?"

"That about describes Paul alright, Michael I'm surprise you're still alive because Paul's pure evil."

"I gathered that from my short visit with him. He's tough as nails too. I popped him in the shoulder good and it didn't subdue him, he kept at it"

"Paul visited me a couple of days ago asking questions."

"Michael if he's the same person from Hong Kong then maybe he's responsible for the surveillance of the mansion."

"Miles it's the same guy. He's here which explains the mystery disappearance of the toads across the street today. This Paul must have been the guy who showed up later and upon spotting me withdrew the surveillance to try put the pieces together."

"You saying Paul has this house under surveillance?"

"No Bishop Terrell we're saying he did have the house under surveillance, he dddiddd." Michael informed the clergy.

"It would appear that he and one of his cronies left about an hour ago. He thought that Michael died while in Hong Kong, but now that Michael's death has proven fallacious he definitely gnawed I'd say." Miles took a drink from his glass and having shared his take on things finally sat back off the edge of the sofa.

"Bishop Terrell what kind of questions was Paul asking?"

"Michael to be honest with you they were strange to say the least. He wanted to know about the "Tables of Testimony," from the Old Testament scriptures and other religious and archeological writings. I told him what was in the documents I had read and studied over the years, but Paul doesn't ask questions unless he wants something and trust me he knows how to obtain answers. I sensed he believed me but for some reason he felt I could help him more. I should've known he'd tail me somehow. Well I can tell you for sure that I'm exposed. He'll press me now about this place."

"You talk about him as though you know this Paul well."

"Michael you're right I do know him well hell I taught him. He was assigned to me as a pupil when the church recognized his true gift. He was never going to make it as a man of the cloth like his ancestors or his cousins at the Vatican. Paul was too headstrong and single minded. This man is I suppose is one of the most deadly men I've ever known. Please Michael I know of the protection and security you've provided to our cause but this man's lineage has seeded him with the innate ability to destroy and rule on a major scale."

"Oh I can attest to that after shooting him in the arm while over in Hong Kong and him reacting as though it was a slight distraction. His performance under injury and duress from heavy gun fire from me impressed me for sure. But why would he be sent?"

"You don't understand. Paul Constantine is the last weapon generally used by the "special works" department of the church. My guess is that he was dispatched to acquire what the church thinks we possess, the Tables of Testimony."

"But that's preposterous we have been on that quest for years now but with no success. Why would they think the Collective had this relic?" Miles felt uncomfortable with the question he laid before his comrades.

Through the course of death and intrigue over just the past two or so weeks Miles was developing as strong inner sense, a sixth sense with acute intuitiveness particularly for when the excrement was about to impact with a windmill; or in lay terms, "when the shit was going to hit the fan."

Miles leaned forward and rubbed his chin in bewilderment.

"I think this would be an opportune time for me to share something with you both. Bishop hand me that bag."

The bishop was apprehensive in picking the bag up but did so. He then ensured a cautious and tense sitting position as he and Miles watched Michael slowly remove the contents of the bag.

"Is that what I think it is?" Miles blurted.

"Dear Mother of God." Bishop Terrell's eyes were dangerously on the brink of eloping. He slowly stood and fell to his knees before the object held by Michael Zarkuhn. It was eighteen inches or so long and about two feet wide at its widest point. The room was eerily dead with silence and a knock on the door brought every thing back to life. Each man took his time looking in the face of the other as to ask the question, "what now?"

"Yes?" Asked Michael, "who is it?

"I'm sorry it's me Margarite. Is all well in the guys? We girls were just getting lonely."

"Of course you are my dear," responded Miles.

"We are just about finished," added Bishop Terrell.

"What should we do?"

"What do you mean what should we do. We should immediately announce this success to the inner circle. I mean it's what we've been searching for, for how long now?" Miles was adamant with his argument.

"You don't agree Bishop. You seem reluctant why?"

"Michael you of all people should realize the danger this find brings to every person in this house, in this organization. We must think this out."

"Think what out? There's nothing to think out. Every person in this house has put their life on the line in order to thwart tyranny and promote an environment for the survival of mankind."

"Miles you're being emotional, you're not thinking with your head, but with your heart."

"I cannot believe you a bishop are saying what you're saying. You must understand my reluctance to believe anything you have to offer to this conversation in lieu of what I've just learned of your history with the very people who are trying to destroy us."

"I take offense to your tone and to your accusation!"

"Gentlemen please. We are loosing sight of our purpose and what's worse we are damaging our respect and friendships.

"But Michael did you …?"

"Miles please one moment. Bishop you make a good point, but in the same vein Miles' correct. Every soul in this dwelling has dedicated in devoted themselves to the cause knowing the risk.

"We were tasked to find this relic and to turn it over to our research department. However, when we are to do this is up for debate. Miles wishes to do it now and he has voiced his reasons for wanting to do so. Bishop wish to wait because of the possible danger it poses to those who know we have this jewel, but Bishop are we not all in danger anyway because certain parties believe we possess the knowledge already?"

"Well yes I suppose you're right, but should any of us be fall into the wrong hands there are only three of us who could actually divulge the truth of the relic's whereabouts or that the Collective even has it."

"That is true Bishop. So should we only inform those with a need to know and if that is what is decided who will those persons be?" Michael Zarkuhn asked as he glared at both men.

"Well Doctor Teranez definitely has to know."

"Okay, so that's a given."

"Well see that wasn't so hard was it? So gents who else should know about this?"

"I think Doctor Martin has to be a part of it after all she and Louis were the project leads and she is the expert on these types of relics and things."

"That's a good point Miles."

"Thanks Bishop, I appreciate that."

"My pleasure Miles It was...."

"Alright guys knock it off or get a hotel room." Michael laughed as he joked with his colleagues.

"I can't think of anyone else who needs to know. At least not at this time do we agree?

Both men leaned back as though they were finally comfortable with what had been discussed.

"I'll take that as a confirmation and now when should we do this?"

"Now, Now!" Popped off both men to Michael.

"I'll call for the two ladies to join us." Miles jumped up and headed for the study door.

"Well Michael that went better than I thought it would thanks to you and God's guidance."

"I don't remember seeing a fourth body in here with us Bishop."

"Oh but God was here trust me."

"Didn't see him and I don't."

"You don't what believe in God or trust me?"

"Bishop both assessments would be accurate." Michael looked into the clergyman's eyes and walked over to his favorite chair and stared out the large window.

The bishop was stunned, he couldn't let it go.

"Michael you don't believe in God? I'm frankly shocked I didn't know. I apologize if I've offended you by sounding sanctimonious."

Michael turned his cold black eyes towards the bishop "It's not that I don't believe in God bishop quite the contrary. I know him very well I just don't believe in him the way you do. I believe in the man you know as Jesus as well as other ascended masters. I've made it a policy over the years not serve tyrants or megalomaniacs. You bishop have been fooled into doing both."

The bishop didn't know what to say. Michael turned away from him and resumed staring out the window. The bishop walked away and took a seat as far from Michael as he could get and still remain in the same room.

"Doctor Teranez how is Mr. Martin?"

"Miles he's sleeping it appears Mr. Martin's going to be just fine. Did you need me for something?"

"Yes, where's Alice we need the both of you in the study pronto."

"I'll get her."

"There she is. Alice we need to meet with you and Doctor Teranez for a closed session in the study right away."

"I'm right behind you let's do it. Miles it sounds important what's up?"

"Well ladies I really can't say. Even if I knew I couldn't say."

"What?"

"Never mind that comment doctor. You'll understand soon enough hurry."

"Miles there you are I thought I heard your voice."

"Margarite my love I can't talk right now we're about to have a meeting."

"Well I wasn't told. I'll get the senator she's in the kitchen with me."

"Margarite that will not be necessary love you see this meeting is compartmentalized, it's closed."

"Oh."

"I'm sorry dear. Trust me it's for the best. You'll understand soon enough okay. I must go."

"Miles."

"Yes, love."

"It is okay, I understand go on. I love you."

"Where's everybody going?"

"Closed meeting Senator we're not invited sorry."

"Well this place is beginning to operate like Washington D.C., damn. Hey J.P. pour me a drink." The Senator shouted as she and Margarite shuffled to the mansion's mini lounge to keep the swaying Mr. Rockdale company.

Chapter 33

What's Oligarchy?

Agent Todd was growing restless when he received the call on his cell phone. As he glanced at the telephone number and name he began to feel the heat. It was the Secretary for Homeland Security and Todd knew when, where, who and what he wanted and what he was going to ask before he answered the call.

"Sir Agent Todd here!"

"Todd what's going on down there in Atlanta. I just got word about two of our boys missing there. This is not the kind of press we need son. Do you know I'm trying to increase our budget and I'm going to be grilled by the senate when I go before them over not being able to account for two agents because their families and the media are on my case.

"Yes sir I know."

"Look, just tell me you have this under control."

"You betcha, I got it sir. I'll send you a full memo explaining the problem."

"What problem. Get the damn agents back on the job and back to their families. That is unless they're undercover? Is that it? Are these guys under cover Todd?"

"Yes sir that's it, but I can't go into it see."

"No, no of course not my apologies Todd just smooth it over with their families okay so they can stop the unnecessary calls to my office and the press."

"I gotcha sir no problem, done, is there anything else sir?"

"Nope I don't think so. Where are you anyway? I called your office and they weren't sure of your location. Does this have anything to do with the undercover thing? No don't tell me. Well good luck son. I knew I could count on you."

"Yes sir you can count on me." Todd stated as the Secretary hung up. Todd was loosing his mind. The senator needed to get to him fast. It was getting late and he wasn't sure what might happen next.

Cardinal Ricci hated flying. He had no control and he savored the art of control. Control of others, control of one's self and control over the destiny of others. Yes control was an intricate part of power without it things often went amuck and caused failure. Failure was not good he thought to himself it was something he was unaccustomed too. In fact he was hard pressed to remember ever performing a "failure" in anything he'd endeavored or ever attempted to do. No, failure was not an associate, acquaintance or friend of his it was as distant from him as Satan and sin. He sighed as he glared out at the heavens with a feeling of joy at such wonderful thoughts about himself.

"We'll land in three hours vir clarissme," Announced the pilot of the private jet.

"Gubernator gratias."

"I refuse to answer anymore questions. What are you looking at peon?"

"Now Mr. Constantine there's simply no need for name calling. Look here we just want you to cooperate with our guest and please be polite okay."

"You no Detective O'Connell you are really beginning to use up your green stamps with me."

"Oh now Paulie, Paulie."

"Don't call me Paulie bastard! Abi in malam rem!"

The door to the interrogation room opened and the room went quiet.

"I thought the detective asked you to be polite Senioror. You're yelling and telling the wonderful detective to go to hell. That's not very polite now is it?"

The brunette was tall with a bake potato brown complexion. She moved as would a large cat on the prowl and although her waist and bottom rolled as a model's taking off the runway her head and shoulders were as steady as Robocop's. She commanded attention for sure not just because of her penetratingly beautiful deep blue eyes and sultry, almost husky voice but because she reeked of predator. This beauty was stone cold genuine feminine predator. No doubt remained in the minds of anyone at the Boston police precinct where she was or in that room where she just walked in.

"Holy shit! Who are you?"

"Mr. Constantine please your language is offensive. I expect more from a man who is suppose to be assigned to the employ of the Vatican, sanctuary of God."

"I apologize for being so common my little beauty but you're obviously not from around this barbarous little town. I'd say Spanish with a drop of Moor for color. By the way I am not a Senioror I'm not much older than yourself I'm sure. I've just had a fast life, very fast that's all, but enough small talk where did you learn Latin my beauty?"

"Church," answered the visitor from Interpol.

She slowly walked towards Constantine and then behind him staring at the wall and one way mirror. He could see her as she walked behind him from the reflection off the glass which faced him. He sat back slowly in his seat intrigued and now amused as he thought of the fun he could now have. This one was interesting not like that damn fat ass cop, O'Connell, who Paul prayed would dismiss himself from the fun.

"Detective would you please leave us," Requested the visitor from Interpol.

"Ma'am I don't think …"

"Detective I can assure you I'm fine."

"Yeah O'Connell can't you see she's fine or are you gay or something?" Paul busted out with laughter as did whoever was behind the one way mirror.

"Hey! Watch that buster, you just watch it okay. Shit can get real harry around here for smart asses."

"Hummm, you cussed I'm gonna tell bad copper, bad copper."

"Please detective if you would," Beckoned the sexy visitor as she held the door opened for the slow retrieving angry Detective O'Connell.

O'Connell was really angry at the joke from Constantine. Being gay was serious taboo in the super hyped predominant Irish police precinct and homophobia was super contagious. Detective O'Connell was overly sensitive due to the fact that his younger brother of five had been involved in a gay rights movement for police officers in the Boston area. He hated his brother and everything associated with him including himself. He'd remembered how the news tore his father's heart out. Poor guy a thirty year veteran from the force second generation proud Irish cop with a gay son. Man that hurt and that damn blonde rabbit had the audacity to joke about him, O'Connell being gay. No way, he thought never, never. Right about then he wished he were married, thirty five years old and never married. He wondered if the guys at the precinct wondered. See that damn Constantine had started something.

"Hello detective," shouted the desk sergeant.

"I hate that son-a-bitch," replied O'Connell as he stormed out of the interrogation area and straight for the coffee and dried out doughnuts.

"Let me formally introduce myself. I'm Contessa Hannabolas and I'm a detective with Interpol as I'm sure you already guessed. I am here to ask you a few questions and I am sure you will try to use your diplomatic immunity status to avoid answering me."

"O contraire my beauty I'll answer your questions as provided I get to look upon your beauty. Please ask away, oh my blood type is ... I was born ... my favorite position ... anything for you dear."

"My first question is how long have you been in America this time?" Contessa asked as she sat to his left side allowing no obstruction to their faces during questioning where behind the mirror she had sat up a camera to film the whole interview so she could review it later in order to observe Paul's facial expressions.

"I got here about three days ago."

"Who is your supervisor Mr. Constantine, who do you work for at the Vatican?"

"You already know this don't you beauty so why do you ask?"

"Answer the question Mr. Constantine."

"I work out of the Social Sciences department."

"Oh please Mr. Constantine there is no such animal answer the question."

"I work for the Swiss Guard detachment."

"Paul I grow tired of your games. Let's try again okay. Who do you work for?"

"I ... I ... worked for Donald Trump okay you got me."

"Paulie!"

That got Constantine's attention as he sat erect and glared at his questioner. He immediately started to try and incorporate his years of training in order to contain his physical and mental composure.

"Madam you know me no? I will only say this once to you and not another time." Paul's Italian accent revealed itself for the first time during his visit to America.

"Don't call me Paulie because the next time you do I will kill you. Do you understand my beauty?" There was a tap on the window to which the Interpol agent held up her hand indicating to the observers on the other side that the threat was okay that she felt no immediate danger. She was learning where the buttons were.

"But of course Paul; I've offended you and for that I'm sorry."

"My boss is Cardinal Ricci."

"I thought as much. Good for he is due here in a couple of hours. My sources tell me he will visit America for the first time and California is his first stop. I know he will love California I do."

"What?" Paul yelled as though he were in trouble. It was sort of like the sister informing her mischievous brother, "Wow moms home".

Mom's home and you didn't complete one iota on her list as she requested.

"What do you mean? The Cardinal is at the homeland not here. If he's here …" Paul was silent and drifted into thought mode.

"Well we're getting somewhere now. Mr. Constantine that's all the questions I have for you for now thank you."

"That's it? You have nothing else for me beauty?"

"Well if you insist. Are you a Knight of Malta or "Nimrod Black Pope" operative or are you a double agent for the Great White Brotherhood?"

"Beauty you already know I'm attached to the Secretary of States Office. What's Malta? Is it some sort of beverage and Great White who. I don't belong to the Klu Klux Klan I love black people. I've spent many hours teaching and instructing wayward coloreds?"

Constantine humored himself with that statement as he thought of all the people color around the world he'd instructed for not showing proper respect to the superior race or the Catholic Church.

"As I stated Mr. Constantine this interview is over and by the way please do not attempt to leave this barbarous town as you so aptly refer to it."

Paul could not wait to get into the taxi and head for his hotel. If what the Interpol beauty said was true he had more pressing issues at hand. He wondered what could get the Cardinal out of the homeland, Vatican City. Whatever it was he would find out soon. This bit of intelligence also provided Paul with an opportunity to complete another part of his long term plan.

He was excited, so excited he almost had an orgasm in the taxi thinking of the great fortune he was just blessed with.

The privileged few had ruled the Earth for centuries. It was no secret who would rule. It was a secret when and over what. The church, businesses and countries all ruled by one big extended family. It was his time to rule. That damn "Narcissistic Complex," was forever creeping into the picture. So what Paul assured himself he wouldn't be so narcissistic if he really didn't have a right to money, control and absolute power; yes just like his older cousin always say's "absolute control is pure power". He didn't mind that for over a thousand years his family had kept power in the family, but now was the time for change. Paul needed to have a talk with his boss, with the Cardinal, with his cousin about his next job opportunity.

CHAPTER 34

MOSES HAD CABLE OR KABAL, AH!

Dr. Teranez joined Alice Martin in the meeting being held by Michael Zarkuhn in the Plantard Mansion study. Bishop Terrell and Miles sat quietly as the ladies entered the room.

"Well ladies I'm glad you could join us. Please be seated as there has been an epidemic of fainting spell associated with our group lately." Miles then took a deep breath and looked at Zarkuhn.

"Ladies please observe." Zarkuhn laid the cracked stone on the table in front of the women.

"I don't believe it!" Alice stated as she walked with both of her hands in the air slowly approaching the object.

Doctor Teranez was able to muster her first words, "I need a sedative my mind is racing back and forth. I mean where, when, how did we get it? Is it safe?"

"This is it? The first Tables of Testimony, well a piece of the first tablet, the Emerald Tablet of Hermes." Miles smiled as he made the statement crossing his arms as though he had himself recovered the jewel.

"Now which one is it? You said Emerald Tablet of Thoth-Hermes and also the Tables of Testimony. Which one is this?"

Alice turned and asked the men in the room. Alice was academically aware of the fact that although both items possessed great power through what was believed to be the same means they were suppose to be different, or at least it was believed so by most in the academic community.

"Doctor please look for yourself and tell me what you think, go on it is perfectly safe." Michael motioned her over to the table where the tablet lay.

Alice Martin gently picked up the artifact and examined it.

"This is extraordinary, remarkable it weighs nearly nothing. It feels like a smooth gem stone and it appears to be as hard as one yet it is virtually weightless. Cheryl come over here you must check this out. Legend has it, if this is the Emerald Tablet of Thoth that his body, the body of Hermes was found clutching the Tablet in a cave."

"Yes he was found by the Greek sage Apollonius of Tyana. So what do you think Alice."

"I think that's most impressive Michael."

"What?"

"I wasn't aware that you were so adept at ancient history. What do I think well it's hard to say? The writing is not Hebrew nor is it Akkadian. It's Sumerian but with some derivatives and symbols that are throwing me off. It appears to be numerical gibberish."

"What do you mean gibberish, could it be "Linear A"? I was reading in a journal …," Miles was quickly cut off by Dr. Martin.

"Miles don't be silly Linear A followed much later and that would make it Minoan or of ancient Greek origin. This piece predates that period by thousands of years based on the cuneiforms and these other markings, hmmm." Alice now revealed a scowl on her face as though thinking about it hurt.

"So what is the problem Doctor Martin?" Asked the Bishop who was almost cowering as the others gathered around the Tablet.

"The problem as I see it is that this form of Sumerian text seems to be number based with just a few statements and instructions."

"What do you mean number based?" Miles asked.

Michael intervened and answered Miles' question. "It seems that the writing may be similar to binary coding not unlike that used in programming computers today. The Tables of Testimony or the Emerald Tablet I might add and as Doctor Martin will attest too are just a few names for this find, other names for this find exist, however, the names are different and the tablets and secret knowledge is used to unravel their secrets. Some believe this knowledge to be contained in mysticism known as Kabbalah."

"Yes Moses himself was trained in not only the ancient Egyptian mystic magic, but also that of the early mysticism, Kabbalah. Jesus himself was a sage and master of the mystic art of the Kabbalah." Doctor Martin got her breath with giving that spill of information as she still held the gem.

"He's correct, Michael is on to something. The lab has been experimenting with downloading data and information into different object for example water, and also gem stones. We've been successful as of this week in retrieving the data. With a specially written program I'm sure my people could write a program to help us tapped into this baby!" Doctor Teranez stated as she also held the gem with Alice.

"I had my doubts at first about Louis, about whether or not he could locate this, but the evidence he continued to produce was so overwhelming. It could only have been that he always knew where to go, where to find the Tablet the whole time that is why I became so suspicious and notified your department Michael. Thank God you were able to develop a security initiative to recover this. I'm guessing Louis was instrumental in the recovery right?"

"He helped me break the ice yes," responded Michael Zarkuhn.

Miles and the bishop knew exactly how helpful he was and tried to avoid eye contact with both ladies as Alice asked her question. Michael had kept Louis Tashido under surveillance early into the project. Even before being flagged by Dr. Martin that Louis' activities overseas were erratic Michael had placed an agent on his tail to verify his trustworthiness. Too much money, too many changes in his itinerary and some meetings with some of the most notorious, most dangerous persons in the world of espionage in existence had over time convinced the Collective that Louis was a double agent. He would at some point in the future have had to be punished and Michael had his opening in Hong Kong after learning from his agent watching Tashido that Louis had indeed located and retrieved the precious find in a village in Syria from descendants of the original tribe of Levi.

"This baby has possibly seen more history than any object on Earth. It was actually handled by the patriarch Moses, hell by God Almighty himself. This is the greatest find in the history of mankind. No other relic, not the Spear of Longinus, the Ark, or the Holy Grail is a greater more powerful find than the

Tables of Testimony." The Bishop appeared to be hypnotized as he made the statement about the Tablet. He too was now under much suspicion because of his strange behavior and reaction to the Tablet's discovery. He was far too defensive and his colleagues sitting on the Collective inner circle were uncomfortable with the clergyman.

"Why would you consider this more important than the Ark of the Covenant?" Miles asked the question of the bishop while everyone else in the room anxiously awaited a response.

However, before Terrell could answer the question Alice Martin, PhD in the Classics with a specialty in Mesopotamian Archeology jumped in; "because the Ark was only a shell, the main frame of what would be called a computer and although it is in its own rights special because on the monatomic properties used in the design it is the programming the CPU that we hold here today in this room. We have in essence God's diskette containing all that there is to know or ever will be known, it's all right here in this baby."

"So If I understand you correctly we might be able to tap into this stone as if it were a computer chip or CD and pull out information. Is that what you're saying Alice?

"That's exactly what she's saying Miles. In fact I'm confident we can retrieve what's in this marvelous tablet right now if we're successful in formulating a code breaker or deciphering the right equations. I wish Louis were here. He was quite an adept Sumerologist and he could probably have read this to us on the spot. Our major issue will be deciphering these symbols," stated Doctor Teranez as she continued to gaze at the tablet before her.

"Michael you know how few hands have touched this relic?"

"In fact Alice I do. As the story goes when Moses returned down from Mount Sinai from his meeting with God he was disappointed to find ..."

"Not disappointed he was pissed Michael, he was fuming!" Bishop Terrell had intervened with what he thought was a more descriptive view of Moses' reaction.

"Yes bishop that probably is a better description of his reaction, yes then he was pissed as the bishop has so amply shared with us. In his anger he tossed the Tables of Testimony to the ground breaking it into two pieces. Luckily one of the young priests picked up the halves and was rebuked by Aaron of all people for touching them. However, as Moses calmed down he asked the young priest to keep the Tablets while he collected the golden calve idols made by the Israelites in his absence."

Michael had a flashback he could see Moses as he directed Aaron and the other Levite tribesmen to gather every idol made and gathered even more gold which he melted down till a white powder mixture was formed and other secret elements added to create "shew bread" to feed to the restless Israelites.

"I thought Moses received the Ten Commandments on two rather large pieces of stone. This is the first I'm hearing about the Tables of Testimony."

"Miles I would strongly suggest you read Exodus and particularly chapter 31, verse 18 of the good book," remarked Bishop Terrell with a noticeable bit of disgust in his tone.

"Most Christians are misinformed or ignorant of the real history that occurred in many parts of the Bible Miles you're not alone in your thinking. Remember most religions as unfortunate as it may be are used as tools to control the masses and that's why the governments support its presence. Giving the sheep too much information would promote the asking of questions which most clergy couldn't logically answer or most governments would prefer the masses not inquire about at all. Remember the greatest form of government is that one governing one's self what better way to do that than through religious indoctrination?"

"That's blasphemous talk young lady you know that don't you?" The bishop stood and faced Doctor Martin as he addressed her. His face was red and he shook his finger at her intensely. Doctor Martin immediately tried to apologize as she recognize she had offended the bishop, but the bishop would not here of it. He was tired of listening to what he considered pathetic educated fools. To him they tried to understand God through logic and reasoning, but he knew as his brethren of the cloth were aware that you could not intellectualize faith or the workings of God. If God wanted you to understand him then he would show you what he wanted you to know. The masses were so ignorant they did not understand that God was omnipotent that no one on Earth could understand him not ever; we were but children to him. Not even children, we were more akin to pets which he loved and took care of and all he asked of us in return was love. To the bishop it was worth it to give love for everlasting peace in heaven with the master. He could not understand why anybody would not want the same.

"Bishop you need to get a hold of yourself sir. Your aggression towards the Alice is unwarranted, stated Miles."

"I beg to differ. She insults all that I stand for."

"Bishop Terrell it was not my intention to insult you I'm truly sorry."

"Bishop it is you who has insulted what you stand for not this lady here. I reiterate a lady with a capital "L" and not only have you failed to exercise forgiveness and tolerance through love and understanding you have been rude, abrupt and threatening all evening. I'm going to ask that you to try and practice what it is you preach or I'm going to practice some Darwinism on you, "you know only the strong survive," something that I preach. Do you understand me?"

With that the Bishop quickly seated himself as Michael made the hair on the backs of everyone present stand. The air in the room was uncomfortable and the members wanted to adjourn. The tension had zapped their energy and they were fatigued by the excitement.

"Michael I didn't realize you're so adept at history especially regarding this piece here."

Michael turned towards Doctor Martin. "Thank you Alice I'm flattered, but I have studied many subjects with great zeal for years. I can assure you I'm only a novice at this. You are all the experts each of you and I'm fortunate."

"I don't believe that for a minute Michael," chuckled Miles Turner.

"Well what should we do now with it? We must secure it somewhere. We must not allow it to be stolen or compromised in anyway. I'm full of anxiety tonight and for that I'm going to apologize to you all I've acted a little off par tonight."

"Bishop we understand, we really do. We are all under pressure and tremendous stress I for one humbly accept your apology. How are you feeling though, I mean physically? May I check you out I'm merely concerned Bishop."

"Well I admit I'm a bit agitated and of course Doctor Teranez I'd appreciate you checking me out, thank you."

Doctor Teranez walked over to the Bishop as she pulled the stethoscope she had used earlier on Doctor Martin's husband.

"I think the bishop is just a little overtaken by all of the hooplah."

The bishop gently moved Doctor Teranez aside as she tried to take his pulse.

"Hooplah! Hooplah you say, this is not hooplah when you're discussing a document forge by God himself. Have you read ever Exodus? God wrote on this stone and dictated to the Patriarch Moses you call these events hooplah. In this gift lies the key to all mankind's sickness, knowledge, our beginning and our end."

The bishop's eyes were glazed over like a thanksgiving ham. Michael Zarkuhn sat quietly and observed everyone's actions it was obvious that the bishop unnerved his colleagues. It was during this awkward moment that he digressed back in time once again remembering that very day when Moses descended from Mount Sinai. Arriving at the encampment he found the Hebrews had transgressed against the commandments of El Shaddai, lord of the Mountain, God of the Christians and Jews. He could see the smashing stone as it hit the ground and broke into two pieces. One of the younger Levite priest picked up the larger section of the stone at the displeasure of Aaron of all people. Michael knew the young priest and he was a good man, a man who had not accepted or participated in the making of the golden calves. This young Levite's family had to have been the missing link in the mystery of the broken Table of Testimony. He recalled Moses asked him to keep the broken pieces until he finished correcting the problem.

Michael helped Moses collect all of the small golden idols and melted them down. Moses then added other elements and ingredients after the gold had been made in a powder form and distributed to the Hebrews as shewbread. The shewbread, their daily bread did the trick it helped the children of God endure and focus as it always did. Michael was Moses' prime and he protected the leader of the tribe of Judea. Moses had to pull him off of Aaron when they first arrived at camp because Michael was so upset at his lack of discernment. A riot almost ensued between the Levites and the tribesman of Judea over the action. As best as Michael could figure it Louis Tashido had located the young Levites' priest descendants in Syria. But Michael also remembered the words of the patriarch Moses when he sat down to eat later that night in his large well lit tent.

"Today my God seemed so human, almost manlike. He was so, so angry. I had to calm him, I was lucky enough to have said the right thing."

"What did you say my pharaoh?" Michael asked.

"I had to remind him of the covenant, of his word he had given my forefathers, Abraham, and Noah. He repented to me."

"What!"

"He repented of the evil he thought to do to his people. I changed my God's mind. It was not what I expected. Sabbathiel I was disappointed and I'm still confused."

Sabbathiel was what Moses called Michael back in the day, these ancient days before western civilization. It was Michael's mystic name and Moses knew who he was before his transformation to human physical form. Michael realized that the reason for Moses telling him about the occurrence was that he desired more insight from him, the former archangel. That insight never came for Michael's disappointment with Jehovah was increasing with every passing century.

Michael ran back threw his mind that day and it angered him. The thought that Moses never even saw the promise land, the land he worked so hard to get his people too vexed him. He was more convinced that the God he had served back then since the day of his creation was a universal class megalomaniac. Although he was thankful that his former master gave him authority over all of his armies and title "King of the Heavens" his many years on Earth provided insightful schooling for him in the ways of control and manipulation of those universal beings around you. But it was not all bad times yes plenty of great battles were to be remembered. Yes awesome battles like the over throw of Sirius and their amphibious inhabitants. In fact, Anu the father of Jehovah married a queen from that star system and there was the battle with the Pleiadeans. Well not really a battle because it was so easy to conquer such a passive people referring to it as battle would've been a shameful disgrace for the then Armies of God. He could see the faces of his brethren Uriel, Raphiel, and his close friend Gabriel. Yes they were the Malachim, the messengers of God and if you lay eyes upon them it was but for two reasons and two only; one that someone was going to have a baby ... always a male from the loins of God, and two to inform some poor race that all hell was going to break loose, someone was getting the crap kicked out of them, no exceptions to that modus operandi. All through the Christian bible the theme proves the same. Michael smiled to himself as he thought about his script, "you will have a son, you are with a man child, kill them all, you must leave or else yada, yada, yada." Then of course hundreds even thousands of none compliant Philistines, Caananites, Amorites or Egyptians would be slaughtered by his master's command. If only those tribes had just worshiped and served him the only true living God that only of course no one ever saw. But those poor unbelievers should've had faith in the strangers God sent to them from foreign lands who could not speak their language, but demanded their allegiance. No, none of what Jehovah did back in those days made much sense when Michael really thought it out.

Perhaps Sammael knew what he was talking about when he rebelled and chose to become the adversary Satan? Or was it some intricate design concocted by his former master Jehovah to amuse his twisted sense of humor. Did he purposely arrange the rebellion led by Sammael and his league of rebel angels in order to make his virtual reality video game more sporting?

It wasn't all bad for Jehovah showed he trusted Michael by giving him the "stones of fire" taken from Sammael in order to provide him protection from other Malachim and Satan who would seek to harm him because of his great standing as General of the Armies of Heaven. However, later the stones were given to Moses to be incorporated into the Levite's high priest ceremonial breast plate of judgment which would protect him from all harm and from the then coveted Ark of the Covenant.

"Michael, hello Michael are you with us? Doctor Teranez was beginning to think a quarantine of the object might be proper protocol with the way everyone in the mansion was behaving since its appearance.

"Yes, I was merely thinking that piece should be relocated to the facility in Atlanta as soon as possible."

"Well I for one agree."

"Miles I'm glad you said what I was thinking".
"Bishop what do you think? Bishop, Oh Bishop Terrell!"

"Oh! Yes. I quite agree, most definitely your place; of course it's an excellent suggestion doctor." But his heart was not in it and everyone wondered where his heart really was.

"I think that settles it then. This precious jewel must find its way to the Atlanta genome lab. Needless to say we will need to beef up security ten fold. I also think it might be prudent Michael if you accompany it to Atlanta."

"I wholeheartedly concur with your proposal Doctor Martin," responded Miles.

"You know this whole sordid business sounds like something right out of a Dan Brown novel, like that Da Vinci Code book. Did any one else read it, it's really quite different rather refreshing from a different point of view kind a way. Well maybe not for the Bishop, but I recom … never mind."

"Miles would you please adjourn us and give it a break I've got to see the senator she and I have some business to attend."

"Michael slow down I was just about to close. Is or are there any other items we should address?"

"Yes. If Michael is not going to accompany the treasure to Atlanta then who will? Who is capable of giving this valuable piece the protection it should be afforded that's what I wish to know."

"The bishop has a good point Michael. Any ideas on who will handle this assignment? I realize that we are not really privy to such knowledge by our bylaws and rules but this is hot stuff."

"Michael, Alice and Bishop Terrell have good points."

"Miles I'm thinking the Asian station chief."

"I thought ... well forget what I thought."

"Look he's proven right? He filed a great report with you last night about his actions in Hong Kong while we were preoccupied he was resourceful and he has the new guy I wish to test."

"Wait I object if this new guy or person. He's never done this kind of level of protection in the past, has he."

"Bishop your objection is noted. Are there any other questions or concerns? Well if not Miles I would like to join Senator Stinger now if that's alright."

"Meeting adjourned, well Michael you can get out of here."
"Michael a word with you before you leave."

"Sure Miles."

"You realize Maurice will be freaked out by us giving him this assignment and even more perplexed by your survival from the Hong Kong shooting."

"That's fine trust me. It will keep him on his toes for the future, but I don't desire him as I indicated I want the new hire Lehchin, the young Asian cop. Lieutenant Lehchin will escort the ladies and the gem to Atlanta. What do you think?"

"I think he's too green."

"He has heart and he proved that by helping us in Hong Kong true enough."

"On that you are correct, maybe he is what we need. The report filed by Maurice on him and the actions he took were quite impressive."

"Yes you're surprised he made it? Trust me on this he's a survivor and what's more he'd rather die than fail he's what we need not a soldier who concentrates on self preservation and his being able to use someday use his pension."

"Okay Michael I'll notify Maurice immediately. I'll also make arrangements to get our agent here and when should we plan on getting down to Atlanta."

"Philippines, Boston then Atlanta, plus a briefing make it happen in forty eight hours."

"It's tight but I don't think we have a choice if what the bishop informed us is true we'll be receiving unwanted visitors soon."

"Miles I've got to get with the Senator thanks for your support see you later."

Michael spotted Doctors Teranez and Martin as he finished up with Miles leaving the study with Bishop Terrell leading the pack.

Peter had disappeared and Margarite called for him over the intercom.

"Peter, Peter …"

"Madam I'm behind you."

"There, so you are."

"Yes, I've seen to dinner and lodging for our guests. The kitchen staff has been directed to serve our guests as they require and to make provisions for room service if necessary. Have you eaten today at all Madam?"

"Peter I'm fine." Margarite hugged Peter.

"Madam all I did was asked if you had eaten it hardly warranted a hug."

"Peter you are so very silly. I just wanted to show you how thankful and grateful I am with how you've handled things and taken care of me, father would be thankful too. Peter I'm happy you're with me. Since father's death, well I don't know what I would have done without you all these years thank you."

"Madam you are indeed quite welcome. Now if you'll release me I can get to my duties, mmm thank you very much and those were truly kind words."

CHAPTER 35

A HOAX! ARE YOU SURE?

"Ma'am is the baby okay now?"

"Yes he was just tired but he's resting now."

"How long must we stay here? This is very uncomfortable for my baby and I so please tell me the truth; are we to be killed, please tell me?"

Merie was running on fumes, zapped of strength. She'd managed to hold on this long only because of Tashi. The anticipation and fear was physically and emotionally draining her spirit. Deep down she knew very well the Cardinal had his hands in this kidnapping. The fact that she and Tashi were being held hostage at a monastery pretty much convinced the young mixed Indonesian mother of this probability. She hoped Margarite would remember her and perhaps become concerned that she and her son were not at the airport in Boston as projected later that day. Why she wasted her time thinking of this was a mystery since she honestly believed no one on Earth could help her now.

The nun was old and dowdy, but there was wisdom and calmness in her presence. Her round red shiny face literally glowed as Merie watched her straighten up the room occupied by her and Tashi.

"Ms. Merie you very special woman, yes. Ms. Merie no one shall hurt you, no never hurt you on this you can be sure. The Cardinal he comes, yes the Cardinal comes for you to see. No my pretty you are not be harmed, are you hungry?"

"No ma'am we are okay for now. I'm just exhausted I shall rest."

"This is California dear, this is the city of Angelos, huh? You and the baby are angels, so you belong, yes."

The frumpy woman spoke strangely, but made surprising sense or at least she put Merie at ease.

The Cardinal's plane had been on the ramp for fifteen minutes, but he felt quite comfortable as he waited for the okay from his security detachment, all twenty of them, that the coast was clear. The Cardinal had plenty of business to attend to in America and he'd been briefed on the decadence and crime that permeated the sinful country, all the more reason for a righteous man like him to show and do God's work. He would visit a few churches, make a couple of special political appearances, get Merie and Tashi and then clean up Paul Constantine's mess. Yes it was time to handle things himself without fail.

"I'm growing tired Marion. Where's my car, how much longer must we wait? Time is becoming my enemy and I have much to attend," the Cardinal said to his assistant Marion, who was opening the door to the plane as the Cardinal addressed him.

Margarite released her grip on Peter. He could make a clean escape.

"Peter I think I'm in love and there's another item."

"Yes madam I've heard something to that effect. Congrats I assume its Miles who's the lucky man; very good I'm so glad we could have this brief talk and unless there's something else."

"Peter I thought you'd be happier for me."

"Oh, but Ms. Margarite I'm elated, ecstatic, much merriment runs through me, I can hardly stand it. If memory serves me correctly and it usually does I mentioned to you ten years ago that Miles Turner, Esquire was the perfect companion for Ms. Margarite, did I not?"

"I feel so much like a mushroom. Yes Peter you did and you were correct. I should have heeded your advice back then, but could you not be so caustic and try and express your elation without hurting me, please?"

"Margie I'm sorry dear. I am happy for you my dear truly I am. Now you stated there was two things you wanted shared one."

"Well Merie Tashido and her baby were suppose to arrive at the airport this evening, but when I called to arrange for her transportation she was not found on the manifest. Peter she never made the flight."

"And of course you've tried to call her direct?"

"Yes and there's no answer. I even had the Los Angeles Airport page her there to see if perhaps she'd missed the flight."

"This is not good. Have you notified Michael or the other board members?"

"That's what I was going to ask you, should I notify Michael and get him involved?"

"I think so Madam. Well it looks as though you may not have too I see the door opening as we speak." With having stated that Peter glanced at Margarite and headed towards the kitchen as though the conversation they had just had never occurred.

Margarite slowly approached the study as the Bishop exited first leading the pack. He politely spoke and headed towards one of the smaller study rooms rubbing his chin as though in great thought.

Next to exit behind him were Doctors Teranez and Martin.

"Margarite I'm glad we caught you. We need to secure a package in the mansion vault as soon as possible may we?"

"Sure. One moment and I'll, alright come on this way."

Margarite could see Miles and Michael Zarkuhn were still discussing something so she'd wait.

"Right this way ladies, it's in the study behind my father's life size portrait. Maragrite grabbed the right side of the large gold framed portrait and pull it open from the wall. It was hinged on the left side and when it opened it revealed a concealed metallic door similar to the one on the old bank vaults. Margarite placed her palm on a lit panel adjacent to the vault door and then placed her eye over a small whole directly above it. She then keyed in a code in the ECD below the bright panel that she had placed her palm on and the door opened.

"Please come on let's find a good place for the item." Doctor Alice Martin carried the duffle bag with the item in it as though it were an infant. The vault was amazingly neat with shelves, metal boxes and cash, so much cash that both doctors were awed and confused, but acted as though nothing was unusual about their surroundings. Each could not wait to discuss the sight with one another later.

"Here's a good spot. Place it in this drawer here."

Margarite took the bag and gently placed it in the drawer. She avoided her natural instinct to inquire about the bag's contents. Questions wouldn't be proper protocol and was taboo in the craft.

"It will be safe here until you need it. Now if I can not be located Michael or Peter can gain access to this vault okay?"

Michael was rushing to get to the Senator after his discussion with Miles. He knew Miles would arrange for the young Mr. Lehchin to escort the precious tablet to the Atlanta research laboratory without fail.

Michael felt awful about keeping Senator Stinger waiting for so long, but somehow he would make it up to her.

"Senator I'm ready come this way I have a limo for us out back." The Senator and Michael snaked their way through the mansion kitchen and jetted out of the underground garage and off the grounds. It was now nine p.m. and they both hoped the DHS agent had not given up and departed. As they parked the limousine both jumped out and darted for the main terminal at Logan Airport.

"I'll bet you a twenty he's at the bar."

"Senator you'll never get my twenty, that's a bet I will not take." Michael knew the Senator was right they'd find the federal agent at the bar. He began to scan the whole area for hostiles or anything that might be suspicious. His eyes darted from the baggage claim area to every shop in the area.

"Well Michael looky there, right over there on the corner at the Samuel Adams bar there's our guy watching the game. Will you wait here and cover me while I deal with him? Wait! Michael would it be out the way to get him back to Plantard Mansion or should we select another off sight like a hotel, what's your advice?"

"The mansion will be fine. I took the liberty of setting up a room for him with Peter before we left and Senator I also installed additional electronic exploitation devices in the conference room to assist us when we question him."

"Mmm you do good work sir, good work. Well here goes nothing I'll be right back with the package."

"Yes ma'am you know where I'll be."

Lieutenant Lehchin lay in his bed staring at the ceiling thinking about all that had happened to him over the past week. He was thankful for his new job and for his new found friends in the Philippines. Maurice was a great boss and the work he had assigned the young former police lieutenant was more than he could ever have dreamed of. He now had a real chance to make a difference not just perform mundane police work. It was around eleven A.M. in the Philippines and Lehchin was going to enjoy his day off. As he dozed off the loud knock on his door brought him to a seated Jujitsu defense position. He laughed at his startled response and answered "who is it?"

"Hey kid it's me get up. You've got an assignment a hot one and you're out of here like yesterday."

Lehchin jumped up grabbed his pants and quickly opened the door.

"Say what's up sir!"

"Look call me Maurie or anything but sir kid." Maurice walked in and looked around the room pulled up a chair and sat.

"By the way kid what's your first name? It's certainly not kid."

"It's Clarence."

"Say what! You're kidding right? Clarence, how did … never mind."
Lieutenant Clarence Lehchin was now gun shy after revealing his name and wanted to avoid any further embarrassment.

"Sir, Maurice, I mean Maurie so what exactly is going on?"

"Well finish getting dressed and pack a bag you've got to get to Boston like yesterday."

"Boston!"

"Yes kid Boston, Boston Massachusetts, US of A."
The young Chinese recruit and Station Chief Maurice Steely were headed to the Manila Airport in no time.

Michael Zarkuhn observed special agent Todd as Senator Stinger approached him. Michael could see the bar was three quarters full and he meticulously watched everyone's actions. He was sorely disappointed at what he observed. He couldn't believe the lousy shape the special agent was in. Todd stood about six feet and weighed somewhere between two hundred thirty to two hundred and forty pounds. Michael thought to himself the agent was entirely too heavy and what was worse he never noticed the Senator walk up on him until she touched him on the shoulder. He was not cognitive of his surroundings, he was an easy target.

"This guy is a bonafide candy ass", Michael whispered.
Todd was startled as Senator Stinger greeted him.

"Special Agent Todd how are you? I'm so delighted you could make it."

"No problem Ma'am."

"Agent Todd I'd like to apologize for the extreme delay. You've been here for hours and I appreciate you just not walking away, you had every right too, thank you."

"Ma'am I must apologize to you for my condition. I've been sucking down Gin and Tonics for at least half the night and I'm feel'n good, good enough to eat shit and howl at the moon; if you'll forgive me for being so blunt in saying so."

"We are clear to go your Excellency. This is California named after the fictitious Spanish goddess. I had a briefing before I departed."

"Yes of course you did your Excellency." Marion replied with a drop of sarcasm under his British accent.

Cardinal Ricci paused momentarily and glared in his direction as he stepped onto the tarmac. He marveled at all of the buildings and cars he'd seen before landing it was magnificent. So many people all over the place his anticipation for the visit grew. Los Angeles was only his first stop and already the sight was overwhelming, wow he thought to himself. Soon he would be face to face with Merie at the monastery where he had given instruction that she be held. He could hardly wait to see the young beautiful, intelligent Indonesian girl from the village where he'd started his first Catholic ministry. Yes he'd be with his secret love the mother of his son soon.

CHAPTER 36

MIND YOUR MANNERS, NO MANOR

"No that's perfectly fine agent Todd in fact I think I may join you for a drink, but first I'd like to introduce you to someone. Michael, Michael this is Special Agent Todd. Todd what's your first name?"

"Christopher ma'am, however I go by Chris."

"Mr. Todd is the Regional Director for DHS Southeast Region and he'll be helping me with some issues regarding Intelligence and National Security."

Michael glared at the DHS agent looking him in the eyes and then slowing moving down his body and then back up to his eyes again.

"That's quite a large and important responsibility you have Agent Todd. It must be quite exciting to be on the ground floor of such an influential organization as the Department of Homeland Security. You know Germany had the first homeland security department."

"I didn't realize that, interesting." Agent Todd appeared bewildered at the statement made by Michael Zarkuhn.

"Yes, but they called it the Gestapo. Senator if you'll excuse me I'll get our transportation."

"Senator now I might be paranoid especially right now, but I don't think your friend cares much for me. He has a bellicose nature to him you know. He's rather intimidating I mean with the big arms, large neck and huge pectorals and all you know."

"You have nothing to worry about Agent Todd, Mr. Zarkuhn is very professional and highly efficient. I won't allow him to harm you."

"Even the guys name is intimidating, Zarrrkkkuhn! What is this person to you? I mean does he work in your office or what?"

"In fact you could say he does. He handles security matters for the location we're headed to and he is a consultant for my office."

Senator Stinger wanted to avoid unnecessary questions about any members of the Collective so she quickly changed the subject matter as she started out towards the terminal where Michael had headed.

"Come along Agent Todd try and keep up."

"Yes ma'am I'm right with you I had to pay my bar tab. Damn thing required me to take out a loan, get it?"

The black senator from Florida stopped in her tracks and turned to Todd. "Yes Todd I got it. Look you've obviously had too much to drink this evening not that its your fault, well that's not true, but tonight try and control yourself. You run the risk of insulting or offending some of my associates so no more jokes and no more booze, comprehenday?"

"Sure thing, but I thought the joke was quite funny I just made it up, just now."

Senator Stinger briskly moved through the terminal towards the outside. "Todd please clam it."

As they stepped out of the terminal into the cold December air Senator Stinger could see their ride moving towards them. A Boston police officer was busy barking at traffic to keep moving. Occasionally gesturing aggressively at drivers who waited too long by the curbside.

"Hop in Todd. Boy it's cold out here. Michael thank you we're ready let's go. Wait! Todd did you have any luggage?"

"No ma'am no luggage I travel light … taste great, no light, taste great, no light …"

Both the Senator and Michael chimed in at the same time, "shut up!"

"This is all we needed, he's officially drunk. I thought we might have an opportunity to chat with him tonight but not in his condition." The Senator sounded exasperated as she turned to look back at her drunken organic package.

"Well he's out for the count and I must say what a relief."

"Senator there will be plenty of time to interrogate the commoner."

"Michael nobody is being interrogated. Agent Todd is trying to help us and we need his help okay?"

"Senator Stinger that's why this country's in trouble, politicians and bureaucrats like that peasant in the back seat there they can't help us their too busy helping themselves. Senator no offense but your government is a carbon copy of the Roman Empire; wealthy representatives and senators with partisan agendas and surrounded by mediocre government servants all working towards the ultimate destruction of the people. They can't take pressure they cannot see the big stage of life. I train my subordinates to avoid hiring that type in the backseat for Collective's security details."

It was quiet and with having shared his feelings with the Senator Michael sat snuggly back in the driver's seat and headed for the Plantard Mansion. He constantly monitored his rear view mirror and took unusual side roads and turns as an added precaution against any possible tails on the vehicle.

It was now a little after 11 p.m. and Peter answered the telephone. The call enticed just about everyone in the mansion to "raw hide" into hall where Peter spoke gently with whoever was calling. Tensions were high due to the events that had taken place and those that were to take place in the near future. Peter continued to look around slowly at the faces of all who had gathered in the hall as he listened intently.

"Well Peter who is it", Miles asked impatiently.

"Yes of course I understand. Is there anything we can do for you?"

"Yes I understand perfectly madam and might I offer my personal condolence for your loss. Yes please hold one moment I shall get her for you." Peter lowered the phone holding his opposite hand over the receiver gesturing to Margarite to come to the phone. She did not want to take the call as she was pushed forward by some of the onlookers in the hall. Margarite began to shake her head from side to side. She knew that look upon the old man's face all too well. In fact, everyone had worn that mask of loss and doom in the last week.

"Madam Margarite it is not good news brace yourself", the old man servant stated to her as he handed her the phone and stood close to her.

It was the eldest daughter of Doctor Amin Sabat on the other end. The elegant lovely held the phone as though it were a contagion, not desiring to hear anything being said on the other end she managed to force herself out of respect to listen. Margarite listened as her eyes welled up with tears. Her large doe like eyes met those of each guest in the hall of her home as she raised her hand to her mouth in an attempt to muffle her sobs. It was no use though she could not hold it inside any longer. The pain was too much another wonderful person and most of his family gone. She cried profusely shouting "no" repeatedly. Miles embraced her and took the phone from her slender hand. Peter also held Margarite as she clutched both men crying hysterically her legs went weak beneath her but they held her up. The Bishop placed his hand on Mile's back patting him as Miles began to explain to the caller the situation with Margarite.

"Hello this is Miles Turner, to whom am I speaking? I'm so sorry Vena. I was also a friend of your father. I must ask if you are alright." Miles looked at everyone and shared with them, "she's fine everyone, she was not there when the incident happened, she was notified by the Gujurati authorities in India of the deaths of her family in the city of Surrat." Miles continued to narrate as he listened to the late Doctor Amin Sabat's daughter.

Doctor Teranez was crying and holding onto Peter as she was sure the death was horrible she reached out for Alice who clung to her husband, but also reached out to Cheryl Teranez as they walked towards each other. J.P. Rockdale stumbled into the arms of all three persons sobbing as well. The four persons, J.P., Alice and Ted Martin, and Doctor Cheryl Teranez approached Peter and Margarite who anxiously embraced all of them and listened to Miles as they slowly moved towards him to consummate to cliché "group hug". Ted Martin's eyes ran with tears as he held Alice tighter. All of the Collective members finally met Miles at the phone sobbing, sniffling, crying, coughing and a whole slew of "no, no, say it ain't so", emanated from the cluster.

"Peter what's going on?" Michael asked about the scene in front of him as he entered the hall from the kitchen, but he was sure he knew.

Peter answered Michael with his usual humor, "Well come on in don't be shy there's literally plenty of hugs to go around Master Michael."

Michael could see the cuddle session was pushing Peter to his emotional limits. Peter was not the sentimental type. His obdurate nature was tough to handle for most and at times his sturdy and witty humor might well offend anyone especially these grieving members in the hall way of Plantard Mansion. Michael took the coats Senator Stinger and Agent Todd as Senator Stinger rushed into the arms of Cheryl Teranez, her lover. The sight of all the different people crying, hugging and the commotion quickly sobered Agent Todd. He was desperately looking for an escape route. What had he gotten himself into he wondered. He'd heard about the wild parties the congressmen and senators in S.O.G, seat of government ... Washington D.C. threw and he wanted no parts of it. It was not that he didn't find one or two of the babes kind of attractive but he was not into orgies and he wasn't about to try it with these fruit cakes, drunk or not.

Michael glanced over at the agent who glared suspiciously back at him.

"They just got bad news it's not what you're thinking Todd."

"Oh yeah, then why is the Senator kissing that chick, huh? Answer me that big guy."

Michael looked at the mesh of Collective bodies in the hall consoling one another and saw that Agent Todd's apprehension and fowl thoughts were certainly valid. It wasn't that the Senator and Doctor Teranez were lip locked or anything, but their affectionate display for each other surpassed mere comfort of a friend. They were hugging, but their comrades were also, however, every other second or so a kiss to face was delivered to one of the women by the other in a questionable area and their hugs were turning Todd on.

"Yeah well that's interesting, so what it looks normal to me I'm of Greek descent though." With that statement Michael glared at the special agent as though he were pushing his patience a little.

"Hey that's funny. I knew you had a sense of humor. Wow! Of Greek descent you know that wasn't bad Mike not bad at all. Hey is that a bar in there? This is nice."

Michael followed agent Todd as he entered the mansion lounge. "I bet you they've got beer here what you think old buddy, huh?"

Todd rushed into the room and darted behind the bar. Once there he opened the refrigerator and grabbed the bottles he saw placing two of them on the mahogany bar.

"Hey Mike let's have one and make up, whoa, but not like those broads in the hall okay, but you're alright and I think we can work together. Hey where's the can opener?"

Michael could feel his blood getting all manic on him, it was starting to boil. Now he wanted to silence the guy just put him to sleep so he could be quiet or hell kill him and apologize to the Senator in the morning for his indiscretion. He would explain the homicide as a really old bad habit, that wouldn't work at least not in this century.

"Look toad if you take one more drink tonight I'll be compelled to break something, something attached to you and very dear to you. You get me juicy boy?" Michael's eyes did that change to gold thing as he loudly threatened the DHS agent.

"Whoa! I get it big guy it's cool, it's cool. I'll sit over here and mind my own business okay? No drink, no drink absolutely no drink at least not tonight."

"Shut up Toad!" Michael shouted and slammed the door to the lounge."

His mind quickly raced to address the image of Senator Stinger and Doctor Teranez's show of affection earlier. He could've cared less about their relationship, because he'd seen it in human behavior for thousands of years and to him it was par. However, it was a possible security nightmare for him and the Collective organization. Questionable values or actions might be used against its members neutralizing their effectiveness in the public arena. He admired both women so he decided he would speak to them in private about the incident rather then make a big to do about it. If other members of the Collective were to question what was observed he would address their issues as needed, but he was sure that after all the time they had been together every member knew the two ladies were lovers and could also have cared less. They were family, extended family and never in Michael's thousands of years on Earth had he been apart of such a large extended family. The emotional attachment he'd developed was felt deep, for he'd never felt so much love of a group since leaving the flag ship of Anu millennia ago where he served as the General of the Armies of God.

On the Mothership and on the planet of Nibiru Michael the Archangel had family albeit not the traditional form of what occupants of Earth would typically consider family. Michael missed his family but it didn't hurt as much now. The pain was eased because of his new surrogate family's presence here on Earth. The punishment that God had sought to use on him was now no punishment at all, but a worthwhile calling, his duty to champion his people. Michael was resolved in not letting the people of the planet Earth become prey to his old employer, Jehovah.

He could still here the sobs and crying from the Collective members in the hall and hurriedly joined them for group hugs as suggested by Peter.

Paul got to the hotel late and as he stood outside lurking in the shadows of the hotel parking lot he could hardly wait to get the report from his soldier assigned to contact Jimmy and his strike team. He needed to know Jimmy's location and when he'd be prepared to strike. Paul experienced chilling shivers as he thought about Cardinal Ricci visiting America outside his Vatican fish bowl. It was perfect timing, Paul thought to himself he would make lemonade out the lemons he'd been given by the bossy Cardinal's unexpected visit to America. He and his team would "eighty six" the Cardinal. Paul began to mumble ...

"I cannot take this task lightly. No, this will not be easy only a fool would think as such. The Cardinal is shrewd as shrewd as me, as shrewd as the Pope himself. However, my blood is purer thus I will prevail. I cannot fail."

Paul was concerned about the Cardinal's elite security detachment, those who would be seen and those who were invisible. Ascertaining the force level and efficiency of his cousin's security detachment would definitely indicate the Cardinal's real intentions in America. Who was he fooling his intentions were obvious, deep freeze Paul and finish the assignment himself, bastard. So much to do in order to pop one man, "damn" he thought as he felt the vibration of his cell phone in his pocket.

"Boss, hello boss it's Jimmy."

"Damn man I was just thinking about you. Where are you? What's your ETA?"

"We're scheduled to arrive at Logan Airport tomorrow at 09:37 hours, Delta flight 332, I think gate thirteen."

"Jimmy when you arrive you call me and I'll give you your instructions and Jimmy did you bring the package?"

"Yes boss. I sent it via the shipping company like you told me. It's already in country. Our guys on the dock over there have been notified to let us know when it's in and boss it's some heavy shit, yeah real heavy."

"Good work meat head, call me when you get in."
Paul put his cellular phone away as he entered the hotel lobby. There in front of him reading the newspaper was the human rodent that ratted on him to Detective O' Connell of the Boston Police Department. Paul Constantine fought the urge to abuse him right there, but decided to have some fun with the desk clerk instead.

"Now look who we have here. You know I was informed someone was murdered here recently and it absolutely shocked me. I couldn't understand why you would've withheld such morbid information such as that from a patron."

"Look sir I ..." the emaciated clerk was shaking as he tried to address Constantine. He laid the paper down and began to step backwards as Constantine addressed him.

"Shut up dweeb I didn't ask you to expound or to even move for that matter. Look here I'm going to make this as easy as I can. I'm going to kill you, but not tonight so make it hard for me, get out of the city we'll play hide and seek. See if you can hide or how long you can evade death. I guess that's all. Oh any calls?"

Paul didn't intend on killing the emaciated sap he just wanted to see the look on his face and also get rid of a potential source for the police in aiding their investigation. The clerk slid towards the back door of the office and shut it. Moments later in his room Paul could see an old beat up Chevrolet pull up outside the hotel. Then he observed the chain smoking front desk clerk frantically jumping into the vehicle with an overstuffed suitcase. The car sped off and Paul sat down to meditate on how he would best execute his plans. He couldn't get the Interpol beauty out of his mind though. Her persona was beginning to haunt him and as he thought about the whole interrogation with her at the station it suddenly came to him that she may not in fact have been who she said she was.

"Mmmmmmmm."

CHAPTER 37

CATHOLIC, PROTESTANT, IDIOT, WHAT'S THE DIFFERENCE?

Peter was now in his room away from the sadness and despair in the hallway of the mansion below. He desperately needed a cathartic experience. He would meditate and assist the loss souls from this realm in entering the next dimension. He began the ritualistic preparation he had done so many times. But first he would rest, yes rest for even though he was not unhealthy he was tired and weary. Why still after so many years had the human race still not learned to love? All they knew was to judge and condemn one another. They chose sides, all kinds of sides pertaining to sports, politics, domestic disputes, philosophy, religion, and basic piss poor prejudices. How could a race of beings be so stubborn? Could they in fact be as stupid as they had reflected over the last couple of millennia? Well the questions weren't really important what was to Peter Stuart was being in Christ, to ascend above all of the toil and chaos he'd been subjected too.

"Please ladies, gentlemen, please may I have your attention? We have suffered a loss I take it?" Miles answered Michael's question.

"Yes Michael I was informed by Doctor Sabat's eldest daughter that her entire family was killed shortly after they arrived in Surrat, India last night. The police do not know who's responsible of course. It's tragic I can make no sense of it, why?"

"Look I know we've all suffered so much in the past weeks but we must hold it together for the rest us, for the ones in this shall who remain alive. Trust me the others who have gone would want us to continue the fight and we must. I believe this very facility may be the next target and for that reason I need all of you to pull yourselves together."

"He's right. Michael's right we can't let this destroy our will. We knew this day might come and now that it's here well?"

"I'm with the Senator and Michael, but I must grieve before I can go on, so please let me alone I must grieve." Margarite continued to cry with having said her piece. Miles hugged her taking every advantage of his new loves vulnerability while the other members gazed helplessly at Michael for direction.

"I suggest we all retire and sleep this over. I for one could use some extra sleep honey how about you?"

Alice looked at her husband and gently placed her hands on his face. She pulled his face down to her kissed him on the forehead and opened her heart.

"I love you so much, so very much please don't you leave me. Let's go to bed. We will see you all in the morning may God watch over us."

Ted hugged his wife and walked her up the long winding stairway to their room followed by Bishop Terrell who was still rubbing his chin and obviously still in deep thought and running a temperature or just nervous about something.

"Michael I think we'll retire as well and thank you again for helping me get our package speaking of which, where's he?"

"I left him in the lounge."

"Oh no not the lounge come on let's get him."

"Well Senator as you would say looky there's your package knocked out." Michael walked over to the bar to see if the "candy ass" had obeyed his order not to drink another drink. To his delight the overweight DHS agent had followed his wishes.

"Michael what are you looking for?"

"Nothing, just checking the area out that's all."

"Are you searching for bugs or something Michael?"

"Doctor Teranez there are no bugs in here I've checked."

Doctor Teranez and J.P. Rockdale broke into laughter.

Senator Stinger stood in the doorway shaking her head at the sight of the drunken agent slumped in the chair before them.

"Well sance thars no bugs in thare I'll jest have me one far tha road, aye."
"J.P. we don't think that's a good idea. Why don't you retire with the rest of us, I mean not with us but go to your room okay, please."

"Doc it's ol'right I'll behave. Hell! I don't won't to think right now anyways my damn head hurts tohiheavan. Think I will go ta bed."

"Well I think I'll just carry our little guest up to his room. Senator we'll meet in the morning and chat with the fat boy here alright?"

"Yeah sure."

"Oh and Senator I'll need to also speak with you and you too Doctor Teranez about your little show of affection tonight in the hall."

"What do you mean show of affection. I was comforting a friend."

"Senator don't get defensive what I saw that drunken master laying over there saw as well and your idea of comforting a friend made Todd there want to hump air, so chill. Understand this that we're alone in this play and I'm in charge of security and intel for this group. I know you two are lovers I've known from the day you both joined the Collective and personally I could give a rat's rectum. However, should your ability to support our cause be negatively effected or your characters be compromised because of your sexual preference it might harm O.W.O.W. thus we would be forced to terminate our relationship with you do you now understand?"

"Michael then what is it you wish to talk to us about in the morning?"

"I don't need to discuss anything with you now; as far as I'm concerned we've had our talk. Goodnight ladies see you in the morning."

"Michael we admire and appreciate your candor and discernment good night we'll see you."

Both Cheryl Teranez and Karen Stinger grinned girlishly at each other. With arms around the waist of the other they walked out of the lounge and into the hall climbing up the beautiful winding staircase of the mansion to their rooms.

Michael Zarkuhn reached down and grabbed his obese package. He heaved the large mass over his left shoulder and walked to the lounge door way cut off the light and walked over to the security pad on the wall next to the hall phone system and set the security system. Michael wondered what more he could do in order to provide protection for his comrades in the house. He knew that a strike was imminent. Attack the mansion is what he would do why wouldn't this unseen enemy. He believed the character he'd confronted in Hong Kong was behind at least some of his organization's loss of lives and desired to meet him again. As he walked slowly up the stairs with his bouncing buddy hanging over his shoulder he faintly smelled the incense emanating from one of the rooms in the opposite wing of the mansion. He suddenly envisioned Peter in deep prayer or meditative cleansing, letting all of the iniquities of the day's events be dissolved from him. Peter had been on Michael's mind and he didn't know why. Michael always shared an unexplainable closeness and had a fondness for Peter since their first meeting a sort of bond that he'd never experience with any other being on the planet. Peter seemed to know Michael and the first time they met September 11, 2001 Peter unnerved Michael at first with his calmness and his familiarity of him. Peter had reminded him of somebody and for the life of him he could not place it which was strange in and of itself for Michael prided himself in his ability to always recall any person with an event, place or thing, etcetera, etcetera; but not with Peter to Michael Zarkuhn the matter was mystifying.

Ted Martin could not rest and he realized his fidgeting would not allow his lovely Alice to get the rest she so desperately needed. Something more was up he just could feel it and he could sense his comrades sensed it.

"There's a fifth column that's it. But who could it be?"

"Honey, Ted did you say something."

"No honey I'm sorry go back to sleep." Ted really felt stupid talking out loud to himself and waking up his wife was exactly what he didn't wish to happen.

"Ted you said column."

"Sweetums go back to sleep okay."

Ted headed for the bathroom but he was not quick enough. The lamp next to Alice was on before his second step.

"Ted that simply will not get it, I distinctly heard you say column."

"Honey you were asleep you heard nothing of the sort."

"Ted I know what I heard and I never sleep so hard as to not hear you talk."

"I didn't realize that I'll make sure to keep that tidbit of information in mind in the future now would you please lie down and got to sleep."

"Teddy."

"Alright you don't have to get rough. The fifth column is a covert or secret way of saying subversive or someone or group working against you from inside your own organization. The term came about during the Spanish Civil War, I believe around 1936 when four columns of rebel troops were attempting to seize Madrid led by a General. When the General was ask by some reporters which column would take the city his response was the "fifth column" of course everyone was puzzled at his statement. They were further bewildered after learning that the "fifth column" referred to sympathizers that never showed up as the General had believed they would."

"You see Teddy, now was that so hard, hmmm?" Alice smiled at her husband holding her arms open towards him and motioning with her fingers for him to come to her. He sat next to her on the edge of the king size bed as Alice pulled away the beautiful lavender comforter. She fluffed her oversized down pillows and crossed her arms around her knees pulling them up to her as though she were at an all girls sleep over discussing the hottest boys.

"Well who might it be? I can't think of anyone who could have taken part in this carnage. The bishop has been rather strange though lately. You should have seen him in our meeting earlier tonight. To be honest with you he literally gave me the willies."

"Yeah I know he's weird and all but the guys a priest for God sake excuse the pun. I'd go with the Senator. I mean she's a politician they have no scruples."

"Ted I don't think you really believe that. I hate to say it but I think your bigot streak is rearing its ugly head in that statement."

"What! Not at all; I really believe she's shaky not just because she's black."

"Well then maybe it has something to do with her sexual preference maybe?"

"You're way off base on this one honey." Ted stood up and started pacing in circles in the room. He stopped occasionally to make eye contact with his insightful wife who was subtly grilling him cerebrally."

"Ted, understand you've come along way from when we first started dating. You were a damn redneck neo Nazi frankly in college. I almost left you because of your views about people of color."

"Not people of color honey just blacks."

"But we've gotten pass that haven't we? Come over here and sit down by me. One of the reasons the Collective brought you on was because of your ultra conservative positions on matters and your connections to the conservative underground networks and you have served the group well. I'm proud of you. You've reflected objectiveness and compassion in your decision making on all levels not ever to my knowledge allowing race to sway you."

"I have always tried to be bi-partisan in my handling of any issue. That is why I helped Makesh Patel in executing justice against those dirty police officers a couple of years ago."

"But until the Collective you hadn't done such noble things for those with different skin Ted."

"What do you mean?"

"Your Mother for instance, I mean the way you treated your mom over the years Ted do you really believe you've treated her fairly?"

Ted was quiet not looking at his wife directly but gazing at her through the reflection of the large dresser mirror at the opposite wall at the end of the bed. He could not only see Alice's image but for the first time he could size himself up eye to eye with his wife's searing question. The answer tore his heart so bad he wanted to scream. Ted and his mother had always been close. He was the closest of all five of her children and the oldest. There was nothing he would not have done for his Mother, but he had felt betrayed by her at the time he turned against her. It all came to him as though he were standing under a Hawaiian waterfall being cleansed only to reveal his bad judgment and shame. He hated his abusive father but refused to support his mother in leaving him despite the beatings he'd dish out every Friday or Saturday night after a good drinking binge. He himself was often the object of his father's wrath by Ted's own design he would challenge his father on his return to the house just to protect his mother and his siblings from his pitiful excuse for a human father. It wasn't long before Ted's father didn't want to come home because Ted looked forward to beating the hell out of him every Friday and Saturday just for sport. The beatings and abuse soon stopped, but the damage was already done. The physical scars received by his mother healed but the memories and neglect forced her to liberate herself and she found another man to comfort her. Ted was hurt not because she was leaving her husband but because she was happy in the arms of a black man. A black man who was well to do, very well educated and for all practical purposes at a better social station than his mother; in fact Ted could not figure out for the life of him why Theodore, the black man, wanted to be with his mother. What his father and friends had said all along while he was growing up must have been true. They said "blacks wanted white women because it was forbidden fruit". Hell it must be true he thought back then. But now looking at himself he could see that after twenty years Theodore had raised his younger brother and sisters to become professionals and after his death just this year from cancer left his mother well off for the remainder of her life. Hell the other Ted had loved her and taken care of her in his absence. Ted felt noxious at the way he saw himself. He was just as abusive to his mother as his father had been without ever hitting her.

"Ted, honey I have Sissie's telephone number if you'd like it."

Ted turned to face Alice and she could see tears in his eyes accompanied by the shame he was so desperately trying to shed. Alice leapt up from the bed cover and ran to him embracing him she explained to him that what he was experiencing was alright, that he was not alone.

"But I was wrong Alice so wrong I hurt her all these years, I've hurt her." He cried as his strong woman held him in her arms. She could now resume the role of fulltime wife and relinquish the motherly role back to Ted's mom. Alice smiled as she still thought of who the "fifth column" could be.

CHAPTER 38

ALAS THE FIFTH COLUMN

Michael noticed the flickering candle lights dancing from beneath the bedroom door of Margarite's bedroom. She was not alone Michael's sensitive ears allowed him to hear her moans of ecstasy as she made love to Miles. He was happy for their new found union, but was still quite puzzled about the whole matter of human sexuality for Michael Zarkuhn had never known the experience of sex. He'd been on the planet almost as long as any sentient being who had made Earth their home; and though Michael had been pursued by the most beautiful women to have ever walked the planet an interest in sex always eluded him.

Michael's large fleshy package dangled from his shoulder as he quietly walked the long wing towards Special Agent Todd's room. As he passed the room of Senator Karen Stinger he heard Cheryl's laughter and the giggling of her lover. His package suddenly became restless and more difficult to handle as he got to the bedroom.

"What the hell is going on dude? Put me down man and please tell this is not some prelude to some homo liaison."

"You know Todd I like you better knocked out and I can arrange that. To answer your question this is not a liaison as you called it this is beddy bye time, now here get off my shoulder you're too heavy and by the way you need to lose that extra weight."

"I'm not obese."

"No Todd you're not obese, you're just plain fat. Now down south that may be how yall like your women and men but really it's not healthy nor is it appealing. I mean have you looked at yourself lately and you call yourself an agent, spplhh."

"Put me down."

"Gladly."

"Is this my room?"

"No dork I just dropped you off here to clean it … of course it's your room."

"Where's my key?"

"Todd does this look like Motel 6? Man its mansion not a hotel go on in and get some much needed sleep. Perhaps tomorrow you'll be on top of your game because right now you're too drunk and fat to play."

"You know something if I could whip your ass I would, but since I know that's not an option I'm going to bed, good night."

"Yeah that's a good idea go to bed Mr. Agent Man."

Michael had thoroughly enjoyed jabbing the DHS agent, but as he turned to head towards the opposite wing of the mansion where his room was located he spotted Peter standing at the corner at the end of the hall.

He was shaking his head and actually grinning apparently at the conversation he'd witnessed between Michael and Agent Todd. He waived Michael to follow him in an under hand motion as though he were tossing a soft ball. Michael followed him to what he realized was Peter's room. He once again recognized and enjoyed the wonderful aroma emanating from the old man servants room. Entering he marveled at the many candles glimmering orange and yellow hues as they radiated intermittently off the walls. The scene was reminiscent of a place he knew yet once again the where eluded him. Peter walked over to him and handed him a wine glass. The glass itself was very rare and embroidered with twenty four carat gold and Michael anxiously anticipated a great wine to match the vessel which would hold it.

Peter presented a bottle of Bordeaux 1953, from Chateau Latour a vineyard in Pauillac located in the Medoc Region of France for their drinking pleasure. Michael lived in the area during the late 1800s recalling that this particular vintage won awards and many accolades as one of the best in all of France and deservedly so. Peter poured some of the fine wine into his glass and handed it to Michael as Michael handed his empty glass to Peter, he repeated the act once more for himself.

"A toast to the success and protection of the Collective."

"Peter I couldn't have thought of a better toast, cheers."

"Now this is a fine Bordeaux Peter."

"What do you think of our present situation? It appears to me we are loosing through attrition wouldn't you say?"

"Peter I don't think you believe that at all. May I sit?"

"But of course forgive me. Over there would be most suitable, that chair there do you recognize its design, the symbol?"

"It couldn't be? That would literally make this almost eighteen hundred years old. You have a chair that belonged to Origen himself."

"Yes, but how would you know about Origen and this simple piece of furniture? Michael I know you have regenerative powers and you also once tried to mention to me that you were immortal, but now let me admit your knowledge has almost convinced me."

"Well I hope so, telling someone you're immortal could only mean you're either schizophrenic or it's true. I admit to being eccentric, but crazy that's debatable. Enough about me Peter it is you who is somewhat of an enigma. I mean just look around this room it is a virtual museum of wonderful artifacts and historical documents. Are those Latin scrolls over there?"

"Where?"

"Right there."

"No those are Greek writings that I've worked on in the last couple of years. I'm researching some church doctrines in order to document the inconsistencies in translation, just a hobby."

"You see that's what I'm talking about, reading Greek and how many other languages? Peter it's not something one expects from your stereotypical man servant or college professor for that matter. Well perhaps a college prof."

"It's really nothing just a hobby," stated Peter as he sipped his wine. He swung his right leg across the left leg and bounced it back and forth with his wine glass resting on his lap.

"I disagree what you are capable of doing very few scholars can do and I happen to know that only few men who've ever lived could do. But how did you come by these things and where were you schooled?"

"Now Michael I find that statement most interesting, it eludes and touches on your being immortal. Shall we discuss you being with some ancients in the past? I'm really fascinated by it all and would like to know more about my collection if you're up to it. I mean you've never really told me where you are from actually and how you came to be here."

"Perhaps some other time when we have the time. It's very late but before I retire I wanted to ask you if you think we have been infiltrated?"

"You mean a spy?"

"Yes a spy. I mean you're right the recent killings of our own and the assault on us from at least two other secret factions that we know of doesn't compute unless they feel it's worth the effort right."

"Michael, just try and remember the golden old rule within every secret order of "cause and effect" okay before you reach any conclusions. If I know and understand the nature of a thing as the Great Solomon beckoned his students to inquire, then I can get what ever answers and truth I desire with time. Maybe there is no spy. Maybe someone wants you to believe there is and then again perhaps one exists but desires you to believe the opposite."

"What!"

"Never mind Michael you're tired we'll discuss this later, but before you depart I wish to give you something."

Peter got up and walked over to the far corner of his room behind some large wooden trunks where he opened one of them. He removed an object from the trunk and approached Michael. In Peter's hands was a long flat box with ancient Hebrew writing on it. Peter held the box as though it contained jewelry in it, a necklace or something.

"That's doesn't have Kryptonite in it?"

Peter and Michael both chuckled as Michael sat his wine glass down.

"May I sit the glass down here?"

"Sure I'll get it later." Peter opened the box slowly as the candle lights bounced off their faces, the shadows and an occasional crackling from the fireplace sang ever so often as the heat warmed both men. The wonderful sight inside the flat box shined brightly; it was not difficult to see the surprise on Michael Zarkuhn's face, for his eyes lit bright gold at the sight of the image in front of him. Michael was not accustomed to being surprised but this presentation weakened his knees and before he knew what was happening he was down on both of them in complete and utter awe.

"It cannot be. What source of magic is this you conjure? They cannot be real for there is no way in heaven nor hell that they could be here before me here now in your room. How did you come by these? Who are you Peter?"

It was late when the Cardinal's motorcade arrived at the Monastery and the Cardinal was extremely tired. He had spent hours being driven around the streets of Los Angles and Beverly Hills because of his fascination with the city sights. He was helped from the limousine by his security detachment and entered through the large stone archway of the old building. The huge wooden doors screeched loudly as they were closed behind him. The rooms smelled of old fire wood mixed with incense and the rustic furniture was complimented by the many beautiful paintings, gold and silver ornaments which littered the walls. The monastery's ambience was already eerie and adding to this was the long heavy red flowing cape which graced the shoulders of the Cardinal whisking back and forth against the cobble stone walkway as he walked down the long dark damp halls. Cardinal Ricci's image unnerved his security entourage as the view was nothing less than that of a scene straight out of a Count Dracula movie.

"Your Excellency welcome."

"Colleeta, how have you been my dear?"

"Excellency finds me most well he does, yes."

"Where are my children?"

"They are here, follow me. They rest so sleepy were the children come this way Excellency, this way."

The frumpy old nun hobbled with great speed as she wobbled down one of the corridors towards Merie and little Tashi. The entourage could barely keep up with her and Cardinal Ricci felt pressured to show the security detachment that he could keep up with the old woman, but the distance growing between them reflected otherwise. The old nun glanced over her shoulder and quickly realized her over zealous movement was embarrassing her superior and she abruptly slowed her roll, literally.

"I apologize, sir it's not much further just right over here."

"Apologize for what? We're right behind you."

The Cardinal was breathing heavy and not alone at this task either as the security detachment inhale and exhaled deeply. The nun turned and continued on her trek smiling to herself at the little physical conquest she'd pulled off.

"Here sir this room here is where the lovelies are yes."

The nun stepped back to allow the Cardinal the courtesy of opening the door to the room. He stepped forward with authority as though to dare anyone else to still the moment from him. He slowly opened the door and walked in to see Merie lying on a large bed flanked by a huge stone fire place to the right of it and nestled next to her chest was Tashi. Tashi was clinging to her left shoulder and her long raven black hair covered most of his torso.

Cardinal Ricci was overcome by thoughts of being a family, but immediately brought his emotions under control. He twisted around and waived the onlookers away as though irritated by flies at a picnic. Spotting a large ornate chair to the left of the fireplace he walked over to it and positioned it a little more towards the bed so that he could view his illegitimate son and the boy's mother. He removed his cape and cap and neatly placed them on the arm of the massive chair. He was quiet so as to not waken the apples of his eye, but in reality oh how he wished they would come to and lay eyes upon him. He realized he would have a difficult time with Merie and that his son would not know who he was, realizing the young boy only knew Louis Tashido as his father. Louis never knew that the Cardinal had impregnated his wife Merie while they had clandestinely visited the Vatican three years earlier. The way the Cardinal saw it Louis owed him and Merie siring a child for him paid the debt for Louis' life. He had commissioned Louis Tashido to locate and bring back to the Vatican a priceless artifact. He'd even gotten the blessing of the Pope himself in supporting the project only to be embarrassed time and time again by Louis' failure to obtain the treasure. Now he had learned that in fact the treasure was successfully obtained by professor Tashido, but that it may have been intercepted by some group in America. However, there was talk of a double cross by Tashido on the deal, but none of that mattered because when Merie woke up the truth would be found. He was confident that his little whore would tell him where his treasure was or else.

Jimmy gathered the seven soldiers that had arrived with him outside the air terminal. Most of them were cussing up a storm at the security checks they had to endure.

"Hey look blokes stop your wining, if you all didn't look so much like bloody criminals you wouldn't get profiled. Anyway it could've been worse, just think if you were unfortunate enough to be black or Arab, huh? Really those folks would still be crawling up your rectums, ha, ha … ha."

"Paul was wondering why he hadn't heard from Jimmy when his cell phone started singing. He looked at the face and felt content.

"It's about time. Did you experience any troubles?"

"No boss, everything was just peachy accept for some of the guys feel a little feminine right about now after being violated by the US of A's finest airport security types, you know cavity searches and all."

"Oh yeah? Hell most of 'em should've felt at home or at least enjoyed it."
"Hell no, I mean we got searched at every point on the entire trip here. Personally I enjoyed mine the guy had small, tiny hands, hah."

"Jimmy you're out of control, you are out of control. It's good to have you here man. Look there are two SUVs waiting for you guys in the North parking area. You'll find the keys taped under the passenger back bumper okay. Are you getting this?"

"Yeah hold on let me write this down."

"Jimmy, Jimmy listen to me don't write shit down okay, do not ever write stuff down are you nuts? Just listen you will find the vehicles at U11 and the other at P2."

"Boss what's U11?"

"Jimmy the parking spots have alphanumeric indicators to identify the parking locations. Wait! Jimmy you do know what alphanumeric means right?"

"Sure boss I got it. U11 and P2 are the spots not a problem."

"Now Jim once you're in the vehicles call me and I'll give you your next instructions."

"Right boss."

"Oh and Jimmy you have the packages right?"

"Still got it boss we picked it up a baggage claim right before we came out."

"Great!"

Michael was no longer in a hurry to get to his room for he was too astonished by what he was being held before him in Peter's hands.

"I see them but I don't believe it. Those are the "stones of fire" from the Breastplate of Judgment right?"

"Yes you are correct grasshopper indeed these are some of the "stones of fire."

"Yes there's only six stones here, you're aware there are twelve stones total?"

"Auh yes, but I only have six so what do you think? So you have seen these before Michael?"

Michael felt fear from Peter's question. All of a sudden he was uncomfortable with where he found himself and with Peter. He decided to be candid and forthright with his friend.

"You know for some strange reason I feel extraordinarily uncomfortable and I can't for the life of me figure out why."

"Well that's perfectly alright Michael I think my questioning was rather abrupt and kind of unfair. I mean, how else could you have known of these stones' but to have read about them or heard throughout all of your wonderful travels?"

"It is I who is being unfair to you old friend. I have not only seen these stones before but I once owned them. They were indeed mine."

"Owned them, how?" Peter now closed the box with the gem stones still inside it and took a seat. His eyes were bright with anticipation and Michael also sat back down and began to explain.

"Wait before you explain Michael I need another drink this is absolutely incredible, my, my. Would like another glass of wine Michael."

"Yes, I think perhaps I need one too. Peter I told you about my regenerative abilities and I've somewhat mentioned my age or times which I was around, but I haven't been completely upfront with you. Peter what I'm about to tell you will seem even more bazaar than anything I've shared with you to date."

"Michael I don't see how that could be possible given the amazing things I have seen already."

"Okay here goes. I was sent here over nine thousand years ago or so."

"Okay and?"

"Well it was kinda like I was to be punished."

"Okay and?"

"I was also being retrained by being sent here."

"Okay I could see that and?"

"Well God sent me."

"Okay we're now moving towards bazaar, but not there yet and?"

"Well I'm Michael the Archangel."

"There! We're definitely there at bazaar."

"No I not finished and Peter?"

"Nope I'm afraid you are Michael, that last bit of info pretty much satisfies the bazaar category in its entirety."

"This secret can never be revealed to the others and wait a minute you've never once said to prove my statements or anything. Now I find that rather bazaar that you've just taken what I've told you and swallowed it."

"Michael I knew who you were all along. I just needed to make sure you weren't a spy that's all. That's why tonight I revealed one of my secrets, the stones to you because I trust that you believe in me. You see Michael, an Archangel would know about the stones, proved to be immortal, but he would also be one other thing and that I don't understand yet for there has been no test."

"What's that Peter?"

"He would be completely loyal, unquestionably loyal to God and the Elohim."

"Peter maybe six thousand years or so ago I would have agreed with you that this poor lost creature would have died for those you mentioned without question, but even Angels, mere messengers can grow up and learn of the arts of treachery, cunningness and deceit."

"You mean you're not as blindly passionate about your duties as you were when you were General of the Heavens, leader of the Malachim?"

"I share that title with many good brethren Peter. I no longer wish to play the role of the blind messenger who delivers news of babies due or destruction cometh I abjure the whole process. No Peter let the God of these people on this planet perform his own evil deeds to those whom he supposedly created or in some cases made in his and his wife's image. I quit."

"I know you do my son. I've dedicated my life to playing in the background the role of "my brother's keeper," in order to protect the innocent though it has not always been that way for me. Many, many years ago when I was younger I dedicated my life to the "Ascended Masters" and to the one called Jesus Christ by Christians. He literally changed my life and the way I saw myself, his death was an epiphany for me. I once desired to walk with God but I too grew up and desire to be as God, however, now I'm satisfied with just doing a good God's work when I can. There have come before me once great men like Enoch who walked with God and was transformed into the mighty Metatron, The patriarch Jacob later known as Israel who is none other than your good friend Uriel and of course let me not forget the prophet Elijah riding his fiery chariot into the heavens only to become the tallest of all angels Sandalphon. They pray for that which they once were, men, but now they have been relegated to delivering messages, galactic messages like whipping boys. It is better to be a man or woman with free will than an Angel with no will at all."

Michael nervously stood up and placed his drink down slowly. He was feeling strange again not quite right about all that he was hearing. Michael was being poked and prodded by all the statements made by Peter and yet it was completely innocent; but he'd never felt this vulnerable before any man and even as an angel only his master and the high council of elders made him this way. No there was one other who bothered him but Michael had discharged him with the help of Gabriel and Uriel at Jehovah's command during the civil war."

"Peter who in Gods name are you?"

"Now Michael that's a funny question."

CHAPTER 39

ITS' GETTING HOT IN HERE

Sergeant O'Connell drank the last of his leaded coffee and threw down an extra dollar for the tip at his favorite diner.

"Hey see ya tomanyana Nance." He stepped out into the brisk bitter Boston morning air. He smelled a rat and he didn't care what anyone said it was in his Irish copper blood to smell such things. He knew something stank with Paul Constantine. The shooting incident that had occurred last week at the old Plantard Mansion on the outskirts of the city and the special visit by Ms. Thang from Interpol didn't add up. O'Connell was losing his grip on all of the cases and that he wasn't going to let happen.

"As soon as I get to the precinct I'm going to rock and roll. I got to get a handle on this mess and today's the day baby."

Merie was hot and removed the covers gently from her legs and torso. Her little baby, Tashi rolled closer to her as if he were trying to suckle her. She peered down at his innocent face and held the small soft hand. His touched induced a smiled for here was some joy in her life through all of the turmoil she'd seen over the last few weeks. Somehow she could feel hope beaming in her, that is until she heard the words coming from the fireplace, "Beati mites qouniam ipsi possidebunt terram."

So much for hope as she frantically fought the bed spread in an effort to cover the exposed flesh. She knew immediately who it was quoting to her that "the meek shall inherit the Earth for they are blessed", in so many words. Her Latin was a bit rusty but she got the gist.

"Your Eminence, Cardinal what are you doing here?"

"Husband, lover, even friend will do my dear. I've come to visit of course, please forgive my staff for bringing you here but security you know these days is paramount."

"I understand Cardinal Ricci, but why are ..."

"All in good time my sweet. I sincerely trust that Father Mitchell's staff has treated you well, no?"

"Yes they have been very courteous."

"Good now would you like to eat or talk first?"

"Please Cardinal I'd like to allow Tashi to sleep longer and I will eat with you later if you will allow?"

"Very well my sweet and I see you still remember your Latin albeit you're a tiny bit rusty, but we shall soon attend to that. I'll meet with you later for dinner then."

The Cardinal took his time putting on his cape and cap and strolled out of the room at snails pace closing the large squeaking door behind him.

Merie knew what the dirty old man was thinking and what he wanted, it made her sick to think of it. She had to escape the monster but how could she. She'd take the next few hours or so to figure out some solution to her dilemma. He was going to grill her about Louis' last project and she had not one iota of useful information and that would definitely motivate the Cardinal to punish her which she believed is what he wanted to do anyway. She froze with panic at the very thought for her last punishment was a baby from the Cardinal's loins not her husband's.

"Thanks Captain I owe you one and I told you I had a sneaky suspicion about her. I just knew it. No broad that goodlook'n stays in this business unless she's some sort of freak or someth'n."

O'Connell was sitting in his car in the parking lot of the station as he received confirmation from his superior that the Interpol agent sent to help interrogate Paul Constantine was indeed their agent, but that she had not been dispatched by Interpol to assist anyone in America. Sergeant O'Connell had used a green stamp with his Captain to call and check the statuesque beauty out. His hunch was right on point, but why Constantine? What was her connection to him? He decided he should ask her especially since the Captain had given him the go ahead.

As Irish luck would have it as soon as O'Connell got to the hotel where the beautiful Contessa Hannabolas was staying she walked out the front door of the lobby and onto the street. Sergeant O'Connell remained in his car and decided to track her. She flagged down a taxi and he followed it to the rather seedy side of town, an area the sergeant knew well, in fact he was just in the neighborhood a couple of days before investigating the death of a young black man who at least one witnessed claimed a white man was responsible for. That white man was Paul Constantine. Being white and in this neighborhood without having grown up there was treacherous in and of itself, but for a foreigner to live there was news worthy and strange.

"Well what do yah know? Why, is she over here this is really getting interesting." O'Connell reached down to drink some of his coffee and realized the Styrofoam cup was old and worse void of coffee.

"Damn no coffee or doughnuts this stakeout's gonna suck."
Contessa got out of the taxi a substantial distance from the hotel in which Paul was staying and walked to a hotel directly across the street, another dive.

"Now that's something you don't see everyday. Now what's my beauty doing here in this neck of the woods? Jimmy I call you right back, you got the info okay, right? Good bye."

Paul spotted the dark, long legged international cop before she entered the hotel across from where he was staying. This would be easy enough to handle, she was either keeping the wraps on him or she was kinky like him, naw, it was definitely the first he thought. No one could be as sick and kinky as Paul he wondered and the thoughts made him hot.

O'Connell would wait until he thought Contessa was in a room and then make his move for a little reconnaissance. This was going to be a cold one because he couldn't chance anyone spotting exhaust continually coming from his parked car from down the street so he turned off the heat.

"I'll wait until she gets nested and then I'll make my move from the back of the building to do a little snooping." Paul said out loud to himself while closing his curtains and proceeding down to the lobby of the roach hotel.

Michael had excused himself from Peter's room earlier due to his uneasiness and his dear friend Peter understood completely. He just needed some time to sort his own questions out and to get back in control operationally. He headed to the security area down in the basement to review incoming COMSEC or communications security messages coming in from his agents around the world. He also wanted to make sure the grounds of the mansion were secured so he monitored the infrared, ultra violet, sound and visual exploitation devices surrounding the mansion for breaches or enemy signatures.

He saw where Maurice Steely the Asian Station Chief had already dispatched young Clarence Lehchin to Boston for special duty detail.

"Good Lehchin will be here tomorrow morning." Michael stated as he laid the message down he noticed a communication from Italy informing the Collective of a special visitor to America from the Vatican, a very high level visitor but not the Pope. This was curious activity and to Michael Zarkuhn's delight he marveled at the fact that all seven American station chief s had acknowledged and tasked an asset to ghost the movements of that visitor when in their sector. Michael typed out a "well done" message to all of his chiefs and asked for them to report any possible zone contamination and what they assessed the contagion to appear to be and what other possibilities there could be based on any past historical data on the contacts they possessed.

Then he saw that the west coast station chief was ahead of his game. The visitor listed in the report was a Cardinal, but not just any Cardinal it was the Secretary of State for the Vatican and he was in Los Angles, California at a monastery on Bakers Street where a Father Mark Mitchell was listed as being in charge of the order. The report further states, "that no less than ten armed guards of a highly trained level" were accompanying him. The apparent lead for the security detachment was listed in the Collective data base as a Knight of Malta member and former British SAS officer. This type of security team was not just used to protect dignitaries, but this caliber of firepower was also used as a strike team. Michael was relieved they were not in Boston at least not yet so he could prepare for them just in case they visited.

"Why go to an obscure church facility that doesn't have any real significance unless there's something or someone you wish to see?"

"Michael good morning I thought that was you. Talking to yourself these days?"

"Good morning Margarite you're up awfully early and no I was thinking out loud."

"Early, oh I wanted to get a jump on some things today."

"Didn't you sleep well Margarite?"

"Michael never better, I had the best sleep I've had in a long time."

"Really?"

"Oh while I'm thinking about it I needed to discuss a matter with you, however, you were rather busy last night."

"Alright what is it?"

"I can't recall whether I informed you that Merie and her son were to arrive yesterday from California and …"

"You say they were coming from California? What part of California were they departing from?"

"Louis and Merie have a home in north of Los Angeles in Lompoc. She was to leave from the airport for Boston for security reasons.

"I wasn't aware that she was inbound, but nonetheless we know she didn't arrive right?"

"I called every airline and she never arrived. There's no record of her canceling and taking another later flight either. Michael I know I shouldn't be so pessimistic but I can't help but think the worst."

"After all you've been through I can't blame you for worrying. I'll contact some eyes and ears in the area and see what we can find out. Margarite I have a feeling it's going to turn out fine."

"Michael, I suggest we all meet at eleven o'clock to bring everyone up to date and to formulate some contingencies do you agree?"

"Good idea! Mmm, it shouldn't interfere with the Senator and I."

"That's right you and the Senator will be talking with the agent from homeland. Perhaps we should just play this morning by ear? Would you like me to have breakfast brought down here to you?"

"Yes, that would be lovely thank you Margarite."

Margarite headed back upstairs via the elevator and Michael fired off a message to the LA station chief. This time he added a specific request for information on Merie and her baby, indicating that a possible abduction may have occurred.

"How much was that again."

"Twenty five dollars missy, yes twenty five a day."

Contessa reached into her designer purse pushing her gun aside and while pulling out the correct currency she inconspicuously scoped the lobby area at the same time. She was very much at home in this setting because most of her time was spent undercover in some of the most remote and dangerous town and cities in the world. It was her specialty whether living in Paris, Tikrit or on the out skirts of Cairo just waiting for the right climate to cultivate her web. A few rags, a little nappy hair from lack of maintenance a few missed baths and she could pull off the typical indigenous female act anywhere; or apply just the opposite in the hygiene and maintenance department and achieve the same results on the upper crust of any society. Of course it helped to be fluent in multiple languages, which was Contessa's special gift. Having no formal education to her credit she was however, a virtuoso in the art of languages, speaking a known twenty different diversified tongues Ms. Contessa Hannabolas was the equivalent to a mammal chameleon in the international undercover arena and known for blending in among the peoples of any community on the planet.

"I will need the use of the telephone there is a phone in the room right?"

"No, but we can remedy that. There's a thirty dollar deposit for the phone." The desk clerk reached underneath the front counter and pulled out a black phone that would definitely need a good cleaning before usage.

"Oh! There's also a twenty dollar incidental charge as well." Hannabolas was pulling out the money while still maintaining her innocent gracious smile as though none of the hassle was an inconvenience. She knew that this desk clerk might be her key for information in the future so she'd appease her as long as the situation called for it. She'd learned that much over the years in the undercover game.

"Here I got it now. Heavy little bugger huh? Oh which way's my room dear?"

"Up the stairs take a left down the hall and last door on the right."

"I'm sorry do you have anything facing the street?"

"Naw sure don't."

"Are you sure hun?"

"Well let's see." The lady behind the counter looked Contessa up and down and seemed to be thinking the same thing Contessa had surmised that she should be nice to someone who had so much of what she wanted, some more of those twenty dollar bills she'd seen remaining in the pretty woman's purse.

"Damn look at that there, I got one for you. Give me that key and take this one and if you need anything you ask for Ginnie. My father-in-law owns the place so I got connections."

"I can see that and thanks so much, you said up the stairs and …"

"Make a right and straight ahead. See ya."

Paul sat on the trash can in the back of his hotel as he smoked a cigarette. His cell phone began to sing.

"Yeah, good now underneath your seat you'll find a map. I want you and the boys to get to know that map real well. The one with red marker writing is the target which located outside the city. The yellow marker is where I want you and the guys to get a couple of rooms. Now Jimmy get two or three different locations in the same area okay, I don't want all of you guys in the same place got it?"

"Got it, I'll contact you when we get settled boss."

Paul put his cigarette out and headed towards the back of an alley adjacent to the hotel between a Dollar Store. He quickly jogged across the street to the other side far enough up the street as not to have been seen by anyone looking out of the hotel across the street from the hotel where he was staying. Once across he made his way pass a warehouse and over to the next street behind the hotel where Contessa had entered. He strolled slowly towards the back of the hotel where he noticed the parking lot and a backside entrance void of security.

"This is good mate, real good." Paul smiled his scheme was going as planned.

Sergeant O'Connell couldn't take the cold inside his vehicle any more and decided enough time had elapsed to start his recon mission. He got out of his car and was relieved to find that it was warmer outside the car than inside. He shuffled down the side walk passed two little old ladies shoveling snow in the front of a hair salon and politely spoke.

"Good morning ladies, good day to yah."

"Good morning sir and thank you."

O'Connell continued as he heard one of the elders say, "now he was a pleasant gentleman too bad my Elsie's not around to have met him."

"Mable your daughter is black that nice man's white."

"Oh was he?"

"Hell yeah Mable, he's as white as Casper that damn ghost."

"O'Connell was holding back his laughter so hard he thought he was going to give up the ghost, Casper."

The Irish cop stopped in front of the hotel and looked up at the front of Paul Constantine's hotel just to see if he was scoping the frontal area then he entered the lobby Contessa entered. A Mexican lady was cleaning the common area of the roach motel, she glanced at him briefly. She quickly turned away which alerted

O'Connell that she probably thought he was there for her. Needless to say when he looked back around she was gone.

"Crap, just like a damn roach. She must think I'm an immigration agent."

"Sir, can I help you?"

"Maybe, I assume you work here?"

"Yeah so what's it to you. I'm trying to locate someone, a woman about this tall with dark black hair, bronze complexion and I can't reiterate enough how bronze her skin is and oh, damn good looking. Have you seen anyone meeting that description?"

"What you want her for?"

"I just want to talk to her, okay."

"How do I know you're not some kind of pimp or someth'n come to whip on her in my place?"

"Will this help?" O'Connell flashed his badge in the clerks face.

"Now enough of the pleasantries where is she?"

"By law I got to notify her and all." The clerk could see all her future earnings from the pretty occupant going out the widow as she picked up the phone to notify Contessa that she had a visitor.

"Hello Ms. Haba, Hayba, damn anyway you have a guest down in the lobby who wants to talk to you."

O'Connell glared at the clerk and showed his badge placing his index finger over his mouth clearly indicating that she had better not let on that the visitor was a cop.

"No I don't know who he is." The clerk's eyes looked for O'Connell's approval at how she'd handled the question she received thumbs up for her effort.

"Okay I'll tell him. She said to tell you she'd be right down."

"You did very well now if you would get loss back there for just a while. Where's the back area? Is there an elevator or just the stairs here?"

"Just the stairs but there's another set of stairs to the back down the hall."

"Thanks go on get loss for awhile okay."

O'Connell knew Contessa might probably try and pull a quick one on him so he headed down the first floor hallway to the back stairwell and stood underneath the stairs and waited.

Contessa locked and loaded her weapon a compact Walter P5. She slipped her heels off and put on flats matching her outfit's color though. She wanted to be prepared but also fashionable. Hell even in the mountains of Afghanistan she dressed fashionably llama hair and all.

Contessa walked slowly over to the window and peered out from the corner of the curtain to the street below. She could see no activity just a young black man on crutches trying to sell drugs on the corner of the hotel directly in front of hers where Paul Constantine resided.

Paul pranced through the back parking lot of the hotel acting as though he were a tenant at the hotel who'd forgotten something inside checking his pockets from to time as though to say "I thought I put it there," to unsuspecting onlookers. As he got to the back door he could see entry was only allowed using an electronic key held by the occupants and this pissed him off. He could not believe this dive across the street from his dive had electronic keys, damn he thought "I should've stayed here."

Paul had a choice either force his way in or wait until someone to provide entry for him. From out of nowhere a white lady with few teeth in the front area of her mouth startled him appearing at the back door from out of the blue.

"Left your key in your room huh? I noticed you from the laundry out the basement window come on in."

She pushed the door open and Constantine entered cautiously. He knew the old toothless hag could be a decoy.

"What room you in hon? I said what room you in good looking I'll let you in I'm head of housekeeping. I got all the keys know what I mean?"

"You know I don't quite remember the room number."

"There's no need to go to the front desk cause, I got my own occupancy list in my office that'll show your room and all the keys right?"

"Sure lady you got all the keys, right." Paul repeated as he surveyed the area with his hands in his coat.

Sergeant O'Connell could here voices around the corner from him and recessed further under the stairs trying to conceal himself from anyone approaching from the direction of the voices.

"Hey is this place private we're going? I mean since you have all the keys and all."

"Damn this is my lucky day. You know I love that accent you got. You don't happen to also have a dirty mouth do yah?"

"Shuuush."

"Right, yeah you're right we need to be incon., incoe, conspit, to hell with it, damn quiet. We can go to my office in the laundry room ain't nobody there. The Mexican chick just grabbed her bag and took off like she seen a ghost or immigration man, come this way goodlook'n."

The battled weary looking woman with her Waffle House fashion guided Paul down one flight of stairs into a large room with linen everywhere and large buggies parked against the wall. The industrial washing machines and dryers all rattled in unison indicating that the lady, although ugly as hell was a hard worker. Paul looked around and noticed an office which he immediately headed for. He pulled a white linen sheet from one of the shelves as he headed for the office. Once in the room he collated his thoughts, the head housekeeper followed closing the door behind them.

Paul was in deep thought. "Lock it."

"Right I need to lock it."

He began to remove his shirt pulling his left arm out of the sleeve. "Come here and sit down."

"Sure baby, sure I'll sit down." The woman was drooling which made Constantine ill.

"Now take off your top ... no real slow and turn away from me so I can relish the moment. You know use my imagination."

"Damn I knew it. I knew you were the romantic type when I spotted you coming from the back parking lot. I done struck gold. You gonna give it to me good right. Now don't take this wrong but, I like it rough not that I'm trying to be pushy or anything hon, but you can hurt me if you want a little."

Paul placed two rounds to the back of the innocent woman's head.
One to the base of the spine and the other dead center in the crown of her head; blood sprayed everywhere to include him, but he'd figured the sanguine spatter in his calculations so he conveniently draped the sheet he removed from the shelf earlier on the front of him from his shoulders down. He gently kissed his silencer and rubbed it across his face while he surveyed his handy work.

"You said you liked it rough. How was that honey? That rough enough for you, ay lass?" Paul proceeded slowly up the cement basement stairs.

Contessa decided she would go out back and make her way around to the front entrance for a surprise visit to see who was waiting for her in the lobby. As she walked down the stairs Paul made his way meticulously up the basement stairs. O'Connell removed his 9mm from its holster and pressed his back hard against the cold stone brick under the staircase as he heard someone approaching.

Contessa Hannabolas felt something was wrong and as she stepped to the floor off the last stair step, she heard someone call out her name.

"Well I don't believe my eyes. Contessa is that you? No it couldn't be you not you in this part of town. I must say you are full of surprises my little Negroid beauty."

"If it isn't Mr. Constantine what are you doing here?" By this time Contessa was not at a disadvantage her weapon was clearly in her jacket pocket pointed at Paul and he definitely saw it.

"What am I doing where?"

"Here, in this hotel? What are you doing in this hotel Paul?"

"You, I long to be with you my beauty, I came to visit you and to talk."

"Now you know that's not possible right? I can not discuss anything with you because this is an official inquiry so I must go now."

"I don't think so. No my littal pritty."

"You're not going to let me go?"

"No, I meant I don't think your visit is that official, nope not at all."

"That's preposterous I can assure you that this is a serious matter and that your involvement in questionable activity throughout Europe and now this country for that matter may be your undoing."

"You're right I've been a little mischievous I'm a bad boy so spank me. The way I see it, is you're a rogue out on your own and if its one thing I know when I see it is a rogue, a pretty one but a rogue nonetheless."

O'Connell wouldn't dare move he was getting more information listening to these twisted killers' quarrel than he could get holding them down at the station. He'd let them continue to talk for awhile then bust them up.

"Paul your shirt's not tucked in and is that lipstick on your cheek? Interesting tattoo that double snake thing on your chest has Paul been naughty as usual?" The beautiful woman walked closer to him trying to get a closer look.

"That's close enough my beauty right there will be just comfy for both of us."

"That's not lipstick is it Paul?"

"Sure it's lipstick it's called "Kiss of Death" would you like to try some?" Paul used his sleeve to wipe the blood from his cheek while holding his weapon under his coat ready to pop the well trained beauty should the need arrive.

The air was deathly still as though everything was in slow motion for the moment. All three parties could feel the other's thoughts. The silence between Contessa and Paul was confusing to O'Connell he was fixated on the snake tattoo description referenced by Contessa. Even more confused was Contessa who wanted this show over like yesterday. Looking deep into Paul's eyes she reaffirmed he was a killer of he purest sort and what was worse he enjoyed it without any remorse. In fact, the spatter of blood on his face suggested he'd played the predator role quite recently.

She didn't find him or his persona attractive in the least bit, but he would never know it; for the minute the egomaniac thought she wasn't interested in him and that he might not stand a chance at a possible conquest of her he would surely kill her. She realized he knew she had another agenda and that it had nothing to do with Interpol. Her task now was to ensure he did not learn what her true agenda really was.

Paul's loins burned at the thought of doing her right there on the stairs in the hallway. His lusty desire was heightened when he remembered being accosted by the hotel housekeeping toothless wonder before he exterminated her in the basement. Paul just knew Contessa found him attractive but he needed to play a little harder to get so as not to appear so easy. If he was too easy and willing she would not be interested in him and well she might even try and kill him. Paul had to play this cool and maybe he'd get to lay her, find out what she was really up to and then kill her.

"Hey mister what are you doing?" The front desk clerk asked O'Connell. "Oh it's you. Did you find …?"

O'Connell was desperately waiving his hand trying to get the woman to go away as he tried to remain hidden under the stairs."

"Ooops!" O'Connell let out the stupid little playful remark as he stepped in sight of the two having the standoff in the hallway.

"Did you see that? Was she talking to you or me? Paul was she talking to you or me?"

"I'd say she was...." Paul placed his index finger over his lips and motioned to the stairs before he saw the Irish cop pointing his gun at him.

"I'd say the clerk was talking to him that poster boy of America's finest standing right there."

Paul approached the staircase in slow, methodical combat fashion, repositioning himself for an alternative shot at the now revealed Boston police detective.

"Okay you two what the hell's going on?"

"My God Sergeant O'Connell it's you. What are you doing here we don't have any doughnuts?" Paul was the only one to laugh at his cliché remark.

"Yes good question what are you doing here sergeant? This is an official matter."

"Bull excrement ma'am I agree with him, your boyfriend Paul there. I don't think your business is official so the question is what is your reason for being here? No sudden moves folks I'm real jittery I've only had three cups of coffee this morning and no doughnuts. Hell I might pull a Los Angeles Police move on your asses so go easy."

The three stood at then end of the stairs, at the end of the hallway at their wits end holding their guns not knowing who to shoot or who would shoot first. All three were in deep thought, Contessa was glad she wore her flats in case she needed to be extremely mobile. O'Connell was glad he hadn't another cup of coffee he was nervous enough; and Paul was glad he didn't make love to the toothless wonder lying dead in the basement. The comical standoff continued.

"Hey! Is anyone else hot in here?" Really is it just me or is it really hot in here."

"Paul you're right it is hot in here, Contessa what do you think?"

"I'm hot too I'm going take my cloths off. What, just my jacket you know you two have dirty minds. Get a life."

Contessa grinned as she removed her coat alternating the gun from one unencumbered hand to the next.

CHAPTER 40

CHANGE OF PLANS NEXT STOP CITY OF ANGELS

"Was that me?"

"No I'm pretty sure it's mine?"

"You're both wrong it's my cell, Hello. Hey Captain. No sir, yes sir well pretty successful. No I mean she didn't give me the slip no."

"Hello. Yes this is he, Paul." Constantine couldn't believe the poor timing of the call to him.

"I'd like to speak with Mr. Paul please." The older female voice requested on Paul's cell phone.

"Is this Mr. Constantine, please?"

"Sister this is me go ahead what is it you have for me?"

Sergeant O'Connell and Paul were easing away slowly from the center of activity but still pointing their guns randomly at one another while attempting to listen to their phone calls.

"You are both pathetic. Look at the two of you." Contessa couldn't believe the scene before her. It was like performing a bad role in a tragic Broadway comedy.

"Hello, Contessa Hannabolas speaking. Oh yes your Excellency I have everything under control." She began to move away from the two men with he same caution they too were exercising. Her weapon oscillated from Paul to the detective as she too listened to the caller on her cell phone.

"What the hell!" The front desk clerk turned around in the middle of the hall as she quickly glanced at the weird group before her.

"You people are on some serious shit, if you got issues get tissues." With that she slid into her back office not even contemplating the thought of alerting the authorities, because one of their boys in blue was in the hallway of the hotel with two other nuts.

Each one of them felt the need to slip away and silence the clerk but for different reasons and in different ways, but for now the telephone calls were obviously important and their first bullet was already reserved for the present company in front of them. They would have to take their chances that time was on their side.

"So honey what was the meeting about last night?"

"Now Karen you know I'm not at liberty to tell you that."

"Cheryl it's me Karen. It must have been serious it took long enough, I swear it reminded me of a damn democratic filibuster against one of the President's "New World Order" assholes."

"No matter I can't divulge the content to you. What does it matter all of the members will be informed soon enough."

"Really?"

"Let's go for breakfast girl. You realize Peter will be calling for us in a minute anyway."

"Miles I think it just awful we cannot have funeral services for or attend them for all of our departed friends and their families."

"Margarite there will be a time for tears and a proper showing of respect, but we, the Collective are under siege and what's worst we don't know from whom."

"It still saddens me."

Miles caressed Margarite around her shoulders as they both sat up in bed reading before heading downstairs to breakfast.

"Knock! Knock!"

"One moment, I'll be right there."

"Hey hi there who the hell are you? I'm J.P Rockdale at yah survace. I jus stopped by to welocum yue to ouwha home and to invot yah to brakefust."

"Well J.P., J.P. right? That's awfully neighborly of you."

"Hey we met befoe, mattafact yue save ma life in Atlanda, I be damn."

"J.P., mmm I don't know J. I don't remember that. Hey have you been drinking?"

"Awh, yeah why?"

"J.P. it's sort of early isn't it?"

"So what's your point son?"

J.P. turned and walked down the hall sluggishly allowing gravity to assist him down the winding stair case.

"Hey J. are you related to Ted Kennedy?" The agent yelled to Rockdale.

"No, why?"

"Never mind J.P. see you at breakfast."

"I am so glad to be with you here this morning for breakfast my dear. Did you sleep well?"

Merie sat back slightly while a white cloth napkin was placed across her lap by one of the monks, a very young, but callous faced man.

"Thank you, no I didn't sleep well at all."

"Oh no, that's not pleasant."

"I did not rest well because I've been kidnapped, forcibly removed from my home and brought here for what? Nobody has explained anything to me and I resent it terribly. You expect me to rest under these conditions?"

"My dear you sound so bitter. You know you are a guest here and well you and I we have ties don't we? I merely needed to see my son. How's he doing? Not still asleep, boy they sleep a lot at that young tender age don't they?" But then I suspect they rather need much rest at that age with all the running and energy they have, yes."

"What do you want of us?"

"Watch, that tone with me my dear, do not become too familiar as to border on being contemptuous. What I want is the relic simply the item for which I and the church paid for handsomely that's all."

"I know nothing of a relic. Please be specific what item did the church pay for? Who was paid, Louis? Is that why he was murdered?"

"You're trying my patience dear eat your eggs they'll get cold."
Merie tried to think of what it could possibly be that the Cardinal was talking about as she tried to stomach her meal.

"More caffei, yes durum excoctum, I like my eggs hard boiled and you my dear more coffee?"

"I don't recall any relics that Louis was looking for. He was working on a project involving the "Tables of Testimony." Merie's eyes bulged as it hit her. "You think Louis located the Tablet? That's why you've disrupted my life? I can't believe this. If Louis had found such an important find he would have told me." She paused as she remembered her husband's ties to the Collective. She tried to relax and gather herself as she realized what her impetuous dead husband probably did, double crossed the Catholic Church or worse Cardinal Ricci.

"Maybe then this could be true? Perhaps your trusting husband kept this from you, maybe?"

"He would never do it?"

"Just like he would never double cross the Catholic Church, eeh? Such treachery! We know he was connected to another secret organization here in this Godless country and you will assist me in learning of them."

"I abhor you I hate you. I will never help you I'm tired of being punished for being female, for marrying a fool, for being a damn slave of the Catholic." She was standing at the table screaming at the Cardinal when his security detail showed up to investigate the yelling. The security detail was too shocked to react as Merie continued to barrage the prominent cleric with insults. The Cardinal's detail stared in amazement at her courageousness and accurate assessment of the German Vatican transplant.

"And another thing I can't believe I sired your child, not with that penis the size of Vienna and I mean the sausage not the city, you sick bastard." Merie was gesturing with her right index finger and thumb about an inch apart still screaming at the Catholic cleric. The security detail were baffled by the Vienna sausage and penis size remark, but were making headway in figuring it out due to Merie's hand gestures. This brought about smiles and grins as each man's light bulb popped on over her anatomical insult.

"What are you just standing there for? Shut her up, silence her now! I'll not be insulted by that whore, shut her up."

Two of the body guards grabbed Merie and she proved surprisingly difficult to control. One of them began to place her in a choke hold much to the displeasure of the Cardinal.

"Don't kill or harm her you fool remove her to a more discrete place where no dignified true believers may allow her ranting to violate their ears and another thing I will hear no more of this matter ever, understood? Is that understood?"

As the body guards nodded in agreement they dragged Merie away. Cardinal Ricci was in disbelief how he'd misjudged his mixed breed Indonesian harlot. To have carried on the way she had was clearly an indication that she didn't know anything useful or that she had gone mad. The question now was should he still interrogate her. His decision of course was to do what he would enjoy, he would practice some Spanish inquisition techniques on Merie that he had read about, after all she'd earned it after her unacceptable tirade.

"Guard where's the old lady Colleeta get her at once."

The guard located Colleeta in her room. She was startled as her bedroom door was opened unannounced by the guard and the expression she presented him told him she was not amused.

"Cardinal Ricci wishes to see you at once."

She placed the telephone down and began to address the guard in a stern motherly tone as she wobbled towards him.

"Young man, don't ever just enter another's room without exercising proper etiquette by announcing yourself and only then after being acknowledge and allowed to enter said party's room shall you enter. Is there any part of this instruction you do not understand dear?"

The young guard gave an affirmative nod and allowed the frumpy nun to continue pass him. He stood dumbfounded by the nun's eloquent articulation, not the usual for her.

"Good morning everyone" Agent Todd greeted everyone as he strolled into the large dining room where he recognized Senator Stinger and a few other faces from the hall gathering the night before.

"Good morning. Everyone this is Special Agent Chris Todd."

"Hello, good morning how are you Mr. Todd?" A smorgasbord of greetings bombarded the hungry confused agent as he sat at the table trying to keep his head from throbbing.

"So how did you rest Chris?"

"Senator that's an unfair question I have a hangover okay, like you couldn't have guessed."

"Excuse me, no one told you to drink yourself into oblivion."

"What's wrong with that, works for me," popped J.P. Rockdale as he sipped his Bloody Mary.

Ted was quick to respond, "we realize that J.P., trust we realize that."

Slight laughter rang out in the huge dining room as the sound of silverware and porcelain cups sang out of tune.

"Has anyone seen Michael?" The Senator asked as she dipped another spoonful of eggs on her plate.

"I left him in the center downstairs earlier."

"Thanks Margarite, I need to meet with him later."

"That reminds me. Is everybody present? Good. We have an eleven o'clock meeting in the conference room."

"Really, this should be interesting."

"Not you Todd, just board members." The Senator glared at Todd like his mother use to do when he was little, so now he felt compelled to pour it on.

"Why not me Senator? Because I'm a guest and even though I work for Uncle Sam I know a lot about business heck I might be able to contribute significantly to your board meeting."

He looked at Senator Stinger with a piece of bacon dangling from his mouth chewing it up as though he was a reptile swallowing prey he offered her a big grin.

"You're not invited don't push Todd."

"Would you like some more crow, I mean coffee Sir." Peter asked Special Agent Todd as he stood to the agent's right side smirking at him.

"Yes, yes I would thank you."

Michael was still going through reports as he was reading about the failed assault which occurred at the mansion while he was in Hong Kong. He saw where his friend Peter had thwarted a home invasion by the assault team that Margarite believed to be Brotherhood connected. Michael was not so confident they were Brotherhood as he reviewed the pictures and the forensics from the attack. It was subtle but the signs were there, the attackers were not from the Illuminati, the church or any other western esoteric secret society but clearly Islamic extremist. This group must have known about the Tables of Testimony possibly being at the mansion although at that time it was not on the premises. He'd made a mistake the day he did the reconnaissance of the mansion grounds and found the two men surveying the property. Michael realized an attempt was made to lead him to believe that the men were affiliated with the "Son of Jared", but they were probably in fact members of a Jihadist group. Michael was now confused and realized that this whole scenario involved a twisted network of groups who would eventually see to it that every member of the Collective perished in an effort to gain the Tablet. But someone had to be orchestrating all of them, perhaps without them knowing it. This would explain the bombardment from so many adversaries.

"If they all keep targeting and killing the members there'll be no one to interrogate or give them information, unless they feel so confident that what they want is in fact here in the mansion and that's what they are trying to do annihilate us here at the sight." Michael knew then a spy had to be amongst them. He was resolute in weeding them out once and for all today without fail. Michael needed to get closer to whom ever it was so he headed upstairs with his empty breakfast tray.

Paul hung up his cell phone first. His posturing became more bellicose after the phone call and O'Connell and their female companion could see it. They both became tense wanting to get off the phones so they could prepare for any of Paul's surprises and so both hung up simultaneously.

"What you guys don't trust me?"

"Should we Paul? Why should we trust you? You're a bloody killer."

"That's telling him Contessa let him have it babe."

Contessa glared at the detective as though he was odiferous and then continued to watch Paul.

"Hey why that look? I don't stink do I? Contessa you're not so squeaky clean here either we did some checking with Interpol out of France there and nada, yep nada. No one knew you were even in the country and you're not known by anyone but some head huncho guy."

"You are as stupid as you look detective. You little puppet, I generally work undercover. Only two persons ever know my whereabouts thus the word undercover."

"Oh, we didn't know that. So we probably blew your cover huh?"

"Yes brainiac, probably." She sighed in exasperation as she backed up from her position a little more to put distance between her and Paul.

"Someone's cell phone is going off again."

"Hey it's mine. Hello Paul here, no not now. Pull over right now, pull over. There's been a change of plans. I'll call you back, okay."

"Are you sure?" The lovely brown woman asked Paul.

"I'm I sure of what. Are sure you're going to be able to return the call to whoever that was?"

"Hey calm down, Contessa don't push any of the wrong buttons. The way I see this is that I'm the law here and I should take charge, so both of yews put your weapons down and we'll go in and talk about this okay? Do it now!" The police officer double gripped his sidearm with a more stringent hold posturing closer to both parties and raising his voice.

Both Contessa and Paul glared at Detective O'Connell and pointed their weapons on him at the same time, he suddenly felt left out and rather stupid.

"Shut up's" were heralded from Contessa and Paul to which O'Connell graciously complied.

"You know here's an idea let's shoot him, I mean face it we're both international with much bigger pictures to attend to and him well he's just a cop, a flat foot on the local beat. I say we both pop him that way we never know which one of our bullets really kills him see and well later should we be caught the authorities shall have a dickens of a time figuring which piece of metal caused the fatality. I imagine it's a minor technicality but surely one that absolutely drives pathologist and the prosecutors bonkers."

"Yes, I could see that. The question will be asked, "which bullet entered first, which killed, on and on, I get the idea." O'Connell had even seen cases with similar issues during his career causing a plea down in the sentencing process for criminals.

"Mmm, Paul that's so Roman of you. I like it though. I mean it's logical and it flows and I'm confident that with you involved in this execution of this little project I will walk away from it with a clear conscience."

"Ms. Hannabolis you can't be serious? You're on the side of law enforcement don't listen to that maniac." That would be murder!"

Once again O'Connell felt stupid as both persons glanced at him with that, "thugh", look.

"You're right Paul's a maniac, but he's right this time."

O'Connell heard the number three whisper off of Paul's lips too late. Paul had some how started a one, two, three count with Contessa without the detective realizing it. Gun fire from the detective's and Contessa's firearms rang through the hotel halls like thunder as the officer attempted to dive for cover. He could not escape the first two hot searing rounds that penetrated his chest slamming him violently against the vending machines across from where he had stood. Glass shattered all over his shoulders and back as the weight of his body impact the machine containing candy bars and other various unhealthy snacks.

Paul's silencer was relentless as it spat hot metal from its' metallic venomous mouth with extreme accuracy, surgically dismembering the human target starting with the chest, then the upper thigh and right above the left eye brow as Paul let out a cowboy, "YAH HOO!"

Constantine true to form then took the liberty of shooting Contessa, however, to his surprise she was already shooting at him at the same time, he proved to be a better shot. She covered her face in the normal reflex motion while spinning in motion away from the gunfire so as to not allow the bullet a clean flat surface. Blood leapt from her spurting in a pinwheel design across the entire hall as she spun and hit the ground. Paul walked passed the bodies placing an indiscriminate shot into both bodies as he passed. The front desk clerk was peeping around the corner of the counter when she loss her eyesight her body immediately went limp. One clean shot to the "all seeing eye" had put her to sleep forever. The telephone lay next to her lifeless body as blood tried to muffle the voice of the 911 operator on the other end.

"HELLO, HELLO MA'AM ARE YOU OKAY, CAN YOU SPEAK TO ME? HELP IS ON THE WAY, DO NOT APPROACH THE ASSAILANT. MA'AM.

"This is Paul we're headed for California. I repeat change of plans we're going to the city of angels."

CHAPTER 41

CONSTANTINE GETS WILD IN THE WEST

"So boss what's up? What's happening? Why the sudden change in plans?"

"Look Jimmy I'll rendezvous in about twenty five minutes." Paul was just three blocks from the carnage he'd created. He couldn't believe how fast the authorities had responded. Sirens were everywhere and the police were swarming from every direction he slowed his pace and covered his face with his scarf as though protecting it from the cold morning air. The hotel obviously had a silent alarm which was triggered by the front desk clerk before he popped her. He couldn't believe it they had a damn silent alarm they didn't even have one at the dive where he was staying. It was a good thing he hadn't stayed at that hotel they had too many amenities for his taste. Electronic keys, hidden silent alarms and a brothel right in the basement, no he was a simple man, none of that fancy stuff for him.

Paul was back on the mission trail now. His informant told him of the whereabouts of the wonderful Cardinal Ricci and now it was time to get that promotion.

"Jimmy yellow on the map. You'll see a street called Jersey off Walker Street. I'm at the Burger King on the Jersey Street side get there and we're out of here."

"Got it boss, we're on our way."

Michael entered the dining room and greeted his associates and friends. Peter made eye contact with him and amazingly realized what he was up too. Michael sat at the end of the table while Peter poured him a cup of coffee. He watched everyone in the room intensely trying to scan them deeper, getting into their heads to try and figure out if he'd misread one of the members and allowed a spy into the sanctuary.

"Hey it's 09:45, Michael, Chris are you two prepared for our meeting?"

"I am." Replied Special Agent Todd.

"Yes ma'am shall we do it in the lounge."

"Is there some other place besides the lounge? I kinda had bad memories of places serving spirits mainly of large imposing figures carrying me away." Michael glared at the guest.

"No problem Todd, Michael let's use the library."

"Okay ma'am."

"Sergeant's in bad shape Captain, real bad. He was wearing his vest but the rounds used on him, man let's just say two inch steel wouldn't have stopped those. He didn't stand a chance."

"Thanks lieutenant keep me informed. Was the detective married? I don't remember was he?"

"No sir never married."

"Well that's one good thing."

"Captain there's two other bodies in there and we think a wounded person was moved. There's blood of what may be a third victim but no body to be found. The CSI team is doing its thing right now and we're checking with every occupant and each room."

"Just keep me up to date alright. Excuse me I need a drink of Pepto. My damn stomach's protesting again. You know nerves."

"Hey officer, officer it was him. It was the abominable snow man that did it. The white dude with the bad ass hands, the guy who...."

"Hold on kid what are you saying? You're trying to tell me you witnessed this?"

"No I saw the guy who did it while I was on the corner over there."

"And just what were you doing on that corner over there?"

"Damn man why you sweaten me I'm a victim. Look I was talk'n to a friend and like he was parked on the corner and …"

"Well does this friend have a name?"

"Hell man how am I suppose to know? Anyway I'm bending down over the driver, my friends window and I see the guy run out of the hotel see and I say to myself, "that's the guy, that is the same dude who did me and Rodney". I'm telling you this guy is the devil man he's bad news, I'm outta here he may come back."

"Not yet, you're not going anywhere we have business down at the station so come on."

"Dang officer I got business to handle okay. Look what's your email address I'll send you what you need later okay?"

"Right wise guy email and all the latest techno shit right? Look kid, get your crutches and your butt in the cruiser."

"Dude you don't know what you're dealing with this. The guy that did whatever shit was done over yonder is way bad, I mean he did me and my boy Rodney in real short order. The guylikes to kill man you can see it in his eyes man. I bet he's a damn serial killer, yeah."

"You mean he did this to you?"

"Have you been listening? Hell yeah! He killed Rodney Benjamin, Jr. and not only dat he insulted my boy's Momma while he kilt him. He called his momma a hoe or cow or somethen. Da dude is murderous man, murderous."

"Son did you report this to the police or were you too busy working?"

"Look alright I wasn't completed honest with Officer O'Connell."

"You know detective O'Connell?"

"Hell man every one down here knows my boy O'Connell he's white as a ghost but he's awhright, cool white brother."

"Interesting you say that because that's him on the gurney there."

"No shit! Awh man, I knew it, I just knew it he kept "F"n with that white haired guy. Personally I played dumb, "I ain't seen nutt'n master suh.""

"Look son what's your name again?"

"Man I neva told you my name befoe, but it's Terry, Terry Hasim Johnson."

"Well Terry will you help us get this guy or not?"

"Dude if this guy's popping the blue team nobody's safe, I'll do it under one condition.

"Okay what's that?"

"There's like nobody to claim my boy Rodney's body and I want your police department to pay for his burial."

"Are you crazy?"

"Awhright just the coffin man, nothen expensive but it's the right thing to do he got nobody man. Even doe the white haired do insulted Rodney's Mom damn man I don't think he ever had one. Please man, come on.

"No promises kid I'll see what I can do. Get in, it's too damn cold out here let's get an APB out on this cop shooter."

"So Agent Todd please share with Michael and I what you know about my page's death and the persons responsible."

"I believe your page was killed because he came across information which revealed certain factions within our government's infrastructure that are aiding in the deterioration, the gradual destruction of this country and the American citizens of our great country."

"What proof do you have?"

"Me, I have been asked to do things over the years, certain details that didn't at the time add up and even now don't make any sense. At least not at the time but now that I look back it was all by design; what I was task to do, things such spying on innocent citizens using undercover agents, wiretaps and even disinformation programs on certain persons. I love my country but we are not supporting freedom or the voice of the people we're way off course man and what's so bad they have no clue."

"Agent all of what you say sounds noble enough but you've offered nothing substantive evidence to support any of your claims."

"Senator your boy was terminated by two of my own agents out of Atlanta and the reason I know this is because those guys were there on special assignment to Washington D.C. that very week of the murder. I placed the same two agents under investigation last year for possible improprieties."

"Still that doesn't prove squatsky."

"Senator how about I found something on one of the agent's desk that can prove he was tracking your young page? Here look at this."

"Well go ahead we're waiting. What is it,"

"According to those papers your page was boinking a staffer out of the Speaker of the House's office, but try this he was also using Meth and he'd contracted aids. All this is in that report, but the interesting part is that the staffer had an accident that same week after your page."

"How's that?"

"How's this, you'd been spying on the poor kid and you got nuth'n. That's how it is? Like that, you just hire losers to follow the people you target for bull crap! How do I know if any of what you've shared with us today is true? These papers prove nuth'n. Even if it is true what does it mean Agent Todd, there's no smoking gun here, well?"

The room went silent but not before Agent Todd's cell phone began to ring and there was a knock at the door. Michael got up to answer it.

"What!" Agent Todd's voice bellowed throughout the halls.

"Peter what is it?"

"Master Michael, Senator I suggest you watch this." Peter picked up the remote and turned on the large Plasma television located on the walnut paneled wall. Special Agent Todd's mouth was wide open and his razor cell hit hard on the hard wood floor as he viewed the picture of himself on CNN news. Senator Stinger backed away from the couch which she had been sitting on and quickly spun towards Agent Todd. Michael looked over his shoulder at the chunky agent and then turned to address him.

"Todd you want to tell us what that was all about."

"What? I don't know what they're talking about. Look believe me I'm being framed I didn't kill anyone. Those two agents they worked for me and they were the same two that I was talking about earlier. Don't look at me like that Senator I'm telling you the truth."

"I can't believe anything you say. You know I gave you a chance, years ago with the hope you would change but you didn't change you got more stupid on top of being a bigot."

The Senator turned in disgust and walked out of the room after angrily addressing Todd.

Peter glared at the agent and spoke, "perhaps you should relax, take some deep breaths and follow me young man."

Michael looked at Peter and then Agent Todd.

"Go ahead listen to him it can't hurt he's wise, he may be able to save you if you're salvageable, go on he'll work on the stupid part."

Agent Todd knelt and picked up his cell phone glancing at it as though it were a broken toy as he followed Peter to the kitchen. Michael walked into the hall and looked for Senator Stinger. He was concerned about her after she had learned of her page's fate and the betrayal of a trusted asset which should've been one of America's finest in law enforcement. Michael was unable to immediately locate her and finally he spotted her on the front lawn talking on her cell phone. He elected not to disturb her and headed down to finish his work in the operations center in the basement.

Once again Michael's innate ability and keenness at matters of security and protection overwhelmed him. He trusted no one and within minutes the directional microphones located in clandestine positions in the front of the mansion were eavesdropping on the United States Senator from Florida.

Michael began to update logs and file reports when he heard what every Secret Service, FBI, CIA agent or Corporate Security specialist dreamed of, catching a mole or an inside traitor. He was intrigued by what he was hearing, hell he wanted to observe her actions so he fired up the mansion's closed circuit television and zoomed in on the unsuspecting Senator filming and recording the conversation. Michael hit the record button and sat back in his chair. The conversation revealed another side to the Senator a cold, calculating and very impatient side. From the conversation Michael wasn't sure if she was in charge or the person to whom she was speaking, but what was revealed was that what Todd had told them earlier was no secret to her not even the page's death.

"Would you like a cup of tea sir? Perhaps a cold beverage might suit you aye?"

"What's your name again?"

"I'm Peter. The butler, man servant, sidekick, boy toy etc., etc," stated Peter.

"Look Mr. Todd what's your pork, or do you Americans say beef? Yes, what's your beef? You are obviously in a pickle at this moment, accused of killing two federal agents in Atlanta and dumping the bodies. My God man you are bold aren't you or rather stupid."

"Peter you have no idea of what happened and personally I don't have the time to go in to it. Look I need to get to Washington D.C. like yesterday. I can't believe this is happening I'm toast here my career is over. All I wanted to do was clean up an already bad situation at the accountant's office, your organization's accountant's office."

"Whatever are you referring too? What accountant? Oh my, that's who's missing Mr. Markovitz, Anish."

"Yes my agents, no those two crooked, twisted bastards killed the poor man I found them in his Atlanta office."

"Hold on, hold one moment Agent Todd I think a very important member of our family should be here to here your side, just wait."

Peter went on the intercom and paged Michael Zarkuhn to the kitchen. Michael was still scanning the Senator and thought to himself that the timing was really poor, but that if it was Peter the page had to be important. Zarkuhn continued to allow the tape to run and set the infrared-sensor on auto to assist in tracking the Senator's movements.

Senator Stinger walked further from the mansion and hid the cell phone in the dead and drabbed thick brown foliage. She nonchalantly turned and walked back towards the mansion. A frosty cloud of exhaust from her breath revealed how cold it was and the Senator hated cold, she longed for her home in Boca Raton, the sun, the sand, the beach. Right now the warmth from all of the huge fireplaces inside the mansion would suffice.

"Karen where have you been I've been looking all over for you."
"Cheryl, come on follow me we need to talk."

"Karen slow down, Karen honey, please slow down honey what's wrong?"

Karen opened the bedroom door and entered with Cheryl following closely behind her lover. The Senator grabbed her tote and suitcase from underneath the bed. She was frantic and moving like a mad woman.

"You're not making any sense and your behavior is scaring me so if you don't mind stopped a minute and please explain to me what you are doing right now?"

"We need to get out of here the FBI, ATF, DHS and God only knows how many others out of the alphabet will be here within the next couple of hours."

"Why, how?"

"How, because at this very minute Michael is interrogating a murderer downstairs; it seems that our Mr. Todd murdered some federal agents in your home town of Atlanta."

"Karen, hold on put the suitcase down for one minute I don't understand any of this. If what you're saying is true we should let the council know so we can …"

"Look baby I, we don't have time for that right now we've got to go and go now."

"Karen I'm not going anywhere and I really think you're making a bad mistake. I don't feel you right now, not at all."

"Try and understand me, just please listen I'm a United States Senator and I'm in a mansion which is harboring a possible criminal accused of killing two homeland security agents. You must realize that is not a good thing."

"Karen you need to explain to me how anyone would know to look here? Can you do that explain that to me and if you can how do you know that information?"

Karen put her sweater down on the edge of the bed and glanced down at her feet and then quickly back up into Cheryl Teranez's eyes. She placed her left hand over her mouth in exasperation and then placed it on her hip.

Before she could say anything the love of her life was storming out the bedroom door.
Cheryl felt betrayed but she didn't know exactly why.
Karen panicked, she felt her future walking out on her and all because she hadn't handled the situation like she would have if it were a press conference. What could she do? It was bad enough she was losing her lover, but any minute the Zarkuhn inquisition could began and she'd undoubtedly be screwed for life. Karen was not about to allow herself to undergo an interrogation from Michael

Zarkuhn. She needed to get away before she could be implicated in the whole sorted mess.

"Captain wait! Captain Boggs wait! Great I caught you."

"Yeah what is it, I was just getting ready to take this young upstanding citizen downtown, so what's up?"

"We found that other body, the third one. A female in one of the rooms upstairs in the hotel found barely alive. They're taking both the sergeant and the other living victim out by chopper like yesterday. Oh and Captain we lucked out."

"I'm waiting."

"The female's cell phone was live. It appears she was in the middle of a conversation before she passed out. How she made it up to the room is a miracle if she did it by herself. Captain the emergency technician told me she has a hole through her hand, shoulder and one hole through her left side."

"What's her chances?"

"Too early to tell."

"She's tough, do we know anything else about her?"

"Yep she's the same woman from Interpol that was at the station yesterday and get this she's got a shit load of nun stuff in her room."

"You're shit'n me? You think she's a nun and if so what's a nun doing down here in Roxbury, Mass., what's she doing working for Interpol. Damn this is definitely a Pepto moment?"

"She has rosary beads and the nun's clothing in her hotel room. Captain presently we're tracing a call from California to her cell phone right now, I'll keep you posted. Oh there were two dead hotel employees inside."

CHAPTER 42

FIFTH COLUMN REVEALED, OOPS!

"Cardinal, I'm sorry I did not know you were on the phone."

"It's okay, please approach I wish to have you attend to a matter for me. Colleeta this is a very sensitive matter which requires the utmost discretion."

"Your Excellency I will never fail the church."

"I know this my dear which is why I'm leaving the health of the child's mother in your capable hands. Do you understand? Can you grasp the importance of this responsibility? Is the gravity of the situation in you? For if it isn't tell me now and I will make other arrangements."

"As I said your Eminence I shall not fail. What is it you desire me to do?"

"I want you get her a doctor, one who shall prescribe medication. Unfortunately the girl is not well and I fear for the safety of the child under her care. Perhaps the doctor should sedate her I suggest this course of action because she attacked me earlier, yes sedation would be good."

"Sister, see to it that this is done immediately and update me when you've completed my directions. Do you understand?"

"Yes I understand perfectly."

"Good leave me now."

Cardinal Ricci turned from sister Colleeta as she humbly lowered her head and left the courtyard. The Cardinal wondered if his face revealed too much to the crafty nun. He was concerned about his mission and the worry was on his face said to anyone looking him in the eyes that "all was not well in Denmark." The phone call he received disturbed him, but could Colleeta have noticed when she entered he wondered? It would not matter she didn't know who he was talking too for she was just a pawn, a puppet to be used as those in power saw fit to use her.

"Bishop where are you headed?"

"Margarite I'm so glad you found me, I was searching all over for you. I was just notified by my assistant that a terrible accident has occurred."

"Bishop no I'm so sorry!"

"Yes. One of my most delightful parishioners has been in a serious accident."

"What happened, no I forget myself I'm sorry."

"It's quite alright, but I have no details at all and that's most disturbing, I need to get to the city."

"I will have one of the onsite staffers drive you to the city immediately. I need to let Michael know and one other council member okay."

Margarite used the intercom to notify Miles and Michael who was about to leave the control center to see Peter as Margarite explained.

"Margarite I appreciate it, but might I use one of the vehicles instead. You have a mess of visitors and the staff is needed here."

"You're right father, by all means take the Aston Martin if you'd like, it can fly."

"Perhaps something a little more low keyed might work better. I was thinking the van."

"The old "Intrepid" clunker, sure but keep your cell phone close in case she has trouble. I can't remember when that vehicle was moved last."

The bishop followed Margarite as she talked. She headed for the kitchen and to the pantry where the vehicle keys were hanging on a wall mount inside the pantry to the right.

"Here you go and Bishop Terrell God speed."

"Thank you so much."

The Bishop entered the huge garage and located the old Mercedes van right where it had been for since he started with the Collective six years ago. He slipped the key into the ignition and she fired right up. The Bishop wasted no time moving towards the automatic garage door which started beeping and rolling up as he approached it to exit the grounds of the mansion. It was cold in the van and the heater fought back trying not to cooperate with him as he adjusted the heat to its highest setting.

Michael paused before heading up to Peter as he watched the monitor's red indicator light and alarm which alerted him that a vehicle was departing the structure. He was suspicious of the Bishop and wished he'd more time to observe him. All of a sudden he noticed the Senator carrying bags to her vehicle in the garage.

"Now where is she going?"

"Knock, knock, Michael I need to speak with you it's rather urgent."

"Doctor Teranez please enter, Doctor I always have time for you. I was just noticing Senator Stinger in the garage loading up her car do you have any clue as to what she's doing?"

"Michael that's what I'm here to tell you. Something is terribly wrong I think she may be in trouble. Earlier she was talking crazy."

"How?"

"She said we needed to leave immediately."

"I know she was shocked and upset to learn about the possible misdeeds of her guest, Agent Todd, but I didn't think she was that bothered."

"There's more she said the mansion would be swarmed by federal agencies, FBI, etcetera. I asked her to discuss her concerns with the council, but to tell you the truth, "sob, sob" and this hurts me to say, I think she's done something stupid."

"You mean she may have given up Todd and in doing so …"

"In doing so Michael she's compromised all of us. The authorities have been hounding us for years and now it will seem as though."

"Right that we're harboring a criminal one that works for us and Cheryl you're correct. That's exactly what will happen it's what I would conclude if I were on the outside."

"What are we going to do? Michael she's leaving look!"

Michael glanced at the security monitor Doctor Teranez was pointing at. The Senator from Florida was approaching the garage exit and the beeping started. Michael hit a toggle switch in the control room and the beeping stop as did the door. It had risen two feet before it stopped rolling up. The Senator could be seen on the monitor slapping the steering wheel in frustration. She quickly jump out of the car and walked over to the manual control buttons located on the wall next to the garage door put the switch in the up position and the door began to rise again. A smile of relief masked her face as she turned to go to her car. The door stopped after only rising three inches. A devilish grin started to infect Michael's face as he over road the manual switch again. The Senator seemed impatient as she slammed the car door spun and returned to the garage's manual control switch. She repeated the action again and hurriedly jumped back into the car slammed the door only to see the door go up only six inches.

The Senator glared at the security camera's at all four corners of the garage then at the garage door. She obviously had not become a Senator by giving up, once again she approached the garage door, spouting a couple of "unsenatorial" expletives she once again repeated the process and zipped back to the car pulled her long cashmere coat in across her lap and slammed the door, again. By this time Michael's grin had fully infected his face and to his surprise proved to be contagious by the grin on Doctor Teranez's face.

But this time the door had started to move and move down not upward; however, the mechanical noise assured the Senator that her desire to have the door rise was not being met. She sat in the car frustrated and rather disconcerted about her ordeal.

"Ahhww! Damn you Michael!"

The Senator screamed out loud as Michael stood up and headed upstairs and out to the garage with Cheryl following closely behind him matching him step for step. The Senator left the car and headed up the stairs and through the kitchen looking for Michael they met in the kitchen as did Margarite, Miles, Ted, Alice, J.P. and Agent Todd.

"What! Are all of you in on this kidnapping?"

"Michael what the dickens is the Senator talking about", asked Miles.

"We heard the noise and wanted to find out what was wrong, so what is wrong?"

"Perhaps the Senator will answer that for us Margarite, Senator?"

"I don't know what you're talking about. I was attempting to leave, but it seems as though someone will not let me."

"I don't wish to be a "kill joy" Senator but where were you going and did you alert any of the members?"

"Alice that's really none of your concern."

"I beg to differ. You know the rules and you're aware of the threat conditions which are facing us in fact, you should understand the seriousness of the matter better than all of us."

"Ted the same goes for you. This is no concern of yours either. I'm a United States Senator and I cannot be found associating with the likes of him."

"Who me!"

"No not you J.P., him."

"Who him?"

"Yes J.P., him the guy to your right, the federal agent who kills federal agents."

"What! Perhaps we all need to discuss the matter. She has a point she is a U.S. Senator and this would kill her career. Hell we won't stand much of a chance either."

"Miles we know that, but that's not the issue. The issue is why didn't she discuss this with us, why did she feel the need to just go and only ask Doctor Teranez to go with her and furthermore how does she know federal agents are going to raid the place?"

"She said that?"

"Yes Miles she said that."

"Michael did you here me say that, well?"

"As a matter of fact Cheryl informed me."

"Well she's lying and there's no proof that I know of agents coming here, but that's neither here nor there, I'm a senator and I'm demanding that you release me now."

"Senator."

"Yes Michael."

"Would like to hear your phone conversation recorded earlier this afternoon shortly after we interviewed Special Agent Todd?"

"That's against the law."

"Senator you're kidding me right? Senator hand me your cell phone please."

"I don't have it I lost it earlier while I was … Michael where are you going?"

"Miles, Ted you all watch her I'll be back in just a moment."

"Michael you'll catch a cold where are you going."

"Maragrite I'll only be a minute."

"Trust me I don't think he'll get a cold."

Peter stated and Miles met his eyes with confirmation of that statement.

The Senator was sweating and Ted Martin was now catching that contagious grin thing that Michael and Doctor Teranez had caught in the control room earlier. He knelt down and whispered in his wife's ear, "I told you I didn't trust her she's a damn politician. Wouldn't have mattered if she were black, orange, or blue you can't trust them. There's our fifth column standing right there."

"Ah Ted hush."

Michael Zarkuhn entered through the kitchen door and scraped the ice and snow off his shoes, the Collective members anxiously awaited resolution to the mystery.

"Very clever Senator, very clever because of your treachery we will now need to implement emergency evacuation and sanitation protocols."

"Whut shay do?"

"Well J.P. it would seem that the honorable, wow that hurts, the Senator accidentally lost her cell phone but neglected to ..."
Ted jumped in, "turn it off, she didn't turn it off."

"I know I'm just a dumb rich old white boy in awll, but I cood give a ratt's rectum whuts it awll meen."

"Mr. J.P. they probably used the cell phone which in all likelihood possesses GPS and triangulated our location verifying she has assisted someone in finding this location."

"You can't prove any of this and why would I do such a thing?"

"Senator shall I review your call and a most interesting video for you and the rest of your former colleagues? Well should I?"

"That won't be necessary Michael. Cheryl how could you, I thought you cared for me."

"About as much as you cared for me Karen."

"I helped you, I stuck by your side all these years how could you do this and not hurt? You don't feel for me the way I feel for you do you? It's obvious so why did you stay with me if you didn't care?"

"Perhaps the sex was great might be the answer, coffee anyone."

Once more Peter's off base humor brought the whole kitchen into gut wrenching laughter and blushed faces, even the Senator and Cheryl couldn't hold back from bursting into laughter both realizing they would miss it, the sex that is.

CHAPTER 43

WAR BETWEEN GOOD AND EVIL

Michael had gathered everyone into the conference room so that the Collective inner circle members could assess their current position. The precarious situations presenting themselves before the Collective were palpable to say the least and Senator Karen Stinger's lapse in judgment hadn't made the team's dismal situation an event of merriment. Senator Stinger agreed to stay in her room until a decision was made about what to do with her. Peter insured she was placed in a room which could be secured and you bet he hid the key. Miles made an announcement and called the meeting to order.

"This is certainly poor timing, taking a phone call Peter. Surely it can wait?"

"No sir afraid not it's the Controller Sir."

The room was still as Miles took the phone and answered the call.

"Miles here may I assist you sir?"

"In fact you may, you can, and you will."

The voice was unrecognizable due to the use of an electronic aid and Miles wondered if Peter had used the proper protocols in authenticating the identity of the caller. He would not insult Peter by asking, fully aware Peter had been doing that very thing before every member of the Collective except Margarite. The other members were keyed to the conversation as they waited.

The voice on the other end continued to instruct Miles as to what he desired from the Collective hierarchy.

"You are to release the Senator immediately, at once without fail. Instruct Michael Zarkuhn to stand down, do not give him any more information he'll understand and finally, I'm instructing you and Ms. Plantard via Mr. Zarkuhn's recommendation to break the seals on the "Emergency Evacuation and Escape Plan, in the event the property is breached you may execute it. Now please place me on the speaker phone."

"One moment of course sir."

"He wants me to put him on the speaker phone does, anyone know how to do it? Hell last thing I want to do is to cut the Controller off."

"Who's this Controller person?"

"You know I'd almost forgotten about you Todd. You have no need to know any of this so come with me."

"Ah you're kidding me man, look my butts on the line and maybe, just maybe I can be of some help to your organization. Mike come on, have a heart I need to be productive and I can't be stuck in here dormant and all, come on."

"I suppose it will not matter in a couple of days anyway so have a seat Toad, I mean Todd and don't say squat."

"Move please, here hand me the phone I'll do it excuse me Ted."

"Margarite pulled her chair back and stepped around Ted Martin and took the phone from Miles. She placed it on the stand from which it was taken, increased the volume and placed the call on speaker mode.

"Sir this Margarite, you're on the speaker now you may proceed."

"Maragrite it is pleasing to hear your voice my dear."

"Thank you sir, likewise."

"I wanted to tell you all that I have not been far from the events that have transpired over the last few weeks and that my heart goes out to all of you. Reviewing the daily reports emailed to me has reflected all of your dedication and hard work in supporting our cause. The suffering over the losses of our dedicated brothers and the pain their families are going through is being felt. But the time is here for us to move forward to the next level. Michael I understand there is some important news to be shared with the council, would you now share it with us?"

"Correct Controller, a meeting was held yesterday with four of the members of the inner circle having an operational impact on the agenda discussed and now I will let everyone present know we have in our possession the "Tables of Testimony. I must clarify that we have approximately half of the first tablet given to Moses and as some of you will recall this was the most important of our charters. What we now possess is the larger of the two pieces, a part of God's little black book."

"Whut!"

J.P. Rockdale nearly fell out of his chair as he put his icy glass of scotch down on the Mahogany conference table. Ted looked at Alice who tried to act as though it was nothing at hearing about this spectacular find.

"This is absolutely wonderful news. We have searched for thousands of years and it has paid off, but not without great losses to our families. I feel with this precious relic we can now move in the direction our forebears outlined for us. Dr. Martin, Dr. Teranez I take it you will be able to begin research on "Project Genesis" a.s.a.p.?"

"We are waiting for our security assignments which Michael will arrange for us, then of course will head to the Gynyxys site first thing."

"Michael when do you expect the security assignments to be in place?"

"Someone from my department will accompany the team two nights from now."

"That will not work. That is unsatisfactory we must begin to find out all we can about this biblical relic and exploit it as soon as possible. This tool will provide us with the ultimate power if we tap into it, it could reveal secrets which will provide us the ways and means of protecting and advancing the human race. It will allow us to identify with ease the genetic markers of our hidden enemies, "the Sons of God," those bastard Watcher abominations, the children of the Nephilim. We will be able to communicate with God himself."

"Sir the detail is imperative. The team will be vulnerable without some security protocol."

"Okay forget the security team. Sending a security team may aid in identifying the team we're trying to conceal thereby hurting them. Send the team with the

"Tables of Testimony" without the so called inconspicuous security team hovering in the shadows, trust me they'll be seen. Our adversaries will pick up the team's scent but not the ladies if they travel alone. I desire them to be in Atlanta by tomorrow night. I realize that I can only suggest and that you must vote on what is I've requested so because of the time constraints I request we put it to the vote now."

"Sir we will comply, but I wish to go on record as protesting this proposed action. I feel it to be reckless especially in light of the fact that we're talking about just one day's delay and my team is competent enough not to tip their hand."

"Michael I'm sure Margarite has duly noted your position in the minutes, correct Margarite?"

"Of course sir I've done so."

"Miles if you would be so kind as to place the motion before the Collective inner circle I'd be most grateful."

"Jimmy what took you so long? Do you know how cold it is out there?"

"Yeah boss pretty damn cold."

"Well hell yeah Jimmy you could say that. We're on our way to Los Angles Dorothy."

"What's in Los Angeles?"

"A little red bird, Cardinal to be exact."

"No shit, you're kid'n right? The Cardinal's in California?"

"That's what I said wasn't it."

"Why did we have to meet you under this bridge, something happen back there kinda bad boss?"

"No o'contraire nothing bad happened. I simply had a revelation of sorts, that's how I know about the little birdy. Stop the car I want you two to get in the other vehicle for about thirty minutes, the lieutenant and I have some business to discuss."

The rental SUV pulled over and the subordinates got into the other two SUVs trailing in the loose convoy.

"Good, you see Jimmy that sneaky SOB sent a mechanic to pop me. Boy she was a Negroid beauty with the most luscious lips, boy mate, whew! Jimmy what I want to know is, is anything sacred anymore? I had to kill that goddess right in the bloody hotel. I should've been shagging the nipper not busting a bloody bullet in her. Life's not fair."

"You mean, "busting a cap" in her boss, it's busting a cap in her ass, like they say in the American movies we watch right? Yo nigga, I go'n ta bust a."

"Whatever! Either way it was not the kind of load I had wished to bust in her."

"Boss how do you know she was contracted to pop you? I don't think the Cardinal would risk it. You're the man in the Catholic black works arena and well he's blood."

"Oh I know he sent her. Interpol my backside … no way in hell they did this, her boss's was named Excellency. Oh I got the drop on her see and now we're going to drop kick that fish hat wearing faggot's side kick, the Cardinal.

The conference room was quiet as Miles stood and addressed his colleagues.

"You've all heard the request made by the Controller and we have had one open objection to that proposal already. What we need now is a vote and we'll keep it simple, a simple yes or no. What's on the floor is do we immediately dispatch our research team from the mansion here to the Gynyxys genome laboratory in Atlanta without a security detail. Is that pretty much it Controller? Accurate enough for a call?"

"Thank you Mr. Turner. I'd say that motion will suffice."

"Before we vote on this matter we'll open the floor for questions."

"Why, for what purpose, the measure is clear enough. It's quite simple an up or down vote is all that is required."

"Forgive me if I disagree with you Controller. Decisions are never as simple as an up or down or yes or no vote when peoples' lives are at stake."

"Touching rhetoric Mr. Zarkuhn, but hardly substantively relative given the big picture. This is a time sensitive issue with grave risks associated with it. By merely sitting there in that room you're each reflecting your responsibility in exercising selflessness in the execution of your duties. Every member present and those no longer with us knew the seriousness of our mission from day one and if they did not, then perhaps it is best that we are no longer plagued by their inept existence. Ladies, Gentleman grow up this sort of business is not easy, but callous and ruthless."

"Begging your pardon Controller but that is a most harsh and insensitive view to have about our dead friends and what each of us has been through."

"Margarite was that you?"

"Yes Controller."

"It was not my intent to insult or hurt the feelings of anyone present, but the reason I'm in this role as Controller is because long ago it was deemed essential that the position of Controller be filled by a member who could distance themselves from the emotional side and deal objectively with any issue facing the group using the sound empirical principles of logic and reasoning, to be tempered with compassion and sympathy when it thought to be reasonably needed."

"You know I just haven't seen or heard from you much of the latter, you know compassion, sympathy and that troubles me Controller."

"Michael need I remind you that you are not a seating member of the Collective's inner circle and thus your role is at most somewhat limited. Your role is security operations and in that capacity you've made your concerns known so please abstain from any further input unless asked a specific question by one of the inner circle, thank you."

"But of course Controller my apology."

"I have a question. How much more significant operational research time do we gain by getting a team to Atlanta by tomorrow as opposed to waiting for an escort as Michael has suggested."

"I think …," as the Controller started to answer the question brought up by Mr. Martin he's abruptly cut off.

"Controller if you please Doctor Alice Martin here, may I answer that question."

"By all means proceed, but Doctor Martin wouldn't this question best be answered by Doctor Teranez, our lead researcher."

"We share that role at the present sir and the answer is not a significant amount of time would be gained, because there would be little or nothing we could accomplish the night of arrival."

"She's absolutely right. I mean although we have an idea of how we would proceed a specific team will have to be assigned to this particular project when we arrived and that would take at least two days."

"Why was a team not already in place before now Doctor Teranez?"

"The circle decided over two years ago that in the event we ever to find this particular relic then and only then would a team be assembled for two reasons; one security and two to decide how the project personnel and resources would be best used. No, haste would not become our enemy but time would become our ally, would be patient."

"Not to mention as I recalled the expertise and staff changes that are made say every two or three years, I think I'm right in that, prohibited us from putting together such a sensitive team too early. It simply wasn't cost effective or security wise."

"Thank you Miles for your miniscule input, but I still fail to see why such an important measure was not taken in advance. Why there was no contingency plan in place. I mean this group possesses some of the most potent minds and abilities on the planet, unacceptable, period."

"Controllar this iz J.P. how are yah?"

"Mr. Rockdale fancy hearing you after all these years. You'd like to share something with us pertinent to the proceedings?"

"Yeah I wood. Yah no I fel tosee why yoo kant trust these wunderfall kids ta do thare jobs. Hell we don't know yah from hill or beans. I aint nevar seen yah matta fack aint nobody here that I knose uv know ya. Sounds to me and I aint da britest lite bolb in da pack dat yah may jest be our biggust securitay risk cuz you jest aint feeeeling us man."

"Well thank you J.P. for that evanescent position of yours."

"J.P. is right and everyone here in this room knows it. What is this anyway your version of Charlie's Angels?"

"Who's addressing the floor? I do not recognize the voice."

"This is Special Agent Christopher Todd of the Department of Homeland Security speaking and curiously none of us are allowed to recognize your voice."

"Why is an outsider at a special meeting, this is a clear violation of security provisions and protocol, Michael answer immediately."

"No I think we should hear what the outsider has to say, he may provide a clearer, more objective view to us. What do you all think inner circle?"

There was a wave of support and "yes's", across the conference room as the modulated voice of the Controller recessed for a moment.

"Go ahead agent Todd speak on."

"What Mr. Rockdale brought up is on point. From this spectator's viewpoint all of you are being taken to the cleaners by whom ever this person on the other end. He's asking that you not provide security for your folks and to move before you're ready. Look for some years I've taken orders from people in Washington D.C. and most of the time their directions are flawed because they're too distant or have another altogether different agenda than the one the agency clearly dictates we should have. You are all in the trenches this person obviously isn't. Who is he? When was he elected the Controller and how? Were any of you involved in the process? Know J.P. you got it on the money baby and I'm sorry this Southern Atlanta boy thought of you as some dumb drunk all this time. You're seeing clearly and if there is anything you all here can do to silence this Controller fellow's authority my suggestion is to do it and do it now."

"Right, are you through Agent Todd?"

"Quite, and thank you for letting me speak." "Thank you for letting me speak Hitler", was murmured under his breath, but Michael heard it and reconsidered his view of Todd for at least a moment.

"Now if there are no more questions I suggest we vote and vote now, time is critical remember."

Miles and Margarite stood up next facing each other and gazed at one another with a smile as they took each other's hand. Miles and Margarite along with J.P. Rockdale were the senior members on the Collective council. Mr. Rockdale smiled at Special Agent Todd, J.P.'s red bulbous nose seemed to glow with glee and he stood up as well in an act of solidarity for Miles and Margarite.

"I propose a motion that we suspend the authority and duties of the Controller, to commence immediately on the grounds that this structure and arrangement no longer works for the Collective and may create an environment counterproductive to the good order of our mission."

"Miles you're out of line, and on what grounds would you even consider such a preposterous motion?"

"Simply because every question brought up by the outsider and J.P. before the board today is logical and merits reason, that's why. You're a security risk, subject to an investigation by the top two senior members of the council. The matter shall be handed over to Mr. Zarkuhn's department and left to his discretion."

"Margarite surely you must see that this is not in line with how the board much less your dear father would have conducted business over the many years of this entity's existence?"

"I'm sure it isn't Controller, but everyone has the right to think, to act and to make decisions for the betterment of their livelihood and in this case the livelihood of the Collective. So we'll be trying to get in contact with you as soon as time will allow unless you wish to cooperate with our investigation beginning now?"

"Sounds to me like he's hung up on us Michael."

"Yep miracles never cease huh?

"People we have a lot to do so let's get to work and by the way does anyone have a problem with me asking Agent Todd to stay on to assist, because I sure don't?"

The up vote was unanimous by all the members. As the maps, pens and files started coming out on the table.

"I need to excuse myself for a moment I'll be right back. Oh and Miles would you join me for a minute."

"Sure, Michael what is it."

"Get in touch with Maurice and ask him to have Lehchin bed down in Los Angeles, California."

"Right excellent plan you'll need the extra muscle. Should I alert Marcus, the West Coast Station Chief so that he may support you?"

"No not at this time this has to be played right off the cuff and very low key with no comm. I'll contact him right before I'm there in his zone then I'll get what support I need from him."

"Okay."

"Hello. I just got out of a conference call with the circle and we still have a problem they would not remove the security detachment as I requested and one of my federal agents is on the premises, for what purpose I do not know. Nothing was mention in the daily reports I received about him being on assignment with the group. This concerns me it could complicate things. I should have caught it but nonetheless."

"That doesn't matter my brother we will still acquire the "Tables of Testimony" and with it power beyond anything known within this dimension or part of the Universe will once again be ours not some petty unforgiving great, great, great, great uncle God."

"By the way did you reach the Bishop? Yes he was contacted before all of this transpired. The task will be carried out as you directed, will there be anything else Nero?"

"No Cardinal you have served well. Continue to press all fronts."

CHAPTER 44

EXODUS ALL OVER AGAIN

"Cardinal what a surprise."

"How's the operation Paul? What is the status with regards to retrieving the artifact?"

"Well we've assemble the team and we're headed for glory."

"That makes no sense at all, speak as though you have some wits about you."

"Where are you Padre?"

"That is no concern of yours now is it. Obviously you're aware that I here in these United States otherwise you wouldn't have asked such an obvious question. You listen to me and hear me clearly your role in this operation is drawing to a close and so far you've produced zed. Your insolent and openly barbaric manner has brought shame on the Church. You have made me appear incompetent before his Holiness by my placing such great trust in you and that's not a healthy thing to do."

"That sounds suspiciously like a threat Padre."

"Listen to me you sociopath stop calling me Padre. Did you come to this land of cowboys just to loose the last of your social graces the few you'd possess? I want you to execute the job we sent you here for."

"I'll handle my operation and I will not fail. I never fail, see you your eminence soon."

Cardinal Ricci was chafed after his conversation with Paul Constantine. He'd wanted Constantine shut down but his effort to achieve that goal had apparently fallen short with the failure of his assassin to kill Paul in Boston. He hoped his new plan would fair better, for he was now being fed failure for the first time, something not compatible with the epicurean in him and he didn't enjoy this palate.

Paul was totally pissed at the Cardinal's treacherous act in sending an assassin to terminate him. He estimated that at the rate he and his team were traveling they'd be at their destination in California in thirteen more hours and then he would anoint the Cardinal with a hail of bullets.

"Jimmy which vehicle has the package?"

"Ours does boss they're right in the back ammo and all. Man we're go'n to partay!"

"You're so right dude, you're so right."

"Captain the kid clearly identified that foreign guy that we had in here last week. You know the one, that the pretty Interpol lady interviewed ah, a Paul Constantine."

"Great! Put an updated APB out on the guy we're already running behind the eight ball on this jerk let's try and make up some time. You know that S.O.B. probably shot O'Connell and get this that pretty broad too. Can you believe anybody in his right mind could shoot that broad?"

Captain Boggs swallowed some Pepto Bismol and frowned as the pink elixir fought its way down his throat. Ten years of drinking the stuff and he still wasn't use to it. It suddenly occurred to him that he should review all of O'Connell's files perhaps there was some more, some information that might assist him in picking up the perpetrators trail.

"Hey sarge how's about getting me O'Connell's files, you know where he keeps them? And check on his condition at the hospital for me alright. I think I'll swing by there later."

"Captain we got a hit on the cell phone."

"Good come on in lets have it, what you got?"

"It appears the phone call was made from a phone registered to ... you're going to love this, the Vatican administrative support office."

"You're shit'n me no way."

"Naw Captain I'm not shit'n ya."

"No way. You mean that beautiful broad is a nun? Wow! Makes a Protestant consider converting. What a waste!"

"That's right Captain no one was going to get none, she was or is a nun, yep."

"Naw you're shit'n me."

"No Captain."

Bishop Terrell was numb he couldn't fathom the mess he was in. He was sinking into the quagmire of espionage and butchery again a place he'd tried to escape by taking an assignment in America years ago, but now he was being drawn into the dark. He knew he would not get out of this spiritually unscathed, he could feel it this was not going to end in his favor. As he drove to the hospital it was all he could do to keep the speed of the car reasonable his nerves were shot. The Bishop was terrified at the prospect of the Collective losing the "Tables of Testimony", he was horrified at the thought of possibly running across his old student Paul Constantine and he was afraid of going to hell for what he had to do in the next hour.

Karen sat on the edge of her bed and couldn't believe how low she had fallen, a prisoner in a mansion held captive by people she admired. She had turned her back on her constituents long ago opting for political survival instead of pushing the utopian ideals spewed from her mouth during her first campaign when she first ran for office eight years ago. Why she did what she did was behind her she needed to get in touch with her contacts in Washington D.C.

The soft knock on the door frightened her.

"Come in, but it's locked."

"It's me Michael. Senator I wanted to check on you and to tell you we were directed to release you by the Controller earlier."

"I would appreciate that I have much to do."

"But we overruled him, sorry."

"I thought you couldn't do that, that he was the final say."

"No that's not entirely true in fact he will now find himself under the microscope. I will know his or her identity by the weeks end and we will find out more. Do you know where I'm going with this Karen?"

"Yes Michael of course but what can I tell you. I don't know anything and contrary to what you may think I am innocent. Try and understand Michael there are things I cannot divulge to you for National Security reasons."

The Senator got Michael's attention and he helped himself to a seat by the edge of her bed. "Tell me what you can Karen we are about to …, your friends downstairs may be killed because of your National Security. We will in all probability be assaulted maybe not today but eventually those people and their families will die perhaps because of what you know and are refusing to tell us."

"Michael I can't, as much as I want too I just can't. This goes up high, too high. It would be treason."

Karen Stinger turned away and Michael could see it was not because she regretted in not opening up to him, but shame was emotionally whipping her at that moment. It did not matter, Michael knew what he had to do and he was focused.

"I'm sincerely sadden by your decision Senator you must realize you are a security risk and a threat to this very old institution, and to what was once your family?"

"Are you saying what I think you're saying, but Michael you wouldn't, you couldn't do that to me. I would never …"

"No Senator you already did. You betrayed us today and I can't let you go and for that I'm sorry. You know the threat our adversaries pose to humanity you know better than any of us."

"Yes damn you I do and you want to know why I know? It's not because I sit on the Collective's inner damn circle, no Michael Zarkuhn it's because I've helped in creating the very thing that the Collective was created to thwart. Remember what committee I sit on, Senate Intelligence Committee an entity that by design helps to promote the dictates of the Brotherhood, Illuminati, hell Corporate America, so on, and so on. Do you get what I'm telling you Michael?"

"More than you realize Senator. I do have some experience in the area you know, the secret world behind the scenes and all causes and affects. But that does not exonerate you from breaking your vow of secrecy and allegiance to the Collective. In fact, the reason you were invited to join us is because your ideology so matched ours we were honored to have you. Tell me you didn't let someone in your government know about the "Tables of Testimony?"

"Michael grow up get a grip, you have know idea what it's like to grow up poor, black and female in this God forsaken country. I have been able to accomplish more for my constituents than any other Senator ever from my state and that's because I'm a realist, practical something most Blacks in this country have refused to grasp. Know they want to pray to God or rely on social welfare systems to provide for them. Well God never gave me crap and I sent myself to school and to law school, no one gave me noth'n and I didn't ask anyone for noth'n. Every time I would go back to my neighborhood I would have to justify why I was going to college or even now answer foolish questions about why the government gives loans to foreigners like the Koreans and the East Indians and not African Americans. Well I guess the others pay their loans and debts off in acceptable terms right? You think Black folk can swallow that? Hell no!"

"Those are valid questions from their view point so what's the big deal? You're there to help them understand, is that too much to ask?"

"Look what do you want from me Michael? For me to tell you the truth, is that what you want, is it? Well I'll tell you what you want to know only if you promise not to neutralize me. You know kill me."

The feisty Senator sheepishly looked up at Michael when she'd asked him to spare her. She knew Zarkuhn would have no problem with abrogating her existence. Even pleading with him was in most probability falling on deaf ears, but she wished to live for she enjoyed life despite the perpetual battles her high profile position placed her in. She started weeping, crying out of fear and with the hope that maybe just maybe Michael might be touched and reconsider this once. Being in the room with him was unnerving he was so callous and relentlessly efficient at performing his tasks. What chance did she stand at being shown mercy? Hell his callousness was one of the qualities she considered his better traits in the position he held and one of the reasons she'd requested him to accompany her to the airport the night before and why he had been invited to escort her on past visits to foreign countries possessing volatile political climates. Now her life would be forfeit because of a misunderstanding or difference of opinion, surely Michael might realize this.

"Senator you know I'm fond of you, but I must do what I must. Please continue explaining to me whatever it is you feel will enlighten me as to your recent lapse in honor."

"My page was killed by the two henchmen working for the Department of Homeland Security, but I knew they were going to kill him. The murder was sanction by a special group which works within the upper echelons of the government. Unfortunately, the poor boy read a document earmarked for my eyes only; it was really more of a sensitive plan. He saw some footnotes and information collated by a few think tanks he shouldn't have seen and it was agreed that he was a threat to National Security."

"To whom was he a real threat? Optimum word here, whom."

"Cliché okay, a threat to National Security of course not a threat to whom and it's always because of National Security. You know how ignorant American citizens are to National Security matters, with all those terrorist and all out there just waiting to attack us again. We can hide anything behind the phrase, anyway the document outlined causalities a course of actions to be taken and reactions expected then counter actions by the secret government resulting in desired results necessary to break the strong spirit of the American people; all courtesy of such corporations as the Heritage Foundation, Lexington, etcetera, etc. Well I was going on vacation and we couldn't allow the possibility that the page might leak or talk with someone about his discovery. To complicate matters and the icing on the cake was that he was a homosexual with ties to an opposing political office so it was determined that termination was the only viable solution for he and his partner."

"Sounds much like the situation you find yourself in right now."
"Michael this is different. You think I've helped some government agencies hostile to us locate you, not you personally but the organization and I haven't. I'll tell you that what I did was contact a person in Washington, D.C. who is vital to ensuring this country's future."

"I'm waiting for this person's name."

"I can't give you that, but I'll tell you how to get it that way I'll have kept my word to my country."

"I have deciphered the mystery of the contact person. It is the Secretary of the Department for Homeland Security his cell phone number was easy enough to trace off your phone. Explain his role and you understand perfectly why I'm asking don't you."

"Harming him would be a big mistake Michael. The Collective is not that powerful. He had contacted Special Agent Todd a day or so ago and asked about two missing agents, two agents that he knew were dead. Special Agent Todd's demeanor and answers during the conversation gave him away. I know this because he's kept me informed, the Secretary that is."

"I don't follow you my interrogation of Todd reflects that he merely tried to cover up the killing of Anish Markovitz committed by the two agents Todd's innocent."

"Yes, but he did not come clean with the SecDHS instead he attempted to spoon feed him a crock of crap which insulted the arrogant secretary."

"You think I'm stupid? Continue."

"Well he realized that Special Agent Todd was trying to cover up the deaths of the two bad apples and that he had been probing the two men in the last few months because of suspicious activities. What Todd would eventually find was that all trails would lead to the top to the Secretary himself and since he had shown himself to be a company man true and blue he needed to be removed. That's where I came in I was to make sure I found out what Todd knew and then get him into the hands of the authorities for the murder of the two agents."

"How is it that the SecDHS knew about the two agent's death? Todd didn't tell him so who else knew?"

"The agents were dispatch by a special group who are contracted by the group the Secretary also sits as a member and they were to scare Anish Markovitz into giving us financial information on the Collective's cover organizations."

"And how did they know to be at Mr. Markovitz' office and what group is this that's so special."

"You know I gave them the information Michael and as for the group you must know that too. What should I say Illuminati, Council of 300 hundred, Black Wolfpack, what's the term you use yada, yada, give me a break. The black bag squad used was probably subcontracted for obvious reasons and you know the government uses them all the time so take your pick."

"I can see you're concerned with maintaining loyalty to your country and the American government, but to the Collective you would forsake us knowing full well that they've designed a long term plot to sterilize Democracy here. I don't mind telling you that this little kiss and tell is not helping your position with me much. In fact, it rather makes my wanting to kill you a mush easier task."

"I do not need to hear that crap right now. I'm trying to come clean here okay, what I'm telling you could get me murdered."

"That would be virtually impossible at this stage of the game, since I want to kill you first please continue."

"When the agents didn't report in as directed we, yes we dispatched two local assets to check out the area of the operation and they reported activity from Special Agent Todd which forced them to survey the area. That's when they saw Agent Todd in what could only be described as a sanitation operation of Anish's office."

"Of course they followed him and yada, yada, yada the rest is history."

"Pretty much."

"So the powers to be in your little secret group couldn't very well let this conscientious agent do his job that would be too much unlike a government employee right. He would be completely out of the woods if he were to have exercised some of that United States Post Office lack of zeal in conducting his duties right? Yeah, government affiliated employees always aiming to please with one hundred per cent mediocrity and inefficiency."

"At this juncture they want Todd okay."

"It would figure they want a scapegoat, someone to toss to the bottom of the cliff onto the rocks. You know nothing ever changes with time or country you're all the same with your games and surreptitious acts to incite future sedition from the American people."

Michael then phased out remembering the rift between Jehovah and his brother. Politics also played a great role in their war and led to the attempt of the Christian God, Jehovah to flood the occupied Earth in an effort to destroy men his brother's creation. The relationship between Enlil or Jehovah and Enki who was later unjustly referred to as Satan after some bad press was tempestuous at best. Michael was familiar with "The Epic of Gilgamesh and the Book of Enoch" eons ago and recalled how it described the petty jealousy of both brothers towards the other, however the Christian God also God to the Jews was the head over the Earth settlement and its mining and exploration operations. He let his brother never forget he was appointed commander not him. But politics paved the way for the older but junior ranked brother to create man as a worker for the garden synonymous with mines of South Africa. Since then politics always made Zarkuhn ill. He was still an angel at heart and they were not created to be cunning and devious as was man. Of course man had little choice since they possessed the DNA of the God's. Angels, the Malachim did not possess the DNA or the blood of the Gods, they needed to learn the ways of manipulation and checkmate strategies. From the Crusades, to the World Wars politics had been the term used to describe the "art of social manipulation and mass control". Michael had been a part of such manipulation during the great wars of heaven when he fought the adversary Sammael, Satan, Jehovak's brother Enki.

In the book, "Secrets of Enoch (Enoch II)" he is referred to as the prince of demons and a magician, thus the term Serpent and Dragon was attached to him to describe his clever and tricky character a clever political move. Michael and his soldiers were deceived into fighting him and his followers by being led to believe he wanted God's thrown and rule over the heavens and Earth. Now the truth had been unveiled before Michael Zarkuhn's face by living the lie here on Earth he'd learned that he played a puppets role much like the Senator was playing for her masters.

"Michael did you here me? You're being paged by Miles."

"Senator excuse me, we'll continue this little chat later."

"Don't rush on my account, I'm in no hurry trust me."

"Now that would be a mistake, trusting you."

Michael closed the door and proceeded down the winding staircase to the conference room where he found the Collective inner circle still busy ironing out the last details to there eventual flight. He thought of them as his new Army and cared for them as he did his former Army although they were in no way as well trained or as dangerous. He slowly approached Miles who was standing at the end of the long conference table speaking with Ted Martin. Zarkuhn realized that every person in that room was in the next few days going to be uprooted from their homes and lives because they'd be unfairly labeled as terrorist being forced to flee.

Ted and Alice had longed prepared for such a day with a contingency plan as did each member of the Collective. Wills were done, trusts were in order, additional cash reserves set away in offshore accounts, multiple passports available, vaccination papers and the likes were in order for each inner circle member as well as each station chief under Michael Zarkuhn's purview. When the order was issued to disband came virtually all remnants of the Collective secret society would be quickly dissolved. What would be left might lead even the most seasoned investigator to believe that a money laundering scheme was at play under the name O.W.O.W. a nonprofit institution headed by a drunk billionaire from Texas with verifiable papers reflecting irrefutable proof that he was mentally incompetent to carry out even his own business transactions. Public records would indicate that because of J.P. Rockdale's clinical diagnosis of mental incompetency a power of attorney had been issued to Joshua Paul Rockdale III allowing him authority to conduct his father's business affairs to include the nonprofit organization. Thus, it was calculated that a search for Joshua would began, but exonerating his poor mentally challenged drunken father a purported member of the Collective.

Michael snickered when he thought of the difficult time the law would incur in their heated efforts to find and prosecute this bad seed standing before him. Last count over one hundred and fifty J.P. Rockdale decoys had been setup all over the planet by the Collective with intricate backgrounds, histories and leading to some trails in foreign countries that were so remote that no western eye's had visited for decades, thanks to Michael Zarkuhn's memory of places long forgotten. Confidence was by the group was abound that not many federal or international enforcement agency gutsy enough to follow through with all the work it capture would entail. These were the same agencies Michael was reminded that couldn't even locate Robert Vesco after his great money scheme involving Nixon. Michael had located him golfing on a so, so golf course down in Costa Rica surrounded by so many body guards the ball struck one on them on every stroke. What a handicap.

"Good Michael I'm glad you're here. I was able to contact Maurice and he was genuinely happy to here you're alive, a little puzzled as to how, okay a lot puzzled but happy. He says he would contact Lehchin and he let us know how you could get in touch with him in L.A."

"Miles that is indeed good news, I like that kid. I know he is a great warrior don't you feel it?"

"Michael the warrior stuff is your department, fainting is mine okay. Please try and remember that."

Margarite and J.P. overheard the comment by Miles and erupted in laughter.

"Peter, can I speak with you a moment Sir?"

"Of course you may speak with me Agent Todd, there's no doubt as to whether you can I'm sure you'll manage just fine."

"Over here I don't want the others to hear me. What exactly does J.P. do? I mean the guy's obviously a drunk and man I've never met a white man who speaks "country ebonics", what's his role?"

"Well his role is quite simple money. Mr. J.P. Rockdale was one of our first members to join the Collective family. Oh my, I don't know if that's classified, let me think no its not. Blazes, doesn't really quite matter at this point now does it? Anyway he was first approached because it was felt that he could provide much needed financing for the cause."

"What cause, I mean I've been here a day and you guys seem like some stuff out of a James Bond flick or that Dan Brown book doing so well on the market right now."

"Mr. Todd please don't ramble it's annoying. As I was saying he was approached by his long time friend Margarite's father who trusted him impeccably. Thus J.P. was eventually persuaded to come in. You see Mr. Rockdale holds a Ph.D. from the University of Texas in Economics."

"Say what, you're kidding that guy has a PhD?" Todd was pointing in the direction of the old drunk as he made eye contact with him at the same time and waved.

"Sir most every member on the Collective council has a doctorate it's somewhat a requirement for the smallest consideration. Please stop interrupting me I'm losing my train of thought. Where was I?"

"Friends, Margarite's father, you were talking about friends, and Margarite's father?"

"Yes, but it wasn't until after J.P.'s son was classified MIA in Vietnam that J.P. was convinced to join the cause."

"Why? I mean just because his son went missing."

"Well he fell out of favor with the war quite out of character for the good old Southern boy, but he was convinced to do so after being made privy to some information which showed him his country sacrificed our young men and women for selfish reasons accomplished by men of like mind to him. He vowed to fight them using any means he could to avenge the loss of his son."

"But with all that money and his smarts why would he become what I see today?"

"And what exactly is that, that you think you see today Agent Todd?"

Todd appeared baffled by the man servant's question to him the question was obvious. The guy was a drunk and rather squalid with no apparent ability to take care of himself.

"Perhaps that is the nucleus of your problem Mr. Todd, in that you cannot see at all. Your long service with the United States Government has indoctrinated you into the mode of temporary blindness. Trust me I'm being kind, extreme ignorance would have been a more accurate description of your symptoms."

"Perhaps, but that doesn't really answer my question does it."

"Let's just say that maybe the son J.P. eventually got back wasn't the one he remembered. Wars have away of changing a man or woman, something the Iraq War shall reflect in good time."

"I know what you mean. So his son had some problems huh?"

"Yes nothing real serious though, but they weren't that close after his return he seemed to be a different person according to J.P."

"Man that's too bad. I mean my father and I weren't close but I still talk to the old guy from time to time."

"Yes it really was bad especially in view of the fact that his son is his only known surviving family."

Peter excused himself and headed for the kitchen after he and Todd had talked. The seed Peter had just planted worked he felt it. He and Michael Zarkuhn knew the agent would swallow the bait. There was that gleam in Special Agents Todd's eyes that read "now I'm getting somewhere." What the poor sap didn't know and Peter wasn't going to inform him of was that J.P.'s son was killed in Vietnam supposedly near the Laos border on a special operations mission with Michael Zarkuhn when both were doing some special work for the government as a sniper. Thanks to some excellent long term foresight by Joseph

Plantard and J.P. a plan was initiated by the two men to replace the loss of J.P.'s son with a former renegade C.I.A. agent and friend who desired to join Zarkuhn's benefactors. The man returned as J. P. Rockdale III and melted into oblivion some years later leaving a Humint, (human intelligence) signature for any future snoopers to track if the need arrived. Peter thought about what Joseph used to say, "a dog that will fetch a bone will inevitably carry a bone back, the dog would be Todd."

Michael had gambled that agent Todd would carry the bones he found while with the Collective back to his master, thereby leaving a scent for a nonexistent lead after the disbandment of the Collective.

The bishop pulled into the parking lot of the hospital. He was irritable, hypoglycemic probably from worry as well as hunger. He decided he would get something to eat from the hospital cafeteria. This would not only give him the nourishment he needed but also help allow him to get his nerves up for the task ahead of him. His cell phone was going off as he stepped out of the van. He quickly stepped back out of the cold evening air and closed the van door crouching behind the van steering wheel.

"Hello, Bishop Terrell."
"And how is your task coming? You should be in place now so give me the news that will give me hope, yes."

"I am in place. I just arrived at the hospital where she's being cared for. I begged of you to please reconsider, release me from this task please reconsider."

It was bitterly cold and the Bishop's finger tips were sticking to his cell phone. He was putting the gloves he'd removed earlier during the trip back on using his teeth to pull them down over his wrist as he struggled to hear his caller talking. Oh how the Bishop longed to be a protestant right about now somewhere down South he began to think. The carefree life of spreading the word of God with no strings attached free of "Corporate Churchdom". He could do a sermon and then have Sunday supper with any of the multitude of women in the church. Possibly some overweight Southern black or white family or he would swing by some widow's home anoint her with a few words of spiritual encouragement, eat a hardy meal, bed her down and get a nice monetary offering for spreading the good word. Oh yeah! The tax free money for the shows he'd put on up at the pulpit; all that tithing collection doe for a few exciting statements like, "can I get a witness", and "you didn't hear me I said you didn't hear me someone testify," all with the James Brown flavor or that Rev. Jesse Jackson intensity. Yes why couldn't he have been born black or a white down South at least serve God as a Baptist even a Methodist would do? No! He just had to follow tradition and join a damn Roman religious cult, a clandestine band of latent pedophile homosexuals, shit it made him want to lose his religion.

The caller was now demanding that he enter and complete the task.

"I will not tell you again and when you have completed this task, you are to return to that mansion and await further instructions."
"I need to go before parking lot security gets suspicious I shall comply."

Captain Boggs was impressed by how much work Detective O'Connell was involved with, but something was strange about each one of his high profile cases although he couldn't put his finger on it. He needed another pair of fresh eyes. The intricacy and fast pace of the files was giving him heart burn and soon he would need his Pepto.

"Lieutenant what are you working on right this moment? Get in here it doesn't matter I need you to glance at something with me."

"Sure Captain, what you got?"

"Take a look see at these files and tell me what you think."

The Captain opened his left desk drawer only to find it empty. Then he checked the right drawer only to find an empty Pepto Bismol bottle. The lieutenant noticed but played it off knowing that soon all hell would most likely break loose. The lieutenant pressed on with the review of the files. The Captain was too calm as he got up from his seat and waltz over to his jacket reached into one of the pockets and pulled out a bottle Pepto, then reached into the large winter coat pocket and retrieve a paper bag with a super family size bottle of Pepto, grinned and proceeded to place it in the left drawer of his desk.

"Captain if these files are correct we may have ourselves a real problem. I haven't seen this much mud and intrigue since Nam. If it's what I think, it might be that we're gonna have feds up the wazoo soon. You got anymore of that Pepto Captain, I might need it."

Chapter 45

Who Invited You?

Colleeta did not like Cardinal Ricci he was not a Godly man. She was not fooled by his air of spiritual hype she was fully acquainted with Ricci's type for she had fallen prey to his type when she first entered the service of the church. Seduced and repeatedly used to please men of the cloth right in the houses of God. She was saved one night from another brutal rape by a man who was not so spiritual, but he was not pretentious either. The man was a member of the Catholic order, but he was a brutal cold blooded killer in the service of the church. Strange how he walked in the room finding Colleeta half naked sobbing with her robe hugging her ankles as the priest of her church devoured her young brown taut nipples. The stranger punished the priest severely as she coward speechless in a corner of the room. Afterwards the priest was made to reveal what he'd done to all the members of the church and to his superiors. It wasn't long before he was called back to the Vatican from the little village in Indonesia. The priest was later found dead at his next assignment. The death by asphyxiation was ruled. What nobody could solve was why he had a robe on pulled down around his ankles or who might have done it. Colleeta knew she knew that her rescuer was not satisfied with the hand slapping from the Church all too often given to their perverts. Paul Constantine had hidden out at her church that night of the murder until the authorities stopped looking for a white haired, very athletic built man wanted for an assassination of an Italian banker in the area also supposedly connected with the esoteric Rosicrucian Order, P2. That particular night he was her Messiah. Paul liberated her and from then on no one in the church crossed her it was as though she had been marked for protection from that day on. That is why she worked for Mr. Constantine and gave him her allegiance as did many in secrecy in the church, for he was predictable and in his own way righteous even if he wasn't so good or clean it did not matter he removed all the filth from the Earth in the name of the Church even the filth within its sanctum.

Colleeta had contacted Paul Constantine and told him that the Cardinal was there in Los Angeles and that he was holding a woman and her child captive. She was glad to hear the joy in his voice and realized the Cardinal might soon be wearing clothes around his ankles the thought excited her tremendously.

"Do not be afraid my dearest I will not harm you. You poor child I'm so sorry you are here under the power of that evil man."

"Who, whom are you referring sister?"

"The Cardinal, that malicious sanctimonious old fart."

"Ha, ha, stop you're making me laugh. Thank you I needed that. I haven't laughed in so long I'd forgotten how. I was under the impression you were a company girl sister."

"The company of God not rapist and abusive clergy like that. He is why the Catholic Church has a bad reputation, his kind. Megalomaniacs, pedophiles and devil worshipers hiding right under the lovely wool of God it's a shame."

"You know you sure speaking with better diction and articulation than you were when we first met. What's up with that Sister?"

Merie had been fooled like many before her. The sister was clever and gutsy but realized to allow anyone to know this would prompt them to attack her spirit thus taking away her strength.

"I've been in the service of God through the Catholic Church for fifty years ever since my fourteenth birthday. The Church is good but riddled with some walking, talking cancers like the Cardinal. Oh! Is the baby his missy? You do not have to answer I will understand."

"Its fine, yes he's Tashi's father."

"He hurt you didn't he?"

"I … ah … yes he took me. I was married and he violated me, my marriage vows and me. I never thought I could hate, but I hate him and I feel guilty for it."

"Because of the baby you feel guilty. You possess immense love for the child and yet his progenitor is a man you hate. It is perfectly normal for you to feel the way you do. Missy Merie it is okay to hate as long as you hate the act of sin and forgive the person. The act is over, yes?" You can not change what has happened you must forgive yourself and him in order to move forward.

Merie leaned forward on the little cot she was sitting on and the old nun Colleeta moved towards her they embraced as Colleeta stroked Merie's hair she comforted her.

"I know you wish to see Tashi so I'll be back. You must be hungry too."

"Yes very much, thank you Ma'am."

Colleeta smiled and left Merie's side stopped at the door and turned back towards Merie. "You mustn't leave the room it would not be safe you are considered a liability to the Cardinal so please stay put my child."

"I understand, I'll remain here sister."

Colleeta gently closed the door and disappeared down the long dark stone corridor.

Lehchin wasn't sure of why the plans had changed, but he was in high gear. He'd not slept once during the long flight from Hong Kong to his destination. He had too much adrenaline pumping through him, Lehchin was wired. "Taxi."

"Where to?"

"Here take me to any hotel near this address please."

"Right away."

"Peter I wanted to share with this with you, you've helped me see Mr. Rockdale in a different light."

"If there's nothing else Mr. Todd I'll be getting on with my duties."

"Well Pete my man."

"What now Mr. Todd?"

"Never mind thank you, Peter."

"I would say no problem, but I'd be lying so excuse me."

Todd gazed around the room wondering about everyone in it. What were their stories, how did they come to be with this group?

Michael was just entering the room when he made eye contact with Todd and called him over.

"How are you going to handle your predicament Todd? You're a fugitive and as much as I enjoy your company you can't remain here."

"I realize that. I think that if I can get into Washington D.C. I might be able to get an audience with the Secretary and clear myself."

"Listen to me, Todd maybe you should consider a different plan."

"Why? Do you know something I should know? What would make you suggest that Michael?"

"You're in the Intelligence business and yet you don't seem to be able to use any of it. In this business nothing is ever what it appears you just try and keep that in mind. Trust me Agent Todd your life depends on it."

Michael walked away and over to others still planning for their eventual exodus.

"Michael when are you traveling to Los Angeles?"

"I was thinking tonight might not be soon enough, Miles."

Ted Martin heard the conversation and told the others gathered around the table. The news of Michael possibly departing bothered them all. He was their security blanket and right now his presence helped give them a sense of peaceful security. For Michael to leave would crush that security creating an environment of anxiety. In fact, the anxiety was already creeping up its ugly head.

"Michael did we over hear you were going somewhere?"

"Hey look Ted, J.P., all of you gather around for a second. I've got to go to Los Angeles, but I will not be there long if all goes according to plan I'll be back with you by dinner tomorrow."

"Yes if all goes well you say, but what if it doesn't? Can you tell us why you have to leave?"

"Alice it's important that's all I should really say."

Michael glanced at Miles and Margarite as they held hands standing over a map of Central America.

"We're getting prepared for one the most serious missions in this organization's history and you are the pivotal pillar in maintaining security and protection for us and you're leaving?"

"Ted calm down, Michael they deserve to know tell them."

"Very well Margarite. I'm going to California to attempt to rescue Meri Tashido and her child."

"Well why didn't you just say so? If you don't mind that's a trip I'd like to accompany you on."

"I don't think that would be a good idea Ted the team may need you here. Field ops work can be very treacherous and fatal."

"Well if he doesn't go may I go?"

"Absolutely not Todd you wouldn't get two feet in or out of an airport anywhere in the country."

"Well let Todd be my muscle here, I want to go with you to save that young lady and little Tashi."

"Alice what do you think? You think Ted can come out and play."

Alice gazed up into her husband's brown eyes and held his cheeks in both of her palms. "I don't want you to go Ted. I don't think it's a good idea, but if you really want too I'll not stop you. I understand why you're doing this and you don't have to prove anything."

Ted kissed his wife passionately which got the whole room sounding off with the customary team, "awe".

"Look Alice I'll take care of him."

"Yes my buddy Michael will get me home in one piece. Michael I'll make the arrangements if you'll give me the details."

"That would be very helpful Miles I'll be right with you."

Captain its Sergeant O'Connell's family, his father to be exact. He's on line two and he says it's important."

"Joe, Richey here, I'm so sorry we're communicating like this after twenty years. Yes it's been twenty, I know man I know. So what's up? How's your boy Joe?"

"Joe, try and slow down, start from the beginning because it just so happens I've got your boy's files right in the front of me, no hold on. I need to get to a pen. Okay say that again the part about the snakes and circle. Okay I got it, but what does it mean. No Joe, I was thinking out loud. Did he mention anything else before passed out, anything that might make a little sense? Hey what the hell! Look will you be there later? I was going to stop by later. Yeah well I'll see you guy."

Captain Boggs placed a picture down in front of him on the desk along with some other photos. He was determined to pass the test, he was on the trail, it was final he was going to need some Pepto.

"Joe had said that his son told him of snakes on the bodies of his assailant? Yeah right a tattoo why didn't he think of it sooner. He'd verified an officer was still outside Sergeant O'Connell's room? This was good because another attack could occur."

"Is that your cell phone Todd?"

"Yes Miles it is. I've got to take this it's important would you get Michael."

"I'll try but he and Ted are getting ready to go to the airport."

Miles scurried out of the room looking for Michael as Todd exited the mansion library through the large courtyard doors. There were stars littering the sky and the moon was fighting to claim its fullness. Agent Todd was numb from the cold winter air but not too cold to notice the beauty of the lights above. He listened intently as he gazed at the heavens completely lost in the beauty of the moment he had to force himself to concentrate on the caller's dialogue.

"Mr. Secretary I'm so sorry about."

"Shut up Agent Todd and listen and listen well. You've caused me a great deal of trouble and I expect you to get your sorry bottom in my office as soon as possible here in Washington."

"Sir I will turn myself into the nearest law enforcement office tonight and request I be sent to the Washington venue."

"No don't do that! I need to verify your location I'll send a recovery team for you to turn yourself in. Your idea may be risky there are a lot of angry police officers out there about hearing of two dead agents found in Atlanta."

"Mr. Secretary I did not kill anyone I."

"I said to listen not communicate. Where are you?"

"Mr. Secretary I'm confused if you really wanted to know my whereabouts I couldn't conceal it. I mean you have tremendous resources at your disposal …"

There was that standard silence during awkward moments suddenly the wheels started to turn and a little faster for Special Agent Todd. He could hear Michael Zarkuhn's voice as he cautioned him that things were not what they always seemed to be. He would need to be delicate in his handling of this matter in the next few minutes.

"Of course Sir I'm in Boston. I was visiting a family friend."

"Bad time to be vacationing, give me the address Agent Todd."

Todd paused realizing that he no longer trusted the system he'd believed in. He was afraid not for himself but for the people who were inside the huge stone structure behind him. He was thinking so fast his head hurt.

"Sir, perhaps there is a better course of action?"

"You've obviously not listened to a word I've said agent. Give me your location, give me your present address?"

Todd couldn't believe he was refusing to comply with a direct order from the Secretary of the Department of Homeland Security. What was more fascinating to him was that the Secretary was too interested in this whole affair, he couldn't help but have his first real free thought since being a federal agent, "why was the Secretary of Homeland Security so interested in this matter?" He would not help "the man" any longer. Todd hung up his phone as Michael walked back through the large French doors into the mansion library turned around and walked back out into the courtyard. Michael spotted Agent Todd his aura was brighter clearer he was happy.

"I'm pleased."

"Now why is that my large handsome friend, tell me what could possibly please you?"

"I am pressed to ask you the same question. Miles asked me to join you, that you requested my presence."

"No I thought I needed you. You know their coming, how could I have been so foolish, sorry?"

"Believe me I've played the role a time to two in my life time."

"Michael I'm talking seventeen years here okay not a drop in the bucket. I think I was set up and I think the Secretary of Homeland Security knows something about the whole mess. Hell everybody knows he's had eyes on the Presidency, he's a war hero and then some."

Michael placed his tote over his shoulder and slowly walked around agent Todd also gazing up at the stars as he addressed him.

"Well what makes you say that?"

"I just spoke with him and it wasn't good. I think we're going to have some visitors from him and I feel their not totally noble in their efforts to get to the truth. I think they want what you've got."

"Good I'm glad you're finally pulling the veil from over your eyes. What woke you up? Would you like a weapon?"

"Now what kind of question is that? The Secretary wants to bring me in, but I volunteered to turn myself in. He insists on dispatching his own private escort to get me back to S.O.G., so if you think I'm going to take arms against the United States …"

"I expect you to protect yourself and my family while I'm away. However, there is another way we can get you free and clear of association with us and maybe clear your good name, it will require that you do two things."

"Go ahead you've got my attention."

"One you'll have to cooperate with the Senator and two give yourself up as a possible traitor for now."

"Oh is that all. Are f"""""n nuts Michael I love my country I'm not going out as a traitor."

"Are you a traitor?"

"No!"

"Do you wish to help all of mankind or America which is more important to you?"

"I never thought about it that way. I mean American versus mankind, the one world stuff."

"Yes that's where you're at it's your decision. Too many people on our planet are attached to their country and countrymen not to the planet Earth and all peoples sharing it."

"You people are into some stuff that I have no clue about aren't you? I'm almost afraid to know. What exactly is it that you're involved in?"

"Now Todd if I answer that I'll have to kill you."

"Michael you crack me up." Special Agent Christopher Todd burst into a little laugh, but Michael wasn't joining him. Things were definitely more serious than he thought.

"What do you want to do, do you have a plan?"

"Captain Boggs you will not believe this."

"Come on in Lieutenant I'm on to something here with O'Connell's files their well, different."

"What you got?"

"Remember the broad that was shot with the nun stuff in her room?"

"She's dead right, damn shame?"

"No, she's in recovery and talking already."

"Say what?"

"Yeah I just got off the phone with our officer down at Beth Israel Hospital assigned to guard her room and he verified she's talking like she just had a cold. Say's the doc said it's a miracle."

"Maybe she is a nun because she's definitely must be living right. Hey do me a favor it's a long shot; ask the officer there to have her doctor call me."

"Sure Captain."

"Great, Agent Todd you hungry the staff has prepared the most wonderful dinner?"

"It's Anne, no Ahhh, Annette, Betty, your name I'm trying to remember your name."

"I'm Alice agent Todd please come in and join us."

"Thank you, will the Senator be joining us?"

"No, not while Michaels not here, why?"

"I need to speak with her later if possible."

"Sure I'll take you up after we eat."

"Miles thank you."

"Wonderful thank you nurse, I really appreciate this it is so very kind of you."

"What was the name again Father?"

"That's just it I know her as Theresa, Sister Theresa."

"My, I bet you're talking about the Jane Doe."

"Why have you had a nun come in injured?"

"We don't know if she's a nun for real or not. Some of the officers were joking about it because of some clothing or something they found in her belongings. She's got gun shot wounds can you believe it poor girl was shot three times, hold on! Here we are."

"But of course."

"There we go room 332 that's our Jane Doe. Father, oh Father she's under a security watch."

The elevator took forever to get to the third floor and the Bishop was nervous it had been awhile since he'd killed, but then always in the service of the church as if that cleaned his conscientious. It could never be cleaned no matter how many hail Maries anyone did. He was doomed by his past sins and now would be for the sin he was about to do. He arrived at the room of his prey but the guard wasn't present which made him pull his weapon premature. The Bishop cautiously entered the room and found no one, but the bathroom door was closed and it was time to pay the piper. Slowly, ever so slowly the Bishop approached the bathroom door and grabbed it opening it quickly. He placed his weapon back under his robe.

"Nurse, nurse, NURSE! This police officer needs medical attention."

"Oh my God what happened?"

"I don't know he was in here on the floor."

"Oh my, this is not good, this is not good at all."

"Bishop I know please move Father."

"Yes excuse me I must contact my church."

"Bishop, Bishop, Bishop, please come back."

The Bishop was looking for a place not the place where his intended target might have escaped to, but a place where he might consider what he was trying to do at the hospital in the first place. As Bishop Terrell walked quickly and aimlessly down the hospital corridor he realized what he needed to do. He needed to be closer to his maker, closer to God surely his answers lie there. How could he have forgotten that his peace of mind and salvation was etched in his faith in, God.

"Excuse me nurse where's the hospital chapel?"

"Just right around the corner last door on the right father, would you like me to show you?"

"No I'll be fine thank you."

The Bishop was nervous and felt his soul slipping from him. He desperately needed to purge the black marks on the "book of life" against him. The door to the chapel was wood with an ornate stain glass window, and Bishop Terrell paused before he opened the door and entered the chapel. It was small, but surprisingly tastefully done he liked the feel of the room. He gazed around after leaving the basin and was suddenly greeted by a friendly familiar face.

"My goodness Bishop Terrell, how are you? What a pleasant surprise oh my, it has been a long time sir."

"Bobby McNamara that is you! I can't believe it, I thought you were in Texas."

"Oh, James I was for some time."

"When did you get here no one notified me that you were to be assigned here in my area."

"I just got here two days ago, but I'm not assigned here I'm merely visiting from Florida. Unfortunately, I have a family member having an operation tomorrow so I'm a part of the cheering squad. You know how that goes?"

Bishop Terrell trusted Bobby, he had known him for a long time and he was going to test that trust with his next request.

"Well my friend what brings you here to the hospital?"

"I'm here to visit you, I need to confess. I must come clean."

"What a confessional! James I don't know that, that …"

"You must old friend, my soul, oh my soul is at …"

Bishop Terrell was shaking and Father McNamara realized this was a serious matter his friend was dealing with and he would not leave him alone at that moment. He put his arms around the much younger cleric and led him over to a bench in the very front of the tiny hospital chapel. They sat and Father McNamara began to pray.

"Bishop I'm ready let's do this how long has it been brother."

"Old friend entirely too long, much too long and I fear for my …"

"I know fear no more of this please enter."

Bishop Terrell entered the small box and sat quietly in the dark feeling lost and scared. He couldn't remember how he'd gotten to the place where he was at this point in his life, relegated as a hit man wearing the cloth of a soldier of the Catholic Church sent to kill another of God's creatures. He heard the father addressing him and he responded opening up to his listener not holding back, not holding back anything. The more he told the better he felt. Redemption, he sought to be forgiven, if only he could be forgiven just to hear the words maybe he could start over and get on the right path to salvation, back in the good graces of the church, no he thought "to hell with the church" he needed to know God forgave him. The church had helped put his soul in jeopardy once, but he would make it right after tonight.

Little Tashi was awake when Sister Colleeta entered the room and he was fussy. It was obvious that he wanted to see a familiar face and that he was hungry.

"Oh little one come on let's get you to mommy, aye."

"Sister what are you doing with the boy?"

"Cardinal I hadn't noticed you there."

"Obvious."

"Yes, well I was taking Tashi to spend time with his mother."

"Absolutely not! I will not have that woman near my … this child, no simply out of the question. I thought I had explained the situation to you. Did you not understand? No it is clear to me that you did not."

"Cardinal the child needs the mother, mother gets better and child is happy. Surely no harm can come from the love between the two."

"What did I say? You are beginning to try my patience and that is not recommended, not at all woman, now get the doctor here as I demanded earlier."

"I have sent for Doctor Rodriguez. He handles all of us here at this place. The doctor will attend to her and your desire to drug her."

"Enough, the next time I see you it had better be under circumstances which make me feel better about your existence here."

"May I depart now your eminence, Tashi needs to be fed."

"Yes feed him he needs his nourishment. He is rather handsome isn't he? ... And he's smart too, what a wonderful child don't you think?" Colleeta turned and walked away from the room ensuring her manner of walk and demeanor were humble in appearance not wanting to insult the Cardinal's fragile ego any more than had been done.

"Who is it? Come in if you have a key."

"Senator I thought you might be hungry or at least desire company."

"Todd nobody invited you. You're sure acting awfully cozy around here these days so what's up?"

"That's why I'm here I'm hoping you can tell me."

CHAPTER 46

BRING IT ON

"Boss we got one hour and …"

"Yeah, look lets just get there okay I need some satisfaction. You know that S.O.B. tried to have me popped and I got some payback. Plus there's a package there that might prove of use to us, yeah it may be what we need to leverage the deal."

"The deal? What deal boss?"

"Jimmy drive the damn vehicle and watch out you almost hit that last car you dummy. All we need right now is some overzealous copper begging for an Irish funeral by messing with me about now so mind your cues."

"What exactly do you want Todd?"

"Senator I want to know how could you do what you did to your friends downstairs?"

"You're talking about my country here Todd."

"Senator the first time I ever met you was in the office of one of your friends and you thrashed me for disrespecting her, what's happened to you don't you have your priorities straight anymore?"

"You listen to me you don't know crap about nothing. This is not a frat game it's for keeps and it's real you understand?"

"Yes, well it's my country too and I want to help you Senator."

"Help me, how?"

"They've said if I agree to turn myself in they'll release me, but the catch is I must be escorted by you."

The Senator sat up in her chair and pushed it back as she stood up and began pacing the floor. She was not happy at hearing what Todd had just shared. She was suspicious, suspicious because it was out of character for the way the Collective operated.

"Why would they want to do that? Wait it makes sense. Pressure, if I get stuck with you the pressure is squarely on me not them, but!"

"But what Senator? It's good for both of us and once I clear myself we can deal with this group with support from our country. Deal, is it a deal?"

"Yes let's get out of here, how, when?"

"Let me verify with Michael and the rest and I'll be back."

"Right."

The Senator was not at all comfortable with the arrangement suggested by Special Agent Todd, but if she wouldn't be killed, she could get her allies to rally and stall an offensive on the mansion so she could somehow retrieve the treasure and the "Tables of Testimony" wanted by American Intelligence community so desperately.

"Thank you Father McNamara you have saved me."

"You have led a very tumultuous life Bishop I never knew, wow."

"Yes and I am not entirely proud of all the things I have done. But this I do know the path I took was paved for me by those in the Catholic Church when I was very young and naïve. Never again will I believe what I am told based on just faith I will think for myself and confer with God almighty and also use my heart to temper my path."

"I don't know what to say."

"Bobby say nothing and thank you old friend."

"James, try and remember God forgives all for we all fall sort of the glory of God. Protect yourself and good luck Bishop Terrell."

Father McNamara left the room and Bishop Terrell could not help but noticed him shaking his head as he departed.

"Bishop, oh Bishop are you searching for me?"

"What? Who, who are you? Don't tell me you're the mystery woman who was injured in the room."

"Enough Bishop you know very well who I am. Why were you sent? Are you really a Bishop?"

"You had to have been listening for quite sometime correct, well then you know I am. As for who sent me, God sent me I was here visiting a friend when I was summoned to attend …"

"You and I both see through your lies Bishop. I have much experience in lying and deceit you can't fool me especially since I overheard you describe your bad boy days. You're a shooter, mechanic, cleaner and I'm your target. I'm going to ask you once more before I become rude. Who sent you?"

"You already know who."

Contessa realized that although the man in front of her was a man of the cloth he was in all probability a seasoned killer and she would need to get his attention and respect to be taken serious.

"Come, you get in the front of me and if you move or breathe to my displeasure I will be forced to do you here."

The bishop was calm and at peace as he walked in front of the young woman. She held the police revolver at his back as he was led to an office in the back of the chapel. Contessa shut the door behind them and told him to sit. Bishop Terrell held no animosity towards her and couldn't understand why he had obeyed the Cardinal's order to kill her.

"Ahh! Oh my God! Why did you do that? It's broken, ahh, ooh."

"Well I did it because I can and well yes it is broken or at least I hope it is. Now who sent you? Oh and Bishop I'll take that gun under your robe you could hurt somebody with that."

"Ricci, ahhh, Cardinal Ricci sent me, but as I said earlier you already knew that. Please hand me something to at least wrap this hand."

"Later, why did he send you, I mean do you regularly kill people when you're not attempting to save their souls?"

"No of course not. You know him, well then you're acquainted with his intolerance for disobedience and failure in following his dictates. He wanted to make sure that your presence in this country could not be traced back to the Vatican no reason given of course, so he demanded I complete the task. What was your assignment? I know you're going to kill me so what harm would there be in telling me why you were here."

"Constantine, a man named Constantine was becoming a thorn in the Cardinal's buttocks. Talk about failure he was starting to pop up all over the grid due to his insatiable appetite for murder and mayhem. So I was pulled in from my part time job to do this job for my church."

"Your church?"

"Yes my church, I'm a member who will do anything to ensure the protection and sanctity of the church."

"What about Ricci? He ordered your death to protect himself."

"Correction, to protect the church and so what I would have done the same. Look there are evil men and good men, but the church does not waver it remains righteous and a path of light."

"How did you survive your injuries? Obviously you were injured otherwise you wouldn't be here and what are you going to do about Constantine now?"

"You've asked all the questions you need to. You too many questions, no more questions. Where do you want it? Head, heart, come on time is a ticking Bishop."
   Contessa was so cold with her request and extremely serious about her work. A curtain on one of the office windows was torn off its rod and wrap around the muzzle of the gun along with a pillow cushion at the last minute. Bishop Terrell

got off the chair and on his knees, his broken right hand shook violently as he gingerly positioned it away from his body and with his left hand pulled out rosary beads from a pocket under his robe. Contessa Hannabolas didn't need to bring suspicion to her by the gun blast. She contemplated garroting the priest but a quick kill without resistance was preferred because she still felt weak from her quick healing wounds.

"Young lady I know Paul better than anyone and if he was the one who did you, he knows Cardinal Ricci sent you he'll be gunning for Ricci next."

"You never mentioned you know Constantine."

"I think I know what he failed at as well, it was something the group I'm associated with here in Boston was searching for. Cardinal Ricci thinks we have it, but we do not. That didn't matter to him he's attacked innocent people in an attempt to get the object an object that doesn't exist."

"Interesting, this object is something the Catholic Church would want? What is it?"

"Ma'am it is something that every person, organization and institution would want. But understand this is in fact not a church issue but this sole quest of a madman. The church would never approve of how the Cardinal has conducted his affairs using the veil of the Catholic Church. I will caution you to reconsider any thoughts of trying to find the relic in question or in toying with Mr. Constantine."

"I have changed my plan. I will not kill you yet I'll wait until you've serve the church in their quests to retrieve the object you are speaking of. Get up, slowly we're out of here and you'll make a great decoy."

"May I suggest a robe for you sister. A head cover and nun's outfit will look more believable and conceal your appearance a quite nicely."

"Great idea and it's not like I wear this outfit enough, I'm in luck there are several articles of clothing in this closet. You don't move or I'll change the plan again. You never told me what the object is. Tell me, is this relic the Holy Grail, because if so forget it. I happen to know where that Bloodline resides. Oh, the

Ark of the Covenant! No Israel has it. The original Breastplate of Judgment now that would be a most profitable find."

"Miss I'm not going to tell you anything, so stop guessing. I simply have to find some medicine for the pain. My hand is killing me."

Michael and Ted boarded the aircraft for Los Angeles. Paul and his crew were now four hours from the outskirts of Los Angeles. The newest Collective security team member settled into his Los Angeles hotel room and then contacted Maurice Steeley who forwarded the information to Miles at Plantard Mansion.

Special Agent Todd walked down the long staircase and into the conference room where he noticed Miles getting off the phone. Todd approached him and nodded to Miles and Margarite.

"She's good with it."

"Great where is she?"

"Getting her bags ready, she wishes to speak with all of you before we leave."

The flight wouldn't take long to get to Los Angeles and Michael couldn't wait. As he and Ted Martin settled into there seats Michael gave intense thought to the open items having to do with the Collective's situation. He had ceased all emails to the Controller and had assigned a local Collective intelligence agent in his Boston cell to work on gathering any information on the Controller's identity and possible location using all historical data from the Collective files. Michael was completely confident that she would learn the identity of the Controller. He squeezed the gift that Peter had given to him for he knew the power of the stones would protect them all. Peter had surprised him and the mysterious old man was renting plenty of space in Michael's head. Michael needed to give his friend some deep thought. The evacuation of the Collective inner circle to world safe havens and the secure placement of the "Tables of Testimony" within the walls of the genome laboratory owned by the Collective raced through his mind. With the Tablet the team could if successful unlock the answers to every question a person could ever ask God. He declined the drink offered to him by the flight attendant and decided to get a nap.

Ted missed Missy, his mother. He could not wait to talk with her again. The anticipation was killing him he knew she'd be happy to hear from him. Ted pulled out his electronic address book and placed the telephone number given to him by his wife into his files. He was almost tempted to call her right then. He had the best wife in the world and to think she had stayed in touch with his mom for all these years without his knowledge. Ted could get a nap with a smile on his face knowing those two special women were a part of his life.

"Captain, boy am, I glad you're here."

"Sorry I don't feel the same way Sarge. Where's the injured officer?"

"He's alright sir just a little droggy. States somebody clocked him from behind, and from the size of the lump on his head they clopped him good."

"And the girl? Any location on her?"

"Afraid not sir she just poofed, disappeared and Captain they stole the officer's roscoe."

"She just poofed, what the heck is poofed? Sarge don't use that word I hate that word.... poof. Look she's wounded they couldn't have gotten far especially if someone is carrying her, so poof will not work for me. I want that girl. Hey there son are you okay?"

"Yes sir Captain, I'm fine sir. I think somebody got the girl. She was asking to be let out before all this happened. I think she was afraid. Sorry about losing my gun sir."

"Tell you what lock this puppy down Sarge. I want this place combed from head to toe now! Where's Sergeant O'Connell's room nurse."

"I'll take you there Captain I know where it is."

"Thanks Sarge let's check O'Connell out and hey do you have a replacement here yet for this young officer? That's right there's no one in the room to guard any longer she went poof. I need some Pepto."

Everybody in the conference room was quiet as Senator Stinger walked in carrying a tote and a large luggage bag. She sat them down in the doorway and began to speak.

"I just wanted to apologize to all of you. I never intended to hurt any of you or to betray your trust. I simply thought that what I was doing was right, I'm sorry."

"Senator for what it's worth, it was a pleasure getting to know you I really mean it."

"Thank you Alice."

"Todd if you're ready."

"Sure senator I'll pull the car around. Peter you say this ones okay to use?"

"Yes Agent Todd that particular vehicle should be adequately serviced and ready for use."

"Well folks I too appreciate everything and if you ever get down South stop by and holler at me in Atlanta okay especially you J.P. I'd really love to see your mug old buddy."

"Ah I bet yah say dat tah all da fellas."

"Just the ones I love J., just the ones I love."

Agent Todd grabbed the senator's bags and headed for the door and down to the garage from the kitchen. Senator Stinger glanced at her lover Cheryl her emotions were easily read by all present in the room. Her face revealed her heart as tears rolled down her face the eyes said, "I never meant to hurt you right now I just need to hear you say it's okay, that you do care, that you've always cared, please say it, please, before I leave, please." But Karen's lover did not see those words in her teary eyes and Karen would not to hear what she longed to hear from the woman she loved. Karen was not forgiven and more importantly she wouldn't hear the words she longed for, "I still love you". In fact, Cheryl was surprisingly apathetic towards Karen, thus utterly stupefying her ex-lover and the curious heterosexual bystanders of the Collective. Karen's mind became a puzzle palace wondering how she had been fooled into thinking Cheryl's love was so true blue. She cut the process off and joined Todd as he descended down the stairs and into the garage.

"Where's Tashi? I thought you were going to bring him to me."

"Sweetie I'm sorry, so sorry but I was directed to leave the baby by …"

"The Cardinal, he wouldn't let you bring him to me. If I ever get the chance I will make him pay. He will pay for the death of my husband and for the loss of my virtue, for putting my son and me through all of this. I realize you tried and for that I'm grateful."

"Your day will be soon my sweetie, shhhh. We have help on the way."
The small, round nun whispered.

"Who, how do you know, when? I'm hitting you with too much aren't I? What should I do?"

"Sweetie listen say nothing, do nothing but what you have done, be still. Do not be sound of mind either, let them think you need the doctor the medicine it will keep them from you until you are free. I have a strong suspicion that the Cardinal's robe shall soon be around his ankles, quite soon."
Colleeta smiled and nodded her head in conformation, her chubby coarse hands folded as though in prayer.

"What does that mean sister? Robe, ankles?"

"It's a very long story my child here eat and by the way a doctor will see you tomorrow morning. Don't worry he is to give medicine, medicine that will incapacitate you."

"What!"

"Trust me love I will ensure you are okay you will be fine don't fret you will be fine."

"I believe you Colleeta don't let me down, don't let them harm Tashi."

"I will die first sweetie trust me no harm shall befall you or Tashi."

"Where to boss?"

"Pull in over there in that driveway at Arby's, yeah I could use some horseradish and beef right about now, well get to it Jimmy."

"Yeah sure thing boss."

"Give me that phone mate I got a party to set up. Aye! Jimmy, get me three beef and cheddars with extra horsey sauce."

"Sure boss that sounds good. I'll let the guys know to eat their fill."

"Yes sir I can get there no problem." Lehchin hung up the phone.

He was still primed and brimming with anticipation. The young man couldn't believe he was about to support the lead team from home base. He was going to back up Mr. Zarkuhn a legend in the Collective organization. The agents that Lehchin had spoken with in the Asian theater all said Michael Zarkuhn was not real, that he was the fastest, strongest and most skillful artisan in the world of espionage and security that they were aware of. Of course if there was someone better the nature of their jobs would be that they wouldn't know of someone better until it was too late. When Lehchin had asked his mentor and supervisor Maurice Steeley about Zarkuhn all he could do was shake his head and say "the man's nuts, the best but nonetheless, nuts and don't tell him I said so."

"Lehchin was there says he'll meet us in front of the South Terminal the Delta section."

"I just spoke with Marcus, the station chief for this area and he will meet us at the base here do you know where that is he didn't say?"

"Sure I do, Marcus probably would've refused to give it to you if you had asked."

"Maybe he just assumed I knew."

"Well it looks like we're going to make the party you up to it Ted?"

"As ready as I'll ever be."

"Senator perhaps would be a good time for me to contact the Secretary to inform him that I'm on my way in."

"Todd you're really going to go to Washington to try and explain your position to your people? You know their going to attempt to use you like a wireless puppet. I think perhaps I should enlighten you, because despite your numerous flaws I like you."

"Well I think "a thank you" is in order, but I don't really know why you're being so cynical about the matter."

"Keep driving get us to Logan and just listen to me. I'm not in this for some lobbyist group or money. I'm not trying to protect a bunch of Canadian retirees and under educated White beach bum constituents from my districts. This is bigger than all of that, because an item that that group back there at the mansion have in their possession is so powerful that nobody on this planet will be able to challenge them. That power should belong to those better suited to handle it."

"Let me guess, you and your group should possess this item right and what item are we talking about Senator? Is it some new kind of weapon?"

"That's not important what is important is that the United States government control such a power for the safety and prosperity for all the peoples future."

"You see that's where you lose me Senator. What people which ones? Americans, White Americans, coloreds who? Senator can you explain to me whose interest the American government going to protect? Well?"

"Boy Todd you have grown up. Don't you think you're taking a rather cynical view of your government, your beloved employer. You're a regular international Boy Scout aren't you? However, your question was valid all except the part where you referred to people of color as coloreds."

"What! Senator you just stated yourself they're people of color. I think you're over reacting, you're being too sensitive."

"Don't use the term colored Todd unless you don't value your teeth around Blacks. Try African American, I believe that's the term we're using this year."

"I don't get it Senator Black, Negro, Colored it seems to me you're talking out of both sides of your mouth you're not even from Africa. African American yeah right, I don't know who you're for or what, but I don't think it's the United States government that's for sure. For all I know you may have your own hidden agenda with some secret group of your own."

"When you get to Washington Todd it will all be made clear, unfortunately it may be too late for you to capitalize on the knowledge."

"Is that why we haven't contacted the Secretary for Homeland Security's office yet? Because you think I won't be able to clear myself?"

"Yes part of the reason."

"What's the other part? What is it that you aren't revealing?"

"A raid will be done on the mansion before they move that item and if we notify Washington that we're no longer at that location they will be hard pressed to support a raid, remember Waco?"

"So we wait and allow the Department of Homeland Security to strike is that why the Secretary did not want me to come in on my own? Wait a minute how would you know that? You're working with him. I mean you sit on the Senate Intelligence committee for Homeland Security, hell he owes his selection to that post to you. You were his biggest supporter."

"No phone calls we keep low until we're called got it Todd? If they realize that I'm out and clear they'll attack for sure, so we buy a little time for me to fix this. Maybe I can resolve this amicably."

"I don't like it those fine folks could be injured or even killed."

Senator Stinger glanced over at Todd as he glanced over at her and he could read that look. She really didn't like what happening either.

"They don't want survivors do they, right Senator? Even if the persons at that mansion were to cooperate and comply with the feds the idea is to leave no one alive, well answer me Senator? How are they going to pull it off, huh?"

"Special Agent Todd you should be concerned for your own safety at this point and yes they want all of you dead just in different locations under different situations."

"How's your hand Bishop?"

"I'm afraid it's pretty bad it hurts like hell."

"Father I'm appalled at such language."

"Please don't be my dear, just get me out of here. I really need some pain killers bad."

"Keep moving down this way into the crowd Father, go on."

"They're checking persons departing the building should I keep moving."

"Yes keep moving we have no choice and try not to do anything that will require you receiving last rites."

"If my hand doesn't get better we may have to give me last rites anyway."

"You're funny Father I can't wait to party with you."

As Contessa and Bishop Terrell slowly approached the exit door of the hospital Contessa concealed his injured hand even more with a head piece she'd pulled from the shelf in the office where they had hidden.

The police were scrutinizing everybody's identification as they exited the building and this was going to pose a challenge to Contessa's effort to escape. She had to think and think quickly about how to address the check point coming up.

Bishop Terrell was indifferent the broken hand he'd been given by his captor was throbbing as though he were holding a rapper's woofer with hot gasoline burning on it. He wasn't sure if it was the throbbing or the burning sensation that hurt worse. Their turn to exit was next.

"Good evening Father your license sir."

Contessa began to jabber in Italian as she held the Bishop's one good hand tightly against her restricting his movement.

"One moment officer I, I …"

The Bishop was wincing in obvious pain as he attempted to calm his companion who by now was pointing at his injured hand while still clutching his good arm.

"Father is your hand hurt?"

"Yes officer that is why we were here getting medicine", remarked the Bishop as he suddenly got the gist of what his captor was trying to pull off. "I think that is what the sister is trying to tell you unfortunately in Italian. Sister Sonja, please momento, one moment sister." The Bishop politely addressed his lethal companion.

The officer began to feel like a ham as someone in the long line requested he not hold the Bishop up.

"Father go ahead sir have a nice day."

Both Contessa and Bishop Terrell couldn't believe the beauty of how well it went. It was too good and they were right about that.

"What are you doing officer? Hey priest hold on, officer did you check these two, well did you?"

"Sarge they were … no sir."

Contessa stood on the ready still speaking a little more Italian that everyone in the lobby could somehow understand. It was apparent from her theatrics she was asking the Father what was wrong. She wanted to know what was happening and Bishop Terrell played the sympathy card acting as though all was well and consoling her with his good left hand as she still clutched it. Her gun still on the ready she would drop the boorish sergeant first then the nice officer.

"What's going on here? Why the bottle neck officer?"

"Oh, hello Captain it's nothing sir I was just making sure the officer here checked the priest's identification."

"You got something against priest Sarge?"

"No, not really Captain."

The Captain removed his unlit cigar from the corner of his mouth, raised a brow and scowled at the burly sergeant. "What kind of answer is that? Let the good Father and the sister out of here. Our apologies Father, sister for the inconvenience, Sarge you're going to hell you know that, come on let's find O'Connell's room."

"Sure Captain, sure."

"Now that was close. Wow what a rush! I'd forgotten how good it felt. The thrill of it all was so invigorating didn't you feel it sister? Whatever your name really is."

"You're an adrenaline junky I should have guessed it. You were in the business because of your addiction? It's sad you don't even know why you get a thrill from almost being beaten, maimed or even killed do you?"

"In fact young lady I do know I'm a thrill junky among other things and I do know why I was in the business. You have already tasted my work as a matter of fact."

"And how's that Bishop, keep moving before they changed their minds, as I asked how's that?"

"You met Mr. Paul Constantine."

CHAPTER 47

"MURDER AND MAYHEM IN CALI"

"Oh shit! Stop that nun quick hurry up!"

"Outside, they just left I didn't see which way did they went?"

"They drove off about three minutes ago Captain. Why, what's wrong?"

"Two minutes into our conversation with Sergeant O'Connell's father he describes the nun we just let out of here to a "T" as being the Interpol chic, alias nun and victim in the shooting."

"Captain if you don't mind me saying so I tried to enforce our policy when we were checking identification but you stopped me."

"So Sarge you're sharing this with me to say what?"

"Come on Captain its Boston for Christ sake, how many nigger nuns you seen here, huh? It was unusual right, I'm right huh?"

"Sarge first of all I've never seen a nigger and the Boston Police Department doesn't have a policy of harassing the clergy or using inflammatory words like nigger. I strongly believe if we had it your way and the way of some bad cops we'd stop every different looking person in the country for identification without cause. Wait, I need a swig of this, now where was I? Oh and I don't like you Sergeant Barkowsky you're a racist and what's worse a lousy cop. Now get an APD out on those two, I'm headed for the station the feds and I have a mansion to visit."

"Mr. Zarkuhn, Mr. Zarkuhn sir it is a pleasure to see you again. I have a car outside for us."

"Lieutenant Lehchin it is also good to see you again. Ted this is Mr. Lehchin. I understand from Miles via Maurice you're not too thrilled about being called by your first name."

"Right, I must mention to you Mr. Zarkuhn that the stunt you pulled off in Hong Kong with your death and all was the most fantastic ruse I'd ever witnessed."

"Yes it was. The things we can pull off with all the new technologies today. When is our meeting with our contact setup for?"

"Mr. Zar …"

"Stop with the Mr. Zarkuhn stuff please. Call me Michael, Lehchin okay after all we've been through. I mean remember I fell for you." Lehchin didn't get the joke at first and politely smiled turning away so as not to insult his idol with an expression of what he really thought of the joke.

"Michael, sir we will head straight to meet our contact and sir that joke was sickening. I just couldn't keep it in sir."

"Now that's being proactive, you were right about this Lehchin guy Michael, efficient and honest with guts to boot. Well alright then."

"I think so Ted, I think so."

Michael was fond of the young Asian man, Lehchin. He couldn't tell anyone a specific reason why he felt the way he did if he was asked. It was a familiar feeling he got from time to time and he'd had this experience about other persons in his past. Each and every instance proved to be the same, those persons he was fond of for what ever reason turned out to be altruistic, completely unselfish and righteous in uniquely special ways. Until such time this pattern changed Michael would always show a certain degree of favoritism towards this type of individuals.

He was pensive as he thought back on the sacrifices made by his own armies in the service of God both on Earth and in far away places never heard of on this planet. He'd lost the most loyal and honorable soldiers in the battle against God's former number one enemy and his former commander. The battles were fought right over this very planet Michael remembered. He could still see the deluge destroying all in its path in order to wipe out man in an attempt for retribution against God's brother for creating man an insolent oversexed, stubborn creature as slaves and servants, having not worked out quite as well as God and the council of elders had wanted them too. It was written, but inaccurately in the first Pentateuch, book of Genesis that God brought about the floods because of man's evil deeds when in fact it was the evil committed by his own offspring against man and an overly ambitious plan by a nephew to eventually gain control of the planet and live as the Gods on it. This plan was crushed by Michael and his loyal Army as always but today Michael was a different being living amongst the "beast of burden" and he found some them noble and as forthright as any of his former soldiers. Today if asked to accomplish the same mission he would be reluctant, no he would refuse for he now realized that the "Serpent, Satan, The Adversary", God's brother a doctor by profession and a being who's Caduceus still exist to this day as a symbol for medicine was right to defend his creation man against the wrath of God his brother.

Briskly walking through the Los Angeles airport Michael made a decision that he would contact the "Great Serpent" here on the planet. He would still be there trapped in a dimensional time tomb located near the Tigris and Euphrates rivers where Michael had imprisoned him. All Michael needed to do to visit would be to use the key "Words of Power" he had used to lock Satan in the tomb eons ago. Yes he now had some questions for the former Archangel about what really happened in his own words. When the Collective was safe and all the dust settled Michael would visit the true creator of man for a real heart to heart.

As the three men approached the Lehchin's rental car Michael's cell phone began to ring and he quickly answered.

"Are you sure Miles. Then you know what to do. What's the status of Senator Stinger and Todd?"

"She and Todd left about an hour ago and yes she bought the plan, it's a go. I will tell you that our vault and most of our logistical requirements have been secured thanks to Peter and his staff."

"Then we shall wait to see if our little plan works. You need to get out of there all of you. They cannot let any of you survive. Secure the relic and Miles keep it with you, don't attempt to get it to Atlanta they'll be watching and watching hard. Miles good luck I'll see you at the Exodus point and say good bye to all for me."

"Michael take care, oh Alice wishes to speak with Ted."

"Sure, Ted it's for you."

"Yes Miles."

"It's me Alice honey, how are you doing my love?"

"I'm fine, so do not worry about me okay I'll be just fine. I'm in good hands trust me."

"I just have, have a, to say I love you Ted see you honey at Exodus point."

Ted handed the phone back to Michael as he put it to his ear there was no one on it. When they got to their car all of them looked at each other over the roof of their vehicle and then submerged as though they had made a pact above the firmament and then dipped for battle into the abyss of chaos.

"Why is it that these cheap American sandwiches appeal to me so?"

"Because they're cheap boss?"

"No dummy it's because they're so damn delicious. How do they do it? Okay let's get the package out so I can ensure they're in working order my man. Get the others let's have a review Jimmy cause there will be a test later."

"Righteo boss."

Cardinal Ricci sat and tried to enjoy his tea as he contemplated his next move. He was tired and found it difficult to concentrate which unsettled him for he knew not the taste of failure. The buzzing under his robe alerted him to a call on his cell phone. Who could it be?

As he gazed at the number he did not recognize it so he ignored it and soon it ceased. Again his phone began to vibrate and again he looked at the number same one. He was annoyed as he could only imagine some common American ingrate with some "pay as you go" cell phone calling his phone number once again he ignored the call.

"I think it is a mistake for you to call him. For god sake sister or whatever your name is. What is your name?"

"My real name is Lilith."

"Most interesting and might I say from a historical stand point it suits you. Well Lilith need I remind you that the man you're trying to call ordered me to kill you."

"I will again remind you that he was attempting to protect the Catholic Church. He should be congratulated for his noble efforts, so please remain quiet Bishop while I shall try again."

"By all means Sister Lilith, by all means."

"I beseech you do not call this number, you have the wrong number."

"Sistere, Stop."

"Who are you?"

"Cardinal Ricci it is Contessa are you shocked to hear from me?"

"Contessa my dear I've worried about you my child. What happened? The last time I heard from you at the hotel you were not well."

"I failed to complete my task your eminence. I beg you and the church for forgiveness."

"For the love of Jesus I think I'm going to vomit." Bishop Terrell stated as he bent over gesturing the act of throwing up.

"Shush!"

"You need no forgiveness for you have not failed me or the church my dear you have failed yourself. You will try again that is my command to you. Are you alone Contessa?"

"As a matter of fact no I'm not alone I have one of your admirers here beside me."

"The anticipation is too much my dear who is it?"

"Here, he wishes to speak with you, go on take it or I will break one of your fingers."

Contessa handed the Bishop's cell phone back to him and smiled sweetly, the Bishop snubbed the smile but knew she meant it ... about the fingers and hesitantly took the phone with his one remaining operable hand.

"Hello Bishop Terrell speaking."

There was no response it was quiet on the other end of the line as the Bishop continued to speak.

"Hello, Hello! No one is there."

"Give me that, hello."

"Yes I am here Contessa. Listen to me very carefully I do not want you around this man."

"Why your eminence? He is one of us, a brother of the church."

"Torture him don't ask me questions, just hurt him."

"Careful Cardinal you should not joke on the cell phone in that manner."

"You're correct I forget my humor, hah! It is bad sometimes, no?"

"Yes you do and yes it is dangerous. Trust me I have Bishop Terrell under control."

"Do you? I wonder, be extremely cautious he is very clever this one."

"Your eminence should take your own advice I believe one Mr. Constantine should be in your city right about now. He feels he needs to settle some debts so perhaps you should make arrangements to settle the debt first. I will try to collect the item you sent him here to purchase."

"Really, that sounds workable, yes I like it, but when you do make sure you settle my debt with the Bishop. He has some open items too. Do you understand Contessa?"

"My very thoughts, Cardinal it will be done."

"Quickly we must finish evacuating."

"Was that Michael?"

"Yes, he says to get the hell out of here so please people let's go. Cheryl, Alice, I'll carry the relic with me as per Michael. Margarite would you and Alice get it …"

"Wait! We can do this. We can get it to Atlanta so why are we delaying? You heard the Controller I think he's right. Alice tell them we …"

"Cheryl we can't it's too hot, don't forget we can regroup per our contingency plan later. Miles and Margarite will take care of the relic."
The feel of the room turned grey and strange. It was though a dark haze glazed it and J.P. rose up slowly to solicit confirmation from the others as to whether he was alone in what he was experiencing.

"It's the power, the electric it has been cut we're now on the back up generators. I'll be back I've got to check the security cameras I'll be downstairs please call Peter."

"I'm here sir and here is the relic to which you mention needing earlier." Once again Peter out thought all in his midst as he stood holding the duffle bag containing the broken piece of Tables of Testimony.

"Peter would you do me a favor and bring that here."

"One last looksee aye doctor, of course madam."

Peter walked towards Doctor Cheryl Teranez and glanced over at the others as he approached and as he did Cheryl did the unpredictable before he reached her.

The gun blast rang out frighteningly loud and everyone ducked all except Peter who was falling while blood spewed from his chest onto the conference table and floor. Teranez grabbed the duffle bag held in his hand and fired a couple of more rounds to keep everyone in the room honest.

"Damn it old man see what you made me do. Miles, Miles get your lard butt out here right now. Get off the floor or I'll cap your fat ..."

"Okay, Okay don't shoot I'm coming out."

Margarite was screaming hysterically as she crawled around the long conference room floor to where Peter lay on his back convulsing and gasping for air. His eyes were shining and turning blue as Cheryl Teranez laid the bag on the conference table in front of her she pulled out her cell phone and made a call. Her gun was rotating back and forth and it was now clearly the main focus of everyone's attention.

"J.P. you get your drunken bottom up and out here as well, you too Miss pris, come on Alice move it. People don't make me shoot the rest of you, I'm on a schedule here and the bus is about to leave."

Doctor Teranez continued her call using her cell phone as she cautiously watched everyone in the conference room.

"Yeah! Got it send in the cleaners I'm tired of this gig it's been long, way too long. By the way you can notify Rahmad that the Senator and Todd are not present they should be at the airport by now. I've got to go so get that chopper in here it's getting hot. Miles where are the other servants, get them out here now?"

"They were released sometime ago because of our evacuation, you know that. There's nobody else here on the premises."

"Don't, do not, do not cry little one I shall be fine. Focus on the task at hand little one, remember."

"Peter, oh Peter! Please somebody help him, please."

Margarite's head was pounding she cried so hard her head hurt. Miles quickly made his way over to where Peter lay dying and knelt beside him and Margarite. He placed his arms around her and held her tight as he too began to cry and held Peter's hand. He couldn't look Peter in the eyes for it hurt too much to see the man he considered a grandfather dying before him.

"Peter I love you old man, thank you for being there for me all those years."

"I'd be, b, be, be lying if I, I said it was my pleasure Master Turner, but it was interesting and some, somewhat entertaining sir."

Peter was coughing and gasping for air as he strained to talk.

"Peter don't speak lie still, I need to thank you Peter you're were always there, you the witty one,"

"Frankly I fail to see the wit in my present situation at the moment, so I must beg your pardon Master Miles."

"Hush Peter, we'll get help for you. Cheryl I beg of you we must dial 911 he needs a doctor. You're a doctor for God sake if you won't help him at least let me call please. You have the relic please Cheryl."

"That's true, but unfortunately for Peter as you can see he's coughing up blood. Right now he can barely breathe and his lungs are collapsing, excruciating pain isn't it my butler buddy. Frankly I'm amazed he's lasted this long. Where's that damn helicopter?"

"Cheryl why?"

"Alice why are you asking me like that? I mean with that indignant tone in your voice? Think about it these people were going to take the most powerful weapon on the face of the Earth and do what? Huh, do what? Exactly!"

"Weapon, why does it have to be used as a weapon Cheryl? For God's sake you're a doctor you took an oath to save lives."

"Baby that's what I'm going to do, save lives the lives of my people."

"Yah peeple?"

"Damn you were so quiet I thought you were dead J.P., yes my people."

"And just who might they be, your people if I may be so bold as to ask?"

"Bold, please don't make me laugh Miles you could never be bold, but in answer to your question the Nation of Islam and the Arab people. You people thought just because I have a Spanish name my heritage was Latino? You see how inept and stupid you are, you see. You never saw it coming you deserve what you're going to get and him that British pig lying on the floor there, well the British deserve to feel the wrath of Allah first."

"This place is quite impressive Bishop are you sure the item we seek is there?"

"No, well yes it is here. You remember the plan right? The plan is the only reason I agreed to assist you. You'll give the item to the church, to the Pope himself."

"I'm no dummy Bishop I've done such things before you drive I'll perform, go on drive. And Bishop I always keep my word, the church shall have the item as you choose to call it."

The Bishop was falling in love with his vixen captor. He was charmed by her pure deadliness of character and nubile nature. It also amazed him that he found a woman attractive being a celibate homosexual.

"Captain I don't mind telling you that your story is so far fetched that it's the only reason we have approved this visit to the Mansion."

"So why are we waiting here five miles out? Let's go in."

"Because as I stated before this is the Department for Homeland Security's dance, got it. How they got involved beats me, but my directions are clear, not to move until they okay it."

"Sure, but it sounds a little too stupid even for the feds. Where's my Pepto, yeah."

"Captain we were just informed that a van has driven onto the grounds, lights off and with two people in it. Have any idea who that might be Captain?"

"As a matter of fact I do."

"Yes."

"Ask if they're wearing Catholic clothing and if one is a nun, go on stop looking at me so crazy I know it's weird just ask already."

"You know you Boston cops are damn weird, you know that right, okay I'll ask."

"That's affirmative Captain what in God's name is going on? I didn't mean to actually say God of course, it was not meant to be a joke. What I wanted to...."

"Don't worry about it. We're all good Catholics here right? God knows you weren't trying to be funny at his expense and if he didn't realize it, well when this raid is over you will no longer be with us will you?"

"Hey Captain don't joke like that. That's not funny that's not funny at all, quiet! We're getting another report of an incoming helicopter and two men seen on the back side on the mansion dressed in black combat gear."

"Is it one of ours? Are they ours?"

"Maybe it's the Homeland Security guys you think?"

"I don't think so. They would have copied us in before now."

"Everyone's here but them what's up with that? You're F.B.I. do you know?"

"Captain I'm F.B.I., but I couldn't began to tell you what those folks at Homeland Security are thinking. Damn everyone knows they're confused."

"Right, if they don't get here or contact soon we need to make a decision you know that right, right? At least one of those persons down there is possibly wanted for the shooting of one of my guys and he's not expected to make it."

"Why hadn't you mentioned that before? Were you too busy thinking about the possibility that just maybe another bad hombre might be in there. Who?"

"A man by the name of Constantine, Paul Constantine and I think he may be in there. Agent he's bad, real bad."

"Right, we saw that come out yesterday on the "want ads" our name for APDs. You think he might be in there too?"

"Who knows? Excuse me I need to take a Pepto break."
"Here have some of mine."

"You know Agent Ford for a Fed you're alright."

"Thanks Captain."

"Bishop what's the safest way in there given our situation?"
The Bishop was so excited he could hardly answer the question. He was once again experiencing a rush.

"Take the van around back I'll show you. We'll enter from the garage door."

"Cardinal we have a problem?"

"Nice to see you Edwin are we ready for the strike? Please brief me quickly I don't want to miss the party."

"Mr. Secretary I think this is a very big mistake, I just want to go on record as disagreeing with you partaking in this raid sir it's dangerous. You should let the field ops team handle this matter, there are too many things that can go wrong and by the way your U.C.O., undercover operative has just informed us that the chopper is in place and that Senator Stinger and Agent Todd should be at the airport. Excellency how do you want us to handle the Senator and Agent Todd?"

"Get me to that sight now, like yesterday you here me? Try and contact Stinger we need to make sure both birds are together before we act and don't call me Excellency. The walls may have ears."

"I understand Secretary, your Excellency. Your bloodline dictates that I express the proper protocols to you my lord."

The Secretary of the Department of Homeland Security smiled at his aid and opened the drawer to his desk. He was beaming as he pulled out his favorite instrument of death, well his second favorite. He lifted the Colt Anaconda stainless revolver as though it would break if handled too roughly.

"That's a large gun Mr. Secretary."

"Yes it is. This is a forty four Calibre magnum and boy it leaves the largest hole." The Secretary pressed the weapon up against his left cheek and kissed the gun passionately which freaked his chief of staff out as he closed the door to the Secretary's office.

"What are you doing?"

"I'm calling my boss is that okay Senator?"

"Todd you really want to know, no it's not okay. Haven't you heard anything I've said to you this evening. You idiot, you are going to be killed and me too. You cannot let that S.O.B. know where we are, not yet, because if you do we're dead, we are dead, do you understand dead Agent Todd."

"Okay now I've had it with your sanctimonious black ass what's up?"

"Know you didn't, you did not just say what I think you said."

"In fact, I did Senator I'm tired of your hubris nature and omnipotent attitude. Need I remind you if you were so smart your skanky ass wouldn't be on the line like mine is got it?"

"White boy you're working on an ass whipping from the sister here."

"I don't think so."

"And where did you learn to spout like that?"

"I am from Atlanta GA, damn ATL white boy or not, I can damn represent when I need too."

Todd pulled the vehicle over to the side of the road and stared straight ahead out the window at the night sky. The Senator paused blew out a frigid puff of air then jumped out of the car into the snow.

"I'm pissed cracker get your ass out of the car, right now."

"Senator what's your problem? This is ridiculous now get back into the car, it's freezing out there. Come on we're losing time so please get back in the car."

"Not until I kick your hunky ass."

"Now see, there you go name calling, what's with that?"

"What do you mean, what's with that? Boy you called me a damn skank."

"Look it's not like I called you bitch or anything. I could've opted for that you know."

"You know Todd this alter ego white boy, black talk thing is about to get yo ass kilt!"

"Kilt! You mean killed right?"

"No, white boy I meant kilt don't mock me. It's a black thing so carry yo ass."

The Senator was now pissed and ran for Agent Todd and he gently stepped aside as she clumsily fell to the side of the road. As she got up very slowly she glimpsed around at her intended target and lunged at him only to greet the hood of the car. She was obviously out of shape, way out of shape compared to her college track days. There would be no ass whippings dished out from the sister this night that was obvious.

"Have you had enough my sister?" Agent Todd was snickering as he leaned against the opposite side of the hood of the car.

"I'm not your sister. Don't just stand there help me up I'm out of breath."

"I can see that."

"Whose phone was that? Todd please tell me that's your phone, please."

"Senator it's not mine, mine is off. Check yours."

"I don't have it. It must have fallen when I was making a fool of myself."

"I didn't here it ring and you haven't used it, but if it was inadvertently turned on the GPS will give our position away."

"Well it's ringing now, hear that?"

"Look answer it what have we got to lose? By the front tire there right by your foot go ahead answer it."

Senator Stinger was reluctant to pick the cell phone up, but as she did she adjusted her tattered clothing as though she were about to go into a job interview.

"Hello, hello Senator Stinger here."

"Senator I hadn't heard from you is all okay?"

"Mr. Secretary this is a surprise of course all is well. I was on my way to Washington."

"Where are you now?"

"Alec please don't be coy with me you know perfectly well where I am. The question is why are you up so late calling me and at this hour? We had set up a meeting for tomorrow right, so again why the call tonight, damn it answer me, why?"

"Is Agent Todd still with you?"

"How did you know the agent was with me I never reported that? Is that why you're so … I hear a helicopter, you bastard."

"Give me the phone Senator, quick give it to me now." Agent Todd grabbed the Senator's cell phone and dialed in a number.

"Who in the hell are you calling it better be Batman because we're about to be …"

"I know kilt, yeah, kilt. Hurry let's get over to those woods and that ditch, hurry, take the damn high heels off Senator come on."

The Senator and agent Todd fell into thick brush and slid down a steep ditch. There hands stung from the impact of the thorns and frozen ground. The ground was wet and hard from the snow and the ice was dampening their cloths. Todd was concerned about the bright hot pink blouse his companion was wearing and debated how he should approach his concern.

"Senator don't take this wrong, take off your blouse it's too bright. I'm not getting fresh with you so stop looking at me that way, come on take it off."

"Help me with this jacket, here pull the sleeve. I'm having trouble it's all wet here, pull here, ouch that's my arm you fool."

"Sorry. There let's bury this. Wow Senator those are quite nice."

"Stop looking fool." The Senator snapped as she smiled feeling somewhat flattered.

"Here take my jacket it will give you a little warmth."

"Thanks."

The helicopter was now approaching from the passenger side of the convertible car. A spotlight was moving in a circular pattern as it got closer. Two figures could be seen by Todd looming from the chopper door one with a gun mount.

"What were you doing with the phone?"

"I dialed a pay phone. I got familiar with a certain phone number sometime ago during an undercover drug sting.

It will keep ringing and I bet those people in the chopper are being fed information that we are in the vehicle there, shhhhuu."

The chopper circled the car at a good distance and then a tremendous blast blinded both the Senator and Agent Todd. They covered there heads as the flames lit the night sky spewing debris and smoke upward.

"Damn an RPG, they were out for the kill no talking, no interrogation, nothing just termination, bastards."

"I told you Todd. That's your Secretary of Homeland Security's doing, nice man huh? So what's an RPG?"

"Rocket propelled grenade. Let's start moving backwards slowly, we've got to put some distance between us and that chopper. I thought you were in some group or something with the Secretary. So why would he be trying to kill you."

"That doesn't matter to them I know too much. I'm a liability to them and everyone in that mansion back there is too. Alec, the Secretary is hell bent on getting that relic in the interest of the United States for National Security reasons or at least I thought that was his reason, but I think it's because he thinks it belongs to him because of his lineage, long story."

"We've got to get back there and warned them."

"Have you loss your damn mind white boy are you crazy. These people are killers and they want us dead. I don't know about you, but I need to get as far from here as possible. Hell I'll live in the woods forever if I have too."

The chopper hovered at a good distance and then all of a sudden it swung North in the direction of the mansion away from the incinerated car which suited the Senator just fine.

"Todd we're too far away, you'd never be able to beat that chopper so stop thinking what you're thinking. You and I know that's where it's headed next."

Todd felt sadden at the thought of all of the occupants back at the mansion being slaughtered and by the agency he worked for.

"I'm going to try. I see a house over there."

"That house has to be five miles away."

"I've got to try. What are you going to do?"

"I'm with you let's go, I'm serious come on white boy and don't you dare be look'n at my breast.

"Then Senator I must suggest you stay in front of me."

"Fine, I will Special Agent Todd."

"Good, cause we Southern boys like our backsides large, yeah just like that."

"Yeah, well you like'm black too?"

Agent Todd did not respond prompting the Senator to glance curiously back at him. He gave her a sneaky smile and raised both hands to his side as though to say "I don't know, maybe?"

"You know Todd your white ass is getting a bit interesting."

"Thanks sister. I just didn't know you had it like that. Whew!"
Both Todd and his congressional companion laughed as they met the relentless snow drifts head on. Their feet, knees and thighs froze from the melted snow as they pushed forward through the crystal glistening woods.

"He's dead, oh my God Miles, Peter is dead." Margarite held Peter's head in her lap with both arms as his head lay in her lap. She rocked back and forth frantically crying.

"Damn where's that extraction team? Would you stop that annoying sobbing, come on Rahmad, come on honey."

"You screw yourself bitch! You killed him, he was innocent he never harmed anyone, so screw you."

"Well Margarite I do say I didn't know you could be so unlady like. The old man was recalcitrant, cantankerous, and spilt tea on me once. No just kidding about the tea, but I really kinda like that dirty mouth of yours makes me hot for you. Just kidding again you're definitely not my type."

"I heard something."

"All of you shut up! That trick won't work on me and I might caution you those kind of tricks might get you where the old man is, dead."

"Okay, but I thought I heard someone in the kitchen."

"I thought no one else was ... Yes Rahmad go ahead I can't hear you. Speak up, you say you're how far out, excellent."

"Contessa over here, take a peep."

"Who is she? The one with the gun."

"She was one of us, Doctor Teranez, but I don't understand why she's got the gun on them and ..."

"You hear that? Wait it's a helicopter."

"Let's get the prize Bishop. I think that helicopter means trouble, come on."

"Where is it? It has to be right in the front of our pretty woman with the gun on the table there, I'll bet your life it's in that duffle bag."

The Bishop took one final look at the monitor in the basement security room and followed Contessa slowly up the stairs his hand still throbbing from her assault earlier that day.

Michael and his entourage pulled into the back of a liquor store as his favorite Asian carefully drove the rental car they'd acquired. The car was quiet as each member of the Collective sat waiting thinking about what was to happen next. A car pulled up next to them and as the window rolled down on the passenger side the Collective's West Coast Station Chief greeted them with too much enthusiasm for the moment.

"Dudes, sir are you ready? We can discuss it at my office. Well come over and get in. This is my office, street office anyway."

Michael had forgotten how unusual this station manager was when he hired him three years ago but he was good, very good and brilliant at least by human standards. Each man was poised to get out of the car and enter the Cali station chief's car but the damn rap music would have to go first.

"Do you mind?"

"What that bro?"

"The music it's a bit loud."
Ted Martin was not so polite in his explanation.

"That music has got to go, dude. This is not a disco or better yet the ghetto."

"Ted that's quite enough." Michael cautioned Ted Martin.

"Sorry guys didn't realize it would offend you know."

"It's alright Marcus, so what you got?"

"The fire power is in the trunk and I have back up on standby should we need it."

"We, what's with the we?"

"Valid question Ted. Marcus you and your crew were to sit this strike out. Trust me it's for the best. You could be implicated by the law and your mirror image blown."

"Sir, I realize this, but our intel on this operation reveals you're going up against what may turn out to be superior firepower for your team. You may need increased support of the crucial kind. Look at most let me hang with you. I got nothing better to do."

"Why? Surfs down at the beach dude?"

"Ted right, you know I like you I really do because I understand you. But you may need me some day real soon so ease up bro."

"Michael I don't think it's a good idea. We know the plan he doesn't and …"

"Well I disagree with Ted sir, I think if a man wants to support his friends or team he's a man most needed that's what I think."

"Well thought out agent Lehchin and I must say I agree. Ted, Lehchin I apologize for not briefing you on our station chief and his credentials before now. Marcus why don't you do the honors and inform the team know a little about your background."

"Sir, I really don't think, well that's whacked. I'm just a man from the streets and well you can if you desire, sir."

"Sure it's my pleasure. Gentlemen to look at Marcus you would think he was a member of some gang from the Southside of L.A. and you wouldn't be too far off, but what is not obvious is the Medal of Honor he received in Iraq for service to his country? Yes gentlemen, we have a true hero on our team."

"I'm awed, but it doesn't change the fact that … okay I'm thinking I'm wrong on this one. Sorry bro!" Ted reached his hand out towards the black station chief and grasped his hand with a firm wholehearted shake.

"Whoa! Bro! Yeah! See team I told you I liked Ted he, "ahw rite."

"I respect you so would you drop the Ebonics routine just while we're working together okay."

"No problem Ted my man. No more raping the Queen's English."

"Lock and load Marcus you're in and hand me that sweet Israeli automatic right there, yeah that's a winner. Well don't just look at me get your own."

Two minutes later Marcus' car was carrying Michael and the team towards Baker Street to the location of the Cardinal and his security staff. Listening to the rapper Emenim didn't help with the stress levels radiating from the car, however, their irritation from listening to the lyrics would ensure each member committed more carnage then was usually accustomed.

"Hello is anybody home, hello?"

"I'm freezing it's so cold. I don't think I can make it Todd."

"Someone's got to be home, I can see the fireplace going hold one moment."

"What are you doing Todd?"

"I'm trying to keep my hand from getting cut that's what I'm doing."

"No idiot you're going to break into someone's house?"

"Senator you've got to be kidding. We were just almost blown to smitherinzes, we're on some secret group's hit list and you're worried about a B & E, woman please."

"B & E?"

"Damn Senator breaking and entering. I thought you were black."

"Todd watch it. Don't start that racist shit."

"Hush somebody's coming."

"Who is it? Who's there I'll shoot."

"It's the police ma'am."

"Todd, the police!"

"Well I am, sort of."

"My! Okay one moment."

The front door swung open. Todd and the Senator were greeted by a four foot eight inch gun toting grandmotherly looking white woman with a real big shot gun, a large double barreled ominous weapon; the size of which could not be expressed enough as it was pointed at their faces.

"Ma'am I'm going to pee on myself and then faint, or faint and then pee if you do not remove that monstrosity from my face, please."

"Son you go right ahead, pee. Do you two think I'm some kind of fool? You come to my door this time of night, no car, all wet. She's black you white your cloths all messed up. Naw, I think it's shoot'n time. Yall step back don't want the mess in the house."

"Wait, I have identification!"

"Really? Does she have identification too. Or are you a wayward woman?"
"Ma'am, this is a United States Senator."

"See you almost had me son, but you messed up. Then why is she walking around looking like a skank?"

"That's it. I'm out of here."

"Senator, wait a moment she didn't mean it. I'm sure she didn't. Ma'am please, we're cold and she may get very sick. Tell her you didn't mean it."

"Mean what?"

"Your reference to her being a skank; please it's a long story."

"All right I'm sorry about the skank remark young woman get in here both of yuse. Damn, I have to believe some of your story cause frankly she's got issues. Hell she must be a Senator or at least in politics."

"Yes ma'am. I felt the same way when I first met her."

Senator Stinger was glaring at the old lady as she shivered in front of the small fireplace.

"I'll get you two some dry clothes."

"Yes ma'am. But what we really need is transportation."

"Well my son is about your size and Senator you should be able to wear his cloths too with that chest and butt you're sport'n. I'll be right back."

The old woman left the room and Karen Stinger was obviously mad enough to chew nails and spit. She warmed her hands as she rocked back and forth. Todd walked over to her and caressed her from behind not completely understanding why. His action was met with an unexpected turn from his partner who reached up and kissed him softly on the cheek. He was frozen and remained so until.

"Hey! You two no monkey business in here, stop this instance. I will not have kinky sex on my property. No sir. That Mandingo thang ain't happen here on Ms. Patty's watch, so stop and put these on, go on."

"So where's your son?"

"He's over there."

"Over there?"

"Yes my dear Senator. He's in Iraq trying to avoid the slaughter lottery."

"Ma'am what are you talking about, lottery?"

"The lottery of death that claims our soldiers, our young girls and boys. Yes harms way for a lie. They come home, maimed, with PT something, that mental problem or dead. The only question is which fate will befall my boy?"

"I'm so sorry ma'am."

"Are you, are you really and how did you vote Senator?"

CHAPTER 48
EXODUS BEGINS

"Your Excellency your phone it's ringing." The Cardinal was startled by his head of security.

"Cardinal Ricci speaking, yes wonderful sir. Well thank you, sir."

The head of security wondered who the Cardinal was addressing. Could it be the Pope himself? Who would this arrogant S.O.B. be kissing up to in such a manner as to almost kneel as he spoke on the phone. The security chief had never witnessed the Cardinal behave in such a passive manner it made him uneasy. The thought that out there somewhere was someone possibly more treacherous than his employer the Cardinal was truly unsettling.

As the Cardinal hung up the phone he rose ever so slightly from his stupor and turned to the security chief with a large smile. Again, the security chief witnessed something new and also unsettling, a smile from the Cardinal.

"Is all well your eminency?"

"Is all well? Never better, all is very well my good servant. Now what is it was there something else?"

"Oh yes, I'm told we will have hostile visitors very shortly and if I may."
"Please you may, after all it is what we pay you for."

"I suggest we remove you from these premises immediately. I have instructed my men to engage any intruders with extreme prejudice even at the cost of their lives. They will not expect the resistance I've prepared."

"I would expect no less, but I want the girl and the boy to be evacuated as well. No harm shall befall either do you understand?"

"Yes, but of course I'll make the arrangements now."

The Cardinal's security chief darted out of the small garden area and down the hall leaving Cardinal Ricci staring up towards the sky as a light misty rain gently embraced his face. He began to talk to himself as he stretched out his arms towards the sky.

"The Black Pope has acknowledged my superior abilities and the relic shall be ours this day, this is a great day, a great day indeed. I shall have my revenge do you here me I shall be redeemed, oh yes!"

"Margarite let go, honey let him go he's gone come on."

"Miles it's not fair, it's just not fair he was so innocent."

Miles gently pulled Margarite up from the floor and off her knees as she laid Peter's head softly on the thick Persian carpet. She gazed up at Doctor Teranez who was still busy tracking the sounds of the helicopter outside the mansion walls.

"How do you plan to proceed pretty lady, surely you have a plan?"

"Bishop I'll handle this, you just do as I instruct understand?" Contessa carefully watched the group as they stood in the conference with Cheryl Teranez periodically pointing the gun at each person present. She was nervous and growing unpredictable by her erratic movement and stressed voice, but Contessa now had a plan.

"Bishop here's what you're going to do." When Contessa finished explaining her plan there was silence and a dumb founded look on the Bishop's face.

"Are you crazy? Hell no! Shoot me now, no you shoot me now. At least with you the kill will be done professionally, quick and painless. With her I don't know what she'll shoot. Hell I wish she'd shoot this hand you broke, damn. The pain couldn't get much worse."

"Look you don't even know that she will shoot at you. She knows you, right?"

"But you want me to take that chance while you flank her from the main hall door, again are you nuts? Of course she'll shoot look at her out there, she's falling to pieces as we speak."

"Look Bishop I'm not asking you, I'm telling you. Do you want a chance at getting that bag on the table or not?" Contessa had struck a cord with having reminded the Bishop of the prize that awaited them. He would take the risk in order to get the Tables of Testimony.

"You'll do it?"

"Yes. I'll do it."

"Give me two minutes to get down the hall then you waltz in and …"

"And get shot while you shoot her. I got it. Oh and thanks."

"Come with me." The head of security for the Cardinal was stone faced as he delivered his request. "Hurry we don't have much time, quickly."

"But my son, where is my son? I won't leave without my son."

"We shall get him, quiet, be quiet."

The man pulled her by the arm as he hurried down the damp, dark stone hall towards the room where little Tashi and Merie had stayed until Merie was removed. Her captor opened the door to find Sister Colleeta feeding young Tashi and the sister rose from the rocker very quickly as though she were preparing for battle.

"What is it? It is young master Tashi's feeding time. Lady Merie what is it?"

"They've told me nothing. Tashi, Tashi." The toddler ran to his mother grabbing her legs as the head of security demanded she and the child follow him.

"Both of you follow me."

"He's here, he's here isn't he? I knew he'd come praise God I knew it."

"What are you saying ol'lady?"

"You shall soon see and oh I hope your pants find themselves below your ankles."

"What! I don't have time for this get away you witch or I'll."

"You'll kill me? Surely you've heard of the rumors go ahead that will ensure your pants shall drop below your knees you swine."

The security agent had heard of the story about the old nun and her rescuer during his time with the church, but they were just that stories he would not be deterred by old wives tales. He pushed Colleeta to the floor and warned her not to try him.

"Old lady don't get in my way and don't tempt me the only reason you're not dead right now is that I wasn't paid to do you, yet!"

The head of security for the Cardinal pushed Merie down the hall towards the small garden area where the Cardinal had been earlier.

It was now raining and the Abbey bells were ringing as the head of security glanced at his watch it was six o'clock. He wiped the rain water from his brow and face and proceeded to the back of the Abbey where a limousine awaited its passengers.

The Bishop waited the time allotted by Contessa and then darted through the door.

"Cheryl what's going on?"

Doctor Teranez was startled by Bishop Terrell's sudden appearance and swung her gun in his direction away from Alice who'd joined Margarite and Miles at the opposite end of the long thick wood table. Contessa was also startled as the massive grandfather clock in the hall she'd just passed chimed. It was now nine o'clock and the hour of indecisiveness for Doctor Teranez for she couldn't determine whether to shoot the clock in the hall that had scared her or the clergyman who'd appeared through from the kitchen door into the conference room.

"You fool what are you doing here, where did you come from?"

"Well my business at the hospital took a turn and …"

"Never mind I don't really want to know Bishop so please join the others. Go on hurry, I'm real touchy here."

During this interlude of conversation Contessa had positioned herself in the hall doorway of the conference room and had a clean kill shot at the Latin doctor.

She paused momentarily as she heard the rotor blades of the chopper right outside hovering in front of the mansion's front doors.

The Secretary of the Department of Homeland Security or Gestapo as Michael Zarkuhn referred to them hurried towards his chopper and began to spout orders as he entered the doorway of the state of the art whirly bird. The events and actions he was experiencing were taking him back, back to a time he missed. Thailand, Vietnam and Cambodia the killing fields where he'd found his calling, where he'd learned who he was and his true essence. He could not see it or even imagine it at Yale a young man not even when he was suppose to have been enlightened by his acceptance as a member of "Skull and Bones". He had to see it, smell it, feel it, taste it and live it even at the objection of his father and fellow Skull mates who did all within their power to protect him during his tour in the Army. Ensuring his rapid promotion and his eventual participation in many key government and business positions, ultimately his connections elevated him to the position of Nero the Black Pope. He knew there had never been a modern leader like him amongst their ranks; a leader who had killed in the heat of battle at the risk of death without there being a need to risk his life, a leader who managed to remain squeaky clean despite his flamboyant mannerisms and aggressive political maneuverings. He was truly the master of the New World Order worthy of admiration from his forefathers those devilish fallen angels, progenitors of the children of the Sons of God.

"The Senator and Special Agent Todd are no more. Our Al Queda chopper destroyed them with the help of the coordinates your friends at NSA provided."

"That's pleasant news did you instruct the Al Queda insertion team to begin the extraction of their operative?"

"Yes sir, but you do realize they'll pull the relic out with her and that may."

"Instruct our advance attack crew to proceed to the mansion. Destroy the Al Queda chopper while it's on the ground, and at the same time notify Rahmad that we've been informed that his operative has turned. Tell him his operative seems to have decided to keep the weapons plans and the jewels for herself."

"I must say that is a most ingenious plan sir."

"Yes it is. We'll be applauded by the American public and commended by Congress for thwarting an Al Queda plot to kidnap and rob one of America's most prominent families. We will have destroyed our adversaries across the board. We'll have every congressman and woman as well as America's corporate wealthy begging for an increase in the budget for fear that the same type of attack could happen to them. Yes, all loose ends in the course of executing this wonderful plan will be tied tightly up. Now, how long will it take before we're in the kill zone? I simply must shoot someone tonight. Why are you smiling?"

"They, this group in Boston, the Collective they still don't know you're the man. It's rather Shakespearian, tragic. It somewhat amazes me that they comprise some of the most brilliant minds on earth and they've acted so ineptly with regard to following the dictates of the Controller for how many years? I often wondered how long it would take them to challenge you."

"That's inconsequential at this moment. Believe me the position served a very good cause when I was elected for it. Let's puff smoke pilot."

"We'll make it in thirty five minutes in this bird sir."

"Make it twenty five and the first beer is on me."

Michael sensed an empty presence and a great loss at the same time. He could feel his eyes changing color as they stung with moisture from the light rain entering his open window. Yeah he was feeling a might froggy, but someone else's ass would be jumping in very short order. Michael knew someone he cared for had been taken from him.

"Pull around the next corner. No over there, yeah right there this is good. Maurice you've sanitized areas before?"

"Yes sir."

"Then please take care of the car. Where's our exit points?"

"Right about two blocks from here you can see it on the map here."

"Point it out to us. In case some of us get separated we will all know how to escape and where to. So study this S.E.R.E. map closely."

"Sere, what's that?"

"Oh, Survival, Escape, Rescue, Evasion equals S.E.R.E. an anagram no big deal."

"Not really, how about speaking something I understand like Latin."

"Sure Ted."

"Anyway there will be a DHL station next to a Krispy Cream around the corner and there's DHL uniforms in the van that'll be out front, well at least a couple of shirts and hats anyway. Look I just want to say thank you for letting me in guys and please be careful."

"Chill Bro you've got me tearing up here."

"Ted you're still okay in my book you bigot you."

"Hey I'm not a bigot. I'm a racist."

"Yeah, well?"

"Well, I'm working on it. Yes I'm a bigot an evil ignorant white boy with issues and I've not spoken to my mother in twenty years because she married a black man. And due to my ignorance it's caused me great pain, but I'm trying here so give me a break!"

Ted's confession was a little too much information for his comrades to swallow at the time and they all stood before him with confused puppy dog looks on their faces trying to figure out what kind of drugs he was taking.

"What in the blazes is he talking about Mr. Zarkuhn?"

"It's alright Agent Lehchin he's really not on drugs he's just crass. Right Ted, you're crass not stupid right? Get a grip man we've serious business to attend to here. Well is everyone ready because I think they know we're here."

"How do you know that?

"Over there on the rooftop opposite of the Abbey. You see him?"

"I do now. Wow I would've missed that."

"Don't worry we got your back brother."

"Thanks, looks as though I might need that."

Todd was wondering if he and the Senator had made a mistake allowing the old farm lady to drive them back to the mansion. She obviously had no respect for snow and ice. The Senator definitely was concerned about her present situation. Her ducking and covering her face brought about frowns from the driver who insisted on making matters more uncomfortable for her guests by smoking in the truck forcing her passengers to choose the cold of the night air over the smoke by rolling down the windows.

"Ma'am, ma'am, uh Ms. Patty?"

"What is it boy?"

"You can slow down if you want too."

"Don't."

"Don't what ma'am?"

"Don't want to slow down. Whatever it was that brought you two love birds to my humble home in the middle of the night must have been pretty important and I don't doubt it after looking at that car on flames back there."

"What makes you think that car was ours?"

"I know the Plantards. Knew old man Plantard for years before he passed, wonderful, giving man he was, yep that car belonged to the Plantards. Seen it around during the years, yep that's a Plantard car, never said it was your car."

"Well my, my we can't pull any wool over your eyes can we?"

"Wouldn't change much I have cataracts and night blindness wool wouldn't make much difference."

"Right, then how did you recognize the burning vehicle as the Plantards?"

"It was yeller right?"

"Yes it was yellow, yellow right."

"Yeller convertible, special agent man and high fallutin senator have to be your car courtesy of Plantard Mansion."

The Senator and Todd looked hard at each other as they attempted to deflect as much of the freezing air off of themselves as they could. Todd finally gave up and attempted to roll the window up but without much success as he cranked the knob.

"Want work once you let it down it'll take an act of the senator's brethren to get it up, sorry kids."

Captain Boggs was getting antsy with the waiting. He wasn't by himself either as the restless bee hive of law enforcement officers located down the road from the mansion stood around in the cold soup of night air. The abrupt appearance of a helicopter over the mansion's grounds made all of them uneasy and they desired answers.

"Damn its cold. I'm about tire of this waiting, has the homeland guys contacted you yet? I don't like the looks of that chopper."

"I'm more concerned about that blast we heard earlier and that glowing light over there. Anyway the Sheriff's department sent one of theirs to check it out. I told them we couldn't spare the manpower."

"Yeah I know the Sheriff he's good people. He didn't have to do that you know. Let's make an agreement here between my Boston Police guys and you Feds. I say we go in there in say ten minutes if we don't …"

"One moment Captain Boggs my guy has something coming in now."

Both men darted over to the radio operator who was waving for the F.B.I. Agent in Charge and handed him the headset. Boggs was even more restless than ever. He thought about Sergeant O'Connell lying severely injured in the hospital and the innocent staff killed at the hotel. Tonight he absolutely had to make a collar to get redemption for those people.

"That was interesting."

"What! What was interesting, tell me come on."

"I just got off the phone with the Secretary of Homeland Security."

"What did he want? You mean this is that hot, damn. Where's my Pep!"

"Hey I'll return the favor take some of mine."

"Thanks. So go on what's going on?"

"Seems that the people in the mansion may be tied into some Arab terrorist group."

"Which one, Al Queda?"

"He didn't say, he was very vague, but one thing is for sure we're not to go near that place he was very adamant about that. Say's his people were on it."

"I don't know seems weird to me. I'm gonna let my superiors know what's up. Oh did you tell him about the helicopter?"

"I mentioned it but the radio went dead I didn't get a response."

"I gotta be honest cause I like you, I don't trust Feds I really don't."

"Captain Boggs me neither. I don't trust us either."

Hearing the Special Agent in Charge of the F.B.I. say it didn't trust the federal government called for another swig of Pepto for Captain Boggs.

The truck raced through the snow sliding and splashing slushy ice up onto the windshield and into the open window as the old farm lady navigated closer to the mansion.

"Ma'am."

"Look if you're going to ask me to slow down forget it sonny."

"No ma'am, I just wanted to inform you that you just flew by a police car."

"Oh then that would explain those pretty blue lights behind us."

"Ma'am."

"What now son."

"Perhaps we should pull over okay."

"No not okay."

"But ma'am you don't want to run from the law that will only make matters worse."

"Ma'am Agent Todd is right surely you don't wish to break the law."

"Already have."

"What! What do you mean by that?"

"I don't have a driver's license."

"You let them expire?"

"Nope."

"Oh no, they were suspended."

"Nope."

"Good I was worried."

"Yeah me too."

The Senator and Todd's relief was short lived as they realized they still had no answer to the question. In unison they both asked.

"Then what law have you broken?"

"I'd say driving without a license."

"Ma'am that's no problem."

"Sure I'm a Senator. We'll simply tell the officer that we're on an urgent mission and that you forgot your license."

"That's a good one Senator."

"Thanks Agent Todd."

"Won't work kids."

"Why not?"

"Never had one. Never had a license."

"You never had a license."

"Nope."

"Awh shit! We're screwed."

"Senator hold on for a moment. Ms. Patty then how did you learn to drive?"

"Haven't, this my first time, not bad uh? Learned on the tractor at the farm."

"Senator we're screwed."

"I know that."

The Senator and Todd put on their seat belts and grabbed any and everything in the truck that wasn't rattling which left very little as the truck sped through the cold, slushy damp of night. The police lights were not getting closer which was clearly and indicator as to how fast the old lady was moving. Senator Stinger began to cry and Todd held his tears back as he tried to reason with the driver to pull over volunteering to pay her if she'd comply. It was to no avail the old lady was enjoying the chase too much now she felt like a Rebel with a cause. She was thumbing her nose at the man for sending her son to that killing ground, Iraq. She increased her speed.

Paul pointed to the old Abbey as his entourage drove by. They soon parked on the next street over behind their target site. As his team unloaded the shipment of AK 47s and ammo Paul noticed two guards on the roof of the Abbey and one across the street on the rooftop on one of the neighboring buildings.

"Well this is going to be no cake walk mates they know we're here."

"I noticed them too boss not a problem though, not with these grenade launchers."

Paul smiled and put out his cigarette.

"What are you doing Marcus?"

"He's setting up the portable police scanner so he can monitor the law enforcement authorities in this area. So we can stand down and escape should he hear they're going to show up."

"Cool. Can you show me."

"Sure, but not now brother."

Michael enjoyed young Mr. Lehchin's zeal and enthusiasm. He'd make sure the young man stayed close to him during this operation. As they checked their weapons Michael had decided that using armament with too much explosive power would bring the authorities in to the game too quick so surgical snipe was in order.

"Marcus the two on the roof."

"Already on it. I got my "long gun" right here and the silencer."

"Can you do it? Can you get both targets?"

"I can do one clean. The other … it could get sloppy."
The young former Hong Kong Police Lieutenant volunteered. The group was silent to his response and it was obvious that they were uncomfortable with the idea of him sniping the other target.

"Look this isn't some theme park where we're shooting tin animals for a teddy bear this is serious."
No response was forthcoming but everyone agreed with Ted Martin's assessment. If the target was missed he'd possibly alert the others inside and the element of surprised would be lost.

"I'm a marksman with the … well I was a marksman with S.W.A.T in Hong Kong. It's been awhile but I know I can get him."
Ted didn't like the fact that Marcus and Michael were now making goo goo eyes.
"Come on guys be serious. What if he misses?"

"I'll back him up."

"Okay Marcus you go for the guy on the farthest end and Lehchin you get the one closest to us. Marcus as soon as you pop your mark go for the second target if he's already down pop him again anyway."

"Got it!"

"I'll take the one across the street Ted you back them. We'll meet at the stone fence by that oak when completed. This will be in three minutes starting now, go."

The Collective rescue team moved towards their target.

Paul took the grenade launcher but he was not really warm to the idea of using it. The noise would cause a delay in the kills because of the loss of surprise.

"Jimmy did you remember to bring any silencers in the shipment?"

"Jimmy acted as though he hadn't heard the question."

"Right that's what I thought. That would explain your grabbing this hammer for a job that didn't require a nail but a thumb tack. You idiot, oh bloody hell, it won't matter we're killing the whole lot of 'em any way. Okay everyone knows what to do? Okay a communications check you copy? Great count down for two minutes action begins now!"

Paul's hit teams moved towards the backsides of the target as he loaded the launcher for the attack.

CHAPTER 49

WARS ON ALL FRONTS

The grandfather clock was just the distraction Contessa needed although it was unexpected. By the time Cheryl Teranez noticed her it was too late.

It was no secret to anyone in the conference what was going to happen next and everyone leapt for cover. The Bishop dropped and crawled under the large conference table in front of him. He thanked God for not being shot by the doctor. He was not praying alone as he could see Alice, J.P., Miles, and Margarite jockeying for positions under the table on the far end of the heavy mahogany table.

"You bitch!" Cried out Cheryl Teranez. The bullet fired by Contessa forced its way through the Hispanic doctor's right shoulder violently knocking off her feet and on to the expensive Persian rug.

Contessa wasted no time in her advance, but was surprised by rapid gunfire behind her as she leaped over Doctor Teranez's body into a gymnastics roll and again leaped over a leather captain's chair pulling it back backwards as she went over it and using it as a shield in the process. The move acrobatic temporarily stunned her pursuers allowing her to return fire.

Marcus was good he dropped his target with a blistering head shot that past right through the preys left eye.

Paul lowered his rocket grenade launcher in disbelief as he observed the hit.

"Guys stand down I repeat stand down it seems others were invited to the party."

Paul rubbed his chin and scratched his head as he saw the bodies on the roof drop like sacks of rocks before his very eyes.

"Boss what's wrong?"

"Bloody hell mate, someone's sniping the guards on the roof."

"No joke? Who?"

"Jimmy how in God's name would I know? I'm just thankful that someone remembered to bring a blasted silencer. You see Jimmy that could have been your good work, but no you had to go and forget the blasted rifles and silencers; anyway let's wait and let our new found friends do our work for us. Everyone copy?"

"Team one copies, team two copies, Roger that sir team three out." Lehchin was ashamed he only winged his target but before he could try and adjust for another shot the wounded man staggered into a bullet from Marcus' "long gun" as he referred to his rifle. The targets lay lifeless on the Abbey roof handy work of Marcus' adroitness as a sniper.

The chopper was sitting on the front lawn of Plantard Mansion as its propellers were rotating slowly through the cold night air. Two of the passengers had entered the mansion and began their assault while several others waited along the outside wall in the front of the mansion. The front door being blown down by low yield explosives was reported by scouts assigned to A.T.F. and local law enforcement teams on recon of the mansion grounds. The road anxiety down the road was further exacerbated as they patiently waited to perform some kind of action.

"I say the hell with Homeland Security we just shouldn't sit around and watch this. Well should we?"

The F.B.I. Special Agent in Charge was rubbing his chin and walking back and forth through the snow barely keeping his balance as he tried to make a decision.

"Well what you gonna do?"

"I need to confer with my superiors first."

"Hell man you know what those candy asses are going to say. They're all afraid to make decisions you know that. Surely you have bigger testicles than that, there are possibly innocent bystanders in that house."

"I'll let them know that there has been gunfire I'm sure they'll."

"They'll what? They'll order us doughnuts and coffee on their expense card and think that we'll be appeased by it. Look if you don't go down there I'm going without you I'm gathering my guys. That's it for me."

"Wait, just wait don't do anything rash. Awh! Hell! You only live once let's go down there."

Captain Boggs was moving so fast he slipped on the ice.

The Special Agent in Charge grabbed his arm trying to pull him up but little progress was being made; however, Boggs finally managed to get to his feet and rested himself across the hood of one of the police cruisers breathing heavily as though he'd just finished running a marathon.

Soon the word was buzzing through the ranks of all the officers and agents and the SUVs and law enforcement cruisers were gunning their engines. Lights violated the night, exhaust and noise filled the frosty air as the officers tried to warm their vehicles up. They desperately tried to keep their vehicles from running into each other as car tires glided slowly off the snow laden shoulders and onto the icy roadway.

"There she is the big house."

"Yes ma'am now if we can only get there in one piece."

The old truck slowed as the old farm woman jetted between the two huge ornate black rod iron gates. The truck suddenly began to slide and the Senator and Agent Todd knew what was coming next for they were seasoned drivers.

"No don't brake!" They both yelled out but it was too late.

As the brakes were applied the truck came alive with a mind of its own and it rebelled against the novice driver handling her by skidding 180 degrees slamming the back driver side bumper and tail light into the left side of the gate and violently crushing the black ornate rod iron gate and knocking it to the ground. The old lady was not to be beaten by the fancy tractor as she called the truck. She turned the wheel away from snow drift which was about to engulf the vehicle. "Not happening", was the truck's response and it made its intent very clear by ignoring the old farm woman's desperate attempts at correcting her bad judgment and continued its course. Both the Senator and Todd wanted desperately to admonish the old woman and well just beat the hell out of her, but it seemed that they would have to take a number because the truck had first dibbs.

The siren from the pursuing sheriff's deputy could now be heard from the opened window and it was right behind them but suddenly stopped its pursuit. The truck slammed into the huge snow drift which conspicuously hid a tree behind it. The tree and truck had conspired against the Ms. Patty; both aided in knocking her out cold upon impact, crushing the driver's side door leaving a monstrous indentation in the frame and breaking her left arm in the process.

"Are you alright Senator?"

"Yes, you?"

"Yes I'm fine, but our driver is not good at all we'd better get out of here this truck it may explode."

Zarkuhn felt the warmth of the stones as they radiated underneath his vest. He'd forgotten that he had placed them in a money belt around his waist as Peter had instructed him to do. The man on the opposite roof the Catholic security guard was Michael's target, he resisted the wire sliding through his neck with all his strength but it was to no avail Michael was too adept at the art of garroting, the Burmese soldiers he'd fought with centuries ago had taught him well. The piano wire melted through the poor man's neck like butter on piping hot pancakes. Michael made every effort to make the kill as quick as he could under the circumstance and his timing it couldn't have been more perfect because the security guard was about to report the disappearance of his fellow comrades from the adjacent roof when he was snared him from behind.

"Boss what's going on? Do you see our other party guys yet?"

"Jimmy, continue maintaining comm. silence. That goes for all of ... wait there they are. Well looka there, Jimmy you won't believe who I'm looking at. I can't believe it."

"Boss who, who?"

"Didn't I say shut up, didn't I?"

"It's that "chink cop" from the alley in Hong Kong. He's one of the snipers and he's with some "jigga boo" with a beauty of a rifle. Team three they're at your nine so heads up."

"We copy sir."

"Marcus great job! Alright, I'm headed to the front Ted join Marcus and Lehchin you flank me, go."

"Gotcha Michael." Ted scampered across the street from his location and slammed against the medieval stone wall. He could see Marcus directly ahead of him and he scooted on his buttocks with his back firmly pressed against the wall until he joined him.

"Whew! Man this is nerve racking, by the way nice shooting."

"Thanks, but limit the talking."

"Sure thing." Ted was sweating profusely yet he hadn't done one iota yet. He was beginning to regret his hasty decision to accompany Michael Zarkuhn in attempting this risky operation. Truth was he was scared, frightened to death about the whole matter. He realized he was out of his element, but what could he do? Ted remembered Michael briefing him as they made their way to meet Marcus, "If either of you wishes to back out or if you have reservations at any time please do say so at any time. I don't care if we're in the heat of battle just don't get yourself or any of us killed. I and the others will not think ill of you for doing so."

Ted thought to himself he should skadattle right back across the street and head for safety. After all that's what a sound and rational intellectual would do and he was an intellectual. He was definitely not sound, at least not at that moment.

"No! I can't quit, I'm not going to let these guys down."

"Ted, shush! What's up with you man? You okay brother?"

"Sure."

Marcus caught a glimpse of Michael's eyes as he shot across the street and rested against the colorful stones next to the front door of the mossy stoned Abbey. He now sported a weapon in both hands as he braced his back against the wall as though trying to hold the stone structure up. He could see young Mr. Lehchin attempting to hold the other side of the wall up as he slowly slid towards Michael periodically glancing from left to right as he made his way down the wall towards the front door of the Abbey.

"Jimmy move your men towards team three, we'll out flank these smart asses."

"Copy Boss." Jimmy motioned to his men to follow him as he raced along the back wall of the Abbey. A door in the back was partially opened and a light could be seen fighting its way through the crack.

"Jimmy."

"I see it Boss." Jimmy stopped and placed his right fist up over his head. Then he turned to his first man and motioned for him to go, then the next, then the next and then the last man was with team three.

"Jimmy look out!" Paul could see the rifle stock and shadow before the guard appeared through the back door.

Jimmy was not Paul's number one for being the sharpest pencil in the class room, but for what he would do in the next forty seconds. Before the unsuspecting guard could react Jimmy cut the man's across throat. The serrated blade entered from the right side; while Jimmy's left hand covered the man's mouth muffling his screams. He grabbed the victim's right arm simultaneously pulling him out the door to the ground. The guard instinctively grabbed for his throat and the blade then made its way to man's groin and sternum. Jimmy continued to hold his left hand over the victim's mouth as he mounted him until there was no life. Paul was proud. He wished he could just sit and watch more of the action from the hill, but duty called.

"Jimmy, that took thirty nine seconds most excellent kill. Guys did you see that? That's the way it's done, textbook kill Jimmy great job. Press on guys and no "F" ups. Hold there. I'll tell you when to move team three. Team two make your advance around the garage perimeter to the side of the building and don't let that limo get away. In fact team leader."

"Yes Sir."

"Sir"
"No team two leader. I want you to mine that limo, but only blow it when I give the signal."

"What if it starts to leave?"

"Blow it only on my signal. I have my reasons, got it."

"Yes sir."

Senator Stinger was drowsy as her legs slid to the ground. Todd helped her out as she held the frame of the door to the truck they both knew enough to stay low even though the cold snow was begging to blister their hands.

"Here help me slide the old lady out. Careful I think her arm is broken. Whoa she has quite a bump on her head we're going to have to leave her and get a Doctor. She's injured worse than I thought."

"Hey I don't mean to be a party pooper but is that a helicopter over on the lawn in front of the fountain."

"Yes, I know what you're thinking but it's not the same one that blew up the car."

"How can you be sure? It was dark are you absolutely sure because if you're wrong than …"

"I know, but I'm positive that's not the unfriendly chopper. Here grab her legs let's get her outside."

Senator Stinger and Special Agent Todd carried the wounded woman about twenty feet before the Senator motioned for Todd to stop.

"I, I, I can't, I need to rest. Boy she's heavy for as little as she is."

"Probably because she's so damn stubborn."

"You ready to try again?"

"What was that?"

"What? I didn't hear anything."

"Well I did and it sounded like a gun."

"You're hearing things and trust me that's alright just don't start seeing things."

"Well I can't promise you I won't comply with that request."

"Ha, ha got to love you Ms.Stinger."

"I hear ya but I wasn't joking. Who are they?"

"Get down."
Three men were in the prone position directly in front of the mansion door. Their positions and low posture is why they weren't seen initially by Todd or the Senator. Two other men were sitting in the helicopter. One was having what seemed to be a rather hot discussion on his cell phone with someone. Todd figured out that he had to be in charge of this operation against the mansion.

"We'd better get out of here those are not friendlies and they have some nasty looking guns."

"Where, I mean where can we go? We've got no transportation."

"Listen to me Senator right now that doesn't matter. All that matters is that we put as much distance between us and them as we possibly can, now start crawling."

The shooting resumed as the gun men shot a barrage of bullets towards the conference room. Their shooting was sporadic and Contessa couldn't understand why. However, she decided to capitalize on the men's poor marksmanship. She began by knee capping the closest shooter bringing him to the hardwood floor screaming in pain. His accomplice retreated to the hall and could be heard calling in reinforcements.

Miles held both Alice and Margarite close as they held their ears and shivered profusely from fear. J.P. was worried he could barely concentrate with all the blasted noise going on. He was anxious as he worried about the fate of the rare bottles of Scotch that graced the corner of the conference room on a small dry bar. He leaned against one of the table legs with his hands crossed in his lap and his legs stretched out as though he were shading under a tree at a picnic.

Margarite and the others were now convinced more than ever that J.P. harbored many unresolved issues.

Alice was not as worried she probably should've been. All she could think about was Ted her loving husband. If she was going through this she could only imagine what he might encounter. She should've been more forceful she thought. He was only trying to make a point a point that was not necessary at least to her. She shook at the thought of losing him.

"We're going to get out of this Alice trust me."

"I feel that Miles I really feel we will. Margarite Ted's right we'll be fine."

"I know but Peter, what about my Peter? We can't bring him back."
Margarite sobbed as she clinched Miles jacket. His whole shoulder was wet with moisture from her tears as she lowered her head and continued to cry.

"On my mark." Michael mimicked with his lips as he leaned just right out side of the Abbey entrance."
Lehchin was ready to explode. His adrenalin was running so intense he felt as though he was going pass out. His palms were wet and he wiped them on his camouflage pants as he watched his mentor for direction. Michael felt the warmth of the sacred stones as they began to radiate their energy along his waist and down through his groin area. He'd forgotten the power of the stones and how they worked. His killing of the guard on the roof acted as a catalyst to the stones awakening. The stones had absorbed life forces from the sacrifices made by the priests of the tribe of Levi and transferred the strength to its possessor. Michael's lower torso felt as though it were in a whirling hot tub he liked the sensation, but more importantly realized he now had a secret weapon on his person. For with each kill within the right radius of the stones Michael Zarkuhn would receive the sacred power of protection. The same protection that was afforded him during his battle with Satan, and to the Levi high priest who wore the Breastplate of Judgment as they carried out the commands of Jehovah inside the tent housing the Ark of the Covenant.

"Sit there and do not move. Keep that child quiet, I mean it."

"Or what?"

"I meant no disrespect to the child or the woman your eminence."

"It was not they that you disrespected. Go see to our transportation."
The chief of security for the Cardinal left quickly towards the side of the Abbey.
"Where are you taking us?"

"Do not worry yourself with such questions my love."

"I'm not your love."

"Then please let us not quarrel in the front of our son."
Merie almost passed out at hearing the Cardinal's muffle the words from his musty old mouth. She would not have any further dialogue with him then maybe he wouldn't talk. She sat holding Tashi who reached out to touch the Cardinal's bright red cape only to be restrained and pulled back by his mother.

"No Tashi no."

"You see my dear he knows, he knows who I am. He can feel it and someday he shall wear the colors, he shall wear the crown."
With that statement Merie covered her child's head and rocked back and forth as she desperately attempted to drown out the thoughts of what the Cardinal had said.
Adrenalin

The Cardinal turned as his cape rode the air as though it were alive moving in slow motion as the old priest headed for the door.

"Never!" Merie shouted. "Never!"
Tashi sensed the tension and began to cry.

"Cardinal they have us surrounded or at least they think they do."

"Well then my little plebeian friend, please invite them in and let the fireworks begin. Is my car ready?"

"Yes your eminence, but I must insist it be checked once more."

"I don't have the time. You ensure my plane is ready. I'll have four body guards plus the chauffer to protect us. You send as many of them away without last rites as you can and please join me when its all over I like your company."

"As you wish your eminence." The head of security for the Cardinal swung open the heavy back door and tapped his security team on the shoulder one at a time. One man to the front of the vehicle and one to the back, the other three men would be dispatched to shield the Cardinal as he carried the child to the limo.

Paul's strike team concealed themselves just behind the back wall of the Abbey where the limousine sat. They would wait for Paul's signal before striking. Jimmy and his teams were now in position to flank Marcus and Ted when they were given the go ahead. Paul walked over to the dead man's body who Jimmy had slain earlier. He peered through the back door that was opened about six inches and saw that it was the kitchen and he could see a guard standing at the kitchen door and an a nun seated with her back to him. Paul suddenly saw that he'd gained another tactical advantage with this opportunity.

"Jimmy whisper two team members back to the spot where you whacked the guard."

"Done boss."

The two men soon joined Paul at the rear of the Abbey. He signed them instructions and they gave the affirmative that they understood the plan with thumbs up.

Michael knew that there incursion had been far too easy and that at some point the lid was going to blow off on easy street.

"Michael you know this has been far too."

"Easy. I was just thinking that."

Ted became even more uneasy and irresolute about his predicament.

"I can't! I can't go through with it!"

"What, Michael standby. Ted what's wrong? Where are you going man? Michael Ted's out, he just hauled ass across the street."

"That may be for the best you sit tight. How's the Police chatter?"

"All quiet right now."

"Start making your way towards us."

Jimmy was now not sure what the hell caused the abrupt movement by one of the attackers from his position. Jimmy was however a born predator and this type of work came natural to him. What was also instinctive for Jimmy Soomers was caution while in hot zones. He'd learned his trade as a young Tyro while operating as a mercenary in unstable African countries as well as running arms for the insurgents on the borders of Syria and Pakistan. Soomers had become adept and keen to ambushes and double crosses accumulated courtesy of his vast experiences not from intellect and Ted's sudden decampment through him off. Red flags were now up and waving in his limited animal mind.

"Paul we've got a little birdie on the move."

"Where'd he go?"

"That's just it he retreated. He went South across the street out of our line of sight."

"Hmmm, don't worry about him. Can you suppress and control the current force."

"With ease boss."

"Michael I just detected movement North West of my position."

"Can you confirm? Are they on to you?"
"I'd say yeah, their trying to flank us."
"Do you remember the ops in Nicaragua the back shuffle, I repeat the back shuffle?"

"Yes, got it. I have two grenades on me and that should do it."

"Good that was my next question."

The snow was taking its toll on Agent Todd and the Senator.

"We can't make any ground this way and did you hear those gun shots?"

"They came from inside."

"What are we going to do?"

"Well it's obvious we can't move her so here help wrap her hands and head with this. Here use my scarf for her hands."
"We're going to leave her here!"
"Do you have a better suggestion Senator, do you? We have no chance of surviving here with her. I know those men saw us crash threw the gate and the only reason their not on us at this very moment is because we're no threat and that Senator could change at least in their minds."
"So the answer is we leave her here in the freezing cold injured like this?"
"I asked you if you had a better idea. Do you want to stay and guard her, well Senator? Then let's pack ice on that shoulder and arm and try and crawl out of here. We'll come back when we can get adequate help."
"Okay, alright you're right. It just seems so cruel."

Several of the attackers from the helicopter joined in on the assault inside the mansion. However, the narrow double doors to the conference room only allowed for a limited assault.
Doctor Teranez was now scooting towards the conference table. Her wound was not that serious to her because the bullet had gone straight through the muscle literally missing bone and the major artery. Her goal was to retrieve the duffle bag from the table.
"I don't think so missy."

"Bishop that's mine get your hand off of it now." Cheryl yelled over the gunfire.

"I'm so sorry lass but that I cannot do that."

The Bishop held a strap to the bag that hung over the table, problem was Cheryl held the same strap. Both now had only one operable hand and thus the tug of war begun under the table and in the midst of gunfire.

Zarkuhn stepped back and hammered the massive Abbey door with his foot. He thought to himself as he heard the thug from his boot, "that was stupid."

The action solicited a puzzled glare from young Mr. Lehchin who struggled with reasoning out his mentor's feeble attempt at crushing such a sturdy door. Zarkuhn now coming to his senses merely turned the door knob and slowly opened the door pushing it further open with his foot and then jetted in guns to the ready.

Lehchin followed his lead. Marcus now readied his RPG launcher as he now saw the shadows moving to his far right in an attempt to flank him. He lobbed the first grenade high over then attackers in back of them.

"Move in Jimmy, I repeat move in." Paul ordered as he entered the back kitchen door he dropped the guard at the kitchen entrance with one shot while at the same time pushing the head of the nun forward to the table slamming her face hard against it. He quickly pulled the guards body into the kitchen and pushed the back door shut. Kill her, he barked at the men who followed him in. He turned to watch and before the blade could taste the nun's neck he shouted.

"Stop!"

"What are you doing here sister? I would've thought you'd be gone."

"Colleeta the old nun looked up at Paul as he approached her and helped her sit up. He wiped the blood from her wrinkled worn face as she smiled at him.

"I knew you would come. Come to reveal the vulnerability of some evil ankles aye my boy?" She laughed out loud.

"Do not harm her, where is the Cardinal Colleeta?"

"He's in motor pool about to leave. He has captives a woman and young boy please do not harm them."

"They are of no concern to me I want the Cardinal. You take point go through the door now." Paul ordered one of the soldiers with him to proceed.

"Master Paul you do not understand. The boy he's the Cardinal's son, your cousin and he is the One, Master."

"How do you know? Are you sure?"

"Master he's the One, the scripture eludes too trust me I know. That is why the pig wants him so badly, not because he's the boy's father. Stop him save the boy."

"You've served well you old witch, but you know what I …"

Colleeta was still shaken up from the trauma to her face as she lowered her head.

"I must end our relationship now my faithful servant. You know it's for your own safety because of what the church will do to you is far worse. I will see that your body be blessed."

A bullet put the nun to sleep forever as Paul hesitated for a moment he was almost saddened. He then followed after the second man as they very slowly pushed open the kitchen door which led into a cold creepy main hallway lined with shelves holding stock supplies.

"They're trying to attack from the rear."
Jimmy wasn't entirely sure if what he heard being yelled was true or not so he favored caution.

"Hold, stand down", he ordered. He then saw a second blast behind his position. Yes he thought to himself attacking from behind made sense, but the choice of ammo he'd use would be good old fashion bullets and he didn't see any. The blasts they were experiencing were mortars or grenades, a decoy, but Jimmy was still cautious.

"You and you cover our rear while we advance towards that forward area."
Marcus was delighted his ploy appeared to have worked allowing him time and the distraction he needed to get to the front door of the Abbey so he could take up position behind Michael and Lehchin.

"I'm on your six now Michael."

"Cover the door, set traps."
"Right, I'm on it."

The lights were now flickering in the conference room and Miles knew it was only a matter of moments before the attackers would locate and destroy the emergency generators.

Contessa was out of ammo and the lights were now off. Silence accompanied the dark and an unknown voice could be heard requesting something. Goggles they were trying to get night vision goggles from the helicopter and Contessa decided that darkness was her ally for the moment. The dark allowed her to get another weapon from the dead man lying just in the doorway of the conference room. Her assailants would not be expecting her to move towards them and she could not wait for them to gain an upper hand by sporting the night vision goggles and more firepower. She snaked her way to the conference doorway without detection. She could hear Cheryl Teranez and the Bishop arguing and tussling with one another as she passed them by the table. Her hands were now wet with moisture as she slithered through some coagulating blood on the carpet.

"Let go you Catholic bastard."

"Try this you bitch." The Bishop released the duffle bag strap and with his good free hand managed to punch the doctor in the neck. He had meant to get hit her face perhaps the nose to break it, but the neck was fine he thought to himself as he felt the soft tissue and bone submit to the force of his fist. She would not survive the blow and he realized it the moment he heard the cracking sound from the fragile bones in her neck. He now possessed the duffle bag or at least the strap. He tried to pull the bag down to him with his good hand until he could pull no more. Reaching up he maneuvered the bag around the chair and down on the floor where he hugged it as if it were a long lost friend.

J.P. just sat in the dark room under the long, wide conference table at the far end opposite the Bishop's location pondering whether or not he should have a drink under the circumstances, especially since probability was great that he be shot in the process, but still was it worth it?

Miles, Margarite and Alice refused to make any sudden movements under the fear that any noise would prompt an assault in their direction across from J.P. They were oblivious to the fact that the attackers were gathering the special night vision equipment and heavier guns. Neither of them spoke as they heard their attackers' conversation, as did Contessa whose proximity allowed her to monitor the chatter by the shooters.

Contessa now sat only a couple of feet from the position of her attackers without their knowledge and to their misfortune she'd commandeered one of their dead man's AK 47 assault weapons.

Someone was truly about to be in a world of hurt she thought to herself. Waiting for what she figured was most of the attackers to re-enter from outside would be the most prudent move on her part. No second chances would be granted. She needed to let as many of them assemble as possible before beginning her barrage from her stealth strike position.

The two men were waving the Cardinal and his security detail to get into the limousine. The Cardinal was not feeling it, he was unusually antsy and he knew enough about his feelings to disrobe his large Dracula looking cape.

"Here you wear this," he demanded of one of the guards who looked at him as though he were crazy.

The man wasn't very bright and all he wanted to do was his job as he kept glancing out into the parking area and back at the Cardinal who was draping his large red cape around the guard and to top it off he placed his head gear on the guard's head. The guard smirked and attempted to resist as the Cardinal shoved him outside towards the limo. He walked crouched over in an offensive stance gun rotating from one side to the other clearly indicating to all watching the fiasco that the garments he wore slowed him down. The Cardinal watched intensely, he sensed a kill on its way especially since the idiot decoy he'd provided was just that an idiot. The guard beat the Cardinal's odds and reached the limo. Now the idiot joined in waving at the other guard and the Cardinal to join him, this only infuriated the Cardinal.

"Do you see that?"

"What?"
"That convoy of cars coming this way up there on the hill."
"Yes."
"Let's stay put maybe they'll get a little closer."
"Why, we need to get …"

"We need to stay put Senator. We have no idea of who they are or what they're here for."

"Look, that's how many times tonight you've been the voice of reason? Why don't we just exchange jobs?"

Todd smiled as he pushed her head down next to his shoulder so they could maintain a low presence.

The Abbey was dimly lit as thousands of candle lights flickered and danced against the stone walls. Michael was soon crawling on his stomach against the cold floor. His shoulder rubbed up on the wall as he scooted his way down the hall. Too easy, he saw the trip wire that eagerly greeted him on the stone floor. He signaled to his young apprentice who lay on the floor directly across from him to stop while he dismantled the toy and then continued forward. Lehchin continued to crawl on the floor making his way over a wooden footing of a hallway table when a man slipped out from a door in front of him and to Michael's right. Michael froze as he realized the man was not cognitive of him or Lehchin's presence. Then a second man appeared but this one hesitated and retreated back into the room. Strangely a different man showed up in his place behind the second man. But then the man seen earlier was spotted by Michael and Lehchin peering at them from floor level smiling as the other two bodies stood at the door and wouldn't press further.

"Hey old buddy, is that you mate?"

Michael braced and tensed up as did Lehchin realizing the voice was addressing them. Michael recognized the voice it was that old white haired killer from Hong Kong.

"Come now mate surely you remember me, come on from the wharf over in …"

"Yes I remember. Fancy meeting you here, you here for a mad man's anonymous convention, but now I can finish what I started back there. I can kill you."

"Yes you did wing me didn't you and it hurts even as I'm speaking to you. How's your wound? It must've been nasty you left enough blood for me to create a picture bad with for the Hong Kong authorities."

"You say your wounds hurting, that's good because that was the whole idea behind shooting you in the first place you murderous bastard."

"See that and I truly believed you possessed better social graces than to resort to innuendo and childish name calling. You leave me no choice, I simply must kill you."

Michael and Lehchin were located in vulnerable positions and they both knew it. Michael waved Lehchin back and removed a grenade from his side vest. Lehchin's retreat was made in haste he was already back where his journey began in front of front Abbey doors. Michael Zarkuhn rolled the grenade at the door and began his backwards shuffle. Paul and his soldiers had already anticipated this action in advance because it was the only logical one. The blast did nothing but destroy the furniture, beautiful tapestry and stained glass in the hall. But it also was the official alert that the fight was now on and every faction, cell, splinter group and law enforcement agency was taking the action hero role in order to annihilate what it perceived as the enemy.

CHAPTER 50

KILL PAUL

Contessa remained still with her back against the wall adjacent to the conference room doors. The room was still dark and there was a total calm no doubt before the storm. She was aware that the attackers were coming back at some point soon and their numbers would no doubt overpower her. She'd have to think fast before they mounted their next attack.

Bishop Terrell could have cared less if he were to get out of the bind he was in for he now was holding a piece of the Tables of Testimony. He reached into the duffle bag and rubbed his good hand over the smooth jade like stone. The surface was like that of Cleopatra's skin, so silky smooth and warm to the touch. Then he saw Peter, he could barely recognize the body with the limited light from outside piercing the massive windows. There he was lying there right next to the edge of the conference table as he still rubbed the tablet. It was Peter, the man servant his friend and the Bishop was ashamed. Why hadn't he noticed him earlier? The darkness of the room was now being overshadowed by the brightness of the reflective moonlight off the snow outside and the Bishop was grateful for it. He shuffled over to the old man's lifeless body pulling the bag as he scooted to Peter's lifeless body. Bishop Terrell reached under the neck line of his dirty white collar and cast out his crucifix placing it on his friend's chest. His own chest swelled with sorrow at the loss, so much death, so much sadness and despair burgeoned in him. Suddenly the Tablet lost it's luster what now became important to the wayward priest was Peter's salvation and he must pray, pray for that salvation after all that's what he was ordained to do, to shepherd the souls and lives of God's flock. There under a table crouching on his knees in the darkness Bishop Terrell had just moments earlier taken a life now he found his own life anointed with purpose his purpose. He had clarity and as he prayed over Peter he finally felt forgiven for all his transgressions or at least he was at peace with himself. Mere confession proved not enough to redeem his soul, a righteous act was.

"Actions do not speak louder than words it is the word in action that matter."

"Bishop get down", Alice saw the silhouettes of the men as they entered the doorway and began indiscriminately shooting the whole room up with their automatic weapons.

Contessa still held her spot not reacting to the tracer fire and bullets passing by her through the door. She knew that a break in the barrage of gun fire would come and well if the others in the room hiding under the table were killed as she witnessed the instant death of the Bishop, then that was the status quo of hostile engagements. Contessa had begun to enjoy the Bishop's company but one of the attacker's bullets had freed her from having to do him in herself and for that she felt relieved. His death was quick and he looked peaceful as his dead body lay in the kneeling position over the lifeless body of Peter who he was praying for when he was struck by bullets in the chest several times. Needless to say Contessa was pissed.

Who was she fooling? She was lying to herself. She hadn't planned to kill the irritating priest because he had grown on her in fact she liked working with him. The more she thought of him the angrier she got until she couldn't take any more. Contessa began to open fire on the attackers. She decided she would kill as many as she could because they'd taken the priest, because they'd destroyed such a lovely mansion, because they didn't know how to treat a lady and worst of all because they weren't Christians.

"Die swine, die you pigs yes ana ismi death, ana ismi death, tiSbah ala kheir, that's right good night bastards."

"Does anyone know what she's yelling?"

"She's saying my name is death and good night, it's Arabic."

"Alice I didn't realize you spoke Arabic."

"Yes Latin and Hebrew as well they were required as prerequisites for my doctorate program. Why in the hell are we discussing this, we're going to probably die here folks."

"Sir our bird is just about over the Al Queda chopper."

"Order the attack, destroy it and tell the gunner shoot anyone in its vicinity. I want a clean job total sanitation, nice and clean, no talkers."

"Oh crap! Now there's the chopper that blew up our car, quick crawl under the brush, hurry."

Agent Todd didn't like the incoming helicopter's angle of approach the tail dipped up and the nose pointed down was standard aggressive posture the same taken by sharks before an attack.

"That chopper's going to attack the other and we're just far away not to get any of the damage."

"What about Ms. Patty she's closer to the truck?"

"We have little choice they probably won't see it of interest unless the gunner goes on a frenzy shooting spree and shoots anything then she's in trouble."

Todd and the Senator's clothing were drenched and they were freezing. They were not going to last much longer but neither of them would openly address their uncomfortable situation.

Rahmad, the Al Queda cell leader ordered the chopper to lift off immediately as he saw the attacking helicopter pop up from over the tree tops behind the mansion but it was too late. The rotors were not spinning fast enough and he quickly exited the door rolling towards the edge of the large circular brick water fountain. Spectacular is all everyone could think of as the ground chopper burst into flames under the dark cloudless sky temporarily blotting out the stars and blinding onlookers. The noise was deafening and the mansion shook as glass on the whole front face of the lovely structure shattered. Contessa was still firing her assault rifle into the hall through the opened doors oblivious to anything but her will to survive.

The Collective "under the table crew" could now see the carnage piling up at the conference room front door as clear as day a gift of the raging fire from the now burning helicopter.

"Miles where's Peter, where's Peter." Margarite was screaming.

"Alice did you see anything, did you?"
Alice was bewildered, "he was there dead lying in front of the Bishop. I don't know I didn't see anything. I mean I ducked when I heard the blast and now he's not there."

"Me too, I ducked and presto he's gone we've got to find …"

"Absolutely not we need to make our escape. J.P. keep up. Let's go all of you follow me to the kitchen, hurry crawl."

The remainder of the inner circle of the Collective followed Mile's lead as he crawled on his knees to the kitchen door leading out from the conference room.

It was pitch black in the Kitchen.

"Hold the door a minute. Margarite the flashlight, is it in the pantry or one of the drawers?"

"I don't, I can't remember. I think the pantry."

"I'll check both places. Hold the door open so I can see."
Miles began to search frantically for the light source.
Contessa had seen the bodies moving from underneath the table towards the kitchen door where she and the Bishop hid earlier. It was obvious that they would know where to go to escape the chaos and she would follow not too far behind them soon enough.

"Holy crappolah did you see that?"

"You're kidding right? All Boston saw that. Slow down a second radio for an update on that chopper I need to know if it's friend or foe. I don't wish to tangle with that sort of fire power."

"Me neither, hell we don't have that kind of muscle on the Boston Police force and I'm just two years away from retirement and this my friend ain't happening, not here tonight."

"Sir, there are no markings on either chopper, but our scouts say there are men shooting back at the attacking helicopter with automatic weapons."

Captain Boggs and the Special Agent in charge spent enough time in Vietnam to earn great respect for air firepower and they knew of that weapon's propensity for inflicting casualties on the friendly side as well without proper communications in place. They both decided to heel to caution under the circumstances. They stopped the convoy's progression much to Agent Todd's and the Senator's disapproval as they desired to be rescued. Both longed to be allowed to sit in the warmth of one of the cruisers which they could now clearly see approaching them.

"There it is sir."

"Yes I see it beautiful, absolutely beautiful look at those flames. Hey instruct the gunner to pop that truck south of it. I want to see how it blows, this is going to be great, watch."

"Roger that sir."
The Homeland Security chopper whirled around at an enormously quick speed and pressed an assault on old woman Patty's truck. One perfectly placed projectile was all that was needed to bring joy to the Secretary of Homeland Security's heart. He watched in amazement as the truck was consumed in an enormous explosion and fire that would've given the God Moloch an orgasm. His satisfaction was short lived, this was an appetizer and he desired hid main course.

"Are they resisting? I see some people shooting back, are they returning fire? They're shooting at us, oh yes, oh yes, action baby!"

"One moment sir I'll verify. Yes sir they are putting up some resistance according to our attack team."

"Well then order the other bird to cover our backdoor to the mansion and we'll take it from here. So Bob you ever seen battle while you were in the Air Force? Of course not, all you fly boys are candy asses why else would you be in the damn Air Force. But you're smart Bob and that means a lot so I'm going to teach you how to become smarter by making a real kill not some kill from a cockpit. This will be up close and personal like, yeah."

"Yes sir, Mr. Secretary, but no sir."

"No sir what?"

"You're correct, I never saw any hot fire per se, but I can learn. I'm ready sir."

The Secretary smiled at his assistant as their chopper lowered itself on the white lawn. White powder was sprayed up everywhere as the blades whipped threw the air above it. The Secretary noticed the multitude of colorful lights afar up at the end of the long mansion driveway and realized he needed to discourage the onlookers from advancing further.

"Bob text message forward, "do not engage, I repeat do not engage Homeland operations hot reign, raining hot under control," send it to the support agencies up there. That F.B.I. agent and the rest, hurry we have work to do."

"We just got a message Captain Boggs that Homeland's got it under raps. They've requested we stand down."

"So now we know who the choppers belong too. Well it's their dance let's watch the light show."

"Who ever would've thought the F.B.I. would have been relegated to sitting on the sideline when something like this was taking place on American soil? Damn I need to retire to Captain Boggs. This job isn't what it used to be."

"Your eminence that's our cue to get out of here your car awaits, please you must leave."

The Cardinal just couldn't bring himself to go to the limousine his nerves were shot. He was turning out to be quite the coward and chinks were developing in his superficial spiritual armor.

"Why do you hesitate, Cardinal? Are you afraid of something of someone, you seem so nervous. God will protect you he protects the innocent, the ignorant. God protects the charitable of heart, well you're protected right? Oh! That's right you possess known of those qualities I've just mentioned. You're not even ignorant, stupid, but not ignorant. It's no wonder you're so fearful you see that Karma may calling." Merie smiled at him as she finished snubbing the unhinged Cardinal. Tashi was surprisingly quiet as he watched his father with an eerie maturity.

"See even Tashi watches in anticipation to see what you shall do your excellent screw up! I can't believe this you're scared, he's scared you men see this? Your great holy man is shivering like a little girl. I pray Tashi didn't inherit your tiny scrotum."

"You harlot how dare you speak to me …" The Cardinal slapped Merie hard with the back of his hand across the left side of her brow and she stumbled against the metal door falling to her knees. She tried desperately not to drop her child, but to no avail. Merie was petite and the Cardinal's hand was almost twice her head size. He was a robustly husky man of German descent and powerful stature. He enjoyed his power over her and hit her again, and again, and once more as Tashi screamed in horror at the sight of his mother being harmed in the doorway.

"Please stop, please stop hitting her I said, please stop hitting her now!"

Soon the Cardinal was huffing and puffing as he tried to get his breath. He leaned against the doorway entrance having exerted himself too exhaustion. He hadn't worked that hard since giving up Choir boys on assignment in South America.

"You, you insolent dog you dare address me and in that manner?"

"I took this job Cardinal because I believe in the Catholic Church and the money isn't bad, but you you're not exhibiting how do they say it, yes "leadership ability", and frankly, well frankly I'm quitting."

"You can't quit you work for the Church."

"Yes you're right I work for the Church not you. You've forgotten the difference and that may cost you. I'll explain my actions to your superior. I doubt as the woman said you have the balls to do the same."

"What?"

"You heard me. Oh and good luck, no I take that back see you maybe."

"You're my security chief you follow my orders as long as I'm alive, you shall follow my demands, do you hear me?"

The security chief for the Cardinal spit on the Cardinal's torso and called the two guards to his side. They removed their knives and Cardinal Ricci could only think of Caesar and the Ives of March.

"No you can't you wouldn't, no you mustn't, you will go to hell if you do this." The Cardinal backed up from the men as they closed in on him.

He yelled out as the slender blade pierced his right side. He looked down to see Merie's hand fall away from the stiletto as it still dangled in his side below his right lower rib. Her blade was the first of the many other punctures he was to receive over the next several minutes from his own security detachment.

"Help me, oh God help me, me, me, mm, m, pleeeaase!"

On his knees he clasped his abdomen and neck the Cardinal Ricci gazed in disbelief into the eyes of his assassins. Each man read his glazed watery eyes as his face conveyed the following, "I am better than you, don't you realize you'll die by the hand of God for this act?"

He was so predictable each man thought to themselves as they put their knives away they realized just one thing this assassinated elitist cleric was a pompous fool.

"Madam we must go, will you and the boy be alright?"

Merie couldn't reply she was in shock searching her psyche for some rationale for what she'd done. Violence of any kind sickened her and she was very ill right now.

"Noli Timere Merie. Beati mites quoniam ipsi possidebunt terram."

The Cardinal was slumped over on his hind quarters his arms stretched out on the floor each now too weak to hold the wounds as they oozed sanguine elixir which fought to match his red raiment. Merie knew his statement referring to the meek had been made to further distress her. "Have no fear Merie", this statement was already eating at her as she held Tashi and scooted back further from the dying clergyman, father of her son, her rapist. Tashi was crying profusely and she hadn't heard him because of the craziness of the moment. Merie now found herself in another room which appeared to be a stock room. She wondered why she hadn't run or tried to get away. Her captor was all but dead and then it hit her that she didn't know where to go or what to do, her friend Colleeta could help. Tashi's little legs gripped his mother's waist as she made her way through the store room to a door and opened it slowly.

"Fancy meeting you here lass. Where's the birdman, where's the Cardinal?"

"He's, he's dead in there, through there at the end in the next room on the floor dead."

"Yes I get it dead, yes dead. Come on guys no not you, you stay with her and the child. Team two is that limo pulling out? If so blow it up I repeat detonate the bomb."

The Vatican security chief joined the other three men at the limo and jumped in. The detonation rocked the old stone structure knocking over the shelves in the stock room as Paul and his team approached the garage area. Flames and debris painted the entire area and the brick wall which shielded Paul's team proved to be inadequate protection causing an injury to the team chief.

Paul could now see his cousin Cardinal Ricci sprawled out on the floor in the doorway of the garage. He could hardly believe the sight laying there before him, this once powerful clergyman of the Roman Catholic Church looked like a regular casualty of war, any war, every war. He was not special in death he died the same way all souls do yet the contrast of his power in life against his posture in death produced serious shock and awe.

"I can't believe he's dead, too easy. Team two I take it none of the holy boys survived out there?"

"Sir affirmative, however, I sustained a minor injury. We're proceeding towards the garage area now."

"Yes I'll meet you there. Jimmy come in, Jimmy do you copy."

"Yes boss I copy my team is entering the Abbey as we speak. They're directly behind the bad guys. Are you guys okay? That was helluva an explosion, so who died?"

"The holy guys."

"Really no shit! All of them?"

"Sure thing."

"Look here boss, I'm in the middle of something right now I'll get back to ya."

"Jimbo are you killing someone? I know that sound in your voice, well?"

"Well if you must know I got that rabbit I reported to you a minute ago and I'm gonna grill him."

Ted ran the whole way back to the car and he was feeling it as he sat down on the ground next to the rental car. Boy he was out of shape. He would have to start exercising as soon as he got home. Ted heard the footsteps running and running hard as he peered up over the trunk he spotted the burly G. O. rilla in black S.W.A.T. attire running towards the car. It was Jimmy coming to satisfy his curiosity about the lost rabbit.

Ted started to panic his heart raced and he looked for a place to run to get away, but there was no place and no energy in his legs even if there was a place to run. Jimmy was closer and he smelled weakness from the man in front of him. Signs of distress were spread out before this hunter like a smorgasbord consisting of fear, fright, alarm, dread and horror a predator could become overweight on such gluttonous weakness. The man had not even moved, had not taken a defensive posture or an offensive posture, he'd taken no action at all, mistake, huge mistake. Jimmy initially doubted his judgment in pursuing the rabbit and he now realized he was right to doubt the pursuit. Weighing his decision against having left his men to apprehend a coward, a person who'd deserted his comrades in effort to save his own meaningless life by deserting friends in battle. Didn't this coward realize he may have had a chance to give his life meaning by helping his buddies, no of course not this S.O.B. ran like little scared child. Jimmy was going to savor this kill he would torture him for at least ten minutes for his indiscretion and cowardice action. Yeah ten minutes would be enough time and it would not hurt his own soldiers for him to be absent ten or fifteen minutes or so. He'd take the man's head back as a trophy and as proof for Paul. Yeah to show his buddies he'd not run out on them, but left to exterminate the coward.

"Whoa!" Ted yelled as he shot at Jimmy and missed, but caused Jimmy to leap abruptly from the path directly in front of him. Ted fired two more rounds again and Jimmy dropped slamming into the rental car's front bumper. Jimmy pulled his weapon and shot underneath the car. Ted yelled and fell to the ground grabbing his left ankle. He couldn't look at the wound. He was not handling the pain or the sight very well. His ankle was barely recognizable with blood and flesh everywhere. Ted was in excruciating pain and fading into shock, but more than that he surprised himself by getting pissed off.

Jimmy saw the body of his prey hit the ground and he couldn't pass up an opportunity to pounce on the wounded specimen ready to be filleted. He holstered his sidearm and walked around to the back of the car where Ted lay in the fetal position holding his ankle moaning and crying in pain. Jimmy immediately looked for the wounded man's gun and kicked it away.

"Damn buddy that must hurt? Does it? I mean does it hurt or what? Sure looks bad, it's gotta hurt like the dickens. I mean damn it's on a string are those tendons look at that nasty, nasty."

"Help, help." Ted attempted to speak into his headset but the jack had been pulled out during his fall. He was cutoff from Michael and his crew.

"Dude I shot you, I'm not going to help you. You must be going into shock or you're just darn stupid. I'll make a deal with you. I was going to take ten minutes with you, but because you're so distressed you may not last ten minutes I'll make it seven minutes. Say thank you, thank you Uncle Jimmy, come on how about a little gratitude here you pug."

Ted was hurting bad his head felt like it was on fire and he was fading fast. He saw the face of his mother just as clear as day and he wanted to say so much to her. He panicked as he realized his on mortality as imminent death was about to claim him.

Ted's messenger of death knelt closer to him poking at his wounded ankle with a bayonet like a small child investigating roadside kill. Ted could swear the man was drooling. Jimmy smelled like musty death and cigarettes as he slowly contemplated how to proceed, he cogitated on what torture would bring about the most satisfaction for him. The man's eyes were dead no light existed in them, what was seconds felt like hours to the wounded attorney and he wanted to cry out for mercy, but he wouldn't he wanted to live and it wasn't because of his children, it wasn't for the understanding wife of twenty years nor because he so enjoyed his work, but because he needed to apologize to his mother for not being a good son.

As Jimmy now straddled Ted's torso in an attempt to demean him Ted squirmed to move out from under him. Ted was a criminologist long before he studied law he would not speak to the animal scooting up towards his chest. There would be no connection with this killer in any form, to do so would empower him and expedite Ted's demise. Jimmy now had an idea of how to enjoy himself with his wounded coward. He suddenly noticed the manicured fingers tugging at his pant legs and reached down and grabbed Ted's hand this verified his suspicion. He was right the man's hands were as soft as doe he was an intellectual, a suit, a fish out of water. The way to proceed for maximum fear was to debase him to attack Ted where he would be weakest and that was his mastery at controlling his animalistic urges. Jimmy reasoned instinctively as higher level animals do that he should take Ted's manhood through the act of fellatio.

Ted somehow sensed this sick scheme boiling in his attacker. It didn't take a rocket scientist based on his present position and the fact that Jimmy was now yelling about knocking his teeth out.

"I found it hold on there it works quick stay behind me." Miles stood up next to the counter and walked quickly towards the corridor with the stairs to the control center Margarite and Alice followed closely in tow.

Contessa was now frantically crawling under the conference table trying to get to the exit where she spotted the others had escape. She passed J.P. under the large mahogany conference table he was pulling at the duffle bag trapped under the dead Bishop.

"Mister you need to join your friends what you seek is no longer in there it was taken."

"How do you know?" J.P. asked as he stopped his search for the Tablet, the powerful relic and attempted to crawl back over the dead priest.

Contessa began her exodus again finally reaching the kitchen door. She turned and answered J.P.'s question.

"I know because the other old man who was under the table took it with him during the gun fight earlier. He appeared to have been injured you must catch up with the others the gunmen will be coming back. I'm sure your friend is okay."

Michael was now joined by Lehchin as he slowly stood up at the door where he had tossed the grenade earlier he entered slowly with Lehchin covering him. The room was small and contained restroom and a table with damaged chairs and debris decorating it.

"Stay close. Marcus SITREP."

"I'm at the front door with some bad guys in very hot pursuit. Don't worry I got them covered, but I picked up chatter from the local yocals on the scanner."

"Was it about our situation here?"

"Couldn't tell too much action was going on, but I'd guess yes."

"Hold your position for ten and then give."

"Gotcha."

"Boy this is an old kitchen look a stone oven. Mr. Zarkuhn oh my God it's a nun!
Who would kill a nun? These men are really a work art." The dead woman was in a seated position with her head face down on the table and it was no secret as to the cause of death. The exit wound on the back side of her cranium told the story.

The "stones of fire" concealed on Michael burned as they had on the "Breastplate of Judgment" centuries ago for the Levites. Michael cautiously approached the dead body observing her body for booby traps. She was an innocent caught between the forces of good and evil and even more a servant of her God.

"Lehchin help me with her here." Michael stood behind the lifeless body of the old frumpy nun placing his arms under her armpits to stand her upright. Carefully he moved her coagulated blood matted hair away from his chest.

"Sir what are we doing?"

"Lehchin I'm going to increase your security clearance. You're a good man son so what you're about to witness will puzzle you and I'm sure you'll understand why, but also as confident you'll want to know how. Hold her up."

Lehchin was extremely uncomfortable the young man had never held a dead body unless he counted holding Michael Zarhuhn's body when he pulled off the fake dead man's stunt in Hong Kong. Michael moved around in front of the nun caressing her small body. His young accomplice held the woman while oscillating his head in multiple directions feeling uneasy about their location in the open kitchen. Lehchin held the woman with one arm as he peered over his shoulder at the door behind him. Both men could hear noises after hearing an explosion in the Abbey. The noises were coming from rooms adjacent to theirs and intermittent gunfire from the front of the Abbey an indication that Marcus was staying busy.

Michael held Colleeta tightly against him and softly whispered in her ear mystical words of power as the stones did their bidding; hidden in the words were secrets concealed in the teachings of the Cabbala and other mystical teachings.

"What tha!" Lehchin pulled his arm from around the woman and jumped back with his automatic rifle pointed at her back. "She moved damn, she moved! Forgive my language sir, but she was, is she dead or what sir?"

Michael held the small portly woman who was stirring and rocking back and forth on her small wide feet.

"Stranger I can't quite see you, but I thank you for praying over an old lady. Let me see Hebrew, Holy, holy, holy is God. Yes he ... oh my, I'm dizzy and boy what a headache."

Lehchin was no coroner or pathologist and the way he saw it he didn't need to be the woman standing in front of him had been dead a minute earlier. His inquisitive mind raced with all the possible explanations including reviewing in his mind every episode of Stargate SG-1, StarTrek, Highlander, etc., somewhere there was a plausible explanation in one of his favorite shows for what he'd just witnessed. However, no matter how he tried nothing worked.

"Lech, Lehchin I'll explain later. Ma'am are you well enough to answer a few questions?"

"Yes I think so."

"We seek a woman and a little boy."

"Merie and Tashi."

"Yes, yes ma'am."

"The Cardinal has them you must save them? They are in the garage area west wing area hurry please, I'll hide go I'll be alright."

"Lehchin you okay?" Lehchin nodded his eyes still bulged as he followed Michael, however, Colleeta the soft spoken nun scared the Michael.

"Michael thank you, you're an angel, thank you."
Michael had a question as his knees wobbled he turned and continued his search and destroy mission there was no time for questions.

"She's right you know about the angel thing, you are an angel Mr. Zarkuhn."

"Sure I am, but I don't know how the woman knew my name."

"What, your name? You told her when you whispered in her ear right?"

"No and you insist on calling me sir so she didn't hear it out you either. Strange."

"What, that I call you sir?"

"No that the nun knows my name. I never told her and well she was dead when we entered the room so how did she know my name."

Miles hurried down the stairs to the control center. Margarite and Alice both ran over to the emergency escape location hidden behind a group file cabinets and communications panels. Miles sat down and started entering codes into the computer. Alice reached down beneath the back of one the cabinets and then pulled out three drawers and pushed them back. The cabinet in the center of the grouping of cabinets withdrew from the wall and remained open. Behind it was a clearance of two feet revealing a deep stairwell well lit from inside it led to a long corridor. They all felt the blast of cold air as the cabinet remained open.

"Miles dear you must hurry."

"I'm going as fast as I can love just another minute or two, there. Done! All files have been destroyed as this room soon shall be in say seven minutes. All operational and EFT transfers were successful all we need do is stay alive."

Alice smiled at both her friends and reminded them of the close danger. "We're out of here. Let's head for the woods to the extraction location. Here are some parkas put them on and well say goodbye at least for now."

The explosion rocked the kitchen and the conference room. The terrorist had taken the conference with the help of two RPGs. Contessa slipped down the stairs as she made her way in the direction she'd figured the others had escaped. She staggered down stairs to the control center in a nick of time, just in time to see the middle cabinet sliding back into to it's deceptive position. Well at least she now knew the escape route was located behind the cabinet her problem would be how to access it.

"Ah halp, I ned halp." J.P. screamed out. The drunk was not fast enough now he found himself buried beneath the collapsed conference table. The weight of the table which had saved so many from the gunfire earlier now knocked J.P. unconscious, but also protected him from the many flying objects and falling debris caused by the grenades launched into the room by Rahmad and his remaining cell members.

"Put her down over there, no over there and let's go hunting," the Secretary of Homeland commanded. He jumped out of the helicopter too early slightly spraining his right ankle. The Secretary's excitement encouraged him to leap prematurely to the chopper setting down making his attempt to be a bad ass as three foot drop in snow. His injury caused him to pause tempering his zeal with a minute of realization that he was not as young as he used to be. His entourage of government trained killers shadowed his every move providing protection for him as well as seeking to destroy the enemy. A few minutes of rest was just what the Secretary needed before reverting back to his alias "Captain America Bad Ass". His aide was shaking next to the Secretary as he lay on the ground covered in snow. He wiped the frost off his face and adjusted his head gear and his actions irritated the Secretary.

"This is not an inspection or a fashion show we're here to kill folks so loosen up and aim straight soldier." The Secretary moved towards the burning helicopter led by four Special Forces soldiers with two other body guards flanking him not to mention a special camera man who was directed to film the Secretary's involvement in the event. This would make him the man in Washington for sure he would have plenty of capital on Capitol Hill in order to run for office when the time was right.

It was dark, cold, and wet all the bad stuff, but Miles and his companions didn't care as long as they'd escaped the mansion. Now they could at least let their hopes fester and maybe someday a story in the form of a life saving memoir would be forthcoming in the future. They all knew the extraction site would have the basic needs to sustain them en route to Alpha Point, once there they'd be safe.

"Over there it should be over, there. Hurry ladies please, hurry the Hummers … is not here!"

"But it has to be here somewhere Miles. Perhaps we've come to the wrong location, maybe?"

"No, this is the spot. I'm sure of it. In fact, I'm positive of it."

"It was moved, you can see the tracks leading out. Point the flashlight back down look the tracks are fresh."

"Alice you are good, but who? Who would know besides us?"
"J.P. J.P. would know, right?"
"Don't be preposterous, I'm still worried about him. He's back in the mansion somewhere unfortunately."

"Then who Miles, who?"

"Me."

"Oh my God Peter!

"Drop the guns, you only have one second."

Guns clanked, and clamored as they fell to the concrete floor. Professionals never tempered fate when about to be shot it's just a job not worth ding for. Paul's men looked like manikins as he and they complied with Michael's demand. Merie couldn't believe her eyes and neither could Michael.

"Who are you? Identify yourself."

"I'm Senator Cheryl Stinger and he's Special Agent Chris Todd. Officer, please get us to whoever's in charge of this operation."

The Sheriff's deputy was baffled but helped the Senator and the agent to his cruiser.

"Deputy there's an old lady that needs medical attention down there near that burning truck."

"Sir, I'd loved to help but we've been ordered not to approach the property. To tell the truth I could get in trouble for helping you right now."

"Deputy get me to whoever is in charge, we'll make sure this mix up gets fixed. Todd shall we?"

"Yes ma'am. I'm right behind ya sister."

Marcus was worried the explosion startled him. However, he had his own problems with Paul's troops threatening to blitz him. He had a surprise. One that would alleviate him of is pursuers or at least the majority of them.

"Michael, Marcus here. I'm en route to you bro. I set up a maze of party poppers for the guests. Hey they're on to us. The local authorities are on the way. I just heard it over the scanner."

"Join us. We're West of you follow the carnage to the garage we could use your muscle right now."

"I'm on it."

"Well mate it's time you and I got to know each other betta."

"I don't think so."

"Damn, it talks. I thought you were mute man."

"It also bites!"

Ted had had it with the homicidal bully so he exercised something he'd learned while doing a thesis for his on inmates in the penal system. His paper was on the survival of inmates while incarcerated. One of the things he learned was to bite while you still had teeth, so he did. He remembered receiving an A on that paper, but he couldn't believe he was thinking about that insignificant detail at the moment.

"You in there. In the mansion please put your weapons down and come forward, surrender now. Give it up Rahmad."

"How does he know my name?" Rahmad asked in an exasperated tone. Years of success blessed by Allah only now he would be martyred as his brethren in Iraq, Afghanistan and Gaza.

"Brothers this is the time. It is now that we shall walk with Mohammed and serve in the garden of Allah. Allen you and Suresh double check your vest ensure nothing goes wrong with the detonation."

"I'm scared Rahmad. I'm sorry, I."

"It is all right my friend. What you are feeling is normal, but I have faith in you. You have been a good servant to God and I believe you will continue to be. All of you brothers, former nonbelievers and brothers of my home do not allow these devils to take you alive."

"I understand. I can do it. I can do it. I can do it."

"Yes, Allen Johnson you can and you will. Take this, it will help. Chew it, go!"

"Listen we've tracked you and your people for some time now. I beg of you not to resist."

The Secretary turned towards the camera man who was filming the event making absolutely sure his best side was visible.

"Are you taping this? Good keep rolling that camera whatever happens." The Secretary for Homeland Security was gloating and his voice dare not hide it. "We know you're with Al Queda. How do you think we got the jump on you? Your inside agent, your girlfriend gave you up."

"You lie. I don't believe you and even if you are telling the truth you know I will never give up. I will die for the cause you pig. Here's my answer!"
The Al Queda cell leader began firing his Russian made weapon at the non-believers and his remaining recruits fired their guns along with him.
Their gunfire was met with an unbelievable onslaught of fire firepower from the opposing force and the filming continued. This was good stuff the Secretary thought as he popped off a couple of rounds while still acting with sincerity in his efforts to negotiate with the terrorists. He'd nurtured this marketing campaign for over three years anticipating the media and American public would eat it up. They would all marvel that America actually possessed a real Presidential contender, someone not afraid to lead or mix it up in the trenches he would definitely appear to be Presidential material.

"Captain Boggs, Special Agent Travis, sirs I'm Sheriffs Deputy Roberts and these two people need to share something with you."

Michael asked Paul to turn around slowly and he slowly complied with an excrement eating grin on his face.
"Don't get anxious mate okay, I'm turning around now and we've put our guns down. Guys the boss has put his weapon down so you should be cool too, put them down now!"

Contessa pulled the middle cabinet drawer out and placed her leg through enough to kick the back of the cabinet. She could feel it giving way and then success. Contessa hurried and squeezed through the small entrance realizing her plan may not have been as well planned as she'd thought which was fine since she hadn't planned anything at all. She found herself falling down five stair steps before being able to get her bearings was a wake up call. She sprained her wrist during the fall but knew it would heal in a minute or two her bones always did. Contessa made a "B" line down the well lit passage way towards the exit. She prayed she'd be able to catch up with those who'd escaped and confiscate their means of freedom for her own use.

"Mexican standoff aye mate?"

"Don't think so Mr. Constantine we've got the guns."

"Yeah you're right so what now Mr. Zarkuhn. That's your name right?"

"Yes and what happens to you will depend entirely on what you do and say in the next few minutes, because personally you vex me and that makes me want to shoot you."

"Cute. I vex you, haven't heard that one since I left the Vatican."

"Ah, ah you're moving, don't. All of you lie down on your stomachs with your hands stretched out. Do it now!"

"Yo Mike my man, Marcus here. Get ready for that big party boom."
Boom!

"I guess that was the welcome blast, huh? I bet that shredded some bad guys."

"You think?"

"Paul what am I to do with you? Do you have others with you?" Michael knew the local police were on their way and he couldn't carry luggage. Three very bad men were on the floor in the prone position and he wasn't about to cap them for convenience sake, at least not while young Mr. Lehchin was present.

"So what you gonna do kill me? Oh and yes, I have a few more boys around. You know the first opportunity I get I'll pop you self professed good guys. So what you gonna do kill me?"

"Constantine sit up, you heard me sit up." Paul was still grinning as he slowly sat up and faced Michael and Lehchin.

"I'm sitting and ...?"

"Good." Michael lifted his weapon up shooting Paul Constantine three times through the heart at point blank range. Paul's upper body fell backwards from the force of the projectiles spraying blood over his comrades on the floor next to him. Every one was silent as Paul's men attempted to glance around to verify if in fact their boss had been killed. Lehchin was trembling not so much from fear but at the coolness exhibited by his mentor in doing the man; the very man who had shot off his big toe in Hong Kong.

Merie found Colleeta where Michael said she'd be, inside the men's bathroom.

"Hi grandma." Tashi reached for Colleeta as she grabbed him and hugged Merie.

"Hello Tashi. I missed you so much. I love you."

"I wuv you grandma."

"He does love you. I appreciate you letting him call you grandmother I never knew my mother."

"Of course you did."

"No sister I." Merie paused and stared at Colleeta and she had to ask what she already felt. "You ever have children Colleeta?"

Colleeta picked Tashi up and cleaned his face while kissing him on the forehead.

"Yes, in fact, I only had you. That wasn't planned, but how many things in life are?"

EPILOGUE

EXODUS

"Don't worry Lehchin. Ted's going to be just fine."

"Do you know this man?"

"Yes his name is J.P. Mr. Rockdale it's Special Agent Todd and."
"Karen, its Senator Stinger J.P. we're going to get you medical attention you're going to be okay."
"He wants his flask. He says it's in his coat pocket."
Agent Todd knelt down closer to J.P. as Senator Stinger walked over towards Secretary Alec Dules. Todd held J.P.'s hand and reached into his pocket to remove the flask while no one was watching.

"I'll take this, you don't need liquor right now, but I do. Hey this isn't booze! It's tea. J.P. you've been drinking tea all this time, just tea? You realize when you get out of the hospital you have some explaining to do."

"Mr. Secretary, Mr. Secretary, Alec."

"Oh Senator I'm glad you're okay. Fine work eh?"

"You know we'll need to talk right?"

"About, oh yes."

"I'm sure we'll be able to protect our interests."

"Like honoring Special Agent Todd and you of course for your assistance in breaking up this Al Queda plot on American soil, yes we need to talk."

"I know we'll all profit from this Mr. Secretary."

"What of the item, any luck?"

"As of yet we have been unable to locate much through the rubble thanks to those Kamikazes."

"Honestly, I don't know where it could be."

"Madam we shall rendezvous with the aircraft in a few minutes. You are all so quiet."

"We're puzzled Peter, that's all, and just happy we're all alive."

"Master Miles I will explain everything to all of you once we reach Alpha Point. Master Michael just informed me that he too is on schedule to meet us as well."

"What about Ted?"

"Ted was injured, but he will be okay Doctor Martin. Your husband is fine."

"And Merie? What of Merie and Tashi?"

"She and the child are safe as well."

"Exodus. We must now complete our trek to Alpha Point folks."

"This is not over. You hear me its not. You should have killed me back there, bitch."

"Shut up Paul. I killed you once already today."

"You summoned me my Lord?"

"Yes, Michael has been away for a couple of years now. Tell me of his progress. I want a full report for the council on him. We are considering bringing him back home."

"My Lord, that may be a problem."

"Problem?"

"Yes, Michael may resist coming back. He's changed my Lord."

"How, in what way? He's a messenger, a servant, he cannot change."

"Lord your answers would require a whole new **Book**."

978-0-595-41687-5
0-595-41687-X

Printed in the United States
81446LV00003B/12